The Straw
That Broke

Gregory Zeigler

RAVEN'S EYE PRESS · DURANGO, COLORADO

Raven's Eye Press
Durango, Colorado
www.ravenseyepress.com

This is a work of fiction. Names, characters, places and incidents either are the product of the author's imagination or are used fictitiously, and any resemblance to actual persons, living or dead, business establishments, events or locales is entirely coincidental.

Zeigler, Gregory.
    The Straw That Broke/Gregory Zeigler   p. cm.

ISBN   978-0-9840056-5-9
LCCN   2013951983

Cover art by Jane Lavino
Graphic design by Lindsay J. Nyquist, elle jay design

Printed in the United States of America
1 3 5 7 9 10 8 6 4 2

Contact the author: gzeigler@wyom.net
Visit the author's website: gzeiglerbooks.com

Dedication

For Dimmie, without whom—
well, frankly, "without whom,"
is, like, unthinkable.

Also by
Gregory Zeigler

Travels With Max:
In Search of Steinbeck's America Fifty Years Later

*If some of the Southwest's largest reservoirs empty out,
the region would experience an apocalypse, "an Armageddon."*
The New York Times

*Lake Mead...[is] headed toward 45 percent capacity,
the lowest level since 1968.*
Los Angeles Times

May 18
Thursday

The damn phone always rang at the worst times. Susan struggled with her belt as she ran to the kitchen to beat the answering machine; she left her police ID badge, radio, pistol, and cell phone scattered on her bed. Traffic reports from a distant city gushed from the television in the living room.

"I'll get it. Get dressed and pack your backpack. Don't forget your art supplies." The phone rang a second time. Susan searched for the portable and found it on the table in the midst of Amy's dirty dishes.

"I can't find my Lip Smackers," Amy called.

"Try my bedroom, but if you don't get moving, you're going to be late again." The phone rang in Susan's hand. "No nine-year-old should be wearing that gunk to school anyhow. And clean up your breakfast stuff." She pushed the talk button cutting off the fourth ring. "Hello. Yes, this is Susan Brand."

Susan glanced down the hall to see if Amy was doing what she had been asked. She wasn't. Amy dawdled in front of the mirror, moving gaudy boas, loops of beads, and her sketches of the Teton Peaks to look at her face. She leisurely zipped up her brown cords and straightened her yellow polo.

"We have what ... when?" Susan struggled to hear the chatty vet's assistant, who had called about an appointment for Cinder, their black

Lab. She looked at the clock and jammed a hand through her hair. Her heart was pounding—a reminder to back off on the morning coffee. Amy left her room, heading in the wrong direction, and Susan could feel her anger rising.

Amy skated down the hall in her socks, humming to herself and practicing her double toe loops. She spun to a stop out of sight at her mother's bedroom door. Spring sunlight shimmered through the room, illuminating all its mysteries and treasures. Everything was soft and smelled luscious. She glanced at her mother's bed and noticed the items there.

"My bed's so spacious, it's like sleeping in Montana," her mother always said.

Amy skated to the dresser and slipped her lip-gloss into her pocket. She opened the top drawer a few inches and relished the aroma of clean clothes and lavender potpourri. She slid over to the bed, inspected Susan's radio and ID badge, and flipped open the cell phone to the screensaver picture of her hugging Cinder. She stopped humming when she saw the handgun. She glanced over her shoulder, put down the cell, and slowly picked up the pistol with both hands. She aimed along the barrel at her reflection in the mirror and made soft popping sounds with her lips. She carefully put the gun back and scrambled up on the bed.

Susan cradled the phone in the crook of her neck, worked her belt through the final loop, and cinched it tight. She quickly ended the call. The rhythmic squeak of bedsprings reverberated down the hall. Amy was refining her trampoline moves.

Susan reached to replace the phone on the wall charger and adjusted her holster with her other hand. The holster was empty. She froze for a moment, threw down the phone on the table and sprinted to the bedroom.

"Amy, stop!"

Amy launched one last hard jump, landing on her bottom on the edge of the mattress. The impact bounced the cell phone and pistol off the bed.

Susan dove.

She bobbled the pistol through her hands and it discharged before dropping to the floor.

Amy screamed. Susan winced from pain.

She stared in horror at her daughter.

She leaped up and grabbed Amy, hugging her, checking her all over, rocking her, squeezing her tight.

A red stain oozed through Susan's fingers, soaking the white duvet.

May 19
Friday

"Break a leg. See you at the top," Fernando said to Don. It was the last in a series of routines Fernando performed before climbing. He glanced across the open meadows below stretching several miles to Jackson, inhaled the scent of sun-warmed sage, and stepped toward the face. A modest rack of climbing hardware, slung bandolier-style, clanked against his slender nylon-covered hip.

"Even a Gumby like me is not likely to break anything on this climb," Don said, preparing to belay his friend. Fernando smiled over his shoulder, adjusted his loose-fitting sleeveless t-shirt, and then turned to the rock and reached, catlike, for the first handhold. At moments like this, to Don, Nando looked beautiful.

Don stood braced at the bottom of the face. At intervals he played out slack and squinted into the morning sun to admire his friend's grace on the rock. Fernando's body flowed over surfaces where Don could discern no holds. The red rope snaked up the limestone route.

Fernando didn't need the climbing hardware he placed at intervals in the cracks that paralleled his ascent; there was rarely any tension on the rope when he climbed. Years of dance training served him well, now only a memory since his rebirth as an environmentalist and field scientist. Fernando finessed the crucial move of the seventy-five foot climb at the apex of an overhang and disappeared from Don's view.

"Off belay," Fernando called.

"Belay off," Don dropped the coil of rope and prepared to follow. It was reassuring to Don to know that once Fernando had anchored himself at the top, he'd protect Don as he climbed by taking up the slack in the rope.

"How was it?" Don called up.

"Excellent! Piece of cake. You're going to love it," Fernando shouted. He pulled the rope taut against Don's harness.

Don tried to slow his breathing while he waited for the signal to make his first move. Up the canyon, a stream, ribboned in green, pooled and fell through steep striated walls and thick stands of conifers. Several patches of lingering snow, tinted a dirty pink from algae, dotted the slope. A red-tailed hawk circled above, its rasping scream echoing across the canyon.

A rock the size of a baseball careened off the top, startling Don, and ricocheted down the talus below. It was unusual for Fernando to dislodge the smallest pebble without calling down a warning.

Fernando shouted, "Fu … oh, no … my God."

Don's focus jerked back to the top of the climb. "Fernando?"

Sounds of feet scuffing rock … a grunt.

A scream echoed down the canyon.

A blur of color hit the edge of the overhang and cascaded down the cliff.

Fernando smashed into the rocks at Don's feet. Trailing rope fell limp on the crumpled body.

Susan left Chuck Simmons sitting in their patrol unit outside St. John's Hospital. As she walked away from the car she noticed his gray handlebar moustache curling around the trademark grin. He was listening to Fox News and enjoying a political cartoon in the daily paper. His cowboy tan started about four wrinkles down from thick salt-and-pepper hair. She envied him. She wished she had something to smile about.

The emergency room doc insisted Susan check back the morning after the accident. Next up on this day of reckoning: facing the chief. Her stomach roiled at the thought. Susan relished the sunshine on her face as she crossed the parking lot to the hospital entrance. The unusual weather was one good thing about this May day.

Susan was back out with a fresh bandage in no time. She opened the car door and slid into the passenger's seat. Chuck was hunched at the wheel looking impatient. "Few minutes ago, dispatch reported a climbing accident in Curtis Canyon." Curtis Canyon lay across the National Elk Refuge bordering Jackson, just beyond the hospital; it offered a popular rock wall near the mouth. "The Sheriff requested P.D. support because everyone at his office is tied up with a semi-truck rollover on Teton Pass. Chief hit my cell a few minutes ago. He's shorthanded too. He wants us to take this last assignment before his little sit-down with you."

Susan glanced down at her tan sweater and slacks. "I'm not even in uniform."

"From the sound of this accident, dressed for your own funeral might be the best call."

Chuck turned on the emergency lights and sped out of town on the unpaved refuge road parallel to the Gros Ventre Range and under the Sleeping Indian Mountain. The summit, which resembles an American Indian in headdress, reclines on the eastern wall of Jackson Hole above the mostly level refuge.

"How's the hand?" Chuck asked.

"Ibuprofen is helping." Susan tucked her bandaged hand down between her thigh and the car door. "I love it out here. Feel like I can breathe."

"Did you get your sorry ass out here this winter?"

"Couple times. Saw wolves working the elk herd. Amazing." Pedestrians moved onto the shoulder away from the police car. "I'm still impressed with that bull elk you got out here last fall," Susan said. "Don't know I could pull the trigger though."

"Hunter or tree hugger. You love animals, you love the Elk Refuge."

"And if you're into mountains." She pushed her hair behind her ear. "It's really the animals and the mountains that've kept me here—that, and the complications of moving a nine-year-old away from her friends. That ole' chief stretched out above us has always been special to me." Susan craned her neck to look up at the Sleeping Indian.

"Didn't you bag that sucker a few years ago? Without even the aid of horse flesh if I remember correctly."

"It was one long, hot slog but gorgeous at the top. Drops sheer for thousands of feet off the backside of the chief's chest."

Chuck's eyes scanned the vast refuge. "Seems all the critters have headed back to the high country for the summer. Sure looks parched for this early."

"Tinder dry." Susan rested her bandaged hand on her leg and stared down at it. "I've had this weird feeling of late. Agitated. Like before a storm. We could use a good rain."

"Yeah, but like as not we'll get hammered with lightning without much moisture. And that means fire exploding in yonder hills." He glanced at her. "Wouldn't you expect to feel a little weird after your accident?"

"That sure as hell didn't help, but this feeling—I don't know—been going on long before that." They sped across the green-gold refuge meadows with the snow-covered Tetons towering to the west.

They arrived at the scene, a side canyon furred with evergreens. Chuck slid the patrol car into a gravel parking lot. Susan grabbed her gear and jumped out. An ambulance sat empty, its rear doors open, its lights rotating, casting a swirling blue reflection on the surrounding sagebrush. A Forest Service vehicle was parked to one side of the ambulance. The only other vehicle in the parking area was a silver Subaru Forrester with Colorado plates. As they hurried to the rock face, Susan mentally reviewed protocol. If the Sheriff's Office could not respond to the call and someone was seriously injured or dead, the police had jurisdiction over the Forest Service. She was in charge.

Chuck and Susan followed a trail through some spruce, up a streambed, and angled through a talus slope to the base of a cliff band. Two Forest Service employees and two EMTs were huddled over a broken figure. Blood was splashed like paint on the rocks around the body. A gurney stood waiting nearby. There was no sense of urgency.

"Dead?" Susan asked. The female EMT nodded. Except for the mocking croak of a raven, the canyon lay silent. A slight young man in climbing attire sat apart from the group and looked off across the valley. The breeze lifted strands of his thin brown hair.

"I'm going up. It would be better if you stayed here. See what you can learn," Chuck said. He scrambled toward the well-worn trail around the cliff to the top. Chuck's taking charge chafed at first, but then Susan realized he was probably just following Earl's orders resulting from her shaky status. Plus she saw it as an opportunity to interview the other man. Susan grabbed a blanket off the gurney and approached the climber. She looked across the valley and, although the skies to the north and south were still clear, wispy mares' tails were gathering around the Grand, the most prominent of the Tetons. She introduced herself. The young man choked out that his name was Don Stein and that he and the fallen climber, Fernando Diaz, were partners.

"I am very sorry for your loss." Susan touched his arm with her hand and eased down beside him. "How long have you known Fernando, Mr. Stein?"

"We've … been together two … two years." He paused to swallow. "We met three years ago in graduate school. I … I'm in shock, I just can't believe my soul mate is gone." He began to shake.

"I know this is really difficult." Susan wrapped the blanket around his shoulders and gave him a moment to regain his composure. "I just need to ask you a few questions. Tell me about Fernando."

"He was intelligent, kind. He was sweet …" Stein's voice trailed off.

"Was he a skilled rock climber?"

"He was incredible!" He looked intently into Susan's face. "He rarely fell. Almost never. It was like watching a ballet. But he had none of the ego of a lot of top climbers. My Nando was a … was a wonderful man."

He told Susan that Fernando had introduced him to rock climbing in Boulder, Colorado, after they both went to work for Dr. Noah Skutches, a field scientist at the University of Colorado. Skutches and his assistants were in Wyoming to study birds of prey in the Yellowstone ecosystem. They had arrived in Jackson Hole a few days ago and Don and Fernando headed out to climb at the first opportunity.

"I just don't know what I'm ... how I'm ..." He started to cry. Susan put her arm around his shoulders until his sobbing stopped. A marmot whistled a warning from the opposite boulder-strewn slope, indicating that death circled above in the form of a red-tailed hawk.

"Don, can you tell me what you remember from just before the accident?"

"Fernando or ... or someone knocked a large rock down without calling a warning. He never made that kind of mistake. He is, was, too disciplined. And, I'm pretty sure I heard a struggle just before he fell."

"You think you heard sounds of a fight?"

"Yes, you have to go up there and look."

"We are up there. It might help to know if Fernando had any enemies."

"Fernando?" He sniffed, smiled and shook his head. "No, absolutely not. You couldn't help but love Fernando. He was such a pure spirit."

Stein said he had been preparing to climb at the time of the accident so he was vague on other details. But he was adamant he'd heard something suspicious.

"Can you describe the sounds you heard?" Susan asked.

"I heard a grunt, a shout, and like a scraping sound."

"But you can't think of anyone who would want to harm Fernando?" Susan asked.

Stein shook his head and stared off into space. Susan gave him her card in case he thought of anything else relating to the incident. He slowly gathered up his things to walk to the parking area. The sun began to heat the rock face as noon approached. Susan sat on a boulder struggling to hold the notebook in her bandaged hand and jotted down some notes. She weighed Stein's emotional state against his memories of the incident. Her concentration was broken, first by the shriek of the hunting hawk, and then by the sound of rocks tumbling down the path.

Chuck was shuffling and sliding down the steep trail beside the rock face. He had some colorful straps in his hand. Once down, he joined Susan and pointed to the top.

"There's a routine belay spot, flat and bombproof, lots of signs of repeated use and wear," Chuck said, still huffing for air. "There's footprints everywhere leading to and from the top of the rock face but the belay for the climb is a shelf of solid rock. Diaz must have thrown these two nylon slings over a boulder for an anchor, but slipped before clipping his harness to them. The slings were all that I found at the top of the climb. He probably tripped on his rope." Chuck had done a little rock climbing for police rescue training and a little was all that was required in any endeavor to deem himself an expert.

"Whoa, buddy, while you were cowboying around up top, I got some interesting information from Don Stein." Susan relayed Stein's recollection of the incident as well as his suspicions.

"Struggle? No sign of that. Unless Diaz was blind, he'd have seen his attacker far enough away to call 911 and give a full description before the guy laid a hand on him."

Seeing that she was getting nowhere with Chuck, Susan said, "You know what, let's wrap this up here and discuss it back at the office."

The EMTs had loaded Fernando on the gurney. Susan released the body for transport to the local coroner's office. Chuck and Susan headed in as well. This time as they crossed the refuge Susan had a better view of the Sleeping Indian lying in repose above the valley as he had for millennium after millennium. Her father, the Reverend Brand, would have referenced Revelation 20 at Susan's mere mention of that word, thundering, "The thousand years during which holiness and great happiness is to prevail and Christ is to reign on earth." If only, Susan thought, remembering Fernando Diaz's broken body and Don Stein's broken heart. And that thought caused her chest to constrict as the horrible events of the previous morning flooded back, accompanied by an undercurrent of concern for Amy.

Susan had Chuck drop her at the office so she could begin working on the report while he went to interview Dr. Skutches at Snow King Lodge. When Chuck had been gone an hour, Susan called him on his cell, putting him on speaker so she could continue typing her report.

"The professor confirmed everything Stein said about Fernando. Nice guy—loved by all. This was an accident," Chuck said.

"But Stein insists he heard a struggle."

"The good professor says that no one could possibly want to kill this guy. He just arrived and nobody even knows him here. What's the motive, Susan? There's no evidence of struggle." Susan stopped typing and stared out the window at a red squirrel clinging to the limb of a pine.

"I have to take your word for that, don't I, because you wouldn't let me climb up to the top."

"Come on. I didn't say you couldn't. I just said it might be better if you didn't. Besides, you're better at interviewing hysterical little girls."

"Don Stein was very upset, yes, but that fact, and the fact that he's gay, doesn't make him less reliable. Stein's sure he heard a struggle."

"Stein's idea of a struggle is trying to put a cork back in a bottle of chardonnay."

"Chuck, goddamnit! Can your macho bullshit and be objective. I can't write this up without mentioning our one eyewitness's perspective. If that makes it so your version is not as neat and tidy, I can't help that."

"Go ahead," he said. "Hell, everyone's a victim, everyone's looking for someone to blame. Jackson hasn't had a homicide in years, Susan. As far as I'm concerned, this was an accident, a climber's error. See you back at the office."

Chuck's redneck views notwithstanding, Susan had to admit that none of the usual suspects—money, sex, jealousy—seemed to apply in Fernando's case. She could think of only one possible motive for his murder. But if you're going to kill someone because of his sexual preference, why go to the trouble of doing it from the top of a climb in the middle of nowhere? It just didn't figure, plus Chuck wasn't buying it. And, if Chuck wasn't buying it, the Chief wouldn't buy it. Given her recent track record, no one was going to listen to her vague suspicions. Case closed. Time to choke down some lunch and suck it up for a wall-to-wall conversation with the boss.

May 19
Friday Afternoon

Susan slumped in a daze on a black plastic chair. The intensity of the morning had briefly distracted her, but the reality of her employment situation came slamming back as she waited outside Earl Meacham's office. She stared at the bandage on her right hand and prepared herself for a difficult conversation with Earl. Her whole being was fragmented. She felt at once cool and detached, hot and agitated. Parts of her were at war: the lucky mother (it could have been much worse) against the guilty one (it was so damned stupid), the smart tough cop at odds with the careless one, the independent woman battling the vulnerable single parent. And her confidence was draining away. No bandage could stanch that flow. She searched her mind for a reassuring thought.

The image of Old Ruth rose up in her memory. She was a Tohono O'odham elder who had lived alone on the reservation in southern Arizona where the Brands used to reside; Reverend Brand had established a Salvation Army Mission there. Though long dead, Ruth remained a shamanic figure of calm, healing, and justice for Susan.

"You are a very brave child, and very strong," Susan remembered Old Ruth saying after school on her porch. Ruth would stand with her back to the sun, bathing Susan's face in her cool shadow, her head encircled by fiery light. "Your pretty hair is like honey," she would say, her gnarled hands pushing flaxen strands behind Susan's ears. Susan always felt small in her father's presence, but she felt like Wonder Woman after those moments with Ruth. Susan often said the exact same words to Amy while brushing back her hair.

It had been awful to see her athletic little girl hobbling home from the hospital on crutches but, my God, the alternative was unimaginable. At least the doctors were predicting a full recovery for where the bullet grazed the palm of Susan's hand and no permanent damage to Amy's foot. Susan suddenly felt the stares of everyone in the station.

A crew-cut rookie on his first day lingered at the coffee pot beside the cluttered bulletin board for his turn to talk to Earl. Until now, her record had been spotless, but Jackson Hole, Wyoming, was a location so desirable, there were dozens of qualified applicants for every job, and she was worried.

What is wrong with this picture, she thought? I recklessly endangered my daughter yesterday. It's two in the afternoon and instead of being out on patrol, I'm out of uniform—dressed up for the dressing down—sitting here looking totally weird with a mummified hand, and I might lose the uniform for good without even an internal review. Oh yeah, there is a whole hell of a lot wrong with this picture. There is only one word—one of Amy's favorites—to describe this situation: it sucks.

She glanced at the frosted glass on the office door that read, "Earl Meacham," and wondered what the chief could possibly be doing in there that was more important than crucifying her. Earl was, no doubt, intentionally keeping her waiting, sweating it out in front of her peers. Her rightful punishment had officially begun.

Earl was a big man, well-loved and generous, tough but fair. He was blessed with thick black hair that belied his six decades, yet Susan had recently pointed out to him that his jowls and slight paunch were starting to blow his cover. Earl had been in the department twenty-three years, serving twelve as chief. Susan could imagine him leaning back against his old leather chair in thought, wanting to get this inevitable chewing out just right. She shook her head, exhaled impatiently, and stared out the window at the grassy lower slopes and evergreens of Snow King Mountain on the edge of town.

At last Earl opened his door. Susan entered in silence and took a chair. Earl's office was simply furnished with a cluttered wooden desk and bookshelves stacked with official binders. He had two pictures on his desk, one of his wife, Rita, and one of his other love, Bob Barker, an aging golden retriever. His walls were covered with diplomas and recognitions. His favorite plaque, however, was a fish that looked like authentic taxidermy until you touched a remote control and it flopped its head and tail. That always got a laugh, but Susan knew today's discussion would be no laughing matter. She sat rigid, waiting for him to speak, her bandaged hand tucked in her lap.

"Susan, I want to tell you a story. Do you mind?"

Susan inhaled. "No, of course not." She pushed a strand of hair behind her left ear. "What is it?"

"When I was a kid in Colorado, my father and I fished and canoed a lot. The spring I turned seventeen, we decided to run a river close to flood stage from snowmelt. After paddling a few flat miles in a canyon, clouds moved in and it rained like hell. I was in the bow and I knew immediately we were in over our heads.

"Long story short, in the first rapid, I was scared shitless. I fought the water rather than working with it, and we capsized. I was trapped under the canoe for a while, then popped up on the surface and, while being pulled by the current, got beat up by the rocks. I finally dragged myself to shore in an eddy below the rapid and, shivering like a damn aspen leaf, dropped onto a boulder."

Susan shifted in her chair and glanced down at her hands.

Earl continued. "My father managed to swim the white water beside the canoe and haul it in about a quarter mile downstream. He made his way back to me and we sat in silence for a few minutes. Then he told me we had to go on before we froze to death. Rapids roared ahead of us on the river. I glared at him and said, 'No way, I'm not going on'.

"My father was pretty savvy. He pointed out that the canyon walls were too steep to climb out and the current was too hard to paddle upstream. He said, 'The only way out is through, buddy.' Only one option—as a kid, that was a first for me.

"I started out tentative, but soon realized that our situation wasn't so bad. If I worked with the force of the water I could conserve energy and avoid another swim. I was stoked by the time we stroked through the final rapid and a whole lot warmer from paddling like a son-of-a-bitch. You see where this is leading, Susan?"

"Umm ... truthfully, Chief ... not really."

"Let me help you. You screwed up big time, Officer Brand. This accidental discharge of your weapon is a career-threatening mistake. Your excellent record helps, but it doesn't excuse you. You'll be the subject of a review, have curtailed duties at the time of year we need you the most, and your fellow officers and I are going to be watching you like a hawk. In fact, I'm assigning Officer Simmons to be your partner. Your life is gonna be hell for a while." Earl took a sip of water from a glass on his desk.

"But the only way out is through. Hold your head up and paddle like a son-of-a-bitch. You'll survive this, and, at the risk of sounding preachy, you'll be stronger for it. I respect you and I'll support you, but I've been very worried about your distracted state of mind since, well, since your divorce. It's going to be tough on you. It can't go any other way." He picked up a paper clip off his desk and twisted it. "Do you have anything to say?"

Susan's shame began to give way a little to relief. She still had a job, for now. "Yes, Chief." She cleared her throat. "For the life of me, I don't know how this happened. I've been planning forever to sell that old Beretta .380 but I needed it because my Glock misfired at the range. The gunsmith is checking it out." Susan sat forward in her chair and pushed her hair behind her ears. "I had a traffic stop the night before the accident, and I got a little spooked when the guy started digging around under his seat and didn't immediately lower his window. Turned out he was trying to find his registration. I must have left the Beretta half-cocked with the safety off and a round in the chamber. I ... I get sick to my stomach thinking about it. But I screwed up and I accept full responsibility for my actions and for Amy's injury. It will never happen again."

"If I didn't trust that, I would be firing your ass, as we speak." He took another sip of water. "You're a good cop and I have thoroughly enjoyed working with you the last four years, but I want my old cop back." They sat in silence for a moment. "Take a couple hours of personal time and go check on Amy." She got up to leave. "Give her a hug for me." Earl picked up a file on his desk and began to leaf through it.

Susan turned at the door, "Chief."

"Yeah?"

"Can I give you some feedback?"

Earl didn't look up. "Feedback is always welcome, Brand."

"That canoeing story…"

"Yeah, what about it?" Earl asked.

"Uh—it was a parable."

"A parable, huh?" Earl put down his papers, puffed up and grinned. "Hmm, I guess it was."

"No offense, but … you can chew me out all day long if you want, but … I hate parables."

Earl's jowls fell and a scowl crossed his face. "It was the best I could come up with under the circumstances."

"I … I get that, Chief. But my father … he … he was a preacher and always lectured us in parables."

"Fine. Thanks for the input. Tell you what, next time I'll simply say, 'you're up shit creek without a paddle,' and help you pack your stuff. We'll discuss this again after the review. Now get your goddamn feedback out of my office."

Susan closed Earl's door, walked through the office trying to look confident, and headed straight out of the building. She paused on the sidewalk and glanced toward the mountains. The air felt cooler even though sunlight still reflected off the windshields of the cars lining the street. Perhaps a front was moving in.

Susan again thought of Old Ruth. It was Ruth's unfortunate end that crystallized Susan's determination to enter police work. In the fall of the year Susan turned sixteen, Ruth was murdered, her head crushed from behind with a piece of firewood. The little house had been ransacked and a few humble possessions and some savings stolen.

Susan's father presided at graveside. She heard the words, "Our beloved Ruth is with Jesus: she is in a better place." But they provided no solace from the gut-deep pain watching her angelic friend being lowered into a hole. Several members of the tribe shoveled dirt onto the coffin—the sound of cascading rocks on wood echoed out of the grave. Susan turned to her mother. Ellen Brand gave her daughter a shoulder squeeze and then wrapped herself in her usual silence. Finally Susan grabbed a shovel, the only woman present to do so, and threw sand in the grave until the flesh on her palms tore.

The tribal police never solved the case. Susan was determined to do that some day.

Looking back, Susan realized Ruth's funeral marked the day the dam broke on her confused compliance, and her questions flooded out. I once was blind but now I see. Eventually her doubts became such a torrent that, if they did not directly erode her father's authority, they certainly washed away some of the sand beneath his firmly planted feet. Her questions were mostly met by biblical references or silence until Northern Arizona University in Flagstaff where she was delighted to find her queries welcome. And it was there that she learned solace could be found in the righteousness of a sweaty pilgrimage to the top of a snow-covered mountain.

Susan strained the grit and grime of her daily police work through the fine mesh that was Ruth's strength and spirit. She tried to apply Ruth's healing ways to the white system of retributive justice. Ruth, schooled in the ways of the church as well as the ways of the earth, was Susan's guardian angel, and right now, Susan longed to ask Ruth what she'd recommend for bringing harmony back to a discordant life. Then Susan recalled something that might help—Ruth had always insisted that when Susan was upset, she should run until she felt at peace. Susan credited Ruth for the fact that she had been an avid runner all her life.

Susan needed to clear her head before heading home to Amy. She started running. For the first block it was a jog, but as oxygen filled her lungs, and the cadence of her feet striking the pavement reverberated up her thighs, she picked up the pace. She sprinted past the log building of Fighting Bear Antiques and into a residential area of modest homes and cabins. Soon she was at the base of Snow King Mountain Ski Resort. The mountaintop was white with spring snow. Muddy tracks under the chairlift to the summit were a vestige of the annual "King of the Hill" snowmobile event. Susan darted around a young woman walking a graying black Lab and leapt over a curb that led to a park near the indoor ice rink where Amy took her skating lessons.

Susan charged into the little park and stopped. She bent over a picnic table and sucked air while her heart slowed. She plopped down on a swing, pushed hard and pumped furiously for several minutes until her injured hand throbbed and the wind chill burned her face. She jammed her feet in the dirt and tried to stand, but the ground was slick and she went down hard on her butt, the swing clipping her in the back of the head. Bending forward, she yelled, "God, I hate parables!" Then dropped her head in her hands and wept.

May 25
Thursday

It was noon. He had been back in Jackson Hole less than twenty-four hours and once again his life was a lot more complicated. He had a raging female tied up and gagged in the motel bathroom and no clue what to do with her. He also had to think of some way to silence her old beagle, yapping incessantly outside in her car.

A deer antler lamp rocked on its points on the bedside table as another kick shook the wall. He checked the bathroom doorknob, tightened the climbing sling that secured it to the lodgepole pine bed, grabbed another sling out of his brown canvas rucksack, and slipped outside the room. Shielding his eyes from the sun, he jogged barefoot down the steps to the parking lot and opened the car door. The dog snarled from the corner of the back seat. The man cinched some nylon webbing around the dog's collar and dragged him back up to the room. The old dog sniffed and strained toward his owner's parka thrown over a chair, snapped at him, and then backed under the bed.

He picked up his cell phone to dial the tunnel office, but couldn't. He felt the tightening in his lungs that signaled extreme stress, grabbed his inhaler off the bedside table, and took two quick puffs. The super had warned him about thinking with his dick, and he didn't relish telling him about this time. The chick was calling it rape. Shit, he'd hardly touched her. Damn college bitch and her damn ideas. She shouldn't have teased him and then turned him down. She thought she was better than him. He hitched up his camouflage pants, flopped down against the pillows on the bed and rubbed the butt of his cell phone up and down his corrugated brown belly. Another hard kick at the bathroom wall and some muffled cursing overcame his inertia. He had to make the call.

"Speak," the super answered. Heavy equipment groaned in the background.

"Hey, man, it's me. I've got a little problem."

"You ever call me and don't have a problem, I'll go back to finding water with a stick. What is it this time?"

"Shit, uh … so how's the straw coming?"

"We're very close to breaking through to Mead. We'll have all the new water Vegas desires and then some to sell. If you can stay out of trouble and keep the ecofreaks distracted, we should finish soon. And just a mere thirty-three million and change over budget, thanks to our thirsty Japanese brethren. Now stop stalling and tell me what the hell you've got yourself into this time while living on my expense account."

"What's the boss up to?" he asked.

"The Water Witch? She's into a genuine CYA covert operation. She's doing everything in her power to avoid swinging for this one. And, of course, the Water Witch is being a water bitch as usual … always on my back because she doesn't spend any time on hers. Now what in bloody hell do you want, lad?"

Even his whitewashed version of the motel affair left the super sputtering. "That's the stupidest thing I've ever heard of anyone with half a brain doing," he shouted. "Are you out of your goddamn mind? Do you know who that chick is? This could blow the whole tunnel deal! Shut down the straw project permanently. Do you understand me, you horny fuck?"

The super raked him over the coals for a few more minutes, and then said he'd call back with a plan. As an afterthought, he threatened to cut off his balls when he got a hold of him and slammed down the phone.

Another miserable hour passed as the man tried to placate his captive. Every time he entered the bathroom and approached her, the damn dog lunged at his ankle from behind. The woman wouldn't listen to reason. He was certain if he freed her, she'd go straight to the cops.

He fidgeted and paced, trying to ignore his hunger because he was afraid to leave the room for long. He allowed the woman Gatorade only after she promised to shut up and stop trying to kick him with those damn long legs. But after she drank, she spat the word "murderer" at him. That really had him concerned. He duct-taped the saliva-soaked gag back into her mouth, dodging bites and kicks. He tried to push her red hair out of the way so he could see her pretty freckled face but she tried to head butt him. He slammed the door and secured it again.

The super finally called. His instructions were to wait until the middle of the night and then transport the girl to a ranch in the mountains above Jackson to meet a plane at dawn. He leaned back against the pillows and uncoiled a little. Felt good to have a plan. His breath came a little easier.

May 26
Friday

She didn't resist; the tranquilizers he slipped into her Gatorade had taken effect. He carried her to the car wrapped in blankets. The dog followed cautiously. The man decided to take him along to shut him up. The car was loaded just after 3:00 a.m. He drove north through Grand Teton National Park.

Along the Teton Front, cirrus clouds scurried across peaks lit by a partial moon. Gray rock massifs, intermittently overlaid by white glaciers, were lustrous in the reflected light. The opalescent spires reminded him of the shark's teeth in the song, "Mack the Knife," and he whistled it as he drove. This was a shitty thing to be doing, but a shit-kicking beautiful place to be doing it, he thought. He'd have to make up a story to explain the disappearance of the girl, something that didn't cause suspicion and involve the cops. The super had said they'd decide later what to do with her. Maybe she could be used to their advantage, perhaps to frame a few tree huggers. He glanced back at the sleeping lump. The dog bared his teeth.

"Freakin' mutt!" he said to the rear view mirror. Maybe after he was paid off and long gone she'd be released alive—but maybe not. Heading east at Moran, the turquoise Mitsubishi climbed out of the valley and turned onto the Union Pass Road. It was gravel, and a washboard hell. The super's directions put the ranch on Kinky Creek Road, roughly twenty-three miles from the pavement. Dawning light revealed dark clouds clustering over the Tetons to the west. After several miles, a mountain squall blew through, settling the dust and opening his brain to a few fresh ideas. He could say she got homesick and went back home. No, that was too easy to check on. Maybe she ran into some old college buddies and went backpacking and was going to rejoin the group later. He'd drive her car until she "caught up with them." Yeah, something like that'd work. By the time they saw through the bullshit, like that roadrunner character leaving that stupid coyote in the dust holding a lit six-pack of dynamite, he'd be long gone. Kaboom! The right lie would buy him the time he needed. He just had to figure out the right lie.

High in the mountains, near the headwaters of the Gros Ventre River, lay the Bar 7-11 Ranch, protected by a cirque of eroded and snow-covered peaks and a full complement of security. Armed guards drove the perimeter twenty-four hours a day; no one visited without an invitation and proper identification. A black cowboy hat atop a yellow slicker stopped the car at the gate. The driver lowered his car window. The dog growled. Long rays of light poked through the scattering clouds and the sagebrush glistened, fragrant with new moisture.

He drove in and parked the car at the end of the landing strip. The main ranch buildings and corrals were faintly visible through the rising mist at the far end of the meadow. Horses grazed adjacent to the strip. He heard a plane. The woman groaned in the back of the car and a mix of dread and relief churned in his stomach. The plane's drone rose to a crescendo.

A small twin-engine landed on the first approach, scattering some of the horses. The plane bumped across the gravel toward the car and turned sharply into the tall grass. The pilot killed the engine and a door emblazoned with an official seal slammed open.

The super squeezed his bulk through the door and lunged toward him. "I'm going to go over this one more time, you stupid loser! Your job is to do nothing to attract attention to yourself. You understand me? Nothing!" The man was staring at his right boot. He rolled a wet horse turd back and forth in the damp earth. A pungent smell rose with each push.

"Your job is to ensure that we can finish the goddamn tunnel unimpeded by the bloody enviros. I swear to God, if you fuck up one more time, I will not bail you out. I defended you to the boss when you slipped up and got made by that nosy spic queer—but now this! You're headed for a fall, yourself, if you don't watch your step. Do you understand me?"

He tilted his head sideways at the super briefly and nodded, "Yeah."

"Well, you goddamn better. This is serious business. If the environmentalists attract attention to the straw, the media and the Feds will be close behind, and then we are dead in the water on the project— that's best case—and facing fraud and homicide charges worst case. Do you understand why you need to keep your eye on the ball and your pecker in your pants?"

"Yup," he said.

"I'll go to bat for you one last time. It's damn fortunate the members of the consortium will do just about any fucking thing to procure more reliable water for their precious businesses. I'll tell them the girl was on to us and that she was sniffing around about sensitive matters. If you're lucky, they'll let me keep her stashed until this is over and you're history, before they hear a word about what you did to her getting your goddamn rocks off." The super's glare was withering. "Now help me get the bitch in the plane. I'm needed back at the straw."

The super's rebuke still rang in his ears as the plane circled up over the mountains like an engorged bird of prey. His only consolation was the sure knowledge that he'd take care of the fat fuck, some sweet day. When he returned to the car, the dog was gone.

"Shit! Now I have to waste more time looking for a fucking dog," he shouted to the sagebrush. Someone else might find the dog and identify him. He had to attend two very important events that day in Jackson and in Yellowstone. All this—and with no sleep. Christ, he thought, this is shaping up as another day from hell.

He searched the length of the airstrip, but there was no sign of the dog. At the far end, he decided the hell with it, no one would find the damn mutt and he'd just be coyote feed anyhow. The man turned and jogged back up the break in the sagebrush to the car, lungs burning from the altitude. While opening the driver's side door, he noticed the turquoise paint had several new scratches, and in the dirt there were drag marks leading under the car. He kneeled down and peered under the chassis. The dog growled and backed up. He was reluctant to reach under in the vicinity of the dog's jaws. He stood, opened the back door, and found one of the girl's shirts on the seat. On the floor was a half-chewed leather bone. He grabbed the bone and wrapped it in the material and held it under the car.

The dog inched forward and he pulled the bone back slightly. The dog moved again and was close enough that he could see his collar. When he reached for it with his other hand, the dog lunged and bit his fingers. "Ow, goddamnit!" He grabbed the collar and pulled the snarling animal out from under the car. In a rage, he kicked the canine repeatedly in the lower back with the toe of his boot.

The dog bleated and tried to shake free. He twisted the nylon collar in his hand cutting off the dog's air supply and forcing him over onto his side. He stomped the full force of his boot down on his ribs. Bones snapped and collapsed like dry sticks. The dog choked and shrieked in pain. His pink tongue lolled out into the dirt and blood gushed from his jaws. The man twisted the collar until there was silence.

He hurled the little body deep into the sagebrush and, heart pounding, gasped for breath in the thin mountain air. His hand throbbed. He straightened, pulled his inhaler from his jeans pocket and sucked on it twice. Suddenly, he noticed a jab of pain in the palm of his hand. Opening his fist, he saw a deep semicircular cut caused by a metal dog tag. He thrust the tag and his inhaler into his jeans, pulled his bandana out of his back pocket and wrapped his injured hand.

He slid back behind the wheel of the car, paused to clear his head, and took a few deep breaths. The inhalant was working; his breath was coming easier, but he still felt like crap. He started the car and plowed backward over sagebrush to turn around, and then realized what was wrong: he'd been up all night, it was almost 7:00 a.m., and so far, no coffee.

June 1
Thursday

"**D**amnit!" Susan grunted from the pain in her right hand as she wrestled the wobbly grocery cart. A tall slender woman studying the cereal boxes looked up in alarm. Her eyes settled on Susan, expressing recognition and pity, and then looked away.

Susan would not return to the front of the store for a cart that tracked straight. She was pissed off at Earl Meacham. In fact, she was fed up with just about everyone in the whole damned department and their insistence on treating her like a kid who had been grounded. It had been two weeks since the shooting accident and there was no end to the patronizing attitudes and phony sympathy. The throbbing from her bandaged hand was nothing compared to her embarrassment at the accusatory glances of the other shoppers.

Jackson is a small town. People read the paper and people talk, and it's not like you can hide while wearing a police uniform. Her nightmare had received prominent coverage in the local press two weeks running. The second article had just come out and was available to all right there in the grocery store. Her carelessness might as well have been plastered over the walls beside the signs for New Zealand apples. Susan searched the aisles for Amy's favorite pizza chips. She was eager to end this ordeal of public humiliation and return to her daughter waiting alone, after school, at home. Two prospects eased her anxiety a little; after spending some time with Amy, she could go for a short run. And maybe later she'd enjoy some email girl banter from her friend Julie.

My amazing little Amy, Susan thought. At least she was doing pretty well. Her classmates had been great; they treated her like a celebrity, like a heroine in an exciting drama. Susan wondered why adults always behaved worse in these situations.

Thinking of Amy conjured up, once again, the wide-eyed look of shock and disbelief on her child's face when the gun discharged. If only I'd flicked on the safety, unloaded the weapon, un-cocked the hammer, she thought.

"Will there be anything else today, Ms. Brand?"

She was surprised to see a plump and pimply checkout girl place Amy's chips in the bag. "I'm sorry, what did you say?"

"I asked if you needed anything else before I ring this up."

"Ah … no, that's all. Thanks."

"No problem. That'll be eighty-six dollars and twelve cents." Susan caught her staring at her bandage. "How's your little girl?"

Susan didn't respond; she wanted to jam her bandaged hand behind her back but couldn't because she needed both hands to extract money from her wallet. She finally clawed out two fifties, handed them over, accepted her change, stuffed her wallet back in her daypack and walked out to her truck to drive home.

As she pulled out of the Smith's parking lot she lowered her window. She sought relief from her memories of the accident—which had just been stirred up again like muck in a stagnant pond—from the view of the mountains south of town and lungs full of high-elevation air. She had always loved how Jackson, though urban, was surrounded by buttes and mountains, and that it was possible to see mountains and hike up to stunning vistas from any place in town. On cooler days she chose sunny treeless south-facing slopes and in warm weather she hiked under towering trees on northern exposures. But no amount of mountain therapy could erase her gnawing guilt for the carelessness that hurt her daughter, guilt that redoubled every time she went on patrol and risked leaving Amy a motherless child.

Susan squeezed into a curbside parking space near her home. Loading up her left hand and hooking her right arm through several plastic bags, she hauled the groceries from the truck. Her little house, set well back from the street, was in the center of a commercial block. She went past the bagel shop and turned at the long path to the yellow saltbox cottage. Tall spruces lined the yard and filtered the early summer heat. She labored up the front walk under the weight of the groceries with the bag handles biting into her arm above the bandage.

Earlier that day, in front of the whole department, the chief had announced the details of an assignment for her. It was a missing person case of a young woman from Las Vegas. The girl's mother had last heard from her just before the daughter was due to arrive in Jackson Hole over a week ago. Susan had jumped at the chance like an over-anxious kid until Meacham went on to say that his buddy, the Chief of the Vegas PD, had called and made it clear the report was groundless. The bogus assignment was all just part of her punishment.

"You know," Meacham had commented while laughing, "adults have the right to be missing. She's probably hooked up with a river guide on a sandbar somewhere." Great! Thanks so much, Earl, for the public announcement of a meaningless position in a lame case. And then she thought, if it was Amy, even if she was grown up and on her own, she'd be just as concerned as that mom in Vegas.

One thing about the missing person report that had caught her attention—although no one else, and especially Chuck, thought it was significant—was that the "missing" woman was associated with the same group as the climber who had died in the fall she'd investigated a few weeks ago. She was unhappy about being given the case assignment, but, still, she needed to mull over the coincidence. Deep in her mind was the nagging feeling that there must be a connection.

As she neared the house, she could hear the television. Cinder greeted her at the screen door and wagged her into the living room where her daughter sat facing away from her on a worn, brown, tweed hide-a-bed.

The house was tiny with a living room, kitchen, two small bedrooms, and a bathroom on one floor. It was cozy, though, and affordable for Jackson. A designer friend had suggested that she go "up," since she couldn't go "out" in her small space, so shelves to the ceiling lined every wall of the living room. They were cluttered with books, trophies, magazines, pictures, a CD player, and mementos.

"How are you, sweetie?" Susan placed the groceries on the floor and smoothed Amy's honey hair against the sides of her head. Amy was wearing a white, scooped-neck t-shirt over blue shorts. She was barefoot. Cinder settled under the split log coffee table that held up Amy's bandaged foot.

Amy muted the TV. "I'm okay, Mom. Those pain pills you gave me are finally helping a little, I think." She put on her sad face. "It's just really hard to sit out soccer and stuff at recess."

"I know, Amers. It won't be long now, honey. Have you kept your foot elevated like Dr. Pockat said?"

Amy checked her bright green over-sized wristwatch. "I've been right here since school, Mom, except for a little fight with this bad dog who keeps stealing the remote." Cinder raised her massive head, pink tongue lolling to the side, as if to deny the accusation.

Susan scooped up the bags and headed to the kitchen. She called back, "Any messages?"

"Yeah, two—both marriage proposals from billionaires. I told them you'd call back."

"Very funny, sweetheart." Susan put the groceries on the counter. "Now, who called, really?"

"Dad called from Alaska. Said the spring skiing has been awesome and he still wants to get me up there soon. You're supposed to call him tonight, if you can. The other guy said he'd call back. I didn't have a pen and didn't want to make him wait while I crawled to the kitchen."

"Amy, you need to keep the phone and pen and paper handy when I'm out. Not to mention your crutches. What if there's a fire or something?"

"Oh Mom, chill. I will next time, okay? He said his name was Jake God or something." Amy turned the volume back on.

Susan smiled. "Guy by the name of God called, huh? I knew I was in serious trouble. Did God say what he wanted?" Amy chuckled at the cartoon. "Amy, turn down the TV. Did God say what he wanted?"

"Oh, something about being an investigator from Utah and needing your help."

"So God is from Utah and doing an investigation in Jackson Hole, and he wants my help. Well, look out Jackson town. There could be hell to pay."

"Huh?"

"Never mind, Amers. Want some chips and a glass of milk?"

"Sure." She put on her best baby-girl voice. "Peeetha chipth are bound to make my widdle foot feel bedda."

Susan smiled and felt her eyes dampen at her daughter's resiliency. Opening the fridge door, she relaxed her shoulders a little, and felt her spirits lift.

While she fixed spaghetti for dinner, Susan's mind turned to caller number one. She and Keith had moved to Jackson from Phoenix when Amy was two, leaving good friends behind. They wanted a safe town to raise their daughter and a more desirable climate for Susan, who hated the desert and craved mountains, and a winter sports town for Keith, who lived to ski and snowboard.

Her mind lurched, recalling once again the "thoughtful" note and one-hundred-dollar bill Keith had left when he ran off to Alaska to be a helicopter ski guide. Nice touch. If it hadn't been for her single and slightly wild hiking pal, Julie, who, given enough wine, could make anything hilarious, Susan wouldn't have survived Keith's abrupt and dramatic departure.

Unfortunately, Julie had decided she could no longer afford Jackson, so she left her nursing position at St. John's Hospital and moved to New Mexico a few months ago. Now Susan had to get her Julie fixes online, but thank God for Skype and Facebook. They were better than nothing. Susan chuckled, remembering how Julie was forever doling out pragmatic advice. Just before the gun accident, as they shared laughs and a long distance glass of wine on Skype, Julie said, "Listen, darling, it's been six months since your divorce and at forty-three, you ain't gettin' any younger. Hell, you ain't gettin' any, period. If you don't have time for a relationship, then just go to a bar and hook-up with some guy for Christ's sake. But don't ask his name and don't forget the rubber."

"Great! How romantic." Susan sputtered after swallowing a large sip and putting her hand up like a traffic cop. "Wait. Stop. Don't tell me your name. Just tell me you're packin' an extra-large Trojan." They both guffawed.

Susan smiled thinking of her friend. She made a mental note to check her email and, if there was no message from Julie, to contact her after a jog and dinner.

Rachel was as mad as he had ever seen her. She tossed his duffel onto the sidewalk in front of her brick Salt Lake City bungalow.

"Thanks for letting me keep my gear here." No response. "Hell, Rach, I said I was sorry for the short notice." Jake Goddard loaded his hip pack and camera bag onto the passenger seat of his car. "I get that you're upset but it's out of my hands. I think the boys will understand." He walked around the rear, threw his duffle in the back seat, closed the door, and stood by the driver's side to lift the wiper and remove dead oak leaves fallen from an overhanging tree.

Rachel stood on the porch, fists on her hips, shaking her head. "You are pulling out of a camping trip with your sons twenty-four hours before you were due to leave. I don't think the boys will understand at all."

"You know I don't have control over when clients need my services, any more than my clients can control the timing of events that lead them to me. This stuff is not done on a schedule. This seems like an important case. A young woman is missing—it doesn't get any more urgent than that. Imagine if she was your daughter. Plus, I need the—"

She cut him off. "We drove by your place last night after getting ice cream because your sons wanted to say goodnight to their daddy. Try to imagine how hard it was for me to explain that we couldn't go in when I saw that convertible parked outside your trailer."

"Hon, that was not ..." Rachel turned on her heel and stormed into the house, slamming the screen door. "... what you think," Jake said to the closed door.

Jake backed out of the driveway. Merging onto I-80 in Sugarhouse, near his home—correction, what used to be his home before he and Rachel separated—was always a pleasure. Today it helped him relax and fret less about his wife's anger. The rugged, snow-capped Wasatch Mountains stood like a pantheon overlooking the valley. It was his favorite view in Salt Lake. Once on the freeway, he was happy to see that on a beautiful, summer, windows-down evening, he could still turn a few female heads, although the younger ones usually lost interest when they noticed his age. That was fine by him—he preferred women with a few miles on their tires.

The little Subaru wagon left the valley and pulled up easily through the mountains. Jake cruised comfortably in the right-hand lane, air currents lifting his left arm. He felt the familiar relief of escaping both the city and the bittersweet pressures of family as he passed the Park City exit and subdivisions gave way to sagebrush flats. His attention turned back to the highway, as several truck-clogged, serpentine curves northeast of Park City required careful braking and steering. He admired the striking red cliffs that lined the road, studied the rock strata as carefully as possible while driving, and tried to recall the names of the formations.

June 2
Friday

L ast night when he had called, Susan had reluctantly agreed to meet
Jake Goddard for lunch as long as it was someplace close to her
office. Just moments ago, he had walked onto the deck of Shades Café
and paused, scanning for her. She saw him notice the uniform blouse and
smile. Heat rose along the back of her neck. She hated that feeling. As he
served himself at the window from the café's kitchen, she couldn't help
but notice that he looked just as good from the rear. Despite the glacial
temperature of the ice tea glass, she had to concentrate hard to loosen her
grip on it. She wiped the wet hand on her jeans, then smoothed her hair
and checked to see that her bandaged hand was hidden under the table.

She hadn't expected anyone so casual—he wore a t-shirt and hiking
shorts—or anyone so fit and rugged looking. She chewed at her lower lip,
thinking neither observation was particularly comforting. She checked
out the opening in her blouse, did up the second button and marshaled
herself to focus on the business at hand. An elderly man and woman,
both carrying full water glasses, sat down at the table next to her.

A breeze stirred pine branches over the redwood deck. Jake, balancing
his quesadilla and a bowl of salsa, approached the table, smiled, swung
a leg over the chair opposite her, and sat. She noticed he was wearing
running shoes with those silly half-socks. A blue and yellow banner

advertising "Pony Espresso" rippled gently on the wooden fence above his beige ball cap. Despite the breeze, Susan's clothing stuck to her skin.

"I don't remember June being this hot when I lived here," he said.

"Consider yourself lucky. News said it was fifteen degrees hotter in Salt Lake."

"Salt Lake can be a bitch in the summer." She caught him staring at her green eyes and quickly glanced away. He sawed at his quesadilla and muttered, "Thanks for giving me your lunch hour."

"Had to eat lunch somewhere, but have to be back at my desk at one o'clock sharp." Susan flashed her wrapped hand and made herself look into his face. "I'm on my best behavior these days."

"I hear that. Me too. These days and every day." He appraised her with another lingering glance and then turned his attention back to his food. "Like I said when I called you—and, by the way, your daughter is great on the phone, very polite. As my wife says, when either of our boys answers, they struggle with anything requiring more than a few short words. Anyhow, I read about your ... your accident in the Jackson paper. I've received it in the mail since moving to Utah."

"It's pretty much the talk of the town. 'Brand screwed up. Big time.' Must be the blonde hair." Susan immediately regretted saying that, smiled briefly, and pushed her hair behind her ears.

Jake raised his eyebrows and grinned at her over a slice of quesadilla. "You said it, I didn't. Actually, I'll bet a good looking blond cop patrolling on horseback stops a lot of traffic around here."

Susan reddened. "Any cop, no matter how spotless her record, is going to get a whole lot more attention than she ever wanted after an accidental shooting in her home." The older couple at the next table stopped their forks in mid-air. Susan lowered her voice. "More attention, I don't need right now, thank you very much." She picked at her salad.

"Well, then, how about something to keep your mind off your problems? A woman named Louise Cuvier from Vancouver has hired me to look into a situation involving her niece. She looks a lot like your daughter, only older."

The casual observation jarred Susan. "How do you know what my daughter looks like?" Jake shrugged his shoulders and held his two hands together in the shape of a book.

"Oh, the Jackson Hole weekly recyclable trash." She took a sip of tea. "What sort of situation?"

"Lyn Burke was supposed to join that Skutches field research team here in Jackson that's also working with the environmental group Lifewater. But on her first day in Wyoming, her assignment changed abruptly. She was reportedly sent off for several weeks of wilderness research in a remote area near the southern Utah border. She failed to check in at home while driving south or before heading into the backcountry. May be innocent, may not be, but Jackson is where Cuvier asked me to start, because this is where Lyn was supposed to be last."

Susan tried to mask her surprise. "Why hire a PI from Salt Lake?"

"Do you know of any in Jackson? Plus, my website mentions my familiarity with Western Wyoming and Eastern Idaho. Course it's been a long time since I lived here."

"So what is it you want from me that is going to, as you so kindly suggested, keep my mind off my problems?"

"I'd like your help. For starters, you really know Jackson and, according to the paper, you're already familiar with Dr. Skutches and his team from that climbing accident you investigated. But, I don't know, something about your story grabbed me. Paper said you had an excellent record, before … well, you know. Plus you're the mother of a daughter and empathy can be very helpful in cases like this. And, uh …" He cleared his throat. "You know as well as I do, to get anywhere, a PI needs local cop cover." He tilted his head and grinned again.

"So you're looking for someone in the department to punch your ticket." She glanced across the deck away from his gaze and pulled on the stud in her left earlobe. "You mean to tell me you didn't know my boss had assigned me this case?"

"Hell no, you gotta be kidding. I had no idea."

"No wonder Amy told me God had called." Susan drilled a look at Jake. "You just figured I was seeking redemption, right?"

"What?"

"Nothing," she said sitting back against her chair. "What the hell, I'm not going anywhere." Career-wise or personally, she thought. She locked eyes with him. "You have my full attention."

Susan walked back to work after leaving Jake at the cafe. The station was relatively quiet for early in the afternoon. Two other female cops were having a muffled conversation in front of the assignment white board, overlapped by the voice of the dispatcher, but it was not the usual rowdy din. Except for her new "partner," Chuck, who was chatting on the phone in his cubicle, most of her colleagues were either still at lunch, in court, or out on patrol.

Susan laid the file Goddard had given her on the upper right-hand corner of her gunmetal gray desk next to a cutting horse trophy. That was her unofficial "for immediate attention" quadrant—well, "pile" was probably a more appropriate term. The folder appeared to contain much more information than she had received from Earl on the same matter.

She reached under the flap of the file and unclipped the picture of twenty-two-year-old Lyn Burke. Lyn exuded the clear-eyed, trusting optimism of a self-assured young woman. She had shoulder-length auburn hair, was tan, freckled, pretty, and appeared to be athletic. Lyn's unassuming sexuality was enough to attract a whole host of perverts, Susan thought.

She glanced up at the pictures of her daughter on the cloth-covered walls of her cubicle: Amy with her arms around Cinder's neck; Amy in her uniform with her foot on a soccer ball; in her pajamas holding up a Christmas stocking. Always smiling—always trusting. A familiar pang of guilt plagued her as she considered the amount of time Amy spent alone at home, and how often, even in this relatively safe small town, she was vulnerable to predation. It caused her stomach to flutter. But then the sad irony hit; she was the only person who had ever been responsible for hurting or badly scaring her daughter. Even Amy's deadbeat ski-bum father had never hurt her.

The folder indicated that Lyn Burke loved rock climbing, yoga, and tennis. Ornithology, especially birds of prey, was her scientific specialty, but groundwater issues such as declining aquifers and depleted rivers, lakes, and reservoirs were her passion as an activist. She also appeared to be a bit of a "techie" and loved animals, never going far without her dog, Mojo, at her heels. She struck Susan as a highly ethical, but unpredictable girl who latched onto short-lived interests and poured her heart into those preoccupations while they lasted.

Susan had pretty much written off Goddard's request right after lunch. The thought of working with a PI, attractive or not, did not appeal to her. In fact, especially because he was attractive—and married, she reminded herself. But being a good Girl Scout, or at least a contrite one, she had run it by Earl when she walked in the door from lunch. Earl said he had just gotten off the phone with his fishing buddy, Brad Wilkinson, the chief in Vegas. Wilkinson was a friend of Stanley Burke, the missing girl's father. Seems Burke was convinced his estranged wife, Florence, who filed the report, was over-reacting and that their daughter was fine.

"But, hey, go through the motions," Earl had said, "and sure, what the heck, can't hurt to baby-sit the PI; might keep him out of trouble. You say the aunt hired him? That's a good one. Don't break a sweat though; my friend in Vegas says everything is under control down at his end."

Great! Politics, she thought. What a waste of time and taxpayers' money.

She finally conceded that the right thing to do was call Goddard to learn more. He appeared to bring a lot of background information to the table that could help her on her assignment. Maybe even help her resolve what was gnawing at her regarding the Fernando Diaz death. Working with a PI would be a first for her, but it might be an adventure and a distraction. Maybe she could make some overtime pay while keeping Goddard company. And he seemed like a decent guy, even if he was a PI. He said he was staying at the Hawkwing Ranch with a friend, Clint Something, the ranch manager, and that it was out of cell phone range. She could try to reach him through the ranch office.

She turned her attention back to the Lyn Burke file. Goddard had mentioned that Florence Burke reported Lyn was happy, a motivated student, not the type to drop out of sight voluntarily without communicating about her plans. It had been Lyn's habit to call each of her parents every few days.

For a few brief moments, Susan took Mrs. Burke's side and indulged herself with the thought of finding this young woman. She fantasized about how wonderful it would be to reunite Lyn with her mother. That led back to her regret that she had never been close to her own mother. She thought of the time she visited her mother in the hospital just before she succumbed to lung cancer. Susan said she loved her, and her mother rasped that she needed to cut her bangs.

"Hey, Brandy! Got those traffic flow projections yet?" A small Nerf football caromed off her desk and fell into her lap. Most of the cops called her Brandy. Chuck peered over the wall of her cubicle. She tried to left-hand the ball back, but Chuck ducked out of range and it bounced off a cluttered corkboard on the wall.

His head popped back up. "It's damn lucky you're such a bad shot."

Susan rolled her hand on her desk and flipped him off. "Not funny, Chucky. Leave me alone for forty-five minutes and I will guarantee a gridlock-free American Indian Festival. I've just got to make one quick call first."

"You got it, partner." Chuck dropped back into his cubicle.

Susan tucked the picture of Lyn Burke back into the folder, picked up the phone, and left a message for Jake Goddard at the ranch. She asked him to meet her at 5:30 p.m. at her house; that way, while they talked, she could be near Amy.

Susan noticed the corner of a small piece of paper had been exposed when Chuck hit her desk with the football. She slipped it out from under the pile. It was a jagged piece of lined notebook paper with the word, "BITCH," scrawled in black ink. Susan glanced around the office. No one was paying any attention to her. I knew I was in hot water around here, she thought, but this ... Try as she might, she couldn't think of a single person in the department who would do this to her. Befuddled, and a little shaken, she tucked the note into her desk drawer.

Traffic on Susan's street was heavy with tourists and end-of-work-day commuters. Jake had to circle the block several times to find parking.

Susan met him at the screen door with two cold beers and invited him to sit outside. Jake's long legs on the tiny front porch caused some awkwardness as they struggled to avoid bumping knees. Amy had a girl friend visiting. They giggled and gossiped while beading on the living room floor.

"A graduate student disappearing on the first day of a summer job," Susan said. "What a horror story for the mother."

"Possibly disappearing. There are widely different views on this case."

"I tend to assume the worst until proven otherwise. Anyone see anything suspicious?"

"Not really. Her supervisor, a guy called Forrest White Wolf, who's still here in the Jackson area, is the one who reported that she was reassigned to southern Utah. She supposedly went with a desert rat friend of his who volunteered to guide her on a research trek."

"Have you spoken to White Wolf?"

"Once, briefly on the phone. These field scientist-types are hard to reach. They spend most of their time camping out and tromping around wilderness areas observing birds of prey."

"Does anyone corroborate what White Wolf said?"

"His boss, the one your partner interviewed about that climber's death, Dr. Noah Skutches. He never met Lyn, but he confirmed White Wolf had called him and told him he was sending Lyn south. Plus, there's been no contact regarding a ransom. Believe me, Dad's got bucks. He owns a gypsum mine near Vegas."

"What about family involvement? You know the stats in cases like these as well as I do. I mean, if she is missing, chances are there is family or friend involvement." She took a sip of beer. "And how can two parents of the same child be so far apart about their daughter's welfare?"

"Since when has it been possible to get warring spouses to agree about anything?" Jake said a little too vehemently. They shifted their chairs as the sun lowered toward the western mountains. Susan noticed the muscles in Jake's tan thighs flex. Jesus, she thought, no wonder he wears shorts everywhere. Cinder panted at the screen door.

"Explain to me again why she was in Jackson. It's a long way from Las Vegas." Susan said.

"She was hired by Skutches to join his field research team from the University of Colorado. They're studying hawks in Yellowstone and demonstrating for Lifewater on their own time. Also, a huge protest was scheduled for a few days after her arrival in Jackson. Lyn was planning to participate, but she was supposedly sent south before it took place. And something else—other than no communication—that's got the mom freaking out, Lyn Burke replaced the kid who died in that rock-climbing accident."

"Really. And, FYI, the dead kid's partner still claims it was no accident." Susan stared at Jake in silence for a moment. "That is the one detail about all this that has my antennae up. Stein made a strong impression on me and I'm still haunted by his certainty that Diaz did not fall accidentally. One kid dies suspiciously and the next one may be missing? Too damn much coincidence."

"Seems like it," Jake said.

Susan got up and stretched across Jake to open the screen door for the dog. Through a small gap in her blue uniform blouse there was a flash of white lace hugging a curve. She sat back down and pushed her hair behind her ears.

"And the Las Vegas police haven't mounted a search because ... ?" Susan asked.

"Because Stanley Burke called off the dogs. He claims his wife is extremely emotional and he believes his daughter is fine and is off doing what she loves."

"Worrying about their daughter's welfare equals too emotional? Interesting. So, why did Louise what's-her-name hire you?" Susan asked.

"Cuvier. My best guess—to get her sister off her back. Actually, Louise shares Burke's view, says Florence 'goes from zero to hysterical in less than sixty seconds.' Right now, Aunt Lou appears to be the most rational of the bunch. She agrees her sister has a tendency to overreact and wants to believe her niece is fine. Still, she feels compelled to ensure that Lyn is okay. That's where I come in. By the way, Lou said if she didn't have a 'hitch in her get-along' from MS, she'd be down here straightening this mess out herself. She's a character, for sure."

Susan took the last sip of her beer and dug at the label with a polished thumbnail while holding the empty between her knees. "Okay. How can I help you?"

"I'd appreciate it if you'd visit every bar in the county and try to find someone who has seen Lyn. I have no clue if Lyn frequents bars, but it can't hurt to ask if anyone has seen her. If you agree to that, I'll check out the campgrounds and cheap motels. It could help to watch for anything related to this case during your regular patrol. And thanks again for agreeing to work with me."

"Let's get something straight. I'm doing this for one reason, because my boss assigned me this case and suggested that I keep an eye on you. Also, my regular patrol doesn't amount to a whole hell of a lot right now." Susan softened a little. "But yeah, okay, I'll hit the bars. I've got a girlfriend who thinks that's exactly what I should be doing right now anyway."

"Sorry?"

"Never mind."

"Great. It should go well for you. You're known here. It's bound to help that you're on official police business. Women can open doors and mouths that a male stranger can't begin to crack."

"Yup, especially if that 'male stranger' is a private investigator. I'm surprised anyone will tell you guys where the men's room is. But unfortunately, I'm a little too well known right now," Susan said.

"Hell, that's nothing but a minor setback." He raised his bottle, "Welcome to the glamorous world of private investigation."

Susan shot Jake a skeptical look. "Hey, my friend, you're in my world."

They heard Amy crying out from the living room, "I'm hurt, Mom, I'm hurt!" Jake and Susan jolted until they realized it was Amy reenacting, with great dramatic embellishment, the morning of the shooting.

"Mom, Mom!"

Cinder barked twice in Amy's room. Susan threw off the covers, leapt to the floor and hurried down the hall. She smashed her bandaged hand on the door jam of her daughter's bedroom and almost tripped over Cinder.

"Shit!"

"Mommy ... are, are you all right?" Amy asked as her mother approached the bed.

"Yes, honey," Susan said through gritted teeth. "I'm fine, I just hit my damn hand is all." She walked to the foot of Amy's bed holding her wrist. "Hey, I'm supposed to be comforting you here. You had the dream again, didn't you?"

"Uh huh," she yawned. "It's weird. I hardly think about the accident when I'm awake, but I can't get it out of my goddamn dreams and it sucks."

"What kind of language is that?" Susan said. Amy tilted her head and waggled a finger. "Never mind, I know. I need to be a better role model in the trash mouth department." She sat on the edge of the bed and touched her daughter's leg through the covers. "I am so sorry, honey."

"Mom, c'mon. We have a deal. No more apologies. I know you're sorry. I'm sorry, too." Amy scooted over to her mother's lap. "I love you, Mom."

"I love you too, Amers. I'm the luckiest mother in the world."

"What were you and Jake talking about tonight?" Amy yawned again.

"Jake wants me to help find some information about a young woman."

"Why? Who is she? What has she done?"

Susan smoothed her daughter's bangs and placed her hand along her cheek. "She hasn't done anything, honey. Her mom is just really worried about her."

"Why is she worried?"

Susan smiled for her daughter but could not look into her eyes. She stood up. "That's all I can tell you right now. I'll tell you later, I promise. You need to go back to sleep. Want to crawl in with me?"

"Sure." Amy pushed down the covers and sat up. "I wonder who was at the door?"

Susan froze. "What do you mean? It's the middle of the night."

"Just after I woke up and called you, I thought I heard the screen door close."

"Sweetie, that's not possible." Susan's jaw clenched.

"I'm pretty sure, Mom. That's why Cinder barked."

"I thought she barked when you yelled. Listen, Amy, you dreamed it, or it was the wind … yeah, it had to be the wind. Come on, let's get some sleep."

Amy shrugged her shoulders and swung her legs over the side of the bed while Susan reached for the crutches that were propped on the dresser. Amy hopped out the door and Susan clutched her daughter's bear and pillow to her chest and followed down the hall.

After settling Amy into bed, Susan called Cinder softly, stopped at the hall closet where she now religiously stored her pistols, and checked the front door. It was closed but the screen door stood slightly ajar. There was a bump and then a scraping sound from outside. Cinder barked.

Susan whisper commanded Cinder to stay and eased through the screen door in her bare feet, holding her Glock 22 awkwardly in her left hand. The motion detector light popped on. There was no sign of anyone out front. The only car on the street was an old black Jeep Wrangler parked on the opposite side.

She crept up to the corner of the house and peered into the semi-darkness of the side yard. Muffled audio from a neighbor's televised baseball game was the only sound. Then there was a loud clank. Something had been slammed against the back of the house. Susan bolted around the corner and ran full force into a currant bush. Staggering back and momentarily blinded, she gasped when something furry brushed her legs. A spooked cat, interrupted from invading her garbage cans, clawed up a spruce tree.

She put her hand to her chest and laughed. She padded to the house, locked the screen and the front door, returned her pistol to the closet and turned toward the kitchen to check the time. When she flicked on the light, she noticed a dirty glass on the table. She rinsed the glass, put it in the dishwasher, switched off the light and joined Amy in bed.

"What was it?"

"Nothing honey, just that stupid old gray cat in the garbage—scared the heck out of me, and I ran into the currant bush. I bet I look like I've been in a fight with the cat."

Susan fluffed her pillow and turned on her side, back to Amy. "By the way, I found your dirty milk glass on the table. You know how I like—"

"Yeah, Mom, dishwasher, I'm sorry. Next time, I promise." Amy pressed against her mother's back and smiled up at her dreamily. "I love to snuggle in your bed. Good night, Mom. Love you, Mom."

Cinder groaned contentedly, settling at the foot of the bed. Susan switched off the bedside light.

"I love you too, honey. Sleep tight."

Amy lay quiet for a while. "Mom, I didn't have any milk tonight."

"Honey, you must have. I never drink it and Cinder sure as heck didn't have a glass of milk. Now go to sleep."

"Okay, I'll rinse next time, okay."

"Thanks Amy, no big deal, sweetheart. Goodnight."

Susan felt her daughter's arms relax and heard her breathing slow.

"But cross my heart, I didn't have any milk. I'm sure of that," she mumbled.

"Amy, damnit ..." Susan caught herself. Her heart raced. "I'm sorry, honey. Just ... just go to sleep. It's late."

Susan rolled over, wrapped her child close, and stared at the flickering reflections of the headlights as they passed in the street. Amy's insistence that she hadn't used the glass preyed on Susan's mind and sleep wouldn't come. After she was certain her daughter was asleep, she slipped out of bed and went back to the kitchen.

As she was reaching for the light switch, she heard a squeaking noise behind the blind covering the window above the sink. She crept up to the counter and felt around in the glow from the light of the stove clock for the drawstring. She yanked and the blind flew up.

A strange man was framed in the window. He seemed as shocked as Susan and sprinted up the alley behind her house. She stumbled backwards and fell hard on a wooden chair. She jumped up and bolted to the door but stopped halfway out. Her police training overrode her anger, causing her to reject charging up the dark alley solo leaving Amy alone in the house.

She returned to the kitchen and sat at the table. When her heart slowed, she made a mental note of the man's appearance. It had been dark but she was sure his head was totally shaved. His thick black eyebrows were the only hair on his head. His nose looked like it had been badly broken and poorly set. He was wearing hunter's camouflage.

She pushed up from the table and switched on the wall light near the door. She crossed the kitchen to close the blind and jolted again. "HCTIB" was scrawled in messy, black, block letters on the outside of the window.

Her first reaction was to call Chuck, but she changed her mind. The prowler was long gone. She considered calling the department but stopped, realizing she'd get the cop on patrol in her neighborhood. Greeting Ronald Cathey in her nightgown was about the last thing she needed right now. Plus she wanted to mull over any possible connection with the note she had found at the office earlier. Reporting the incident could wait until morning.

Called a bitch twice in one day. What's up with that?, she wondered. She broke her new rule, got her Glock out of the living room closet, and carried it to the bedroom. This bizarre day suggested a little extra company would be in order.

June 3
Saturday

Chants rose from the Jackson Hole Middle School's ball fields and reverberated off the nearby buttes. The Consortium of Native Dancers was performing the traditional finale to the annual American Indian Festival that, for many locals, marked the official start of summer. It was a perfect afternoon, clear skies, no wind. Throughout the crowd, brown and white children playing together had shucked their jackets and vests, and in some cases shoes and socks, and danced around the chairs and blankets of their spectator parents.

Stirred by the display of power and spirituality, Susan Brand straightened in her saddle. The percussion of the dancers' feet, the kaleidoscope of colors, the crescendo of the drums, as well as the children's spontaneous response to the music, transported her back to her own childhood. She'd been one of the few white girls on the reservation. Her Indian friends had taught her much, including an appreciation for their dances, like the Eagle Dance and Rain Dance, at the powwow called O'odham Tash.

The performance helped distract her thoughts from Lyn Burke and her concerns for Amy's safety that had once again bubbled up after the previous night's events. But, try as she might, she could not get the image of that bizarre man at the window out of her mind. Her gut was telling her there was a connection between the prowler and the Burke case.

"Probably a random peeper getting his jollies," Earl Meacham had said when Susan reported her visitor. "I'll have a night patrol car keep an eye on your place for a while."

What the hell, Susan thought, why not add Officer Ronald Cathey getting *his* jollies to the man already peering into her house? Chuck, being a good buddy, invited Susan and Amy to spend a few nights at his house. She was grateful, but declined.

In anticipation of the conclusion of the festival, Susan positioned her horse at the first intersection along the exit route from the ball fields. She was determined to keep her corner moving and was eager to see her traffic flow plan work. The horse shifted her long chestnut legs and settled in for the duty, stretching her sleek head sideways at some grass sprouting next to the pavement.

"Sorry, Cassie. It's not dinner time yet." Susan pulled on the reins. "We need to look sharp for the folks." She creaked forward in the saddle and patted her horse's neck.

She was wearing her dress-white blouse and jeans with her favorite silver belt buckle. Her hair was pulled into a ponytail beneath her white straw cowboy hat. She felt good and, considering all she had been through recently, knew she looked good, too, even with a bandaged hand. Tourists love the cops-on-horseback thing. They had no clue how very practical and maneuverable a well-trained horse can be in a crowd, and how intimidating they are, she thought. Being a person of average height and build, she was grateful for the great advantage Cassie offered her.

As traffic flowed out of the school parking lots, she studied every male face. Not that she expected her nocturnal visitor to appreciate American Indian culture, but if he was a pervert, as Earl suspected, he might possess the criminal predator's inability to resist a crowd and all its prurient possibilities.

Several men stared back at her hopefully. In your dreams, boys, she thought. Nothing helpful emerged from the steady stream of cars that passed her corner. She noted blonde hair, white hair, red hair, black hair above hairless faces, but no bald heads.

Suddenly, a shaved head drove past in an old black Jeep Wrangler, clean face as well. The driver grinned and ogled her. Something about the forehead and nose tugged at her. While waving traffic through, she called up the mental snapshot of the peeper; there was a definite resemblance. She wanted to gallop after the slow moving vehicle. It was just a few cars away from the intersection with Jackson's main thoroughfare. She could dig her spurs into Cassie's sides and catch the Jeep in thirty seconds flat, but she didn't dare leave her post, especially on a hunch. The car was too far away to see the plate.

She tried to raise Chuck, stationed at the intersection, but there was only static. Had he forgotten to recharge his radio again last night, she wondered?

"JHP50, do you read?" No response. "Chuck, Chuck, come in, damnit!" Nothing but static. The Jeep made the turn and disappeared into traffic.

If he's the pervert who had been at her window, he could be heading back to her house right now, she thought. A car horn brought her attention back to the corner. She hadn't noticed a mini-van was waiting across the street from her for a signal to turn. She stopped traffic and waved the van around the corner, still searching the distant cars with her eyes.

"Shit—I had him," she muttered to no one in particular.

The Jackson Hole Fitness Club had a warehouse feel, but it was friendly and only five minutes from the police station. Susan liked working out, just didn't like working out surrounded by mirrors and men. She had taken out the membership in a fit of January remorse and resolution, not planning to like it, but actually warmed to the place quickly. She had even allowed her competitive nature get the best of her and entered a club challenge. A t-shirt and three months dues were being offered as prizes to the first female member to bench press her own weight. Six weeks ago she had added a graduated regimen of free-weight chest workouts to her routine. The competition was one thing that she determined would not be affected by her accident.

Jake had been complaining about stiffness from inactivity, so she called him after finishing her Indian Festival duty and invited him to come to the club that afternoon. She told him about the bald guy in the Jeep, promising to fill in all the details while they worked out. The invitation seemed natural. She was relieved that she wouldn't have to sit facing him across another tiny space, trying to keep her legs from brushing his.

Four muted televisions played different channels above the treadmills. The room echoed with the clank of heavy weights and smelled faintly of sweat and cleaning products. Jake stood in front of a rack of dumbbells and a full-length mirror doing bicep curls. Susan sat nearby at a leg machine working quadriceps. She had chosen her black Spandex shorts and a Marine Corps t-shirt with the sleeves cut off after pulling out and rejecting every piece of attractive athletic clothing she owned.

Jake wore his ball cap everywhere and she wondered if thinning hair was the motivation. Noticing his big chest and large, well-defined arms under his loose t-shirt, she realized just how long it had been since she had touched a man's chest, and then reminded herself, once again, that he was married. She pulled her eyes away, counted "twelve" out loud and released the tension in her thighs. Jake started another set. The more she tried to look away, the more her eyes were drawn to him. Look away. Look. Look away. She felt foolish and finally gave in and settled on the mirror as a safe way to watch him lift.

"You trying to impress me?" she asked.

"Of ... course. Is it ... working?" he said, continuing his curls.

"Not really, but keep up the good effort," Susan said, standing now and leaning on a Nautilus machine. "I wish to hell I'd been a little quicker on the switch today and gotten the Jeep's tag. The more I think about it, this guy has to be related to the Burke thing."

"Since I ... haven't turned ... anything up," Jake said, exhaling stabs of air. "Your hunch...about your new best friend at home ... long shot as it is, is ... all we have to go on ...." Jake finished his set and replaced his weights.

"Damn, I wish I had snagged that tag. If he is the kidnapper, he might have been heading straight back to his prey."

"Give yourself a break. There were thousands of people there. You had a few other vehicles to worry about. Help me out here. I get your reasons for suspecting a link between Lyn Burke and Fernando, but what makes you think the cue ball guy is in any way connected to those two?"

"I don't suppose you'd buy women's intuition?"

Jake shook his head.

"So let me try something slightly more logical."

"Okay," Jake said.

"This is a small town. Most cases of harassment or voyeurism involve men as the perpetrators against women who are known to them and vice versa. Now, in a big city like Phoenix, I'd buy that a guy could become fixated on a woman and the woman may have never laid eyes on him, but in a small town—unlikely. Plus in my time here, to my knowledge, there has never been a single similar complaint lodged with the PD. I mean, one involving a male writing bitch backwards on the outside of a woman's window. Those pervs are usually repeat offenders and they generally follow a pattern."

"There's always a first time."

"True, new guy comes to town and quickly becomes obsessed with a little honey working at the sub shop, or a bimbo at the convenience store, but a forty-something cop, armed and dangerous, just to get his jollies? I don't think so. There has to be an ulterior motive. And all I've been doing since the shooting accident is playing traffic cop and the Diaz and Burke cases, and it's not likely to be some problem the jerk has with how I direct traffic. I admit it's just a hunch but there could be a connection. And I'm pissed I blew it on the goddamn plate on the Jeep."

Susan kept her eyes on Jake as he removed his hat and smoothed his damp brown hair back with his hand. A look of admiration spread over his sweaty face.

"Okay, I see what you're getting at. But like I said, go a little easier on yourself." He picked up his towel, ran it over his head and flopped his hat back on. "Now, we just got to find the Jeep with the bald guy in it. Long shot as it is, if it was Lyn's abductor, we know something about him: he likes crowds. So what's the next big event here?"

"Wild West Days is next weekend. But hey, maybe we need to be a little harder on ourselves and maybe you need to stop patronizing me. I get all of that I can stomach at the station these days."

Jake smiled. "My apologies, Officer Brand. I read you loud and clear."

"We don't have another single thing to go on here and that plate could have made a huge difference. That young woman could be in trouble and, assuming she's still alive, might be in worse trouble every day. And we're supposed to sit around waiting five days for the next big event?"

"No offense, but can we slow down a little? Even the woman who hired me is not certain there's anything wrong. It might be a good idea if I forward you Lou Cuvier's emails. It will give you a sense for her and her level of concern. But, believe me, we won't be sitting around. Tomorrow is Sunday and we'll be watching the bars, gas stations and food stores." Jake picked up his towel. "You know what, though—I'll bet you a lunch the next time your cue ball pokes his flattened nose out of his hole will be at the Old West Days celebration." He grabbed his water bottle. "You ready to get changed?"

"Just a few more minutes. Mind spotting me on some bench presses?" Susan asked.

"Benches? With a bum hand?"

"'No pain, no gain.'"

"I guess." Jake shrugged. He followed her to a short bench with a straight bar perched above.

Susan worked her way up quickly from a warm-up of several reps at 60% of her body weight to a few at 80%. Jake helped her add the plates. Then she stood and prepared the bar for her final lift.

"My day's goal is one clean lift at 95% of my weight." Susan checked the weights on both ends and readied herself on the bench again. "If I nail this, it'll be one step closer to the prize." She positioned her bandaged hand under the bar so the weight was away from her injury. He stood at her head, legs spread-eagle, hands ready if she needed him. She lay with her feet braced on the floor on either side of the bench, shoulders back and her hair spread on the bench. She glanced up at Jake and noticed him checking her out.

Susan took three deep breaths, snatched the heavy bar off the stand and lowered the weight. She hit her chest hard and blew out air for the final lift. The bar started to rise slowly and then stalled. As she struggled, her shoulders and pecs popped veins. Her back and chest arched under the strain. The weight did not budge. Jake started to reach for the bar when Susan forced out through gritted teeth, "Not yet."

Her chin dropped, her eyes widened and focused and her cheeks began to tremble. Her face resembled a warrior's mask. The bar started to slowly rise and then with a shout she thrust it up and slammed it back on the rack. She jumped up flushed, eyes sparkling, triumphant.

"Yeess! I knew I could do that weight." She shook the pain out of her bandaged hand and then held it against her chest, wincing and smiling.

He congratulated her with a high-five on her good hand. "Not bad. I thought you were finished when you got stuck. And with an injured hand."

"Don't underestimate me, Goddard," Susan said with a wink. She grabbed up her towel, snapped it toward him, and picked up her water bottle. "I'm feeling good. I think I'll do a little bar hopping tonight."

They walked past the aerobics studio toward the locker rooms. Susan flashed Jake a big grin in the mirror and caught him studying her again—this time from the rear.

June 4
Sunday

Cars and pedestrians outside the Brand cottage began to thin as the weekend wound down into the easy hours of Sunday evening. Amy was settled on the couch with her social studies textbook and a large bowl of Oreo ice cream. Susan was preparing to go back out.

The bars she had visited, three Saturday night and two that afternoon, had turned up nothing. She asked bartenders, bouncers, and regulars; nobody recognized the picture of Lyn Burke. Susan wanted to check out one more saloon before Sunday ended and work interfered with her investigation. She had arranged for a neighbor, Kelly, to hang out with Amy and make sure she didn't stay up too late doing homework. Kelly was in the kitchen talking on her cell.

Susan zipped on her blue fleece vest over her uniform blouse, hugged Amy, waved to Kelly, and walked out to her pickup down the street.

It was a clear cool dusk; several stars had already made their debut in the eastern sky. A few blocks from her house she passed the town square. The tree-covered park was full of the usual tourists jockeying for photo-ops under the signature elk-antler arches adorning the corners. She saw a woman walking with her hand on the shoulder of a boy about Amy's age and was struck again by the irony of her situation. In order to help Florence Burke find her child—in order to do her regular job and help anyone—she had to leave her own child injured and vulnerable. It was a no-win. She'd left Kelly her cell number and strict instructions to call if she heard or saw anything suspicious. That provided Susan some small comfort.

She headed north past several motels, a visitors' center, and a shop with wooden cigar store Indians fanned out in front of it. Near the edge of town was the Elk Country Bar, a popular spot for tourists and locals alike. As she approached, she saw the blue lights of a patrol car pulsating against the bar's corrugated log front. The Elk Country neon lights blinked in accompaniment. Beside the cruiser stood the unmistakable figure of Officer Ronald Cathey.

Unconventional for a cop in a town of outdoorsy jocks, Cathey looked like a sack of laundry cinched at the waist by a gun belt. He had no butt. The topography of his face was round and flat as a dinner plate, the only relief being the contours of his nipple nose and scraggly red mustache. Even in Wyoming, the black cowboy hat and boots looked out of place on Cathey. Susan parked in the bar's lot and grabbed her straw hat and notebook.

"Hey, Brandy. Didn't expect to see you here."

"Hey, Ronnie. What's up, the usual brawlers at it again?"

"Nah, this is pretty weird, even for summer crazies."

He pointed his flashlight at a Honda Civic and then at a Ford Escort. Both were sitting at odd angles to the other parked cars. The Civic had Wyoming plates and a Wilderness Society bumper sticker. The Escort had Utah plates and a cracked tail light.

"According to a witness, this whacko comes out and finds his Jeep parked in a little tight by the Ford and the Honda," he said. "So he slams his bumper up against them and shoves them out of the way."

"Ford looks like a rental."

"Sure is, and the lady's inside crying on the phone to her husband. Weird thing is, the hothead only had two beers according to the bartender. I'd hate to see him after six or eight. Must really get a hard-on," Cathey said.

"Did you say he drove a Jeep?"

"Yup. Black Wrangler, fairly beat."

"Plate?"

"No such luck," he responded. "Witness saw a bumper sticker, though. 'Save a rancher—shoot a wolf.' "

"Description?"

"Of the driver?"

"Yeah."

"White guy, average height, high thirties, early forties. Not a hair on his face or head. Totally shaved."

Susan felt the thrill of a scent. "Did anyone see where he went?"

"Same guy—the witness—played vigilante, followed him for a few blocks, and gave up the chase when the Jeep headed out toward the Elk Refuge."

Susan backed toward her truck. "Looks like you've got everything under control."

"Definitely. I am so-o-o good with hysterical females." Ron scratched another note into his report book propped on his knee. "Hey Brandy, what are you doing here anyway? You don't strike me as the drink-with-the-wannabe-cowboys-and-tourists type. Especially with that bum hand and a hurt daughter and all."

The male cops just love to turn that screw, she thought. "You know what, Cathey, I don't need you to remind me of that." She smiled mechanically while opening the truck door. "But, you're right, for once. I would rather be curled up with my kid and one of her vampire books, but haven't you heard—I thought everyone knew—I've picked up a little overtime work. I was just following up on a hunch. Looks like it's not panning out." She got in her truck, backed up a few feet, and ignored his wave as she sped out of the lot.

Susan left the pavement and headed out the darkened gravel road of the Elk Refuge. She rolled down her window to inhale the grassy odor. The night air made her shiver. Normally, this was one of her favorite places to hike or cruise around and look for animals like the big horn sheep that make it their winter home. Normally, but not tonight. She shivered again. A meandering stream stitching the two halves of the expansive preserve together glowed with a dull sheen. The crescent moon above the Gros Ventre Mountains illuminated several nearby buttes. There were no other cars on the road.

She assessed her situation. She was already in deep shit, and here she was breaking all the rules. She had no back-up and no one knew where she was. She was pursuing a man who was probably armed and could be dangerous and she didn't have the full use of her gun hand. Wanting to call Chuck, she touched a button on her cell phone, but the face lit up and indicated there was no service. This is not good, she thought, not good at all.

The road rounded into total darkness behind a butte. She coasted to a stop, turned off her engine and scanned the refuge for headlights. She was immediately enveloped in a high-western-mountain-valley silence. It was intense, almost palpable. Eventually, it was possible to make out a few vague shapes. Skeletal sagebrush in an old burn dotted the slope of the butte and a lone cottonwood tree stood off to her left next to a boulder.

Being alone outside was not difficult for Susan; she had ventured into the Arizona desert by herself many times as a young girl. She had come to think of the towering saguaro cacti, with their human-like arms, as guardians. When she stayed with her friends on the reservation in the summer, they always slept outside because it was cooler. She had fond memories of trying to stifle giggles while sneaking up in the dark on unsuspecting buddies. She remembered the firelight glistening on the round faces of her Indian friends and joking that her marshmallows, which came out of the bag resembling her, were done to perfection when they looked just like them—toasty brown. She'd often wander off for a while, and felt safe and secure alone under the immense sky. Old Ruth had taught her many skills, including how to read the land to find water, how to dress for the extreme temperatures of the open desert, and how to tell directions at night without a compass.

To Susan, this was just magical lore at the time, and as a child she had not stored it for easy recall. But every once in a while, like now, she'd sit and review some skill to control fear and clear her mind. Tonight it was star reading, and it helped her focus. She picked out the North Star off the cusp of the dipper handle, and leaned out her window to find other constellations. Consumed by her sky search, she jumped when a coyote yipped nearby. It was time to head home. When she drove back around the end of the butte into the moonlight and could see the lights of town, she relaxed into the seat and began to hum one of Amy's favorite songs.

Suddenly, a large black mass bounced down through the sagebrush to her left on the point of the butte. It was headed directly toward the side of her truck. Susan stomped on the gas and just barely cleared the bumper of the Jeep Wrangler as it lurched onto the gravel road and wrenched sideways behind her. The driver flicked on his high beams.

He hung on Susan's tail; if she sped up, he sped up; when she slowed, he slowed. The blinding lights drilled into her mirror. She winced from the pain of locking the passenger window with her lame hand and clawing open the glove box in case she needed her Glock. Sweat trickled down her back. She gradually slowed to a crawl, the Jeep right on her bumper, its vertical grill slits menacing in her mirror.

She fumbled for her pistol but it slipped out of her bandaged hand onto the floor by the passenger door. The Jeep shot around her and raced ahead, spitting gravel onto her windshield. Susan was increasing her speed in pursuit when the Wrangler slid into a u-turn and sped back toward her truck. Susan stood on the brakes, braced for the impact but angrily popped on her high beams just before the driver swerved and missed her, only to spin once again to take up his place behind.

She had seen a bald head in the second she had him in her headlights. He tailgated her for a few seconds. Her neck snapped back when he jolted her truck with his bumper. She gunned it to get away. The Wrangler chased her onto the pavement and back into town. She checked her phone and saw the tower strength had gone up. Between glances in the rearview and ahead at the street, she scrolled down to "station" and hit the call button. When she lifted the phone to her ear, the Jeep driver jerked a hard left and was gone.

"Jackson PD dispatch."

"Wanda! Good to hear your voice. Let me pull over and catch my breath."

She stared up the side street, took a few deep breaths, and licked her lips. The street was lined with houses and parked cars but there was no sign of the Jeep.

"Okay, okay, I just had a vehicle following me and harassing me on the refuge—white male, alone, in an older black Wrangler. I think it was the one Ronnie was looking for earlier for that hit-and-run in the parking lot of the Elk Country. Might also be the perv who was drawing on my window a couple of nights ago."

"Oh my God! Where is he now?"

"He shot south off Broadway onto Absaroka."

"Did you get a plate?"

"No, damnit, it was covered with mud. I could go after the son of a bitch."

"I know I'm stepping over my boundaries here, Susan, but don't do that. I'll notify Officer Cathey. It'd be best to just go home, unless he starts to follow you again, then call me back immediately, okay? I'll put out a surveillance request on the Wrangler."

"That's really what I had in mind, Wanda. Thanks. Good night." Susan threw her cell on the seat next to her and rolled her shoulders and stretched her fingers. She picked up her pistol and placed it on the passenger seat next to her cell. She looked up Absaroka and saw a white pickup turn into a driveway and park. Nothing else was moving.

Despite what she'd said to Wanda, she drove around the neighborhood until her heart rate returned to normal. A few television sets flickered in living rooms. Seeing no sign of the Jeep, she headed for home. As soon as she had checked on Amy, she planned to call Goddard and report her little game of tag with the jerk in the Jeep.

June 5
Monday

Jake drove his Subaru out the Elk Refuge road. The sun was climbing hot toward noon and he and Susan had the windows down.

"So, partner, what the hell possessed you to come out here alone last night in the dark?" Jake asked. He sipped at his now cold to-go coffee.

"I don't know. And I had just left Amy at home. I guess I feel comfortable in the Elk Refuge. I spend a lot of time out here alone. Crazy as it sounds, it might be because no one in the department is taking this guy or this case seriously."

"Sorry to state the obvious, but you're no less dead if killed doing what other cops view as frivolous business. Call me first next time, okay? This is a partnership."

"My partner's Chuck Simmons. When I'm in trouble, I call him." She searched the sloping sage-covered terrain ahead with her eyes. "Of course, it would help if that bonehead took this thing more seriously." A magpie stepped away from road-kill rabbit to avoid being hit by the car. Susan pointed. "Here's the place."

Jake pulled off by fresh ruts running up through splintered sagebrush, switched off the car, and turned toward her. "Do you feel confident using your pistol in your left hand?" He waited a few seconds and, getting no response, shook his head. "Look, please don't misunderstand me. I'm saying this out of concern for you. You shoot skeet, right? You must own a shotgun." She nodded. "Put something in your pickup's gun rack that's a little more lethal than the fly rod you keep there."

"I told the chief I can handle a gun and I can. I know you're just trying to help but, like at the Fitness Club, when I need you to take the weight off me, I'll let you know, okay?" She opened her door and paused. "I'm pissed Cathey didn't catch him last night after I called it in. Of course, Ronnie's never been known for speed." Susan gulped her coffee, tossed the cup on the floor, pushed her hair behind her ears, and tilted her head toward the butte. "Let's go get a little exercise." She started up the rise. "And yeah, I'll start carrying a shotgun in my truck," she said over her shoulder while climbing through bunches of knee-high green grass. And then looking down at her feet to avoid tripping, she muttered, "Thanks for your concern."

Finding nothing but tracks, they sat in the sagebrush at a small plateau halfway up the hill. "Looks like the driver shot up the slope like a high school kid hell-bent to tear up some terrain," Jake said. Across the valley stood the white-capped spires of the Teton Range. Streaked clouds attached to the peaks like white flags.

"Do you think he harassed me because I happened to be the only car out here, or because he knew who I was and I was following him?"

"What a view, eh?" Goddard shifted his gaze from across the valley to Susan. "I have to believe he was just being a jerk. How could he know you were following him? But he may have recognized you after he got on your tail."

"It was bizarre. I've only seen that 'hunter becomes the prey' stuff in movies. And if it's the same pervert that came to my house, now he knows where I live *and* that I drive a red truck."

"It had to be spooky as hell. But the good news is, well, first, that you weren't harmed. Second, if, as you have suspected all along, this guy *is* related to our case, he has crawled out of his hole again just as you said he would. He has revealed himself." Jake pushed up the bill of his ball cap. "And since he seems to be fixated on you, what do you say we use you as bait?"

Susan was incredulous. "What?"

"What difference does it make if we pursue him or he pursues you? We grab him up all the same and find out what, if anything, he knows about Lyn Burke." Jake grinned, plucked a sprig off a low bush, sniffed it, and handed it to Susan. "I love the smell of sage." He looked at his watch. "We better get you back to that desk you're riding."

"Traffic control, desk jockey, and fifth wheel on totally routine investigations. That just may explain a lot," she said, pressing the sage to her nose. "I miss the adrenaline." She crushed the leaves between her fingers and thumb and smelled the sage again. "But still, I'm not sure how I feel about being 'bait' for a psychopath."

"The adrenaline probably does explain why you came out here last night," Jake said while rising and brushing off his pants. "And I have this feeling when the 'cue ball' approaches you, thinking you're an easy target, you're gonna love the rush." He grasped Susan's arms and pulled her to her feet but because of the steep angle she tipped forward and her chest accidentally bumped his. Jake laughed nervously, Susan pushed back hard on his arms, smiled an apology, and pulled her hair behind her ears. They avoided eye contact and, after regaining equilibrium, hiked down the slope to the car.

Susan suggested they drive to the site of the climber's fall before returning to Jackson. "Can't shake the feeling there is a connection between Diaz and Lyn Burke. Maybe we'll see something Chuck and I missed."

"Can't hurt to look," Jake said.

Jake drove north on the refuge road to the access for the climbing area. They parked and followed the trail to the foot of the climb. There was a rope snaking up the face. Susan and Jake scrambled up the trail around the cliff to the top. They watched an athletic woman complete the climb, belayed from above by her male friend. After a quick look around the top and a scramble down the trail, Susan and Jake were back in the car and heading toward town.

"What do you think?" Jake asked.

"I didn't learn anything new but seeing that flat, safe belay spot at the top only increases my suspicions." They passed several people jogging and biking with dogs as they neared the edge of town.

"It didn't seem like the sort of climb that would be any problem for an experienced rock jock like Diaz," Jake said.

"My feelings exactly." Susan fired a look at Jake. "Unless push came to shove."

Jake dropped Susan at the station, drove through Jackson and the southern end of Grand Teton National Park on the main highway, and then turned right along the Gros Ventre River. He slowed for a cluster of RVs and cars—tourists parked helter-skelter to view and photograph a moose browsing in the stream-side willows. Jake didn't stop for the moose jam; he drove on through the little town of Kelly and followed the road that paralleled the river and led out of the park to the Hawkwing.

As his tires crunched on the gravel of the dude ranch road, two blue-gray Australian shepherds loped out from behind the sagebrush and cottonwoods. Their demeanor was one-part threatening and one-part curious, but when they got a whiff of Jake's hand hanging out of his window they wiggled with excitement and worked their butts as if they had tails to wag. It's nice to be remembered, he thought, even if it is because of my distinctive odor. He parked in front of a small log cabin behind the main ranch buildings, slid out, stretched, and dug his fingers into the ruffs of the dogs' necks. A breeze rustled the trees that surrounded the cabin and streaks of sunlight slanted down to the grass. The air was scented with warm pine duff. There was no one around and the only sound was that of the nearby shoals of the boulder-strewn Gros Ventre River.

Jake briefly soaked up the sight of the rushing spring run-off and then followed the dogs across the hollow-sounding planks of the cabin porch, stopping at the screen door to detach a handwritten note from Clint. It said, 'Back at 5:30 with the dudes for dinner. Beer in the lodge fridge.'

Jake and Clint had been friends since their ski bum days here in Jackson. Before Jake and Rachel separated, whenever Clint needed city time, he stayed with them in Salt Lake. When Jake needed time in the Hole, as long as there was room, he was always welcome at the Hawkwing. Now that Jake was living in an Airstream trailer, housing his friend had become more complicated, but Clint told Jake not to worry. He assured him he would find ways to even the score.

The beer and the shaded porch were tempting, but it was only 3:00 p.m., and Jake had a goal to search two nearby campgrounds before dinner for some sign of Lyn Burke. He prepared his camera in hopes of seeing something of interest to the case, or at least some interesting wildlife, and grabbed his Browning 9-mm pistol. He got back in the car and headed down the river to the little settlement of Kelly. While driving through town, he saw a woman hanging laundry that billowed in the breeze by a cluster of white canvas yurts.

After an unproductive visit to the National Park Campground west of town, he turned around and drove north through Kelly again, past the road up the Gros Ventre to the Hawkwing and past the entrance road to the Teton Science School. He had seen no wild animals, just sage flats, tree-covered Blacktail Butte in the foreground, and the spires of the Tetons behind. He cruised by a hay meadow dotted with horses.

Jake had learned to love animals growing up on a farm in central Pennsylvania, but horses were the exception. He always joked that he appreciated horses for aesthetic reasons only, as in standing in someone else's pasture. When he was twelve, a run-away stallion dragging an empty wagon reared up, damn near trampled him, and seriously injured his older brother, Seth. Jake had never forgotten it nor forgiven the species. He could think of no sane reason to ever try to crawl up on the back of a horse.

His other anomaly for a farm-raised kid, besides disliking horses, was that he didn't hunt. He was a meat-eater and had participated in the slaughter of dozens of farm animals as a child, yet, try as he might, his father could never make him a hunter. He couldn't reconcile his love and admiration for the majesty of wild animals with the sight of them terrified, bleeding, and dying. This farm boy/meat-eater/non-hunter paradox was something he had long since stopped questioning since repeatedly being forced to defend it by liberal vegetarian friends and hunter friends alike in college. He smiled, remembering how dismissive those same liberal friends had been with his love of high-stakes poker—the one aspect of the hunting trips with his father and uncles that he had relished. In fact, he often joked that poker had been his major in college and his second love, geology, his minor.

As Jake rounded a bend near the intersection with Antelope Flats Road, several hundred dark brown shapes were clustered loosely in the belly-high grass in the meadow ahead. A bison herd was moving toward the pavement. He drove closer and stopped right in the path of the animals. Jake checked his rearview to be certain he wasn't blocking traffic. A green Park Service vehicle that pulled over a few hundred yards behind him was the only other car around. Jake grabbed his camera.

Massive, and shaggy, the bulls and cows worked their way past his car within fifteen feet of his lens. Jake was aware of a few successful attempts to domesticate buffalo, but he had great respect for their wild, powerful natures. As the area's most dangerous beasts, they were hell on fences and the incautious curious. He was glad to be inside his vehicle.

Several years ago, he had arrived on the scene shortly after the trampling of an eager tourist in Yellowstone. The poor guy was posing for his wife's video camera, when an old bull hooked and gored him from behind. According to the paper, the man had survived with one good kidney, but it sure ruined his vacation. It must have made one hell of a home video, Jake thought.

An enormous bull paused on the asphalt, eyed Jake, and ambled on. In a moment the whole herd, several hundred in all, had shuffled past, producing a chorus of muffled and contented grunts and snorts.

A few cows lagged behind with light-brown calves butting at their udders. Jake raised his eyes in gratitude for the region's abundance of these atavistic creatures, once hunted to near extinction. The sun was moving toward the Tetons; it was time to get back to work. After pulling out, he noticed in his rearview that the Park Service guy seemed to have the same thought—he followed Goddard the few miles to Shadow Mountain, just outside the eastern park boundary.

Jake returned to the Hawkwing feeling successful. He had some excellent bison shots. Plus he had lucked into some information regarding Lyn Burke at the Shadow Mountain National Forest Campground. He was anxious to email Lou Cuvier and Susan and tell them he had confirmation that Lyn had camped at Shadow Mountain.

Clint allowed him to use a computer at the ranch office after business hours. He clomped across the big porch, past the screen door to the dining hall, and in front of several empty Adirondack chairs to the far end of the log lodge. The office was unlocked and dark except for the glow of a booted-up computer that was left on for guests who couldn't wean themselves off email even for a week.

He plopped down in a swivel chair, accessed the internet, and opened his email account. He had several spam messages promising greater male prowess and heft that he quickly deleted. He glanced at a chain email from his wife titled, "End all that worry—put faith in Him" that promised heavenly rewards if the recipient didn't break the chain and serious consequences if he did. He hit delete again.

Through the window, Jake noticed two ranch vans full of guests turning into the parking lot. A delicious aroma emanated out of the lodge kitchen. The day was drawing to a close.

Looking at his inbox reminded him he'd promised Susan he would forward the original exchanges with Louise Cuvier. He opened the Cuvier emails and reviewed them.

From: cuvier@vanhartours.ca
Sent: June 1, 9:08 am, PT
To: Jacob Goddard
Subject: Inquiry
Dear Mr. Goddard,
I hope you don't mind me contacting you out of the blue like this without the proper introductions, but as you get to know me you will realize "proper" is not my style. I'm Louise Cuvier (Lou) and I'm Lyn

Burke's aunt. Florence Burke, Lyn's mother, is my little sister.

Jake, (I trust you don't mind) I'm long divorced and I have no children. My sister Florence and her three children are my only family. Lyn and I are very close and I'm a little concerned about her.

Her mother has not heard from her for almost a week. That is very unusual. I want to help ease my sister's mind and would come down there myself but I'm wheelchair bound, for the most part. The last time Florence heard from Lyn was when she was in Utah recently on her way to Jackson Hole to start work for a Professor Skutches. Well that's not entirely true, Flo got an odd voice message from Lyn that sounds like a benign accidental dial to me, but my sister is convinced it was a distress signal. As you can see, I'm not as concerned as my sister but Lyn's father, Stanley Burke, seems to not be concerned at all. My sister will not let this matter rest and frankly, is hounding me about it.

After several useless attempts to get Stan to act, Florence filed a missing persons report. Now the Las Vegas police appear to be doing nothing. Could that be Stan's influence? My solution is to hire you if you are available.

You must wonder how I know about you. I found you on the web. "Personal Advocacy, Document Research and Discrete Investigation." Very classy. Kind of an upscale "dick" (if you'll pardon the pun). Bet you own an iPad. Well, I hope you're as good as advertised. Lynnie deserves the best. I also hope you work fast. If she is in trouble (I'm frankly not certain that she is), I'd do anything, Jake, to ensure her safe return. You must not tell Stan Burke I've contacted you. I can shed light on activities and interests of Lyn's that might be useful. Please reply ASAP. Thank you for caring about this girl.

Louise Cuvier

From: jgoddard@earthlink.net
Sent: June 1, 5:25 pm, MT
To: Louise Cuvier
Subject: Lyn Burke
Dear Ms. Cuvier,

Thank you for contacting me. I'm very interested in what you have to tell me about Lyn's status and, if she is in trouble, I want very much to determine her whereabouts and ensure her safe return. Any help you can give me toward that end is welcome. It should give you hope to know nine out of ten adult missing persons cases turn out to involve no harm and no foul play. This is almost certainly true with your niece. As you requested, I won't contact any of Lyn's family members. I look forward to hearing from you again soon.

Jake Goddard

From: cuvier@vanhartours.ca
Sent: June 1, 5:15 pm, PT
To: Jacob Goddard
Subject: Lyn Burke

Jake,

Thank you for responding so quickly and keeping our correspondence confidential. Suffice it to say, Lynnie, somewhat because of my influence, and I, are the more liberal members of this godforsaken family. I was the person who recommended that she work for Professor Skutches. Noah and I used to collaborate back in the Pleistocene period. Noah has assured me Lynnie is fine but that will not satisfy my sister. She is adamant that Lyn is in trouble.

Lynnie is a scientist—a good scientist. But she is also a kid with a big heart and a deep abiding passion for the declining health of this ol' globe of ours. In fact, Lynnie has been a volunteer for Lifewater. Lifewater is a mainstream environmental organization that stages non-violent protests of activities that they deem counter to the best interests of the declining global supply of fresh water. For what it is worth, Lynnie's concern comes out of the relationship of climate change to less runoff water and increasing mean temperatures, and the cumulative effect on birds of prey alpine habitat.

Lynnie has always remained on the fringes of extreme activism, but I have worried (as a person who chained herself to an old growth tree or two in her younger days) that she could easily be pulled into more dangerous operatives. She told me that she was planning to join a protest at the summer home of the President of the United Global Bank in

Jackson scheduled for around the time she dropped out of sight. This adopted country of mine is planning bulk sales of groundwater to drier regions, if you can believe it, and the United Global Bank is funding it. If any of this is of interest to you, I will be happy to share my information about an even larger protest that is being organized in Utah and my gut feeling that somehow these are tied to Lyn's situation.

I lead harbor tours here in Vancouver, B.C., but can check email most days. Let me know if you'd like to know more about Lyn's activism.

In the meantime, I recommend you start in Jackson but do not worry too much about Noah Skutches. He is a good man for the most part. Stanley Burke is a different story altogether. There are turbulent waters beneath that calm surface—a veritable riptide. I recommend you handle him with kid gloves.

Stay in touch. Find my girl. Send me information regarding fees, expenses, etc.

Lou

Jake immediately forwarded the Cuvier exchange to Susan with a message that read, "Cuvier correspondence as promised. Good news! I got corroborating information today that Lyn was in Jackson on May 24th. More later." He typed a message to Louise Cuvier regarding what he'd learned at Shadow Mountain.

Lou Cuvier sat on her boat in Vancouver with nothing to do but fret about her sister and her niece. She had waited all day, but no harbor tour customers were biting. Not even for the shorter and cheaper evening cruise. It had been one of those sleepy days in Vancouver, everything dripping and suspended in mist—the clouds parked on top of Grouse Mountain like fat old ladies sinking onto sofas.

Lou inhaled, deep and slow, stretching her arms as she did. The breeze across the water carried the familiar aroma of oil and brine. She grabbed her coffee and smokes, pulled up the old lawn chair on the forward deck of the Minerva Too, and watched her new neighbors on Pier 27A of False Creek returning to their boat on foot carrying supplies.

Rod and Doug were single brothers, deep into mid-life crisis, whose version of the red sports car was the salmon fishing boat they'd just bought and were living on. Big smiles, big talk, and big chests housing big hearts. Every morning they called out sweet offers to help Lou put out the trash and reminded her, laughing at their joke, that they were from the interior and good at things like snow shoveling and lawn-cutting, as if that were any help to a lady living on a boat. Silly, really, but it felt comforting to have them near.

The whole area had become a little more upscale in recent years, attracting larger leisure craft, fancy seafood restaurants, and even sporting a little park with an impressive Kwakiutl sculpture in its center. And the occasional ambulatory psychotic. Strange new world, but she still did her best thinking and writing sitting on her deck in her slicker, staring northwest over the water and the skyline.

Today, as smoke curled slowly up from her nostrils, she could think only of Florence and Lyn. Normally Lou's powers of concentration were formidable. But today, fear and suspicion jammed the gears on her mental processes, and she had to wrench her whole being into thought. Her email alert dinged. Might be Jake Goddard. She looked around for a pad to jot notes just as a cell phone whined inside her anorak, draped out of reach across the transom seat. She slid around and rooted through pockets for the phone, hands fumbling with her cigarette, then squinted at the number: Florence. From her place in Vegas. Now what? One call a week three months ago had jacked up to one or two a day since Lyn's disappearance. She said her friends were all around and helping out, but Lou knew better. Florence didn't have many friends. The poor girl was a wreck, a prisoner. She decided her email could wait and answered her cell.

After finishing his work in the ranch office, Jake ate dinner in the lodge with the guests and then caught some time with Clint. They were alone in the rockers on the porch of Jake's cabin. Clint was wearing his "uniform," a flannel shirt rolled to the elbows, a black bandana tied tight around his neck, jeans, and cowboy boots. The golden light of early evening illuminated the logs of the main building and nearby guest cabins. A sprinkler turned in rhythmic jerks and spat streams across the lawn behind the lodge.

Clint's formula for getting the paying customers out of his hair after dinner had worked flawlessly. On trail ride days, he rode them hard on the horses and then filled them up with food and booze. "Nag 'em and bag 'em," he called it. On river trip days, his goal was to "float 'em and bloat 'em." Today they had rafted the white water of the Snake River Canyon and most were already in their cabins. Delicate shadows from quaking aspen leaves danced across the faces of the two men.

Clint asked after Rachel and the boys and Jake found himself unloading.

"I don't know Clint, Rachel has been so stressed lately. Seems her worry over finances, and, well, everything, equals constantly being pissed at me."

"How do you see this separation thing ending?" Clint asked.

"Not well. Rachel used to be more fun and spontaneous, but lately she's become a classic *molehill mountaineer* and suddenly so self-right-eous and certain about everything. Jumping to conclusions all the time. The other night she saw a new convertible parked outside my Flying Cloud. She assumed it belonged to a woman. Belongs to Frank, my buddy from Geology Club who's into vintage Airstreams and wanted to see my '57."

"Besides imaginary women, what are her issues?"

"You know, the usual. My work and pay are unpredictable, sure, but it's what I'm cut out for. What I love. Just my luck to marry a numbers-crunching woman who does everything on a rigid schedule, except, of course have sex—that never seemed to get scheduled."

"Sounds like numbers aren't all she's crunching lately. Have you talked to anybody?"

"We've gone the counseling route, but Rachel tried to convert the counselor and then suddenly refused to go, insisting we had to see her minister. I refused to do that, cuz I feel her minister's partial to her." Jake watched the sprinkler turn. "It just feels like we are light-years apart. The bottom line, old buddy—I just wonder how our marriage can turn out when we no longer turn each other on."

"Hmm. I hear that," Clint said. The men stared in silence at the Tetons shooting up in the distance above the rounded hills surrounding the ranch. Finally he asked, "How're the boys?"

"They seem fine, actually. You're going to love this. They've really gotten into horses. Rachel got them riding lessons south of Salt Lake."

"Must not be related to you," Clint said, biting off his words like gnawing on a stick of jerky.

"Yeah. Excited about horses, damn. Makes me wonder. It gets worse. Matthew's wearing his toy six-gun to bed every night, and saying he's going to be a cowboy when he grows up, just like Clint."

"'Mamas don't let your babies grow up to be cowboys,'" Clint crooned in a very poor imitation of Willie Nelson.

"I have no problem with him being a cowboy. I just hope he doesn't turn out to be anything like you," Jake said. "Or that his born-again Mama doesn't make a preacher of him."

Clint smiled, bobbed his head in agreement, and thrust his boots up on the top porch rail, crossing them at the ankle. "So while we're soul-searching here, how're you doing with your program?" The sprinkler began a new cycle slapping at the base of a lone pine tree, drenching its lower branches.

"Jeez, cut to the chase, why don't you, Dr. Phil? I'm doing pretty good. Rachel still handles all the money and keeps me on the path of righteousness. I mean, she's … she's my anchor, and I still love her, or at least I think I do." Jake tore a sliver of wood off the rail and picked at his teeth while looking toward the river. "Sometimes I get tired dragging her along behind." He looked at Clint. "But hell, anchor or no anchor, how much trouble can a sinner find in Utah? We don't even have a state lottery." He flicked the sliver off the porch. "Didn't Kenny Rogers sing, 'You gotta know when to fold 'em?' I folded them permanently over a year ago."

"What brings you to paradise?" Clint asked.

"I've got myself a missing person case, well, a possible missing person case. I've partnered up with Officer Brand at the PD. She was assigned the same case."

"She? Wait ... Brand ... Susan Brand? Isn't she the babe who's in hot water? Shit, when I see that woman in uniform, I just want to throw my hands up and say, I confess, officer, I'm aroused in public—cuff me." Clint slapped Jake on the back.

"You wish, buddy. This is strictly professional. But I have to agree, Brand's the whole package—smart, capable."

"Not to mention hot. Watch your step, bud. She's armed." Clint slipped a tobacco tin out of his back pocket. "You said, possible missing person case."

Jake told Clint what he knew about the case.

"But why possible?" Clint asked. "You think she's missing or just off playing in the mountains? You gotta love these elitist protesters. It's like summer vacation. If you were a preppie activist, where would you rather demonstrate, in hot and gritty New York or D.C., or at the poor prick president of the United Global Bank's summer home in Jackson? You know, protest a little, rock climb a little, not bad. I'd sure as hell pick Jackson Hole."

"At this point, I'm really not sure what she's doing or where she is. According to her boss, she was sent to a remote corner of southern Utah to do research. Weird thing is, she had just come through that area on the way up here. Why have her turn around and go right back? Piss poor planning if it's true. She travels with a cutting edge device for email and cell and regularly hits cafes with WiFi. Yet, she hasn't posted on Facebook or contacted her parents lately."

"You know as well as I do that out here sometimes the only cell service is the type with bars on the windows and rusty hinges on the door, and the next cafe could be a whole day's drive," Clint said, squinting at Jake.

"I did read about that protest at the United Global Bank president's home. Used to call those guys monkey-wrenchers—now they're called 'ecoterrorists,' and rightfully so." He sat back and put his hands behind his head. "And it's not long before the FBI's got their eye on them big time. Not to mention anti-environmentalist groups like Sage Use." Clint clomped his boots down on the porch, rocked forward, and spat between the balustrades. The splash of tobacco juice beaded brown in the dry gray duff.

"Jesus, when are you going to quit that disgusting shit?" Not expecting a response, Jake continued, "The Lifewater organization isn't that radical. Hell, brother, your business depends on fresh water in the Gros Ventre and Snake. You might even like them."

"Might like 'em for target practice," Clint said sighting an imaginary rifle at the river.

Jake ignored him. "But yeah, I guess things got a whole lot more serious after those ski area fires in Colorado protesting for lynx habitat. Caused twelve mil in damage."

Clint sat back in his rocker. "Twelve million," he whistled. "I don't think I heard about that. Check out that nighthawk!" Clint pointed to a miniature stealth bomber—striped wings perpendicular to the ground—diving at an insect above the gravel path to the lodge.

Jake nodded and propped his elbows against his knees. He considered telling his friend that deep in a corner of his soul he sympathized with radical environmentalists. That he'd much prefer lynx had ample range than snow bunnies had more habitat. But he could never apply the torch himself. Hell, sometimes all he could manage was to recycle and send a few meager donations to mainstream environmental groups. Jake knew revealing these feelings to his opinionated and conservative buddy would only spark an argument.

"I don't think this kid's into anything that major. It's hard to say at this point. She's just into Lifewater big time."

"But didn't you say she's from Vegas? With Lake Mead right there, they seem to have all the water in the world," Clint said.

"There are upwards of forty million people from Arizona to Mexico who depend on the Colorado River. It's just a matter of time before demand way exceeds supply. Mead's at less than half capacity and, up river, Lake Powell's in the same—"

"That's a bunch of enviro-bullshit! They recently had a record snowmelt year."

"Goddamnit, just hear me out before you jump to conclusions. One good year of water is a drop in the bucket in a desert that has had a dozen years of drought racked up. Ninety percent of Vegas's water comes from Mead. The city is constantly angling for ways to suck more water through their tunnels, which they call straws. I'll just take a wild guess and say they couldn't give a shit about going through proper channels or what happens to the millions of thirsty folks downstream."

"Fuck, I get flyers about Vegas all the time. They say the city is boomin' and bloomin'," Clint said. "Gorgeous waterfalls everywhere."

"I suppose you also believe that load of crap from your outfitter buddies about the moose population being destroyed by wolves when the science points to cars, development, and disease." Clint grunted his disagreement. "I don't have the whole picture yet, to tell you the truth," Jake said. "But I did have some luck today. I met a couple at Shadow Mountain who saw Lyn Burke two nights before the protest and they told me what all the fuss was about. Said the United Global Bank has approved funding to build a pipeline across Northern Canada from well up the Mackenzie River to the Beaufort Sea. But not for oil ... for water."

"For water?" Clint asked.

"Yep." Jake recounted that the plan was to ship the water in tankers and in huge rubber bags, "giant condoms," he joked, from the pipeline terminus through the Northwest Passage. The man at Shadow Mountain had said China and some smaller Asian countries are desperate for potable water, and Canada has plenty to sell.

"I'm sure the tree huggers aren't happy about all this transporting water stuff," Clint said.

"Nope. Nor are they happy about the impact of the pipeline or that the passage is navigable thanks to climate change. My client, the girl's aunt, told me her niece was supposed to be involved in the demonstration but, according to the couple I spoke with at Shadow Mountain, she never showed up."

"All this agua-talk is making me thirsty," Clint said. "What do you say we make a trip to our local watering hole? I got a buddy who works for the paper. I'll bet for the price of a few drinks at the Cowboy Bar, he'll tell you all you want to know about The United Global Bank protest. I'll call Hunter."

"Great. I'll contact Susan Brand and see if she can get away and meet us there. Might be your lucky night, maybe she'll arrest you."

"As in cardiac arrest. I just hope she knows CPR." Clint leered with a tobacco-filled maw. "But, meanwhile, city slicker, see if you can put something on that doesn't have 'Certified, Citified Utah Asshole' written all over it. Hell," he continued, jabbing his finger into the logo of Jake's t-shirt, "Utah Jazz? Isn't jazz against the law in Utah?" Clint swung up and started to walk off the porch but stopped and turned. "Water, huh?" He spat in the dirt. "You remember what Mark Twain said about water in the West, don't you? 'Whiskey is for drinkin', water is for fightin' over.'"

"Yep. People are killed here every year over water," Jake said. "What would this ranch look like without water rights and irrigation?"

"We just better follow old Twain's advice and drink us some whiskey. See you in a few." Clint crossed the compound to his cabin. Jake remained lost in thought in the pooling shadows of the porch while the sprinkler completed another rhythmical rotation.

June 8
Thursday

It was opening night at the Wild West Days celebration held at the Teton County Fairgrounds and Susan Brand caught the duty. The venue was just down mountain from Snow King on the edge of town adjacent to the rodeo arena. The Wild West Days event consisted of one city block crammed full of western arts and old-style crafts. The living historians—mountain men displays of period tools, weapons, and clothing—were a big draw. Two additional blocks were occupied by animals in metal pens. Wild West Days would conclude on Saturday evening with the first rodeo of the summer. As Susan rode around the fairgrounds, she was relieved to know that, because she was on duty tonight and the next night, she would not pull the weekend rodeo duty and would be able to spend it at home with Amy.

A chilly wind kicked up close to 6 p.m.; cotton candy wrappers and drink cups blew around the feet of excited children. Susan guided Cassie through the crowd and looked for Jake. She rode slowly past a pack of teenage boys waiting their turn while a friend bounced around on the mechanical bull. The boys cracked up when the machine sped up and tossed their buddy to the mats.

It was Susan's ardent hope the jerk in the Jeep was lurking somewhere at the celebration and that he would show himself. She wore her tightest jeans and uniform blouse, but threw on her blue nylon jacket as the evening grew more bitter and threatening. Susan had suggested that Jake pose as a tourist and that they keep their distance from each other to provide two vantage points from which to find their suspect.

Chuck Simmons patrolled the fairgrounds in the opposite direction. He wore a brown leather cowboy hat and a matching multi-pocketed jacket buttoned up to his red neckerchief. As they stopped to chat, Buck, his mount, danced sideways.

"Hiii, Buck! Damnit, Buck, settle down!" Buck relented, and steadied a little. "I'm lousy on a horse and you have a hurt paw and are a terrible shot anyway. Between the two of us we make up one decent cop," he said.

"Yup, and I'm the better three-quarters. Even with one hand wrapped like a mummy." Susan shook her head, smiled, and rode on. She feared Chuck might discern she was preoccupied with her missing person case and rib her about it because everyone knew it was just a punishment from the chief. A few minutes later she saw Jake standing by the Bowie knife throwing booth. She nodded and glanced away.

Susan loved the western displays, especially the mountain men with their oily buckskins, long beards, and frontier rifles. The musty barnyard odor coming from the 4-H pens was a harbinger of the Teton County Fair that she and Amy attended every July. The fairs, like Wild West Days and the county fair, were Susan's favorite events of the very busy Jackson summer. The lights of the rides and booths, the smells emanating from popcorn poppers and deep fryers, and the carny barkers pitching their attractions always made her feel like an eight year old again, coming into Phoenix from the reservation for the first time to the Arizona state fair. The state fair was one of the rare times of the year her austere father allowed her a few extra indulgences.

By 10:00 p.m., the wind had sharpened and the fair was shutting down. Most of the games were closing for the night and only a few brave souls remained in the arts and crafts booths looking for deals. Chuck radioed that he was going to ride Buck the few blocks to his house, pasture him there for the night, and turn in.

Several days had passed without any significant leads in the Burke case and there was still no sign of the bald guy. Susan went in search of Jake and saw him in the illumination of a covered livestock arena. Even in the dim light she couldn't miss him in his red mountain parka, signature ball cap and hiking shorts. She tied Cassie, entered the wooden shed, and walked behind the central ring and adjacent bleachers, and past several aromatic metal pens housing sheep and goats.

"How's it going, Jake?"

"Hey, Susan. Any luck?"

"No sign of him or the Jeep," Susan said. "Looks like you gave it up to spend some time in stimulating conversation here."

"I figured if he wasn't here by nine, he wasn't coming. Just been waiting for you to finish your duty. And I like these critters, that is, everywhere but high in the mountains where their grazing is so destructive. I'll take one of these humble beasts over a horse any day. Look how cute those sleeping lambs are." Jake pointed to two well-groomed lambs lying in clean straw nuzzled up against their mother. "I used to raise lambs on the farm," he said. Susan looked skeptical.

They walked out by Cassie and sat on hay bales. A whirling dervish of straw spiraled across the hard pack.

"What'd you make of Louise Cuvier and her emails? Sounds like quite a character, doesn't she?" Jake said.

"Very interesting lady. Hard to say how worried she really is about Lyn but she sure doesn't like Stan Burke." Susan pulled up her collar against the wind.

"No question." Jake nodded toward the animal pens. "I'm gonna guess she's the black sheep of the family but she probably wouldn't have it any other way. It will be interesting to see what else develops with ol' Aunt Lou." They sat in silence for a while, watching the lights in the booths go out one by one.

Susan stood. "I think I better call it a night. My sitter likes to be home by eleven and I still have to put this girl to bed." She patted Cassie's neck. Jake rose, giving the horse wide berth.

"I must admit you look … really … good on her … strong and in control." Jake approached Cassie tentatively and stroked the tips of her ears, standing close enough by Susan to smell her clean hair. "Can I help you put her up for the night?"

Susan pretended to ignore the compliment. "No thanks. I've done it a thousand times alone."

"Even with a stoved-up hand?"

"Thanks for offering." Susan reached for Jake's hand, covered it with hers, shifted it to the base of Cassie ear and moved his fingers up and down. "You need to be more confident. She loves it, right there." Her hand lingered briefly on his, warming it.

Jake scratched below the ear. Cassie leaned her head into his hand like a dog. "Looks like I hit the spot."

"The big gal knows what shuh likes," Susan said in a country drawl.

"Sure I can't help you?" Jake asked.

Susan shook her head. "But let's meet in the morning and map out our next moves. How about Cowboy Coffee near the square around eight? Best place for coffee. I'll go straight there after I drop Amy at the school."

"No problem. Sounds great." Jake said.

"Sleep well, Jake."

"Hey, the Gros Ventre runs right by my cabin—real soothing. I probably won't even need to count sheep. Catch you in the morning." Jake returned to the arena for one last look at the sleeping lambs.

Susan loaded Cassie in the trailer and drove to the edge of town to the police barn and pasture. Several horses huddled in a corner of the dark corral under a cottonwood tree shifted nervously. The wind had increased and leaves and seedpods blew off horizontally with each new gust of air. She backed the trailer up to the paddock, jumped out, and fought her hat and hair as she lowered the back of the trailer. Cassie balked and sidestepped while backing down and off the ramp. Susan sensed something behind her and turned quickly, but she saw only tumbleweed and paper blowing against the side of the building. She exhaled and turned back to Cassie, stroking and reassuring her while leading her into the barn. She removed the saddle, blanket, and halter and hung them on pegs, then brushed Cassie vigorously and gave her some grain. Susan closed the horse in for the night and bent to unhitch the trailer before heading home.

Dark clouds raced across the face of the three-quarter moon and the wind leaned on the spruces lining the yard. Susan's hands were stuffed in her jacket pockets for warmth and she tried to concentrate on relaxing the tension in her neck as she walked to her cottage.

Jamie met Susan at the door. The teen zipped her fleece jacket to cover a flat bare midriff and navel ring. The screen door banged with each gust.

"Wow. Must be a big one coming out there." Jamie flipped her brown hair out of her collar. "Amy has been sound asleep for over an hour. I'll see you tomorrow. Same time, right?" She turned to go, then turned back. "Oh jeez, I almost forgot—a friend of yours came by tonight. A man."

"What friend? I wasn't expecting any friend."

"Don't worry," Jamie said smiling. "You've trained me well. Even though he was your friend, I didn't let him get past the front porch. But, yeah, he said you're old buds. I mean he knew Amy's name and where you worked. He said you'd talked to him about buying life insurance."

"Life insurance! I'm not buying any life ins … wait, what did this guy look like?"

"A bowling ball with a smashed nose is the best I can come up with. Scared me to look at him at first," Jamie said.

"Shaved head?" Jamie nodded. "Black eyebrows?"

"Yeah, I think so … yes." Jamie said.

"Did you see his car?"

"He drove a Jeep. Black Jeep. I noticed because I always wanted a Wrang—"

"Young lady, that man is not a friend. Do not talk to him. Call me immediately if you see him anywhere, understand?"

"Yes, ma'am. I just thought, like, you know, when he knew where you were, at Wild West patrolling and all."

"He did? I can't believe this. Christ!" Jamie bit her lower lip. "Look, it's not your fault. I'm not upset with you. But I want you to go straight home, okay? Keep your cell phone on and call me when you get home.

I'm not sure who this man is, but he's certainly no friend and he may be dangerous."

"Yes, ma'am." Jamie turned, went through the door and trotted to her yellow VW bug in the street. Susan watched her until she pulled away. She picked up the portable phone in the kitchen and went into her daughter's room. Amy was sleeping deeply, as Jamie had reported. Susan stepped out in the hall and dialed. A member of the kitchen staff answered at the Hawkwing and went to get Jake.

"Jake, Jake," she hissed into the phone when he came on. "He was here. The son-of-a-bitch was here again. At my house. He came to my house tonight and spoke to my sitter." She turned toward her daughter's room. "Yes, damnit, please come over, now." She re-entered the bedroom, stretched out beside her daughter and slid an arm across her body.

Jake arrived in less than an hour. He and Susan sat close together on her couch, whispering over coffee mugs. "Why is he harassing me? What the hell does he want?" Susan asked.

"I've been mulling that one over since I got your call. There are only two possible explanations. He has either randomly fixated on you, and, uh, on Amy—"

"Oh shit!" She said, setting her jaw and jamming her hair behind her ear. "I just realized he might have been in our house before. The other night when he was at my window, there was a dirty milk glass left in the kitchen that Amy denied using."

"Susan, come on, a dirty milk glass? Plus, no one could enter your house without Cinder raising a ruckus."

Susan turned to Jake with a blank look. "She didn't bark at you tonight. She didn't bark at you because she's familiar with you." She rubbed her hands on her thighs and turned to stare at the front door. "Now that I think of it, she did bark a few times that night, but I thought it was because of a cat in our garbage." She beat her knee with her left fist. "I can't believe that fucker has been inside my house!"

"Now, wait," Jake said, gripping her shoulder, "we still don't know for certain what this slimy stalker's intentions are. At least he hasn't tried to hurt either of you." The wind whistled through the spruces. The screen door banged.

"How does he even know about Amy and me?" Her hand shook on her coffee mug.

"He either knows which cases you're working, or, like I said, he picked you two at random, or ...." Jake sipped his coffee. "Or, he has been following me, and he followed me ... to you."

"And now my kid is in danger." She looked at her bandaged hand. "I've hit my limit. Screw this. I don't need this. I've got to tell Earl to take me off this Burke thing. Amy's safety is too important."

"You know as well as I do, whether he's connected to Lyn Burke's disappearance and Fernando's death or not, and whether you're on the case or not, he'll probably be back."

"You really think he was following you?" Susan asked.

"Hard to say. It's one logical explanation. But if so, for some reason, he didn't reveal himself to me. I suppose I don't interest him in the same way when it comes to power and control. Like we said at the Elk Refuge, that makes your role all the more important."

Susan took a deep breath. "Forgive the momentary jitters. It's just that, well, you know, it's tough with a kid ..."

"You're talking to a parent." Jake sat back against the cushions. "Speaking of parents, I talked to Louise Cuvier about Lyn's parents tonight, to try and understand their opposing views."

"How're they holding up? Any news about Lyn?" Susan asked.

"According to Lou, the mom is a wreck. Calls Lou daily in hysterics. Dad seems okay, considering. Almost too good. I mean there can't be much else in his life that could go wrong and, yes, there is some news."

"What?"

"Stan Burke told Florence, who told Louise, that in a recent show of support, some of his cronies sent a helicopter to the Parunuweap Canyon trailhead in southern Utah where Lyn allegedly started her trek. The pilot reported that the car that they supposedly drove down in, the one that belongs to her guide, is parked there.

"How do they know what she drove down in?"

"Good question. Beats me, unless they talked to Skutches or White Wolf. They saw no sign of his daughter, but that's to be expected if she's in the backcountry. In that convoluted country, you can get totally lost in a slot canyon a half mile from your car."

"Yeah, if they're in the backcountry. If we don't turn something up soon about Lyn Burke, southern Utah should probably be your next stop. What else is wrong with the guy?" Susan asked.

"Oh, let's see: separated from his wife, stock dropped through the floor, business off dramatically—"

"So his business has tanked?"

"Big time, and that's not all." Jake relayed the details of some online research he had done into Burke's gypsum mine. Lou had directed him to environmentalists' websites that condemned Ashland Mine for outdated extractive practices, such as using open pit mining instead of low impact rotomilling. Also, the sites asserted Burke was making no effort to reclaim his old pit outside Iron Springs. Jake said the websites also accused Burke of indiscriminate use of potable water and experimentation on some of his properties with sulfuric acid injections in limestone aquifers, a quick and dirty way to make instant gypsum.

"They'd like to put him out of business permanently and are blocking any attempts on his part to acquire new mining permits," Jake said.

"And on top of that, his daughter's missing."

"Possibly missing. But definitely proof 'when it rains it pours'," Jake said.

"So what's he like?"

"Lou claims he's greedy, arrogant, and untrustworthy. His belief that Lyn is fine is the chief motivation for Lou to suspect otherwise."

"What kind of father do you think he is? Could he be behind all this?" Susan said.

"Who knows? He's probably as devoted a father as any distracted CEO."

"Any chance his daughter's disappearance is tied to his other problems?" Susan pulled a couch pillow onto her lap and stifled a yawn.

"I wouldn't rule it out. It doesn't seem like the sort of tactic that even the most radical environmental group would stoop to. But, you never know. They up the ante in that game every year." Jake rubbed at his eyes and covered a yawn with his hand. "Sorry. Late. For that matter, her liberal politics could have prompted an abduction from the anti-environmentalist side."

"But, if there was any political motivation, the media or someone should have heard from the perps by now."

"Same is true if this was kidnap for gain. No ransom note and no call. Unfortunately, either of those two choices might bode better for his kid than the only remaining logical explanation," Jake said.

"Which brings us right back to the perv stalking me, who may have helped himself to milk from my refrigerator and gotten his woody tonight by chatting with my teenage sitter within thirty feet of my child."

"Sad to say, but it does," Jake said. "I really need to call Cuvier again tomorrow night and tell her you are being stalked and see if she has any clue who this wacko is or why he might be in play in her niece's case."

"Whatever the guy's motivation is—whether he's trying to scare me off Burke, or even off Diaz, or not—he's mine. I'm sick of this. I'm gonna clean his frickin' clock!"

Jake saw the look in her eyes and believed it—screwed-up hand or not. "I hear you."

"At least I get this off tomorrow." Susan raised her bandaged hand. "Just in time for the results of Earl's inquiry into the accident. And assuming I still have a job, I'll update him about our encounters with the ugly bald guy in the Jeep—who's about to get uglier when I get my two good hands on him."

"That's great news. I mean about the hand. It'd be real nice if you could comfortably use your pistol again." Jake looked at his watch. "It's pretty late, do you mind if I spend the night on the couch?"

"Well … no, no I don't mind." She smiled for the first time since Jake arrived. "It'll give the neighbors something to talk about."

"'Let's give'em something to talk about. A little something to figure out.'" Jake sang quietly. "Do you like Bonnie Raitt?"

"I used to, until I read somewhere that you know you are middle-aged if Bonnie Raitt was the last concert you attended. Which it was, in my case." Susan grinned. She rose from the coach and yawned again. "Oh, excuse me. It's not the company. And, I ... I do appreciate your offering to spend the night."

Jake leaned back and stretched while Susan went in search of some blankets. When she returned with her arms full of bedding, Jake said, "I've got an idea. What do you say we bag that bottom feeder tomorrow?"

"There is nothing I'd like better. But only if you let me gut him and grill him."

"I'll tell you over breakfast what I have in mind." Jake took the blankets from her. "Night." Jake yawned again and bent to untie his shoes but Susan surprised him by plopping down on the couch, putting her head on his shoulder, and giving him a firm hug before jumping up and heading down the hall to her room.

June 9
Friday

Susan waited outside Earl's office while he finished a call. She felt it in her bones. This was the day they'd catch the jerk in the Jeep. She didn't know why he was stalking her. Maybe it had to do with the missing girl, maybe the rock climbing accident, maybe both, maybe neither. She was damn well, with Jake's help, going to find out. After the scumbag's second visit to her house, her best guess, after a good night's sleep, was that he was trying to get her to back off the Burke case. Not going to happen. It only strengthened her resolve to find Lyn Burke and to catch him.

Earl put down the phone and waved her into his office. As she entered he chuckled and hit the remote control to his authentic-looking, electronic, wall-mounted bass. Its tail and head flip-flopped rhythmically. Always a good sign the meeting would go well.

"How ya doing, Brandy?"

"Pretty well, Earl, I'm doing pretty well. Much better than a few weeks ago. How're you and Rita?"

"We're good, thanks. Your hand looks better." Earl tossed the remote on his cluttered desk.

Susan flexed her fingers. "It feels pretty good, considering. Great to have the bandage off."

"Got some good news. The shooting has been ruled an accident. We'll decide in a few days if there will be any further sanctions against you." Earl ran his hand through his hair.

Susan sat back in her chair. "You just made my day, Earl."

He held Susan's gaze for a moment. "I've gotta say, I'm proud of how you've handled this, Brand. I feel like you heard me when we talked." He grinned. "Since you like my preaching so much, let me just say kudos for paddling like hell to get through this mess. Performance of duties and professionalism under duress noted. Keep it up."

"Yeah, well, some days it felt like a dog-shit paddle, but I guess I did hear you, Boss and ... I, uh … I appreciate the professional example you set. Plus, what choice did I have?"

"Lots of cops would've gone straight to the bottom. Give yourself more credit."

"Maybe I should, Earl. Thanks for saying that, and without even coming up with a new parable." Susan smiled.

Earl sat forward in his chair. "I need all hands on deck on some important cases. You can stop wasting your time on that Burke thing. Tomorrow I'll toss it to the rookie—"

"What? I … um … Chief, I know you think you're doing me a favor but I … I honestly don't feel it's a waste of time. Let me bring you up to date."

Twenty minutes later, Susan walked out of the chief's office smiling. The day had started out very well. She had the use of both hands, although the one was still tender and weak. Then there was Earl's good news and the fact that she had convinced him to give her a few more days on the Burke case. Events, both good and bad, were supposed to happen in threes. Her ardent wish for a "third" on this banner day was the bald guy under questioning.

Since he had obviously put Jake and Susan together and seemed aware of their movements, Jake had suggested over breakfast they try to lure him into the light long enough to hook him and book him. They speculated that he had to be centrally located in the town in order to monitor them and react so quickly. Was he involved with Lyn Burke? If so, what kind of shape was she in? It was anybody's guess. Today had to be the day to answer these questions. Susan agreed it was worth a try and ran it by her partner. Chuck felt it was a solid plan and even offered to have Amy spend the night with his kids. Of course, he had to rib Susan about going on a fishing "date" with her "friend" from out of town.

At 7:00 p.m. Jake and Susan were dressed for their parts. Jake parked his car in front of a sporting goods store on the town square. They came out twenty minutes later with some new fishing supplies. They drove out of Jackson west toward the Tetons, through ranchland dotted with horses and cattle and, before crossing the Snake River, turned onto a dike that paralleled the shore. A long strip of level ground like a raised railroad bed, the dike was wide enough for a vehicle to go forward or backward only. They pulled up on it and headed north along the river. Evening light played on the rippled surface of the water like a thousand silver fish. The peaks to the west were splashed with the saffron light of the early evening sun moving toward them. Jake drove a few hundred yards, rounded a blind bend, and stopped in a copse of conifers. An osprey hovered above the deep channel, poised to dive for dinner.

A little spring creek flowed out of the trees, ran parallel to the levee, and rushed under a culvert to join the Snake. They unloaded their rods and gear. The river ran high and slapped noisily against the large rocks lining the dike. Boulders clacked under the current. Just downstream, one thick spruce, uprooted, lay horizontal out over the water, half-submerged. Its branches danced, straining and lashing the surface of the water.

Earlier Chuck had hidden Susan's truck in the trees about eighty yards back from the river. It was Jake's idea to keep his weapons in the truck so there'd be less chance of spooking their prey. They agreed Susan would hide downstream and carry her shotgun, just in case.

Jake prepared to fish the creek in full view of any vehicle that approached.

"I'm going to prop my backpack with my pole on top behind this tree." Susan said. "If he drives up, that should give us a few seconds of the illusion that I'm here with you."

"Sounds good. What the heck, toss your line in the water. You might catch something."

As Susan worked her way to her truck through the cool shadows of the grove, she heard a hermit thrush. The melodious birdcall took the edge off her tension. When she reached the truck, she slipped her shotgun out of the rack in the cab. She walked up the two-track in the direction they had come to get behind her stalker if he showed up. She struggled back toward the water through a tangle of willow bushes and tucked in next to the dike, about sixty yards downstream from where Jake cast his fly rod. Through the willows she could see his pole flash and the line float on the air above it.

An insect hatch filled the air with winged sunlit specks. Birds chattered. The rush of the river was beginning to soothe Susan when the whine of an approaching vehicle snagged her out of her reverie. She spotted the black Jeep. She held her breath as the car sped by within ten feet and bore down on Jake. The driver had a shaved head and wore a camo jacket. Susan scrambled along the inside of the dike trying to stay out of sight. Jake didn't budge; he waited for the vehicle to stop.

The Jeep slid to a stop and the driver sat motionless for a moment, apparently realizing he could not get around Jake's car. Susan slipped on the dike's steep gravel bank and drove both palms into the cinders and pebbles. She bit her lip and puffed air through her nose to avoid crying out in pain, but the noise of the water absorbed the sound of her fall. She brushed off her palms, rechecked that her shotgun was on safety, and inched closer to the Jeep.

The bald guy looked from Jake to the "figure" behind the tree. It slowly dawned on him that he might have driven into a trap. He spun backwards.

Susan was within five yards of the Jeep. She climbed onto the dike, the shotgun leveled at the driver from the passenger's side. Before she could order him to stop, he caught her out of the corner of his eye, braked, and jumped out of the car, scrambling down by the rear tire. She charged around the Jeep. He lunged up at the weapon, twisting the barrel out of her weakened grip. She hung on with her other hand and they wrestled for the gun.

Jake dove over the hood of the Jeep and grabbed the attacker around the neck from behind. Susan kicked at the assailant's knees. Jake hooked a leg with his foot and twisted him around, chopped the gun out of his hand and shoved him down the bank of the dike.

The sun glinted off the stalker's head as he danced for footing, but a small avalanche of gravel carried him into the river. A look of surprise, then fear, gripped his face. The force of the water spun him around and pulled him toward the sweeper tree lying across the surface. He lunged for an upstream limb, but was washed under the trunk and pressed hard into the submerged branches. He was caught. He drove his head to the surface to breathe, but only partially cleared his mouth out of the water. With each gulp, waves broke over his face and water flowed down his throat. He choked and sputtered, spitting out water and sucking at the air, and flailed at the branches with his hands.

"Son of a bitch is in serious trouble," Jake yelled.

"We've got to unhook him somehow," Susan shouted.

"I've got some line in the car. Hold your gun on him." Jake was back in an instant with an old climbing rope. He stripped off his fishing vest, sunglasses, and hat. The drowning man continued to gasp at the surface like a dying salmon.

"What if you get tangled?"

"Got my fishing knife." He patted his hip.

Jake tied one end of the rope around the bumper of the Jeep and the other around his waist and fought his way out into the water balancing on the trunk and sidestepping through the exposed branches of the tree. The current rushed around his knees and tried to rip him out of the tangle. When he reached the drowning man, Jake dropped into the surge on the downstream side of the tree and unsheathed his knife. After gulping air into his lungs, he held the trunk with one hand and dove down. He slashed at the tangle of clothing and tree limbs. When he was coming up for air, the force of the current jammed the man's legs under the trunk and they wrapped around Jake. Jake wrestled the legs, but they locked and pulled him under. He pumped his arms and pulled up on a branch but could not breach the surface. A second attempt failed. The pressure in his chest sharpened into pain. He jabbed the point of his knife into the man's thigh, causing his legs to recoil in pain and release. Jake popped to the surface, sucked more air, and dove again. He cut at the clothing until it tore away. Finally, the man was free and his head was above water, but he hung panting and exhausted in the branches. Jake jerked several times and finally dragged him over the tree. The two men washed downstream and swung into shore on the rope.

The man sat shivering on a log by Susan's truck. She aimed her shotgun at his back. He held up one hand to block the low sunrays through the trees, and the other gripped a growing crimson stain around the cut on his right thigh. "Goddamnit, I'm freezing out here and my leg is killing me."

"You're lucky to be alive, buddy," Jake said, laying the pistol he had retrieved from Susan's truck on a stump and slipping on a dry t-shirt. "What's your name?"

"Name's Moody ... Ranklin Moody," he muttered.

"Mr. Moody, you get dry clothes and first aid after you tell us what the hell you're up to," Susan said.

"Shit! I just came out here to scout a good fishing spot." Moody rubbed his shaved head, tucked his hands between his knees and rocked back and forth.

Susan came around and glared into his face. "Bullshit! You've been watching me. I recognize you from that night at my kitchen window. What kind of a dumb-ass game are you playing, sneaking around my house?"

"Okay, it was stupid, I admit it. I wasn't armed—never have been. I knew you two probably wouldn't a' shot an unarmed man. I didn't mean no harm."

"Oh, really? You think harassment, trespassing, and terrorizing people in their homes is harmless?" Susan stared at Moody. He looked embarrassed and avoided her eyes.

"What's your involvement in Lyn Burke's disappearance?" Jake asked.

"Whoa. Wait a minute, I don't know anything about that … I haven't laid a hand on her. I haven't even seen her."

"So you know who she is," Jake said.

"Yeah, I know who Lyn Burke is," Moody said. Susan and Jake exchanged a look.

"So what the hell have you been doing around my house?" Susan asked.

"The guy I work for paid me to come over here and play grab-ass with you. He told me to report your activities and scare you a little. That's all I know. He didn't say why and I didn't ask."

"You were following me too, right?" Jake asked.

"Well, yeah, it was pretty obvious you two had partnered up. When I reported that, you were added to my surveillance list."

"Who put you up to this?" Jake asked. Moody hesitated, looking around wildly for a way out of answering.

"We can stay here all night to see if you bleed out before you freeze to death if we have to. Who?" Susan demanded.

"You've gotta promise me you won't arrest me."

"I'm not promising you anything," Susan said. "Now, who hired you?"

"Uh … oh … shit. I was, uh … hired by Stan Burke."

Jake and Susan looked at each other in disbelief. "That's a bunch of crap. Now where's the girl?" Susan asked.

Jake caught Susan's arm with his hand. "Wait a minute Susan, crazy as that sounds, it'd explain a lot."

"How do you think I knew who you were and how to find you? Burke knew you were the cop assigned to his daughter's case, and like I said," he turned to Jake, "you were just an add-on. I've got pictures of you two in a dozen places—campgrounds, the Elk Refuge, watching the buffalo on Antelope Flats Road, the Indian Festival, the Wild West … whatever."

"Why would Burke hire you to stalk and harass Officer Brand when it's her job to find his daughter?" Jake asked.

"I don't know. I … ever heard of Sage Use?"

Jake picked up his rope and began to coil it. "Yeah, of course—the pro-growth consortium of businessmen and ranchers. Everyone who can read a newspaper is familiar with Sage Use."

"That's what I do, among other things. I do legitimate R & D for Sage Use's board of directors—Burke is probably the most powerful member. He got me my job with them. But this ... I have to say, this was his most whacked assignment."

"So why'd you do it?" Susan said.

"Like I said, Burke pulls a lot of weight with the group that pays me, and ... he offered me some serious add-on jack."

"And what could possibly be his motivation to pay you to break the law and distract people from his daughter's case?" Susan asked.

"Burke? Shit! He makes his own laws. I dunno, maybe it keeps the heat offa him while he deals with his other problems. He's obviously not too worried about his kid. Burke loves to pull strings."

"You're lucky I didn't shoot you," Susan said.

"Believe me, lady, I'm not stupid. That occurred to me when I saw you come out of the house with your pistol the night I was in your kitchen. Burke had specifically told me to enter your house and leave a sign to give you a good scare ... so I left the dirty milk glass."

"And the window—why the window?" Susan asked.

"I wrote on the window because I was afraid you'd miss the milk glass, what with a little kid, and all. Swear to God, though, from the beginning I haven't liked the feeling of this whole deal. I've never done anything like this before." He wrapped both arms around his torso. "Last night at your house, when I saw your little girl ... I ... I lost my taste for the whole game, money or no money. I even began to suspect maybe Burke'd just as soon see me blown away and out of this. When I saw the shotgun today, I guess ... I just got rattled." Moody bent double and convulsed in a long coughing fit.

Susan jerked him up by the neck of his wet shirt. "You ever pull this kind of crap again or come near my house or my daughter, I will rip your head off."

Moody wiped his mouth with the back of his hand. "I'm sure you could—like a black widow spider." Susan smacked him hard on the side of his head with an open palm. It got his attention. "You won't have no problem from me, I guarantee it, lady. I'm a independent businessman with a reputation to maintain." Susan walked away from her prisoner in disgust. "Hey, I'm really cold. I think I'm getting hyperthermia," Moody said, rocking on the log.

"We are getting nowhere fast with this whiner, Jake," Susan said from behind Moody. "What do you say we take him to the station and get him some dry clothes and find a Mickey Mouse band-aid for his scratch and then maybe he'll tell us all about his arrangement with Stan Burke. If he convinces us he really didn't abduct Lyn Burke, it'll save us another trip out here and the hassle of throwing him back in."

"Oh, you mean like catch and release? Good idea," Jake said. "How about you drive my car so I can keep an eye on this creep while he drives his Jeep? We can pick up your truck tomorrow."

They packed the gear in Jake's car and ordered Moody to get in the driver's seat of the Wrangler. With the sun down, the temperature had dropped at least ten degrees. Moody was shaking all over. Jake trained his pistol on him, hunched behind the wheel. The vehicle reeked. Several empty beer cans and assorted fast food bags littered the floor.

The two cars headed up the dike to the next access point that led back into Jackson. Dusk enveloped the valley. They drove off the levee and past a cottonwood tree-lined marsh surrounding a small pond. Mist was beginning to rise on the surface, like ghosts chasing each other across the dark water.

June 10
Saturday

Jake closed the driver's side window against the early morning alpine air as he and Susan switch-backed up Teton Pass. Long slender shadows cast by tall trees fingered the road. They were heading west over the mountains to Idaho to have another chat with Ranklin Moody, this time at his cabin in Victor. Jake did a mental review of what had happened since they had fished Moody out of the river.

At the police station, Moody's story had actually checked out. And his bravado had fully rebounded once a shotgun was no longer trained on him and he had some dry clothes, hot coffee, and a few stitches from the hospital emergency room. Moody boasted that he was one of the most knowledgeable people in the West when it came to tracking the movements of radical environmentalists. Stan Burke's paranoia about an ecoterrorist attack on his gypsum mine in Nevada had originally led him to Moody. As a big supporter of the anti-environmentalist watch group, Sage Use, Stan Burke had seen to it that Moody be added to the payroll for the purpose of scrutinizing the actions of activists like the Lifewater members. When Burke thought up his scheme regarding Susan Brand, Rank Moody was right at hand. Following Goddard was an easy add-on and it all meant some very attractive money. Moody told Jake and Susan he had spent most of his down time recently, and much of Burke's money, sitting on the balcony of the Rancher Bar overlooking Jackson's town square, drinking beer and watching Susan and Jake's every move. After several hours of questioning, Susan had released Moody with reluctance, telling him she would reserve judgment on pressing charges, but that he should expect a visit soon.

Jake and Susan had then gone to her house to regroup. They had spent an hour at her kitchen table sorting through their new information and coming to grips with the reality of being set up.

"Well, at least we might not be alone," Jake had said, "Moody seems to feel used, too. Or at least that's what he wants us to believe."

"Yeah, if he's to be believed ... about anything. I still think he may know where Lyn Burke is."

"But you have to admit that after what we learned from him, that seems very unlikely. It could prove useful—his being fed up with Burke, I mean. We could use Moody's expertise with environmental groups to help figure out what the hell is going on with Lyn Burke."

"He's too unreliable. At best, he might play both sides. What I totally don't get is what motivates Burke to try to get me to back off his daughter's case?" Susan had said.

"No clue, but it certainly makes him appear suspicious in his daughter's disappearance. That could be another reason to try to turn Ranklin. He knows Stan Burke very well. If you ultimately decide you like Burke for this, Moody could sure come in handy. Of course, we'd have to get him to go along and then we'd have to watch him like a hawk."

Susan had not been convinced of Moody's usefulness but Jake asked her to try to reserve judgment until they spoke to Hunter, the reporter. Jake figured if Ranklin Moody was, as he had bragged, a media darling, the local journalists would be aware of him. Jake had called Hunter on his cell and reached him at the bar. Hunter said he knew all about "Mr. Moody" and invited them to join him.

A hard bump from a pothole jerked Jake back to the present. After only five hours of sleep, his head still vibrated from the pounding beat of the Cowboy Bar country band and the jolt from the pavement reminded him he had just the suggestion of a headache. The car hit another pothole.

"Oh, my head."

"A little reminder from last night's excesses?" Susan asked.

"Can't be a hangover—couldn't be the margaritas. When I was in college, I developed a theory that margaritas don't cause a hangover because lime juice replaces electrolytes and salt prevents dehydration. I used to be able to swill 'ritas all night and never have it effect my judgment or my poker."

"Did you say, your 'pecker'?"

"Ah, no, my po-ker, with an, 'o.'" Jake grinned. "But now that you mention it—didn't affect Mr. Johnson either."

"Just checking," Susan said, straight-faced. "The way you look this morning suggests reconsidering that theory, regardless of how much field research you did in college. We all get older. I try to stick to two beers and lots of water. You should drink more water."

"Thanks for that. Rachel would love you for it. That's what she's been telling me ever since she quit alcohol over a year ago."

Jake considered what Hunter had shouted about Rank Moody last night in the bar, over the music, chatter, and clack of pool balls.

"I've interviewed him many times, often as a spokesman for Sage Use," Hunter had said. "Fifty percent of what he tells you is right on the money, forty percent is harmless bullshit and ten percent could get you killed. The challenge is figuring out which is which. Moody is, well, moody. He can be a kitten or a cougar—depends on the day. But he always lands on his feet. Don't underestimate him. He probably does know more about environmentalists than anyone else in the West, a real self-styled crusader. And with Moody flattery and money, of course, will get you everywhere—he has an ego the size of the Grand Teton and an extended hand as big as a collection plate."

Hunter also told Jake and Susan a few more things he had learned about the Jackson Hole UGB protest. He said that environmentalists are convinced the United Global Bank-financed Canadian pipeline will tear up tundra, destroy animal habitat, and degrade native culture—and that was just the construction. He said they had a whole separate laundry list of reasons why it is a bad idea to transfer large quantities of water from one end of the continent to the other. For starters, they claim the weight of water already trapped behind dams has caused the earth to shift slightly on its axis and that havoc can result from further disruption of hydrological cycles. Hunter said that, predictably, Sage Use and others in favor of the pipeline had their own version of the truth to counter every single one of those claims.

A bushy-tailed coyote standing right beside the pass road snapped Jake's attention back to the job at hand. They descended the Idaho side of the mountains and entered Victor, a quiet ranching community populated mostly by Mormons and workers who commuted daily to Jackson. Main Street offered gas and a few concessions to the thousands of tourists who poured through annually on their way to Grand Teton and Yellowstone National Parks. Jake checked the napkin with Hunter's directions scrawled on it, went two more blocks, and turned.

"Let me take the lead and try to establish some sort of comfort level in Moody," Jake said. "There might be a way to keep him from warning Burke. Might even win Moody over."

"I just don't get why you are so intent on turning him, Goddard."

"Like I said, I just have to believe his information about Skutches and Lifewater, and Stan Burke for that matter, could be useful in finding Lyn."

"Go ahead, knock yourself out. Play good cop all you want. Personally, I think you're wasting your time. I'm still too pissed at the asshole to want to make him comfortable about anything. I'd probably skip the small talk and go straight for his throat." She reached for her hip pack. "You have a pen? I'll try to keep my cool and just take some notes."

"Ah, I don't think that's such a good idea. We want the guy to relax. He sees you writing stuff down, he'll worry it's going to be used against him. Let's just stick with my plan for now." They pulled over behind a large Mormon church. Across the street was a small log structure. "This must be the place," Jake said.

A Forest Service green Suburban and a red Ford truck with no tailgate or right front fender were parked outside the cabin beside the familiar Jeep with the anti-wolf sticker. There was no sign of activity. The silence was disconcerting. Even a barking dog would have been better. They squeezed between the two older vehicles and looked for the cabin door. It was partially hidden by the long lower limbs of a tall spruce.

"What the fuck you want?" A male voice demanded from behind the tree. Jake turned back to Susan with a quizzical look. He couldn't see anyone through the tree and wasn't certain he recognized the voice.

"Rank, is that you? It's me, Jake, Jake Goddard," he said, peering cautiously through the thick greenery. "I'm here with Officer Brand."

A familiar face popped up between the branches. Moody hadn't shaved, jaw or head. His small dark eyes glanced briefly at Jake and Susan.

"Pull up a chair," he said, coming around the tree. He was garbed, as usual, in hunter camouflage from neck to ankle.

Soon they were seated in weathered wicker chairs between the tree and the cabin. Jake and Susan had been provided with mugs of tepid coffee. Moody addressed Jake while avoiding his gaze and ignoring Susan.

"I guess you figure I owe you something for fishing me out last night and not arresting me, although I could a done without the poke in the leg." He rubbed his thigh through his pants. "What do you want?" he asked, looking down at his coffee cup.

Jake spent several minutes giving the background on the case. He sprinkled in generous amounts of complimentary blather to keep his host's interest. Moody never looked up.

"I've been doing this stuff professionally now for over ten years," Jake said. He pulled out his wallet and got up and handed Moody a business card. Moody slipped the card into his shirt pocket without looking at it. Jake sat back down.

"I've been tracking terrorists for about the same amount of time, but no rich paranoid wives hire me to catch their husbands in the act," Moody said. "And nobody pays me to ride around on a horse and direct traffic, either." Susan kept her gaze steady, ignoring the taunt.

"I don't agree with your views, but I really appreciate the dedication you have to your personal cause," Jake said. "I guess the closest I came to that level of involvement was when I was on that Mormon historical document forgery case that was all over the news. I really wanted to catch that bastard. You know, the one who killed several people in Salt Lake City with pipe bombs." Moody looked past Jake's shoulder, but his expression did not change. "Maybe you heard about it. The fool ultimately set off a bomb in his own car by accident and damn near killed himself." No reaction.

"So, anyhow," Jake said, trying desperately to play him, "friends in Jackson tell me you're very knowledgeable about these green protests and I thought you might want to join us." Moody maintained a blank and distant look. "We need your help, Rank. Susan and I have decided this little ruse of Burke's is only going to slow us down. She plans to complete her assignment and," he shot Moody a conspiratorial look, "you could continue to cash your checks from Burke as well as pick up some additional money from my employer if you work with us." Moody shifted in his chair. Jake sensed he had finally gotten his attention. "Think of it as sort of a double-agent kind of thing. There is one new twist, however, that being that it looks like your boss is now just as suspicious as anyone else in this case." Moody scratched his chin and appeared at last to be thinking about what Goddard was saying. "We need you, Rank. Not certain we can do it without you." Jake waited to see if Moody had bitten.

When Jake got no response, Susan broke her silence. "Of course, if you refuse, or tell Burke that I'm on to you, I will have no choice but to take you in and report the arrest to the chief in Vegas. I would guess getting nabbed by the person you were stalking could affect future work for Mr. Stanley Burke and Sage Use. I don't see many want ads for anti-environmentalists these days."

"First of all partner, don't get me wrong," Moody directed to Jake. "I am an environmentalist. I'm a hunter and a fisherman and I hate clear-cutting and animal habitat loss as much as the next man. But I'm a law-abiding citizen of the United States and I just don't like—"

"*Law*-abiding?" Susan snapped.

Moody turned on her. "Look lady, like I told you last night, I never done anything like this before!" He turned back toward Jake. "As I was saying, I don't like to see good people bullied and threatened and property destroyed by radical tree huggers. So I just view myself as a regular guy doing his duty—an anti-extremist, not anti-environmentalist."

Moody paused, finally looked Jake in the eye and probed his shaved head. A white minivan passed the cabin on the street. "And shit, except for Sage Use, I don't get a dime for doing it. I've written two books on the subject of ecotage and have been interviewed by NBC and more radio stations and newspapers than you can count. I've helped the FBI solve a dozen cases—they consider radical enviros to be the biggest domestic terrorist threat—including the Unabomber case, and I can't get serious money for my effort."

"Unabomber, no shit?" Jake said. "Wow, that's major—makes my pipe bomb stuff seem like child's play. All the more reason, what with you tracking every move of these groups, you can help us find Lyn. And hey, maybe what you said last night is true. Maybe she's fine. That should make finding her easy." Jake forced himself to pause and sip slowly at the mug cupped in both hands before he continued. Moody stared down between his boots. His head started to bob and a flush crept up from his neckline to the top of his scalp. Susan shot Jake a look that said she was not happy about the way this was going. He had no choice but to keep on.

"Burke is bound to be pretty pissed when he learns you were reckless and got caught like a fat and lazy old bass. His motives are totally incomprehensible to me, but our catching you was clearly not what he had in mind."

Even the insult failed to get Moody to focus on what Jake was proposing. Rank was on an ugly roll; his face reddened as his right foot tapped out every point. "These green assholes claim my information is useless and that anyone can get it off the Internet. Sure, I read all their inflammatory crap on my piece-a-shit ten-year-old PC Sage Use gave me, but then I photograph them when they congregate, and write down their plate numbers and collect other identifying info for future reference. It ain't brain surgery. But it works." Moody jerked forward and fired the dregs of his coffee into the bushes.

"When they take 'direct action'—their term for arson and destruction of property—I'm there sometimes before the cops. I'm on them like a hungry sumo wrestler on sushi. I can even predict their attacks, which is pretty good, considering they really have no leadership or chain of command. Are either of you familiar with the leaderless resistance model?"

Jake noticed Susan glance away toward the Big Hole Mountains to the west. He shrugged. "No, I –"

"Well, here's how it works. It's sorta like those Islamic fundamentalist cells. One of the cells identifies a target—be it a car dealership, mink farm, Forest Service office, or ski lodge—and they burn or blow the shit out of it. The next day a 'spokesman' receives an untraceable email from a public computer terminal claiming credit for their organization— usually Planet Earth Alliance. The spokesman forwards the email to the media but he or she is always clean. No specific leader or particular cell is ever identified. Sure as hell, if I don't stop them, they're going to kill somebody someday! Recently some of them have cranked up the cyber rhetoric and are advocating using bombs and killing people to make their point. I wonder if the chicken-shit assholes will take credit for that!" And just as quickly as he had redlined, Moody downshifted, took his foot off the accelerator and asked, "Want more coffee?"

Susan shook her head.

Jake said, "Sure. Half. Thanks, Rank."

Ranklin limped back with a fresh mug for Goddard and sat, quietly cleaning his nails. Susan inhaled slowly, "You must be concerned about Lyn Burke's safety—"

"You know what, you're really pissing up the wrong tree." He gestured with the pointed metal stick he had been using on his nails. "I don't have anything on Burke's little granola bar and he didn't hire me to find her." He stood. "Guess you wasted time drivin' over the bump." Moody walked toward the house without offering his hand.

In the car, Susan said, "I tried to keep my mouth shut like you asked, but that was pretty much a total waste of time. I'm going to see Earl about jurisdictional issues. See if I can put Moody away for a long time."

"I think he can be useful if we can just figure out the right angle. This is about Lyn Burke, not Ranklin Moody. In jail he does our case no good," Jake said as he turned out of the driveway.

"Christ, Goddard, useful how? Tell me that! The guy's devious and deranged. Are you trying to be some kinda social worker? He has been in and around my house and harassing Amy and me for days. We don't even know for certain he's not the abductor. There is no way I will work with him."

"I'm just asking you to be objective, Susan."

"Oh, and now you're going to accuse me of being unprofessional." She glared at him. "You'd feel a little different if it had been you—your house and your kids."

They drove in silence until they had crossed back into Wyoming and were about to head over Teton Pass. The ridgeline at the top of the pass bristled with communications towers looming above the conifers. Avalanche chutes and high clearings still held snow.

Susan's mind lurched and she insisted Jake pull into the parking area at the summit. She sat staring at the cars of late season backcountry skiers while the Subaru's engine idled impatiently. The whole way up the mountain, thoughts gnawed at her. Which was the bullshit, which was the truth? What were the signs they had missed? Her gut told her Moody was still playing them—testing them. She realized Moody had been cleaning his nails with a stylus. He said he had a ten-year-old computer. He had purposely picked up the distinctive metal stylus when he went in for more coffee. She shot a look at Jake.

"What?" Jake asked.

"That son of a bitch was cleaning his nails with a digital pen from an electronic tablet. I've seen them advertised. It said in the Burke file that Lyn owned a, a … what's it called? It combines a smart phone and a tablet … a Note, a Samsung Note. Florence gave it to her." She hit the ceiling with her left fist. "Unbelievable!" She shook her head. "Don't say I didn't warn you about him."

"What is going on inside that cue ball? What does he want? I've never dealt with anyone like him," Jake said. A large stock truck full of hay labored over the pass and ground down through the gears for the descent into Jackson Hole.

"Well, that part is fairly easy," Susan said. "What motivates Moody is ego, money, and hatred. But you know, even more than that, I'm convinced he's a few beers short of a six-pack. Totally whacked. What else could possibly explain his constant babble? And you want to convince him to work with us?"

"It seems a little crazy, I admit. But we're hanging out here alone, Susan. Nothing we've been told from day one makes any sense. At least Moody's brand of insanity is manageable, as far as we know. I think we need to go back down there."

"Yeah, manageable as far as we know. I'm so sick of his games." She thrust her head back against the headrest. "All right, I'll agree to go back on one condition. This time I take the lead and I won't be sipping coffee and talking about the notches on my belt." Jake thrust the car into gear and they raced back down the mountain.

The Subaru braked and slid on the gravel in front of Moody's house. Jake slammed his fist on the dash. The Suburban was gone. But Susan noticed an envelope on the windshield of the old truck. It had "Goddard" scrawled on it. She jumped out and tore the envelope open.

Susan read the note to Jake at his open window. "If you'd caught my clue I might've admitted you're a hell of a PI, and I might've led you to the kid. But you blew it, didn't you? A bungler like you is lucky he didn't get his dick blown off by that Mormon forger. Of course, if you'd missed the clue altogether you wouldn't be here now. The fact that you're reading this note means you're a fair investigator, or was it Miss Piggy who got on the 'stick'? But, in this game, fair might not be good enough. So, read the tag, and tag, you're it! Lyn Burke is having a good time and is right under your noses and you haven't picked up the scent. I'm off to Yellowstone to do a little … I can't make out the last word—it might be 'hunting'. What an asshole!"

Susan shook a small piece of pressed aluminum out of the envelope. It was a dog's rabies vaccination tag from Las Vegas. The city and the serial number were the only things that hadn't been scratched off with wear. Not knowing what else to do, they decided to exchange the tag for Susan's business card and put the envelope back on the windshield. Susan got back in the car.

As they drove up the west side of the pass, Jake pushed his ball cap back and squeezed his forehead. "How does Moody have Lyn's dog's tag, assuming that's what it is, and her stylus?"

"All I can say is, he has a hell of a lot to explain, and yet he continues to jerk us around. And what's he 'hunting' in Yellowstone? You can't hunt in Yellowstone—not legally anyway. Unless ... he is hunting Lyn Burke. If he's convinced Lyn Burke is free and unharmed, no wonder he wasn't worried about being implicated in her disappearance." Susan stared at the road ahead. "Rank Moody is paid by Stan Burke to get me to back off the hunt for his daughter when she is supposedly, according to Moody, off somewhere having a good time. This is like banging around in a maze blindfolded."

"Could you check records in Vegas and see if that's Mojo's tag?" Jake asked.

"Of course I could, but maybe Lynnie's mother could verify if it's his tag. It'd give me an excuse to talk to her and see if I can learn anything helpful about Stan Burke."

"It could also put her in a panic and send her running to her husband, but that's a risk we might have to take," Jake said.

"If she does identify it, I could arrest Moody for suspicion in Lyn Burke's disappearance along with the other charges. That'd give me great pleasure," Susan said.

After steering through the pass they could see Jackson, the Elk Refuge, and the Sleeping Indian. Jake dropped the car into a lower gear. He shielded his eyes against the glare of the sun, lowered the visor, and tried to concentrate on staying on the steep winding road.

"Don't forget we need to pick up my truck at the dike," Susan said. She slipped on her dark glasses and rested her head against the passenger's window. "Damn, I wish we could haul Moody out there and throw his ass back in the river."

He chuckled all the way to Yellowstone. He entered the park, drove for thirty-five minutes high above the rapids of an evergreen-lined river, and turned down a rarely used service road that was off limits to the public.

He parked out of sight of the highway and crept a few hundred yards to a slanting mound of sparsely vegetated boulders on a ridge overlooking a geyser basin. No one ever seemed to notice the Forest Service Suburban was lacking the official seal, or questioned if it was on official business. Charred trees, like mummified hands raking the sky, surrounded the island of rocks, a result of the Yellowstone fires of the late 1980s. Steam from gurgling aquamarine hotpots wafted across a small group of people gathered below on the surreal landscape.

He slowly panned his binoculars across the vehicles in the parking area. There was a blue car with Nevada plates. He noticed an attractive young woman with binoculars around her neck wearing tight gray athletic shorts and an orange halter-top. A smug grin twisted Ranklin Moody's face. Predator locked on prey—always the most satisfying moment of the hunt. Once again he had anticipated their next move. "Gotcha," he whispered to himself. "I knew you were still with Skutches, little Lynnie."

As he was setting up his tripod and camera with the telephoto lens, he heard a scream. A powerful looking man was dragging the young woman toward a boiling pool. "No, no Forrest, no please, I'm too young to die!" the woman yelled as she struggled. A few yards short of the edge, the man released his grip and the two began to laugh. The woman turned and punched her companion playfully in the stomach, then hugged him.

Still giggling, they rejoined the group moving toward a tall pine that had somehow been spared by the fires. An older man with a white beard, Dr. Skutches, wearing a safari hat and jacket, pointed toward the top of the tree. A large solitary hawk stood guard on a branch just above a nest.

By the time his camera was ready to shoot, the young woman had shifted behind her companion. He stood in full profile to the camera. He wore a denim shirt—sleeves rolled to the biceps—and jeans. He had on a tan straw cowboy hat, upswept slightly at the sides, and a thick black braid hung down to the middle of his back. Light reflected from his muscular olive cheek. Dark wrap-around glasses hid his eyes.

After about fifteen minutes, the scientists walked back to their cars and drove off. The dust from their tires wafted toward him, but not before he got several shots of the car with the Nevada plates containing the playful couple. He packed his equipment into his car, reached in the passenger side window and grabbed his cell phone and Jake Goddard's card. He relished calling Goddard as soon as he had cell service and telling him he had just photographed Lyn Burke.

As the lights of Jackson receded in the valley below, the truck's headlights stabbed into the trees—cloaked sentries, guarding a dark abyss—lining the pass. It was a clear night and, as they climbed, the stars became more vibrant. Susan was driving. Jake observed her silhouette in the driver's seat. She rested her hands on the top of the steering wheel.

Jake and Susan had eaten dinner at the Silver Dollar Grill and discussed Ranklin Moody's call and the strategy for their third visit to his cabin. Susan had surprised Jake by showing up out of uniform. She had just left a children's art show where Amy's beadwork was on display and was wearing a tight lavender turtleneck and khakis. Following the line of her hair to her shoulder and chest, he realized he had never seen her looking so unguarded and feminine. She arched her back to stretch and yawn. Jake imagined her breasts unencumbered, then quickly changed his head channel from Playboy to Discovery and checked out the passing scenery.

"Oh, excuse me," Susan said. "It's really been a long day and we were up pretty late last night, weren't we?" She pushed a few strands of hair behind her left ear.

"It won't be long now. About another thirty minutes should put us back at Moody's. You okay?"

"Yeah, I'm all right. Do you think the jerk really saw Lyn? God, I hope so, but then how do you explain her not calling home for weeks?" Susan topped the pass and braked around a curve. Dirty snow banks lingering from the winter's plowing flashed by.

"Stranger things have happened. When he called, he seemed certain he had photographed her. I'm not sure how much stock to put into anything the crackpot says but he did have that dog tag. He knows Skutches pretty well. Hunter told me something about the professor that concerns me—"

"Oh shit, what now?" Jake saw resignation in her shadowy face.

"While you were in the ladies' room last night, Hunter said that not only is that guy Skutches a charlatan, but he is a womanizer with a taste for young grad students. I wonder if Lynnie could have fallen under his spell. Who knows, maybe he made up the southern Utah story to clear the way for Lyn to be his girl toy in the Yellowstone hot springs for awhile."

Susan dropped her head briefly, looked up and checked the road ahead and then locked eyes with Jake. "Great! Now we've got a lecherous professor to worry about. If he's got that young woman holed up somewhere, I swear to God I will ..." She looked straight ahead. "I guess I've lost my objectivity about her." Then back at Jake. "I'm feeling a little raw right now."

"I know, I know," Jake said, reaching across to the middle of her shoulders with his hand. "If it were one of my kids or your Amy, well, can you imagine how we'd feel? It's hard enough like this. I just wish we had more to go on. Maybe Moody will have some good news for us." Maybe, Susan thought, but knowing Moody, probably a fifty-fifty at best.

This time Susan took the lead. Jake watched her square off with a man who sensed he was out-matched every way but physically. Moody responded with forced bravado and excessive consumption of beer. He had removed his camouflage shirt but still wore the pants with a plain white t-shirt. Susan tried to be polite at first, but things deteriorated quickly. "Just exactly what is your purpose in spying on these protestors, Mr. Moody?"

"These protestors are destroying property, and last time I checked, that was against the law."

"I agree, arson and vandalism are criminal and should be punished, but I've never heard of a private citizen stalking demonstrators, who, by the way, have the legal right to assemble and protest in all fifty states."

"But they don't have the right to 'assemble' bombs and 'protest' by doing millions of dollars in damage. This is not some friggin' flower child free-for-all, you know. Lyn Burke may be playing with fire with the big boys for real."

Jake looked around the cabin. He saw a crumbling corkboard: attached to it were several notices, news clippings tacked one on top of the other, a few FBI "Wanted" posters, and a curling Sage Use bumper sticker. Two old metal filing cabinets and a dented and scratched brown metal desk without a chair took up one dark-paneled wall. On top of the desk sat an ancient boxy computer monitor. That was pretty much the living room, if you included the tattered couch and two stained overstuffed chairs that sat circled around a battered coffee table covered with newsletters and inexpensive publications. A closed door to one side of the room led off to what Jake assumed was a bedroom. Through an opening at the opposite end from the entrance was a kitchen with a sink piled high with dirty dishes.

Susan was running out of patience. "Where did you get the dog tag?" She demanded. Moody glared briefly somewhere near her face and then looked away.

"When I follow these activist groups, I photograph them and their cars, and I …" He paused, searching for the right words. "I examine their droppings looking for clues to identify and track them. A dog tag is as good as a license plate number. I found the tag and a bunch of other crap after the United Global Bank protest in Jackson and I thought it might be useful. You can't believe how much litter these 'environmentalists' leave."

"Wait … wait. We're not sure Lyn attended that protest."

"Lady, I'm not saying she did. I'm saying I found that tag, and this—" he picked up the metal stylus off the coffee table, "—after that protest, on the ground. Remember, I had the same information you had. I knew Lyn Burke traveled with an old beagle and that she was a techie and—"

"You mean you paw through other people's garbage looking for tidbits, don't you? Just like you sneak around innocent people's houses." Susan's face flushed.

Jake could see it was time to change the subject. "Rank, show us the shots you took today in Yellowstone?"

Holding the desired stack of prints in his hand bolstered Moody's courage. He took a sip from a beer can that looked like it had been sitting on the coffee table for days and fixed Jake with bloodshot eyes. "Hey, I've got proof of the whereabouts of the Burke girl. Whatcha got for me, hotshot, besides a raft of shit from Blondie here?"

Jake answered before Susan could react. "Oh yeah, I almost forgot. Hunter, at the paper, told me where Skutches and his groupies are going next. And I'll tell you, after you show us the pictures, that is." Moody paused briefly, apparently weighing if he was being taken. Then he pushed a stack of prints toward Susan, brushing her knee with the back of his hand. She tensed at the brief contact before looking with disdain at each print. Susan slapped the photos down on the table one by one like a vindicated poker player, her lips a thin bloodless line.

She fixed Moody with a stare full of loathing. "This may be her car, but I'm almost certain this is not Lyn Burke. Even if I could see this young woman clearly in your shots, and I can't, I can tell you that is not Lyn. From what I have learned about her, she dresses more sensibly and her dog Mojo, assuming he is alive, would be right at her feet. I know more about this girl than you do and you work for her father, for Christsakes." Susan stood, placed both hands on the table and leaned into Rank Moody's face. "I'm tired of your bullshit. You and your rich buddy Stan Burke are pissing around here while his child might be in serious trouble. Hear this, Moody—we will find her. And as for you, I'm going to have a little chat with my boss about jurisdiction and I will be back with a warrant for your arrest." Susan's voice dropped low and menacing. "I've got you for leaving the scene of an accident, criminal trespass, and assault with a deadly weapon." Moody looked at her quizzically. "Your Jeep, jerk! You're going to jail." She spun on her heel and walked out of the cabin.

"Rank, think about it," Jake said. "She can get you on at least three serious charges, maybe more. The judge isn't going to care about how you stumbled into this mess. You're going to pay and you are going to lose your livelihood. You think Burke will bail you out of this? If it turns out he is involved in his daughter's abduction, you're an accomplice. You could be talking life in prison. But if you agree to help us, maybe I can convince Susan not to press charges." He left without closing the door.

"Yeah, sure, I'll think about it." Moody called after him from the door. "Hey, wait a minute. Where's Skutches going next?"

"The Howl at the Full Moon Festival near Ely, Nevada."

"I figured as much." He sneered. "See you there, Goddard, if the black widow doesn't kill and eat you first." He jerked the door shut.

Jake eased into the passenger seat of the truck. Susan sat behind the wheel with both hands clenched on her knees staring into the empty church parking lot across the street.

"I think it was the right thing to do to let him go for now. We have bigger fish to fry," Jake said gently. Susan did not respond. She started the truck and drove out of Victor without saying a word, her jaw clenched.

"I still think we can get Moody to help us." Jake said. "Who and what he knows could be very valuable. I told him I might be able to convince you not to press charges if he joined us." Susan shook her head. "Just give it some consideration. That's all I ask."

They got behind a slow RV with Georgia plates lumbering up the mountain to the Wyoming border. "Well, let's see now. What shall we talk about to pass the time at twenty miles per hour?" Jake said. Susan jammed her hair behind her ear and stared straight ahead.

"Okay, lacking any takers for conversation, and considering it usually requires a minimum of two people to communicate, now what? Hmm, I've got it. I'll look for the elusive Bullwinkle constellation in the beautiful night sky." He craned his neck to look up through the windshield at the stars but not before he noticed Susan's face relax a little.

Jake sat back, looked out his side window and thought about Skutches's entourage migrating next to The Howl at the Full Moon Festival in Nevada. He had read The Howl was a huge, annual counterculture happening for new-agers. Its organizer chose the high desert near Ely because of lax Nevada laws and because participants could get wild in the wild without bothering anyone. "Rage Against the Machine" types from the coastal cities loved The Howl and often made the festival part of their summer vacations. Plus, he mused, it's supposedly easy to pack for, since people apparently wear so little clothing. He also thought about Stanley Burke; with Lou Cuvier's approval, tomorrow might be a good day to book a small plane and do recon on Ashland Gypsum Mine.

Jake checked his watch. He wondered if Rachel and the boys were at home. When he got around to telling her that he'd be required to travel to Nevada, she'd fret and probably pray over his self-control around the casinos. He wondered if he would ever adjust to this new righteous Rachel, transformed by the loss, two years ago, of her younger sister to breast cancer. But he had to admit he, too, was a little worried about himself in Nevada. What the hell, he'd been pretty good lately. He should be able to handle it. Plus, Susan would keep him focused on the job.

He pushed up the bill of his ball cap and glanced with admiration at Susan. Damn, what a charge she'd made at Ranklin Moody. She was powerful. Assuming she could get Earl's permission to continue this investigation in Nevada, Jake had no doubt, with or without Moody's help, they'd bring back Lyn Burke.

Susan slammed her hand on the steering wheel, startling Jake.

"What an asshole! I can't believe how violated I feel by Rank Moody, and how Burke set me up." She rubbed her hand on her pants leg and pushed her hair behind her ear. "But sure, why not? I'll agree to use Moody if it can help us in any way. Tell me this, though: if Moody isn't the kidnapper, then who is? And where is Lyn Burke? I've got to do everything in my power and use all my resources to find out. I'm going to get the green light from Earl to go full bore on this and I will find that girl. And I will determine what really happened to Fernando Diaz." She bore a look at Jake. "And I need your help to do it."

"You got it, partner." Yeah, he thought, recognizing the set to her jaw from the time she nailed that lift at the Fitness Club—powerful as hell.

June 11
Sunday

Jake shouted into his headset over the engine noise, "Man! The Grand Canyon is awesome from the air." The twenty-something pilot flashed him a clean-cut smile and shot a thumbs-up. "Some of the most gorgeous rock strata on the planet, don't you think?" The pilot nodded in response. Through a slight haze, the red and white cliffs and anvil mesas of the canyon stretched away, soft and sculpted. The Colorado River looped and coiled, a silver thread at the base of the plunging gorge. Jake wished the little four-seater could fly lower over the park, but regulations prohibited it. In any event, it was the Ashland Gypsum Mine he needed to check out, further west, just east of Vegas near Iron Springs.

In less than fifteen minutes, the terrain went from scenic to barren and Lake Mead stretched below. Jake heard the pilot's voice crackle in his headphones. "Mead is the world's largest man-made reservoir." Jake looked down and noticed the surface of the lake was well below the high watermark on cliffs and promontories. The water was a deep blue-black, and smooth and flat as glass. Several large powerboats etched graceful white lines on the surface. The roar of the plane's engine vibrated into Jake's body. The artificial beauty of the lake notwithstanding, the increasing desolation of the terrain heightened his sense of urgency about the case. Jake had no time to waste that day. He had driven the five hours to the Salt Lake City Airport, caught a commuter plane to Page, Arizona, and booked this scenic flight. Time was even more critical now. With each passing day, if Lyn was in danger, the likelihood of her safe return diminished.

Susan had to remain in Jackson for a few days to convince her boss she needed to travel for the Burke case and, if he agreed, to make arrangements for Amy. In the interim, she planned to call Florence Burke and see what that might turn up. With any luck Mrs. Burke wouldn't tell her husband about the call, but it was only a matter of time before Stanley Burke suspected that something was not right. Jake gnawed on his thumbnail, stared out at the desert, and racked his brain for some sort of clarity and consistency in this mess.

Stan Burke had been having serious problems with his Nevada mining business, and environmentalists wanted to shut him down. He was influential with Sage Use, the pro-development organization that paid Ranklin Moody to spy on green activist groups around the West. Burke's daughter, Lyn had gone to Jackson Hole to work for Noah Skutches, an old friend of her aunt, Louise Cuvier. Lyn had dropped out of sight, or had been reassigned, depending on who you believed, on the first day. She had replaced a young man who had died in a mysterious climbing accident.

Lyn's mother was certain her daughter was in serious trouble. She'd filed a missing persons report and convinced her sister to hire Goddard. Susan Brand had been assigned to the case in Jackson where Lyn had last been seen. That's when it got really weird. Stan Burke paid Rank Moody to harass Susan Brand, whose job it was to find Lyn, all the while claiming his wife was hysterical and his daughter was on an assignment in Utah. Not even Moody, if he could be believed, seemed to have a clue why Burke had hired him to bother Susan.

Moody had found evidence pointing to Lyn Burke's presence at a protest she supposedly never attended. He was convinced she was fine and was hanging around the region with Noah Skutches, but Jake and Susan were pretty sure that it was not Lyn Burke Moody had photographed in Yellowstone. Susan, just that morning, had gone to the hotel where Skutches was staying in Jackson to question him further about Lyn

Burke. She later called Jake and informed him she had missed Skutches. He had checked out and his van was gone.

That was all they knew, really. If Jake went to the Las Vegas police with that, what with most cops' enmity toward PIs and considering Stan Burke's influence there, they'd laugh him out of the building and call Burke before Jake made it to his car.

Jake stared down at the blank face of the lake. He had to admit that nothing was adding up except frustration and the number of hours he and Susan had invested in the case. At least they had bought some time when he told Moody in a phone call from the road that Susan had agreed to let him go free for the time being. In exchange, Jake insisted that Moody not contact Stan Burke. Moody actually seemed to be considering joining them, but hell, who knew what the price tag for that might be? Susan's outburst had not helped make their case with him, but he was unpredictable and there was still hope. He was probably already following Skutches and his groupies to The Howl. That would be Jake's next stop, and Susan's if she got the green light to join him. If they did not find Lyn there, then it was straight on to the wilderness of southern Utah.

The plane crossed the western shore of Lake Mead and climbed over the desolate and denuded Muddy Mountains; the mine lay on the western slope. Las Vegas sprawled to the southwest beneath thick gray air. First the dust from Ashland came into view, and then the open pit. Seeing the huge gouge in the earth and noticing the white haze from the plant drifting east toward the Grand Canyon, Jake understood the environmentalists' problem with Burke's operation.

They dipped closer to the site; Jake began snapping pictures through the polluted air. The buildings and the surrounding terrain were brown on brown, fading to gray in the distance toward Las Vegas. Through his lens he counted roughly a dozen metal structures perched helter skelter on the edge of a deep spiraling pit at the base of a bald mountain. Water towers on stilts stood on the rim, in four separate locations. Tanker trucks worked around the mine spraying water and settling the dust created by the constant digging, then returned to the towers for refilling.

Jake got the pilot's attention and made a circle in the air with his finger to indicate he wanted to go back around a few times. Bulldozers and dump trucks were scattered about. There was some odd-looking machinery with distinct appendages meant for boring, gouging, and pulverizing rock. Everything lay beneath a coat of fine white dust. Water gushed out of an enormous pipe into a catch basin near a central building that had large dirty windows across the front and a conveyor belt attached on the north end. A long chute jutted off the other end to a stockpile of sparkling white gypsum that was continuously wetted down by massive sprinkler heads. White mounds covered every available flat space and all had large sprinklers playing on them.

It struck Jake that Ashland Mine had implemented extensive measures to hold down dust and thus airborne pollution that could drift toward Grand Canyon National Park, but the effort was only partially successful and it was requiring a lot of water.

He noticed one low structure just beyond the security gate. The building was landscaped with scraggly bushes and slender trees and had an adjacent parking lot. Several vehicles, mostly pickups, sat on the asphalt.

A single gravel road led to Iron Springs, no more than a cluster of buildings and a few trees. But just beyond the town, Jake made out a crater the size of a professional football stadium. There was no sign of activity around the hole. He assumed it was Burke's abandoned and unreclaimed pit that had environmentalists so up in arms. His eye followed the road past Iron Springs on to the interstate and Las Vegas.

Jake's camera was indicating a low battery. He signaled the pilot. The young man nodded and the plane banked around for the journey back to Page. Jake sat back, relaxed, and pulled out his phone to scroll through his kid photos. He smiled, looked out across the desert, and thought about the boys. He was eager to return to Salt Lake City and have a few precious days at home while he waited for Susan to arrive. He wished she had been with him—to see the mine from the air. He hoped they could join up again soon. He decided to try to connect with her that night to hear how things stood with her boss and what she had learned in her call to Florence Burke.

Susan dropped Amy at Chuck's house mid-morning and returned home, intending to make her call before packing Cinder up for a visit with a dog-loving friend on a big spread in Star Valley, which was on the way south to Salt Lake. She sat on the couch in her living room with a cup of coffee—a pen and a spiral notebook lay nearby on the table. She punched the numbers and the phone was picked up after the fourth ring. Florence Burke sounded out of breath and anxious.

"Hello, Mrs. Burke, my name is Susan Brand. I've been assigned your daughter's case by the Jackson, Wyoming, Police Department."

Susan sipped her coffee.

"Susan Brand, with the Jackson Police. I'm working with Jake Goddard who was hired by your sister. May I ask you a few questions about your daughter's case?"

Cinder came over and begged for an ear scratch.

"That'd be me. I've been assigned the case. Please call me Susan."

Cinder panted audibly.

"I'm sorry, I have nothing new to report but I would like to ask you a few questions."

Susan heard rustling and what sounded like the phone dropping at the other end of the line.

"That's all right. I drop my phone all the time. I've read the file and your report but I must ask—Mrs. Burke, do you feel everything possible is being done to find your daughter?"

Susan scratched down some notes.

"But wait, Mrs. Burke," Susan said. "You were saying if she has been taken against her will, you hope she is being treated well. Is there anyone you suspect in this?"

Susan checked her watch and sipped her coffee.

"Yes, I know they say on television that abductions usually involve someone close to the child. I can assure you, we are being very thorough in looking at, well, at everyone Lynnie came in contact with."

Susan shooed Cinder away.

"It is good that you filed the police report, even against your husband's wishes. You did the right thing. I'm on this case as a result of your report in Las Vegas. I have to ask, do you have reason to suspect your daughter was abducted by someone close to her?"

Florence Burke seemed to be steering Susan toward Lyn's father, Stan Burke. Cinder returned for more attention.

"Yes, it's natural to begin to suspect everyone. Even people you know in your heart love your child. Are Lyn and her father close?"

Cinder flopped her hot heavy body on Susan's foot. She heard sobbing.

"Mrs. Burke, we are doing everything we can to find your daughter." Susan waited. "Are you okay to go on?" She waited. "Good. I know this is hard. Are Lyn and her father close, ma'am?" Pause. "Yes? Does he treat her well?"

Susan detected a sudden odd tone in the woman's voice—strident and defensive.

"Do you have any reason to suspect he's involved in your daughter's disappearance?"

Florence Burke had switched gears abruptly and now was defending her husband and claiming he spoiled his daughter and that they were very close. Bizarre, Susan thought.

"I'm sorry, but I had to ask. We look at all angles." Susan paused, hoping more information would be volunteered. It wasn't.

"This probably doesn't mean anything because dogs lose their tags all the time, but could you find out if your daughter's dog had a blue tag with DAN1RR on it? I have one that was picked up near Jackson."

Florence's voice had become meek again.

"This may amount to nothing, Mrs. Burke, but we should check it out." Susan paused. "You'll call the vet? Great. Thanks so much."

Susan gave Florence her contact information. "If there is anyone else I should question or if you think of anything else we should know, call me, and if you can't reach me, call Mr. Goddard, okay?"

Florence Burke thanked Susan profusely—too much, really.

"That's an easy one, Mrs. Burke. I have a daughter of my own."

Susan listened to more thanks and nervous small talk about how wonderful girls are.

"God bless you too, Mrs. Burke." The line went dead.

Salt Lake City was hotter than usual for a June afternoon, and busy with traffic. As he turned into the cottage-lined streets of his old neighborhood, Jake switched off the air conditioning, lowered his car windows, and hunched his shoulders to loosen the muscles. He could hear the excited voices of children. One thing he enjoyed seeing on sunny evenings was his boys and their friends playing out on the grass in the center of the cul-de-sac near their home. His sons had a sprinkler going and were jumping through it with a neighbor boy and his sister.

He parked on the street in front of the house, climbed out of his car, and was tackled with wet hugs. Mathew clinched him high around the waist and Timothy wrapped himself around his dad's legs. The usual game was to see how far dad could drag them beyond the oak tree toward the porch. They always tried to grab the tree with one hand while clinching their dad with the other. Today Jake begged for mercy a few yards short of the house. The boys ran shouting back to their two friends. As he climbed the few steps to the porch, Rachel and another woman in jeans and a raspberry t-shirt emerged from the shadows of the living room. It was Susan.

Rachel came through the door with arms outstretched. "So, now I know what kind of cops you've been hanging out with in Wyoming, Jako."

"Hey honey," Jake said, hugging Rachel. Her shoulder length brown hair was pulled back in a tight ponytail. She was wearing a green sleeveless blouse that bulged and gaped at the waist, over gray walking shorts. A silver chain with a cross dangled around her neck. Jake turned to Susan. "How the heck did you get here so soon?"

"You said get down to Salt Lake ASAP. I'm here and I'm going to solve this case," she said, smiling up at him.

"Where's Amy?" Jake asked.

"Chuck's. Partner's got to be good for something."

"And ... your boss?" Jake asked.

"Earl could see I was distracted and wasn't good for much else right now. And get this—I finally convinced him there's merit to this Burke thing. Says there's no one else he'd rather have on it. Guess I'm totally out of the doghouse, or maybe he just thinks your play requires a lot of backing. He gave me personal leave with pay—since this is so far out of our jurisdiction—to see what we can come up with."

"No doubt about the backing part. But you want to spend your leave in the summer heat of the desert howling at the moon? Yep, folks ... she's gone." Jake touched Susan's forehead with an open palm.

Susan glanced at Rachel. "'Addle pated,' my grandmother used to say. I remember her repeating it several times while shaking her head when I told her I wanted to be a cop." She walked over to the railing to watch the kids play.

"I've invited Susan to stay with us. Apparently we are reciprocating for when you stayed with her," Rachel said, cocking an eyebrow at Jake. "Keep your eye on the boys, okay? Dinner will be ready in a little while." She went inside.

"Oops, sorry buddy," Susan said, turning.

"Don't worry about it. Not your problem. Good to see you, partner."

An excited shout turned their attention back to the boys. Timothy did a running flip through the spray, landing with a splash on his backside just beyond the sprinkler. Susan laughed. Jake shook his head.

Traffic droned on the main route a few blocks from the neighborhood. Susan paced back and forth on the porch. Jake sat on the swing and fanned himself with the evening paper.

"Hey, dig the t-shirt—'Jackson Hole Fitness Club's First Lady of Fitness.' You musta pressed your weight. Congratulations."

"I was hoping you'd notice. I forgot to mention it yesterday on the phone. Not long after the bandage came off. Not bad, huh?

"You would've loved it. After I nailed the lift, I was required to get on the scale to prove my weight matched the pounds on the bar. I whipped off my shirt and jumped on the scale in my jog bra. Turned every head in the gym."

"I would've loved it. Very impressive. No way I could do it." He gave her a high five. "Tell me about your call to Florence Burke."

"Not good."

"Why do you say that?"

"I know an abused wife when I hear one. I've interviewed hundreds of them. Florence Burke is a basket case."

"Christ, put yourself in the woman's shoes—"

"I am, damnit," Susan said, stiff-arming the porch rail and leaning over it. "I am putting myself in her shoes. That's why I'm here and not with my child, because I can't think of anything else. And I'm telling you, that is a physically, or at best, a psychologically abused woman. She's meek, has no self-esteem, can barely speak a full sentence without checking herself, and she is guarded when her husband comes up. She's afraid of him. And she knows something, fears something, or suspects something she hasn't reported. I'd bet on it. She seemed to be leading me toward Stan Burke and then got way defensive when I asked her if she thought he could be involved."

"What are you suggesting?" Jake asked.

Susan started to pace again. "I want to confront that scheming son-of-a-bitch Burke. I'd like to ride into his mine and call his bluff."

"Well, you're the police woman and I'm just a PI, ma'am. But let me suggest a downside. One, if you confront him, the cat is out of the bag as far as Rank Moody's helping us goes. Two, if Burke is involved, he will immediately start to cover his tracks. Three, he could hide his daughter so far underground you'd need some of his mining equipment to dig her out. That's the downside. Upside? You maybe feel a little vindicated for a very brief period of time. For now, I think our time is better spent following Lifewater to The Howl at the Full Moon Festival."

"I've told you not to patronize me, Goddard." Susan snapped, then slumped on the swing beside him and pushed hard on the porch with her boots. Jake noticed a faint aroma. Her body odor. It wasn't unpleasant. A woman on the hunt. "Shit. I hate it when you're right," she said.

"So do I, Susan." Rachel poked her head out the door. "So do I. Time to start the grill. I'll meet you two in the backyard, okay? Jake, you're saying grace."

"Tell you what. Let's sleep on this tonight. Tomorrow may bring new insights," Jake said.

They sat rocking silently until Rachel called again from inside the house.

Jake was preparing to head home to his trailer when Rachel had surprised him by whispering that she wanted him to spend the night. They lay on their backs in her king bed with only their hands touching. A breeze cooled the night air and played across the sheets. Jake was trying to remember how many months it had been since they'd slept together.

"Susan seems nice," Rachel said.

"Yeah, intense, but nice," Jake said.

"From the little you two told me at dinner, this thing has gotten really complicated."

"Christ. I guess—it's a veritable Chinese puzzle."

"Jake, watch your language. I don't suppose you've considered praying for the girl."

"Actually, Rachel, it hasn't crossed my mind."

"And I guess, knowing stubborn you, that quitting is not an option."

"I'm afraid it's not an option. I mean, it's just a business arrangement with Louise Cuvier, although her niece sounds like a fine person. But, I wouldn't know how to face Susan. You can bet she won't give up on this until there's resolution, one way or another." Jake moved his hand over to his wife's hip. "I'm really sorry this whole job came up with such short notice and that I have to leave again so soon but now that Susan's here—"

"The boys were hoping to get you for a few days this time. It is kinda funny how your business trips occur at the worst possible times for our family. And you're going to miss several more of Matt's baseball games. But … we'll manage fine without you." She rolled toward him. "Keeping your books straight is one of my bigger challenges, but I have other clients backlogged now as well. I'm pretty busy but I should be able to manage the boys. Don't worry about us. We'll be fine. We're used to it. You can catch up with your sons when you get back." Rachel adjusted her nightgown to close a gap at the top. "So, where do you go from here?"

"Susan and I think our best bet is to follow the Skutches entourage to The Howl at the Full Moon Festival in Nevada. Rank Moody's convinced Lyn is with Noah Skutches, who Moody is being paid to spy on by Sage Use, whose biggest contributor is Lyn's father, whose sister-in-law hired me. If Lyn Burke is with Skutches, she certainly is staying out of sight. And for what reason? Like you said, complicated. If we hadn't wasted so much time on Burke and Moody's little distraction in Jackson we might be way ahead of the game by now."

"I'm sorry, but it worries me, Jake. I mean you going to Nevada and all."

"I'll be out in the boonies, Rachel, a long way from the nearest casino. We aren't convinced Lyn is with Skutches, but we don't have anything else to go on, so we'll follow him and see if that proves useful and if it doesn't, head immediately over to southern Utah. The Nevada desert in June and a counterculture festival—believe me, this is not my idea of a fun time."

"Did you get the camping gear from the basement you need?" Rachel asked.

"Yes, the boys were a big help, especially with dessert held out as their reward, but they're mighty disappointed they're not invited. I'm going to miss them. I'm really not looking forward to this, hon."

"Oh, I know you. You'll get into it once you get there." She rolled onto her back. "And, I know Susan is the kind of person you like to work with. She's awfully pretty and … athletic." Rachel paused. "And … I know what you're doing is all in the line of duty, but promise me … you'll be careful, you'll stay out of the casinos, and you'll behave and keep your clothes on, okay?"

Jake turned toward his wife to see if she was kidding. In the pale light he could see her thin-lipped, half-smile, wrinkled-forehead look. That generally meant her comment was both kidding and totally serious.

"Rachel, come on. What's that supposed to mean?"

"Do you think I'm stupid? Do you think I can't see what's going on?"

"There is nothing going on."

"WWJD. Just do what's right, Jake." In her fashion, she had tossed a lariat around his neck. Before he could respond, she rolled away from him without saying goodnight.

The springs squeaked when he flopped across his bunk. It was dark outside his cabin but he was still dressed in his dust-covered work clothes. He was smiling content. Another successful day at the quarry—an honest day's work blowing rock into gravel and scoring fifty sticks to boot. Lucky the boss is what's known in the business as "a big shot." He wanted every shot to count, cost be damned. He called for three hundred sticks when two hundred-fifty odd did nicely. Powder Guy—they called him Powder Guy and he liked it—had started by holding back five, then ten, then twenty-five. Now he was so damn good he could blow a perfect shot and drive away with fifty sticks of dynamite give or take under the back seat of his crew cab. Fifty sticks that were taken off of inventory because they had been used in a shot, right? Drill, coupla sticks, ammonium nitrate, coupla sticks, caps. Boom! Raining rock. It was getting too easy. He was looking forward to the real challenge—now just over a week away.

He loved the desert. It was clean, uncomplicated and elemental. He had been lost in the desert. He had known thirst. Absolute thirst. It was good for the soul. The desert had defenses but not against developers. A quarry was one thing—it was a sacrifice area. But seeing a new butte bulldozed every day? Sucking Mead dry while looking to build a pipeline two hundred and fifty miles to the north through pristine desert and highlands so 'Las Vegas can continue to grow'? He would fight for the desert. He wanted the fat cats destroying the desert to feel absolute thirst, metaphorically speaking. He wanted them to feel that deep-in-the-bone-marrow longing. He would be one of the people to put wrong to right.

To see the fat cats sucking sand through a straw. He stroked the itchy stump on his left hand where his pinky and ring finger used to be, rolled over with a contented sigh, and sank, fully clothed, into sleep.

June 12
Monday

Jake whispered into the cracked door of the guestroom so as not to disturb Rachel. "Susan ... Susan, get downstairs and check out the TV." In Susan's room, the early morning sun shining through the curtains created a lacy pattern on the wooden floor. She sat up quickly, threw on her blue cotton bathrobe and stumbled down the stairs behind Jake, adjusting her hair with her fingers.

In the game room off the kitchen Jake had the local news on the television. A teaser just before a commercial had caught his attention. Susan stepped over a remote control toy car and joined him on the couch. A camera was panning over a large metal structure surrounded by debris. There was fine white dust everywhere. Some smaller metal outbuildings were flattened. A woman's voice pronounced, "The Ashland Gypsum mine near Iron Springs, Nevada was attacked last night. It appears that radical environmentalists attempted to dynamite a large conveyor system and torch the main processing plant." The camera panned over the wall of the main building. "As you can see, it is possible to make out the letters P, E, and A painted on the main wall. According to our FBI sources, that is the mark of Planet Earth Alliance, a known cell of radical environmentalists. However, to our knowledge, Planet Earth Alliance has not taken credit for the attack. Mine officials say the damage was mostly superficial." The picture switched to the perfectly coiffed head of an early morning anchor. "Stay with us for a related story. A loaded truck from Northwest Trucking Company jack-knifed and overturned in the northbound lanes on I-15 early this morning just south of Provo, causing traffic delays. We will be right back with more news."

Jake said, "I know the guy owns that trucking company."

Susan was still not fully awake. "What? Are you serious? Burke's plant was torched by environmentalists? And they call these guys tree huggers?"

"No, like Moody said, they call them ecoterrorists. Some moderate greens say they are necessary to the cause, others worry they are wild-ass extremists that damage their image. Personally, I don't know what to think."

Mathew walked past in his briefs on the way to the bathroom. "Hey, buddy," Jake said. "We're watching some really interesting stuff about the father of that woman we are trying to find. Don't wake up mom, okay?" Mathew smiled dreamily and closed the bathroom door. "Let's pick up a newspaper report of this incident and print my pictures of Ashland from the flyover. This is amazing. Maybe we should head down there after a few days at The Howl."

"And a little hard to believe," Susan said, focusing.

"What do you mean?"

"What I mean is, any man who hires an unstable loser like Moody to distract a cop who's supposed to be helping his family is pretty much capable of anything."

As Jake went into the kitchen to pour Susan a cup of coffee, the news anchor relayed the details of the 18-wheeler accident.

Jake handed Susan her mug and gestured at the television. "The owner of Northwest Trucking Company, Bev Witt, is an old partner in crime and other vices. Wait a minute. Did she say 'gypsum sludge'? She said, 'the truck was carrying gypsum from the mine that was just attacked.'" Jake and Susan stared at the television and then at each other as the talking head on the screen prattled on about other news.

"Hey Dad, there's no tp," Matt called from behind the bathroom door. Susan chuckled as Jake went to do his fatherly duty.

Jake and Susan briefly discussed their next moves over cereal. Then Susan dressed and left for a nearby mall to buy some clothes that would be more comfortable than jeans in the desert. Jake drove to his Airstream and packed his cooler with wine, beer, a jug of iced tea, and snacks for the road. He dumped his dirty clothes out of his duffle onto the floor and replaced them with clean ones from his bedside dresser. He pulled on a faded green polo shirt and tan cargo shorts. Just as he was leaving the trailer, he noticed a stack of bills and receipts and stuffed them into his pocket.

When Jake returned to Rachel's house he found her up and dressed. She said very little, but she collected Jake's recent business receipts and replenished his supply of cash. Jake and Susan were ready to go by eleven.

The boys clung to their dad's arms trying to stop him from leaving again so soon. Jake hugged them, rubbed their crew cuts, and explained the best he could why he had to go. He could see the wisdom in Mathew's sensitive eyes—he understood a person's life might be at stake.

"I really wish I could spend a few more days at home, guys, I really do, but we have to find a young woman. Her family is worried about her," he said, with an arm around each of the boy's shoulders. "Imagine how your mom and I would feel if anything happened to one of you."

Rachel gave a desultory wave from the porch as Jake and Susan left the driveway. Matt and Tim ran beside the car to the end of the block. Jake honked and turned off their street.

"Rachel looks worried," Susan said as they joined the flow of traffic toward the interstate.

"Yeah, she is. Just a lot of pressure from several different directions, right now."

"I hope your friend Bev is game," Susan said.

"When I called, Bev said he was excited to see us and would put the beer on ice. If I know Bev Witt, he'll like you and jump at the chance to drive you to the mine as soon as he can set it up." Jake glanced at his windshield-mounted GPS. "Shouldn't take us more than ninety minutes

130 • GREGORY ZEIGLER

or so to get to Spanish Fork. From just south of Bev's, we can head straight across Highway 6 to The Howl."

Soon they were south of Salt Lake. Thermal updrafts from the Wasatch Mountain Front buffeted the car as cumulus clouds grew into towers over the western desert.

"I would give anything—anything—to at least know whether we are dealing with an abduction or not," Susan said.

"That'd sure as shit help." Jake lifted one hand off the wheel to point. "See the State Prison over there?"

"It'd be hard to miss it in this tree-starved terrain."

"That's where Gary Mark Gilmore uttered his famous last words."

"Last words?" Susan asked.

"While facing the firing squad that he had insisted was his rightful punishment for murder. He refused to let his attorneys go forward with appeals."

"And those words were?"

"'Let's do it,'" Jake said.

"Hmm, balls."

"Major balls."

Susan watched two scarlet-winged paragliders play on the updrafts above the foothills. She turned her gaze on Jake. "And you? Under similar circumstances what do you think your last words would be?"

"Let's not do it!" Jake said, smiling sideways at her.

"I hear you. But you know, I'm curious, what is the Jake Goddard legacy? What would you point to as your best accomplishment?"

"Seriously?"

"Yeah, seriously, I'm, like I said, just curious after seeing you with … with your family and all."

"I'd probably say I was a good dad and, believe it or not, a fair-to-good husband. Let's see, what else? That I did my professional best to help people solve problems and that I mostly conquered my demons. Caught a few damn big fish on a few damn small flies, too."

"Demons? Rachel made some vague reference to that last night. You don't strike me as a guy with many vices, Jake. Unless you mean drinking the occasional beer in Utah."

"Like most of us, I'm far from perfect."

Susan was lost in thought. Jake saw other paraglider pilots launch off a large promontory of land jutting perpendicular from the Wasatch Mountains and pointed them out to Susan. After watching for a few seconds, she turned back to Goddard.

"What are your demons, Jake? You sure have seen mine in the short time we've known each other."

Jake adjusted the air conditioning and then straightened his hat by tugging on the bill. "Temperature good?" he asked. Susan nodded. He glanced into the side-view mirror and then to the road ahead. A minute of silence passed. "I'm a gambler ... an addict, but I'm in recovery now. I grew up around it on the farm and then got hooked by some all-night, high-stakes card games in college. I got pretty good at faking it instead of making it. Almost flunked out and often lost the rent and text book money." He flashed a crooked smile at Susan. "Of course, I had some pretty good nights, too. That's what keeps you coming back. I'm staying away from it now. Even though it may be too late to save my marriage. Helps to live in a squeaky-clean state like Utah. Bless these saints. Like Gary Gilmore, I'm a sinner among them. But I have to admit, it has helped to have an anchor like Rachel."

"I'll bet it has. Let's just hope you never have to face a firing squad. It'd be a waste of a fair-to-good man."

"Thank you, I think. Truth is, that's how I know Beverly Witt. When he was just a truck driver, before buying the company, he was a gambling partner. We used to hook up in Nevada border towns and play until you could turn our pockets inside out without dropping anything but Kleenex and keys. Bev was one compulsive, impulsive sucker, but fun, a hell of a lot of fun. Raised Mormon, believe it or not. Bev hit it big on a megabucks slot machine and has a trucking company to show for it. I got nothing but debts. The luck of the draw. Although, I have to say, I've had to take a lot of long shots as an investigator and for the most part my instincts have paid off."

"This was pre-Rachel and the boys, I take it," Susan said.

"Let's just say, *mostly* pre-Rachel and the boys and leave it at that. Now, even though we're separated, Rachel keeps the books for my business and handles all the cash."

"Well it's great to have a partner … and family is so important."

"My turn."

"For what?" Susan asked.

"To interrogate the interrogator."

"Fire away."

"Have you ever discharged your weapon on the job?"

After a long pause, Susan said. "Yes."

"Can you elaborate a little on that, officer?"

"Chuck and I approached a female in her car inside a garage. Another officer was providing backup by the garage door. The female held a gun in her hand and was threatening to kill herself. She turned up the music and started her car so I couldn't talk with her. Chuck decided to distract her by smashing out one of the car windows. When he did she discharged her weapon in his direction and I fired. We rendered first aid. The paramedics took her to the hospital. The investigation began. I was back on the job a month later after it was ruled a good shooting. It took me almost that whole month to believe I was the one who had shot her. I was convinced it was the backup officer by the door. It was all foggy for a time. Funny what the mind does to protect."

"You did your duty but took some time to convince yourself you had. Did she live?"

"Yes. Diane lived. Two years later I walked into an interview room where she was scheduled to be questioned for a suspected drugs violation. I said hello and she looked at me funny and said, you're the one who shot me, aren't you? I said yes. She told me she was sorry she made me shoot her. She was distraught over a man and wanted me to end her life. She even showed me the scars, you know, woman-to-woman. Ironic in many ways."

"How so?"

"Women rarely use weapons in suicides. Women rarely shoot other women. We were trying to prevent her from killing herself and I almost killed her for Christsake." Her hands balled into fists on her lap. "And then there's my fucking father …" She shook her head and stared out the side window. "Here's the exit for Spanish Fork."

"Just a few miles to Bev's place." Jake didn't want to push her. "Thanks for sharing that stuff."

Susan leaned back against the seat pondering why she had revealed so much and what Jake had said—and not said.

In a few minutes they left the freeway and sprawl near the exit and entered a residential area of perfect lawns and bungalows.

Beverly Witt owned an enormous white and brown ranch-style home with an attached garage as big as the house. The garage contained a boat, a jet ski, a snowmobile, and a huge late model pick-up truck—big man, big toys. His perfect lawn was larger than most in the neighborhood.

Bev, who felt it was never too early for beer because, as he often said, "If you're drinking beer, you're not really drinking," had set up a cooler full of Jake's favorite Mexican brand next to the picnic table on the patio behind the house. A trellis provided some shade from the bake of the mid-day Utah summer sun.

"Figured this'd save several steps," Bev said, prying off the cooler lid.

He pulled three beer bottles out of the ice and popped the tops off with an opener on the key chain that hung from his leather belt. Bev Witt was a man who looked like he preferred any sitting position to walking. He had short-cropped brown hair. A huge firm waist, like a watermelon, pressed his polo shirt against the table. His handsome round red face, perched atop the egg-shaped body, reminded Susan of Humpty Dumpty. Yet, he looked powerful and anything but fragile.

Introductions and pleasantries having been exchanged at the front door, Bev Witt took a long pull on his beer followed by a cooling swipe with the bottle across his broad forehead and got right to the point. "What can I do for you two upstanding citizens?"

"Heard about your truck jack-knifing on I-15 and wanted to ask you a few questions about it," Jake said.

"Whoa, am I being investigated by my old buddy?" He held both meaty hands out, palms up. "My truck licenses are all current, my drivers never exceed the speed limit, the driving time limit, or the weight limit, nor, I might add, do they so much as take No-Doz to stay awake, and I just mailed my alimony check to the 'ex' yesterday. You got nothing on me, pard." Bev grinned and sucked on his beer. "Plus, that spill is already cleaned up. Even HazMat is impressed, and believe me, brother and sister, that ain't easy in Utah."

"Glad to hear you're such an upstanding citizen," Jake said. "Guess my colleague here can put the cuffs away, relax a little, and enjoy her beer."

"I'm relaxing more with each sip," Susan said. "No, Bev, we just want some information. The news said your truck was coming from Ashland Mine in Nevada."

"Yeah? What about it?"

"Have your drivers mentioned anything unusual there? That is, before the recent attack by Planet Earth Alliance?" Susan asked.

"Not really, but you know how curious the average truck driver is: 'What's the speed limit? What's on the country station? Who's winning the game? Wonder when I'll get home. Wonder what the wife's up to.'" Bev took another swallow of his beer. "It's no accident that those country songs are so simple. Say, did you hear what happens when you play one of those songs backwards?" Bev asked, turning his high beams on Susan.

"No, what?" Susan asked.

"Guy gets his house back from the bank, gets his wife back from his best friend, gets his truck fixed, and his dog comes back to life." He howled and slapped the picnic table with his palms, bouncing the beers.

"Dog comes back to life, I love it," Susan chuckled.

"O.K, Jeff Foxworthy, here's what we need from you," Jake said. "We need you to climb back in the saddle of one of those big rigs and drive Susan to Ashland Mine for your next shipment of gypsum. And, if you trust me, and who better than the guy that used to get your back and cover your stake in Vegas, I'll explain to you over the next beer why we are doing this. I guarantee no one will suspect and we will not tarnish the shining reputation of your, as you describe it, spotless company."

"Damn!" Bev looked from Jake to Susan. "Hellamighty sounds interesting. Do I get an assistant PI badge, or license, or anything official like that?"

"Of course," Jake said. "And your very own decoder ring and miniature camera. It all comes standard with the license."

"Do I get a pretty side-kick like yours, Jake?" Bev winked at Susan.

"Well, actually, Bev, I'm the boss and Jake is the side-kick but if you play your cards right, I might be able to get you a cute guy like him to tag along with you. I have to warn you, though. They're not as useful as you might think."

Bev slapped Jake on the shoulder and hooted. Jake just shook his head, smiled, and said, "I was thinking it might seem more natural to have a woman in the cab with you, seeing as so many drivers travel with their wives."

While considering Jake's offer, Beverly leaned back and squinted over his guests' heads at the Wasatch Mountains. After a few seconds, he said, "Oh my heck, why not? I can cancel all my hot dates and social engagements for a few days for a pick-up at Ashland. Let me grab my cell and check with my dispatcher for the time and date of our next shipment while you two have another pop. Then I want to hear all about this deal." Bev jumped up with surprising grace for a big man, opened the sliding door to his living room, and went inside.

"Told you he was an impulsive SOB." Jake looked directly at Susan with his best hole card face. "You two should get along great." He tilted his head to the side, grinned, and reached into the cooler for three more beers.

"Hey, Florie, what's up?" Lou grimaced at her fake falsetto cheeriness in answering the first of what, no doubt, would be several Skype calls from her sister today. Florence's thin face filled the iPad screen. Even the usual screen distortion couldn't explain the deep facial lines barely disguised by hastily applied make-up, and unkempt dyed-black hair. Lou was beginning to regret introducing Flo to Skype.

"I heard from the policewoman in Jackson, Wyoming assigned to Lynnie's case. Thank God, my missing person report has had some effect—but a woman, Lou. How much can a woman do to find Lyn?"

"Oh, sis. You're such a feminist." Lou flicked her cigarette over the side of her boat. Fortunately, Vancouver Harbor was enjoying a quiet morning for a change and Florence wasn't doing her usual carping about the background noise. "You've been complaining nothing was being done. Now you're complaining about the person assigned to do something."

"Also, Louise, I'm becoming more convinced by the hour that something is wrong with Stanley. He has gone off the deep end. He is just not himself. This morning, he wouldn't—"

"Whoa, Florie, slow down. C'mon, honey. We can sort through this. Take a few deep breaths."

Florence sighed and Lou waited while her sister took a moment to collect herself. "This morning I … I phoned him to talk about money. He cut me off and hung up. He's been rude to me before, like cold and distant, but he's never hung up on me. What do you think of that?"

"Not much. Could be anything. Sounds like the same old Stan to me."

"I think he doesn't want to be confronted about money because he's spending ours like crazy. He was so civil about all this when he bought the condo. For the first couple of months after he moved out, I got my usual allowance. In the last three weeks, he has practically forgotten me. I can't get him to talk about money—or more recently, about our daughter. He is totally distracted and totally ignoring our little girl, as if she just stayed out too late or something." Lou could see the tears coming. "You're the strong one, Lou, you have to do something. Lou, Lou, you have to—"

Lou modulated her voice and tried to keep her sister collected. "Listen, Florence, when you insisted for the hundredth time that I do something, I hired Jake Goddard. What else can I possibly do?"

"I don't know, Lou, I don't know … Can you at least contact Mr. Goddard again and see if he has anything new?"

"I contact him every day I can—" Florence started to protest. "But … I'll send another message in a little while. You have to hang on to what Noah Skutches said. Remember, Florie, the people who work for him reported that Lyn was fine."

"But that garbled cell phone message. It's haunting me. I just know she's in trouble and that damn Stanley refuses to support my claim to the police." Lou knew no good would come out of going over that infernal voice message again. It had come from Lyn's phone but, as described by Florence, sounded like a typical butt dial with odd sounds and no voice. It was the last communication Florence had received from her daughter. Lou tried a new tact.

"You have to find a way to deal with this more assertively, Florence. You have to stand on your own two feet. Patrick and Margaret are still at home and they need you right now. They must be worried about their sister."

"Lou, I entered a way different world when I married Stan Burke and I knew it. I live a privileged life because of him, not Daddy, and I make a difference in this community. We have three beautiful children. The rules are set. Separated or not, we are partners and I can't upset the apple cart. Especially now. I have to stay on his good side, you know? I'm not as strong as you are, Lou..." She was sobbing now and daubing at her eyes with tissue.

"Florie, if you can't be assertive with Stan, then do something else, but do something other than just calling me. How about talking to your banker? Maybe Stan just isn't hauling it in like he used to. I've always found his various investment schemes and his paranoia that he never has enough money bizarre. And you know what else? I admit this is your big sister talking, but you need to pamper yourself a little: go shopping, go out with friends. They can take your mind off things."

Lou might as well have been talking to herself. "I just hate dealing with banks. I just want things back to normal. I'm so scared, Lou. So tired. And my pastor has got to be sick of looking in. He's due here any minute. Oh, here he comes now up the walk, and uh, okay, Louise. I'll call again soon."

The Skype window closed. I'm sure you will, and you and this situation are becoming very weird, thought Lou. She rolled inside the cabin and turned on her laptop. She needed to line up all the players in this drama and look them over. Clearly, Stan was not acting rationally and her sister was getting even more hysterical. So, what else was new? She hungered for solid information that might help determine what was going on with her niece. She sent Jake Goddard a short message as she had promised Florence, and then thought about Noah Skutches.

Lou had moved to Vancouver from San Francisco in the sixties when her then husband, Roger, was avoiding the draft and the war. She met Noah Skutches in the early seventies, when he was an ascending star—in hindsight she realized he was building a reputation that masked poor judgment. As a younger professor, his groundbreaking findings on climatological trends earned him her admiration. He took many risks in subsequent years, and focused on the studies of the nineteenth century entomologist, J. W. Tutt, on *Biston betularia*, the fragile peppered moth. He began to watch small bush birds, using a similar hypothesis, and saw that certain species' feathering was adapting better than others to changes in water and air quality. His work was innovative, but only the most knowledgeable in environmental circles took notice; financial support was weak.

They met in Vancouver at a Sierra Club fundraiser when she was writing for the journal *Mother Jones* and they hit it off. Eventually he hired her to be his communications expert and Canadian media agent. In that role, she encouraged him to cast his net more widely and to associate himself with higher profile causes. He followed her advice and his reputation started to broaden. They were lovers for a time, but the man's penis got in his way. Just like her ex-husband. The co-eds eventually got more of Noah's attention than the research did. They fought through four projects before she quit. Christ, she mused, the men in her life were feeble.

In the last ten years, the professor had become almost pathetic. He had been resting on his laurels and the young Turks were publishing more frequent and better work. His graduate seminars were thinly attended and invitations to speak less frequent. Thinking he still had much of value to share with his students, she had persuaded Lyn to join him for the summer after she learned from one of his sporadic emails that a young man on his team had died suddenly. Lyn had a chance to follow her favorite bird, the northern goshawk. Lou didn't want to dampen her niece's enthusiasm with negatives and wanted to believe that Noah would be on his best behavior with her niece because of their history. Noah owed her a great deal and Lou still had a soft spot for him in her heart.

Remembering Skutches' innovative work on water quality brought her attention back to the Lifewater organization. She accessed the Lifewater website and stumbled over another rather unpleasant memory, a picture of Forrest White Wolf. He was the son of Willy White Wolf, a Nootka rabble-rouser-cum-union-steward for the teamsters, and a white mother who had abandoned him early. Alcohol had been a demon dancing through the lives of both Forrest's parents—two bright people embittered and wasted. Willy White Wolf was a product of one of those desolate Canadian Indian boarding schools that had been funded by the government decades ago; loneliness and abuse were the only lessons those kids learned. Willy was not a good single father. It had taken the village and then some to raise Forrest. At the age of twelve, he made an indelible first impression on her.

She and Roger were writing propaganda on behalf of the Clayoquot tribes, meant to stir up rage against clear-cutting on Vancouver Island. One Saturday, she headed up to Gold River, a protest hot spot, to find that the native folk were pissed at her. They were making big bucks driving logging trucks across the island, and were way more concerned about losing income than about angering the tree spirits.

Willy White Wolf was speaking for the truckers and a bunch of the kids were hanging around the scene on their bikes. Forrest wanted to impress Dad and his buddies, so he marched up to Lou and spat in her face. The boys howled. Willy cuffed Forrest on the back of his head and sent him sprawling into the dust. The boys howled again. Forrest stared blackly at Willy, then at her, grabbed his bike and took off up the hill to the village.

When she saw his image in a promotional photo at the Lifewater website, the same pale flashing eyes and aggressive jaw line stared back at her. So he was an activist now. She could see that anger had been transmuted into righteous determination. Or had it? His father had been a smooth, if volatile, opportunist, and here was Forrest, smiling, long black braid displayed, arm tattooed, ear pierced. Very handsome, but he looked like another incarnation of the trickster raven to her. Nothing in the Lifewater archives gave her more information on him, except one reference to his role as "consulting historian." Good grief, she thought.

Her next step was to go to the northwest tribes' website and see if his name popped up anywhere in connection with policy-making. Nothing. Finally, she found a reference to him at the First People's Environmental Network. He had been a founding member, working on water rights and land claim issues. From there, she was able to follow his trail by searching water rights groups. He had worked for four or five of them over the years, but seemed to move around a great deal. Then she tracked him to the Paiute Water Conservancy Actions site. He was advising a consortium of nations who were reopening century-old land and water treaties, negotiating what was known colloquially as Winter's Rights. That had been just last fall. She went back to dig more at the Lifewater site and after a few minutes of searching recent postings jolted when she found him listed as a "field supervisor."

Knowing that Lifewater was one of Lyn's favorite causes, that she was supposed to be with Noah Skutches, and that Forrest was within range, caused her great concern. She didn't believe in coincidence or luck. She believed in action and planning and understood the chess game. But how do you anticipate your opponent's moves when you're not sure who your opponent is? Was White Wolf friend or foe? And with Lyn's father, planted clearly on the side of the enemies of environmentalists, was he friend or foe? Her idealistic niece could be in for some surprisingly tough education. Who was Lou to believe: the charming and untrustworthy father who said Lyn was fine or the hysterical mother who was convinced Lyn was in serious trouble? She'd go with her sister's instincts over Stan Burke's assertions any day. At least she felt, with some assurance, that she could depend on Jake Goddard's expertise and Noah's friendship.

She had heard that big protests were happening soon near Zion National Park, though the recent hype on the discussion boards seemed way too alarmist. The news on the sites held that native groups, environmentalists, anti-capitalists, and farmers would all be converging to try to stop more pouring of the water from the Virgin and Colorado rivers down the insatiable throat of Las Vegas. In the southwest, pro-development forces—like Stan's pet, Sage Use—were rich and ruthless, and their political battles over water fierce. Forrest was sure to be there and Lyn could easily find herself under his spell. She'd bet a million that Forrest, too, had a thing for the ladies.

As cigarette after cigarette burned down to a long tube of ash, Lou arrived at two decisions. The first was to get off her ass to do more to find Lyn by linking up somehow with Jake Goddard. The second was to return to her research into the Zion area protests, to dip as deeply as she could into her well of information about eco-activism, dig until her network of contacts brought her to some kernel of truth, some essential and familiar clue. It was a huge risk to her Planet Earth Alliance status to act independently without organizational sanctions. The role of messengers like her was clearly defined; they were to relay information about "direct actions" without ever knowing anything about the participants, other cell members, or the cell's future plans. It was fundamental to the organization's success and secrecy. For that matter, it was fundamental to protecting her from culpability. But she couldn't help herself. She had no choice but to try and unearth information that could ensure Lyn's safety.

She picked her way back and forth across the web all day and well into the night, stopping only to light cigarettes, pour coffee, and wolf granola bars. Finally, two sets of information popped up in front of her—a sequence of symbols like Anasazi rock carvings and charts detailing Las Vegas's water consumption and growth rate. She had seen this kind of pattern before. Then it came to her: Planet Earth Alliance had somehow figured out that the dams were a ruse. Everyone else had been fooled.

"You have missed an essential move, you morons! You've been tricked by a subterfuge! It's not about the Virgin, goddamnit to hell! It's not happening there." She hit print, rolled back from the desk, and reached for cigarettes—out. She shut the laptop. She was exhausted. She rolled out for one last look from her deck at the night sky and the harbor to calm her down before turning in. Tomorrow was going to be a busy day.

It was late afternoon when Susan and Jake left the shade of Bev Witt's backyard, Susan behind the wheel. The heat showed no sign of diminishing. Still and heavy, it squatted between two mountain ranges, causing the pavement to appear wavy in the distance. As she drove, Susan's beer-buzz departed and the desert encroached. The aridity lodged on her skin and in her throat. After dozing for close to half an hour, Jake broke the silence.

"Oh … uh … sorry about that." He stretched and yawned. "Bev and beer are a lethal combination midday. His name really ought to be 'Beverage,' not Beverly. You doing okay?"

"Doing fine, Jake."

"I forgot to tell you, I checked my email just before we left my house. Had another message from Lou Cuvier. Nothing new, just asking if we'd made any progress. I didn't have time to respond." He studied her profile. "What are you thinking about—other than your daughter, that is?"

"Other than my daughter and Florence Burke's daughter, honestly, I was thinking about you—Rachel, your sons, your neat little house—guess I'm just a little jealous of the family scene. Does your sleeping together last night mean you're getting back together?"

"The 'family scene,' as you call it, sometimes feels like it's held together with duct tape. Guess it's obvious but Rachel and I have some pretty serious challenges right now. I was shocked when she asked me to stay. I figured later, when it really wasn't about sex, that she did it for your benefit." He stroked his chin and cleared his throat. "And of course she would never want to pass up an opportunity to lecture me. Seems I manage to screw up, at least in her eyes, on a regular basis."

"How do you—"

Jake interrupted. "Speaking of screwing up, that's exactly what I don't want to happen at this shindig. It might help us blend in at The Howl if we understood more about the issues the Lifewater members are so fired up about. I've been reading up on it." He reached for the daypack between his feet.

"And what have you learned?"

"I'm only just beginning to understand this in any depth," Jake replied. "I actually found most of this info in Lyn's file, which you've seen, and online. Oh, and I called a professor of mine from college. I admit this stuff could be biased but you know, the more I read, the more I felt those old college activist juices flowing again."

"You were an activist in college?"

"More or less—marched in several American Indian and green protests. Three Mile Island was the first thing that got my attention as a kid. Scared me big time."

"It wasn't, by any chance, a way to appear sensitive and attractive to certain braless members of the Earth Day crowd?" Susan asked, pushing him on the shoulder.

Jake smiled and stretched one arm behind his head. "Not to change the subject but, what have I learned? Let me check my notes." He pulled his iPad out of the pack. "Let's see. Most of this is from the Lifewater website and it definitely gets your attention. 'Aquifers are dropping down all over the planet because of being pumped without any acknowledgement that they recover slowly, if at all.' It said, 'Whole sections of Mexico City are sinking because of dropping water tables.'" He looked up. "One of the world's largest cities is freakin' sinking. Blows my mind. 'Unless there are major changes in the distribution of ever-scarcer water supplies, two thirds of the world's population is expected to be living under severe water stress conditions by the year 2025.' Lifewater got that quote from the *Scientific American* website."

Susan took it all in while negotiating traffic through a mining town. After resetting the cruise control, she said, "Those are pretty scary statements. But before you get all wound up and join protests, are they for real, or are they just propaganda?"

"They seem bona fide, endorsed and cross-referenced by several international groups and scientists. Lyn Burke had it all indexed." Jake pulled out her file and flipped a few pages. "Okay, get this, I'll summarize it for you. China has four hundred million farmers—four hundred million. All of them need water to produce crops and survive. But the interior is facing desertification problems. It says northeast Chinese water tables are dropping at more than a meter a year—mostly because of wasteful irrigation." Jake looked out the front window. "Water scarcity and fear of mass migrations to cities, or a full-on farmer revolt, has Chinese officials scared shitless. Most people view access to potable water as a basic human right."

"Yeah, and with us North Americans, the right to waste as much water as we want. I'll try and remember that the next time I shampoo my hair." Susan said, studying a strand of hair and then pushing it behind her ear.

"So what's your best guess on why Skutches is so interested in The Howl at the Full Moon Festival?" Jake asked. "Do you buy that it's about recruiting?"

She exhaled slowly. "I'm at a loss on that one. What I know of The Howl is pretty limited. I hear that it's a latter-day love-in for aging hippy baby boomers. All I can say is, thank God Bev is coming for me in his truck in three days. The desert has never been my favorite place in the summer, so at least I'll be traveling with him in air-conditioned comfort again soon." A Mack truck passed in a rush on their left. "Heck, it might be fun to be up in the cab with Bev feeling like the captain of the highways. You and I will just have to sort out The Howl and Skutches' interest in it when we start howlin'. I really hope Moody is right and Lynnie is there and is fine, but I just can't believe something hasn't gone wrong, or else she'd have called her mother."

Jake pointed to a sign. The next exit was for Winston, Utah, and the junction of U.S. 6 and 50. The sign claimed that 6 and 50 through Nevada was the 'Loneliest stretch of highway in the United States. No services for the next 75 miles. Last gas ahead.' Jake looked for that gas station.

"You better pull in for gas when we see it."

The problem wasn't blinking and missing the Mormon town of Winston. You could barely find it with your eyes wide open. Jake and Susan came up on a small clapboard post office with a weathered and torn American flag. There were a few trailers scattered about. There was one gas station/rock shop/café/store—an assortment of old whitewashed and pockmarked concrete block buildings sitting back from the road and surrounded by tumbleweed. A battered sign, a phone booth with no phone, two pumps, and a few abandoned vehicles on blocks crowded up against the central building.

Suddenly, a metallic blue coupe with two people in it squealed around the back of the gas station and headed broadside for Jake's car. The oncoming car swerved and missed sideswiping the Subaru by no more than six inches. The car bounced over the curb before fishtailing down the road toward Nevada. Susan and Jake uncoiled and looked at each other with amazement.

"What was that all about?" Jake said.

"You've got me. The driver looks too old to be a hell-raising teen trying to impress his gal," Susan said, easing her grip on the steering wheel.

"I wonder if that was Lyn's car," Jake said. "It fits the description. Why don't you go ahead and pull in there?"

One other car was visible. It was snugged-up in the shade of a lone cottonwood and Jake immediately recognized it: Moody's green Suburban. Before they could get out of the car, Moody came out a side door of the building, wiping off his face with paper towels. He was wearing a blue t-shirt that was soaked in the front and black jeans. He had a battered canvas daypack slung over one shoulder. He stopped and glared at Susan and Jake.

"Christ, look who's here. It's like getting something stuck to your shoe," Susan said.

Then, flinging his towels in a fifty-five gallon drum, Moody strode over. Susan fought the urge to slam her car door open into Moody's knees, but instead she lowered her window.

"You have any idea what kind of people your Lyn Burke is hanging out with, lady?" Moody demanded.

"Nice to see you too, Ranklin. The point you seem to be missing is if we weren't concerned about these people, we wouldn't be anywhere near this godforsaken road." Susan smiled hard. "And you're lucky you're not out on some road rockin' a day-glow orange leisure suit."

"Susan, don't let the local bishop hear you call this paradise 'godforsaken.' What's all over your shirt, Moody?"

"Was lemon meringue before I washed it off," he said with disgust, pulling his t-shirt out from the bottom. "I was following Skutches' van and that car with Nevada plates for several hundred miles when I finally had to pull in here to take a leak. As I came out of the men's room that damn half-breed, White Wolf, hit me in the face with a pie and said something about 'pie, rhyming with spy' and if I followed them, 'I might die.' Jerk circled back specifically to harass me, I know it. He jumped in the car and left with your supposed kidnap victim, flipping me the bird. He's the one I photographed in Yellowstone."

"They almost broadsided us on their way out," Jake said.

"Oh, Ranklin, has someone been harassing you?" Susan said. "I am so sorry to hear that." Her light mocking tone turned hard. "I realize that Lyn and Forrest White Wolf were both working for Professor Skutches but I don't believe Lyn was in that car. I don't believe Lyn is currently with this group. It was probably the same woman you mistook her for in Yellowstone. If she is with White Wolf at all, it's not voluntarily and if she isn't, I want to know where she is and why he has her car."

"Did you see a dog in or around the car?" Jake asked. A raven landed on the rim of the garbage drum searching for food.

"No, but then it was a little hard to see anything through the crap all over my face."

"Lyn Burke got into this because of her love of birds. My best guess, if she is wrapped up in something this volatile, she has been drugged or brainwashed. I'm going to ask you one more time, Moody." Jake said. "Will you help us find her?"

Moody paused and looked over the car to the horizon. "Well, I'm committed to my Sage Use backers and to Stan Burke—"

"Christ, don't you think finding Stan Burke's daughter is fulfilling your obligation to Stan Burke, even if you are working with us without his knowledge?" Jake demanded. "Just imagine you're wrong, that she's in trouble and you help rescue her. Burke will love you for it, assuming he's not involved. He'll owe you big time. And if he is involved, you're an accomplice to kidnapping. Joining us is a win-win, Rank."

"Beats going to jail," Susan said.

"But, as I was about to say," Moody continued. "If, in fact, Lyn Burke is somehow caught in this against her will, it'd please the shit out of me to get her away from these pie-throwing jerks. And, if the pay is right, I might be interested."

Jake said, "All right, but you damn well better earn it. I thought you just might be up for a little double-dipping, Moody." His tone eased a little. "Why don't we get a mad cow special in the café and talk? I just hope they have coffee." He turned to Susan. "Some Mormon joints refuse to sell it, but they will pour enough Coke to keep you awake and peeing for a week."

They walked through the store into the café and found a battered table near the back. Moody half-hid himself behind the stacks of soft drink cases and sat with his back to the entrance. The wall was peeling and covered with framed photos of the desert. Many were faded shots of hunters on horseback—various prey slung across the saddles. Susan took several thin paper napkins from the dispenser and dabbed at a pool of Coke dotted with two drowned flies.

A large woman in a hairnet and stained white uniform managed to take their order while uttering little more than, "Yup." After she headed for the kitchen, Moody started in.

"They all know me and fear me, you know. The extremists know I'm watching and it makes them nervous. Thing is, now that I've been spotted, they'll all be watching me too. But you two can go undercover and blend in. No way White Wolf will remember you from the brief encounter you just had here in the parking lot. He was having too much fun laughing at me."

"Blend in," Susan said as she stood to throw away the used napkins in a waste bin by the back door. "Maybe Jake can blend in wearing Birkenstocks and a smile, but how the hell do I blend in?"

"Looking like a has-been country-and-western star?" Moody said, pointing at Susan's tight jeans.

"That has to have it all over looking like a wanna-be private investigator, slash 'anti-extremist'—to use your words—covered in lemon meringue." Susan pierced Moody with a look and sat.

Moody backed off. "Most folks come from cities and pretty middle-class lives. They cover the logos on their cars and trucks with duct tape and eventually shuck their regular clothes in favor of body paint, makeshift costumes or whatever, sometimes their birthday suits—sun block's a big seller every summer. Christ, a few years back, I twisted my ankle and the Doc in the med tent who checked me out was dressed like Tarzan. I don't think you're gonna have a problem. There were thirty-five thousand of them at The Howl last summer. Shouldn't be hard to hide in a crowd like that."

"So, what do we 'howlers' do all day—besides get sunburned?" Jake asked.

"Performances, speeches on all sorts of whacko subjects, games, mime, sex and drugs, pretty much. They pitch it as a celebration of art, dance and personal expression, but it's really high school in the desert for grown-ups."

"So how do you suggest we approach this Lyn Burke thing?" Jake asked. "I mean, considering that we might be looking at a Stockholm Syndrome, Patty Hearst type deal."

"If she's there, you grab her up and throw her in the car, with or without her permission. If, as you suspect, she's not there and you have proof she's not on a legitimate assignment, you infiltrate White Wolf's little party and sign on for the next opportunity to throw a monkey wrench, or whatever. If they learn to trust you, they may slip up and give you some leads to the girl. Or, better yet, we may be able to find someone in the group willing to turn and share what they know." He thrust his jaw at Susan. "The worst thing you can do if Lyn Burke is not there, is be the mama bear and go for their throats the way you did me in Victor. She may never see the light of day again."

The big waitress brought three hamburger plates on one arm, and had her massive finger through the rings of three coffee mugs with the other. Moody snapped a bite out of his burger almost before the plate touched down.

"Observe, and then make a move when the timing is right," Jake said.

"Standard missing person investigative technique," Susan said, shaking her head. "Brilliant."

"You got it," Moody mumbled to Susan with a full mouth, while reaching into his daypack for a file folder. "Now look at these photos—I mean, really *look* at them—so you know who the players are. I was going to show you them at the cabin before you got so pissed." One by one, he held up pictures of the Lifewater/Skutches team. When he got to White Wolf's picture, he cautioned, "This is Forrest White Wolf, the pie guy. I'd be especially careful around him. He is one mean hombre—definitely meaner than your average tree-hugger."

"And if people ask questions about us?" Susan demanded impatiently.

"Cardinal rule: base your bullshit on as many facts as possible. What can you tell us about your 'ex,' or whatever?"

"There is nothing to tell," Susan fired back.

Moody chewed his meat and stared defiantly at the table. "Okay, tell them you met in college, the one where Jake really went in case someone knows it. 'Moved out West, then came marriage, then came baby in a baby carriage'—you know people never question that old fairy tale. Tell 'em you live in Salt Lake and let Jake handle all questions about college and Salt Lake. Work it out on your way there. Believe me, there won't be much else to do on this stretch of highway."

"What will you be doing?" Susan asked.

"I'll be around stirring up the usual crap. I'll photograph any 'howlers' with a suspected track record in illegal eco-actions and monitor general sessions that are pro-environment. I'll get a message to your tent about where we can meet, compare notes, and plan our next move. My fee is two-fifty a day plus expenses, one day up front," Moody said, and for the first time made brief eye contact with Susan. Jake slid the money out of his wallet and across the table to Moody.

"The first day's on me. If you earn this, I'll contact my employer and see if she will approve keeping you on the payroll after day one," Jake said.

Jamming the bills in his front pocket, Moody added, "And, uh, beware, okay? All is not as it seems with these people. Remember, the radical ones are criminals." He stood up. "See you happily married folks at The Howl." Moody turned and went into the store, spoke briefly with the owner, and left before the check arrived.

Jake and Susan finished their burgers. Susan stepped into the store to choose some last minute supplies while Jake went out to fill up the car. When Jake returned they both went up to the counter to pay the bill. The owner, a gangly fellow who looked like Jimmy Stewart playing Ichabod Crane, asked, "What brings you two down the loneliest road?"

"We're on our way to The Howl at the Full Moon Festival near Ely," Jake said.

The owner looked them up and down. "You don't look the types."

Susan turned to Jake, arched an "I told you so" eyebrow and asked, "Why do you say that?"

"Lotta ungodliness at that pagan orgy—why, there's drugs, nudity, fornication, and..."

"Oh, that. We know all about that, but we aren't going to get nude and fornicate, even as a couple bound by holy matrimony." Jake slid his arm around Susan's shoulders. "We have no intention of indulging in shameful behavior. Do we, honey?" He squeezed her to his side.

"Certainly not," Susan said.

"We have been sent to The Howl to proselytize," Jake said.

The proprietor looked over his reading glasses for a few seconds, presumably to determine if he was being had, and, deciding his customers were legitimate, said, "Well, now, that's a great relief. God bless you both. May you travel safe and be successful in your mission."

Jake gave him his most earnest look. "Thank you so much, brother. What do we owe you?"

"Oh, ah, sorry, of course. Let's see." He rang up the sale. "Including your friend's gas. That will be $122.64." Jake snorted and shook his head. "And gosh, let me throw in a six-pack of Coke to support your efforts. I've made a ton of money off them heathen howlers needing gas and such on their way through."

"That's very kind, sir. With prices as high as these, I'm certain you are making a lot of money. We'll pass on the soft drinks though, thanks just the same. But I got forty bucks worth of gas." He slid four fifties across the counter. "Have a nice day," Jake said, picking up his change. He and Susan grabbed the bags and headed toward the door. But just after the screen door banged shut, Jake turned back and asked, "By the way, where's the nearest casino after we cross the Nevada border?" The owner's face dropped. He turned back to his shelves. Susan grabbed Jake's elbow and steered him to the car.

Jake chuckled as they got in. "You gotta love it! The Utah-Nevada border. Saints on one side—sinners on the other—both looking to make a buck off each other."

"That was kind of a childish thing to do to that poor man, Jake."

"I know. But I can't stand the hypocritical bullshit. Too much religion distorts folks' perspective."

Just after Jake pulled away from the store, Susan said, "Jake, I just want you to know I hear you on the hypocrisy. I had my fill of that as a minister's kid."

"Yeah, but you grew up and moved away. My wife and family reside in this self-righteous state and Rachel's getting more righteous by the day." Jake stared at the highway. A range of treeless, boulder-strewn mountains loomed ahead across a flat sage-covered basin.

"Would you like me to read some more stuff from your notes?"

"Knock yourself out."

Susan scanned through some digital pages on Jake's iPad. "Says here that after Gorbachev left Russian politics, he turned to humanitarian concerns and begun to write about water. For instance, he wrote, 'This century's wars will be fought over water rather than oil.' " She pondered that for a moment. "If there is such a shortage elsewhere, what's the downside with a pipeline in Canada and sales to needier countries?"

Jake said, "Seems the problem is make-a-quick-buck, bureaucratic maneuvering. In Canada, environmentalists fear that once water becomes a salable commodity, there will be no stopping it or controlling it because of NAFTA. That old prof I told you I contacted was one of my more radical geology instructors at Carnegie Mellon."

"What'd he have to say?"

"'Like dam building in the past, this pipeline idea is a similar example of thoughtless engineering of natural systems.' He said that even the United Nations was now concerned about widespread social upheaval that studies predicted would be directly related to global warming and drought but that the Canadian pipeline was not the solution."

"You know there is a whole disprove man-caused global warming movement out there," Susan said.

"Yeah, I know. But no one in their right mind can deny drought, the scarcity of water, and the more extreme weather we are experiencing. All you have to do is look at the bathtub ring around Mead. Do you remember what Hunter told us at the bar about the United Global Bank the night we caught Moody?"

"Sure, he said something about that the UGB is often misguided, but even they won't fund dams anymore," Susan said.

"Right, and that the idea of borrowing a huge amount of money from United Global Bank and building a pipeline to fill fossil fuel guzzling tankers crashing through the Northwest Passage is driving the environmentalists nuts. And even more so because they believe that it is now navigable in the summer with an icebreaker because of, and only because of, man-caused climate change."

"That's why I don't see Lyn Burke passing up a chance to demonstrate against the pipeline in Jackson." Susan looked out her window at a spooked jackrabbit on the fly through the brush. "Damn, where in the world can that girl be?"

"So, what do we know for certain?"

"We know that Skutches' main interest in The Howl is recruiting for the big event which follows," Susan said. "And that's a huge protest planned for the official announcement of two highly controversial dams to be built on the Virgin River, just across the Utah border in Arizona, and more importantly, just below Zion National Park."

"A remote area that environmentalists love for its wilderness value and that Lyn is supposedly studying," Jake said.

"Exactly. Skutches is going to The Howl to recruit more troops. Certainly not to indulge in sex with co-eds, drugs, and rock and roll," Susan said.

"No, no, certainly not."

The highway began to climb beside a tree-and-grass-lined stream up through the mountain range. They wound around blind corners—cuts blasted for the road in the steep rock. Jake pointed out the swirling limestone and shale strata in the convoluted canyon walls and then, as they headed down the western flank to the sage flats below, the conversation inevitably turned back to Rank.

"Moody seems to be enjoying his role as hired gun," Jake said.

"Desperate times, desperate measures," Susan said. "We must be damn desperate, that's all I have to say."

"You referring to hiring Moody or being my wife?"

"Ha. Hiring Moody. As for being your wife, I'm not that desperate."

"You should be so lucky. I was once known as a guy who could make the gals howl at the moon."

"Don't flatter yourself, Jake," Susan muttered and looked out the passenger window to hide the flush in her cheeks. She turned back to him wide-eyed. "Aaaooooou," she mock howled. They both cracked up.

They were driving through basin and range country and soon were climbing again to a tree-lined pass very close to the thirteen thousand-foot, snow-covered heights of Wheeler Peak in Great Basin National Park. They descended to a valley floor studded with modern white wind turbines and came to the junction with U.S. 93 South. Jake slowed for a stock truck turning on the highway ahead of them. It had a bright red bumper sticker emblazoned with the words STOP SDWA'S WATER GRAB.

"What do you think that's about?" Susan asked.

"Let me put it this way. That first mountain range we drove through, that was the Confusion Range. This last one was the Snake Range. The folks scratching out a living in the Snake Valley, like that rancher ahead of us, are a bit confused about why the Southern Desert Water Authority is thirsting to snake sixteen billion gallons of their water per year through a fifteen billion dollar, two hundred-mile long, pipeline to Vegas."

"Hmmm. I suppose I'd be a little confused and a lot pissed," Susan said.

"It's been all over the Salt Lake papers. A spear into the heart of Nevada's most beautiful mountain ranges and close to her only national park. That's not likely to be popular up here in this scenic rural country."

The road stretched dead ahead into the sunset. Red rock blended into fiery clouds without apparent demarcation. Except for asphalt, posts, and poles, they saw nothing that was man made. The dim light of dusk began to fill in the crevices of the cliffs lining the highway. Again they began to climb and soon topped another mountain pass. A halo of alpenglow outlined the distant mountains and the green of sporadic junipers and pines was muted by the approach of night. On the subsequent descent to the desert floor, they passed a small herd of mule deer grazing a grassed slope. Homemade signs that said "Howl" and depicted a stenciled profile of a wolf against a large moon pointed the way.

Jake switched off the air and dropped the windows. "I love the smell of the desert," he said. Susan gathered her hair at her neck and watched the yellow blur of rabbit brush along the shoulder.

In the distance, flames reflected on a sheer sandstone wall. Jake turned off the pavement onto a well maintained but dusty dirt road that wound around boulders and through arroyos, then descended into an enormous natural bowl of rock containing a makeshift town. At one end of the encampment, in front of a concave sandstone face, sat a portable stage flanked by scaffolding stacked with massive speakers. Abutting the stage were several concession tents, water trucks, and a line of blue portable toilets. The center of the amphitheater was covered with thousands of cars, tarps, tents, trailers, and battered RVs. At the back of the bowl, beyond the campers, a towering papier-mâché wolf was engulfed in flames. A fire truck with 'Ely, Nevada' painted on the door and two security vehicles were parked a safe distance from the heat. The radiant blaze from the wolf's snout licked upward at its bright complement, the moon rising full.

Jake paid their admission and registered for a numbered campsite near the porta-potties. They drove around for a few minutes and found their spot. Human "wolf" howls and several strains of music filled the air. Cheers and whistles erupted across the camp as large chunks of flaming wolf streaked to the ground. Soon the fire from the wolf effigy died down; only a smoking metal frame remained.

Jake and Susan started unloading the car. Jake hadn't noticed the tent selected by his sons in Salt Lake was an old nylon one he'd bequeathed to them two summers ago because it was now too small for the family. Jake and Susan pitched it. Their attempts to interact like an old married couple seemed laughable and transparent to Susan, but their neighbors didn't seem to notice as they went about finishing dinner and starting their campfires. A bare-chested electric guitar player strolled by in a brown kilt and boots with what appeared to be a battery-powered amplifier strapped to his back. Moonlight and long soft shadows played on the surrounding rock walls and on the campsites.

"This doesn't seem so wild," Susan whispered as Jake bent down to stuff two sleeping bags in the stained orange tent.

"It really doesn't, particularly since it's a 'full wolf moon' tonight. I expected a little more lunacy."

"June is the Strawberry Moon. January is the Wolf Moon," Susan said.

"Oops." Jake straightened and looked around. "Things could still pick up, it's only the first day and the night is young." The spicy smell of marijuana wafted over from a nearby tent. "Now we're talking," Jake said, inhaling deeply. "Let's get the party started. After we set up, I suggest we follow our noses and meet some of our fellow campers." When Susan frowned, Jake said, "Now honey, you know it's the polite thing to do." Then more seriously, "Soon as we locate Skutches' campsite, we search for Lyn."

They crawled into the tent to arrange their sleeping bags and duffels. It smelled like it hadn't been aired for years. Jake unzipped all the windows and doors and switched on a battery-powered lamp.

Susan sat with her arms around her knees and brushed sand off her pant legs. "Great, sand in the tent already. Next it will be in the food and the sleeping bags." She swept sand toward the door with her hand. "Which direction do you want your head to point? Not that you have too many choices, but…"

"I like to have my head uphill. I sleep deep, really don't notice much once I'm under," Jake yawned. "So whatever you want, hon, is fine with me. And, uh, been meaning to say I'm sorry for my behavior at the store in Winston. You were right, it was … a little childish and I feel like I snapped at you."

"Thanks for that, sweetie," Susan said, raising her eyebrows. "Married couples shouldn't go to bed mad." She brushed some more sand toward the door. "Seriously, I love the outdoors, but give me a fist full of high forest dirt over sand any day. Don't get me wrong; I can handle the desert, most seasons. I did it, what, like a hundred times as a kid. I just can't stand sleeping in a dusty tent city. My dad used to take the whole congregation into the Sonora Desert once a year for a mandatory communion with God and nature. More like a survival weekend. Always four days since forty days and forty nights in the wilderness would have been impractical. Bad cooking and lots of boring 'sword for the lord' lectures on God's creation, and parables, loads of parables. I learned to fend for myself and hated it all the while." Susan pushed up the roof of the nylon tent with her hand. "You know, I'm going to have to get up to pee in the middle of the night, for sure. I don't think you want me flopping over you as I crawl out to the john."

"Your relationship with your father reminds me of mine with Rachel. What happened to your dad?"

"Well, speaking of hypocrisy—and irony. He died about ten years ago from a self-inflicted gunshot wound to the head."

"That had to be tough."

"I never picked up on how depressed he was after losing my mother and then my brother. He always seemed so strong. I thought it was hardest on me."

Jake held her gaze and it seemed for a moment like he might go on but then he changed the subject. "I don't mind if you crawl over me. I'm used to the kids jumping into our bed at night. Just depends on where you land," Jake said.

"Ha, ha. You're a laugh a minute. I'll take the door." They heard shouting from a nearby party. Susan muttered, "Shit, I'll never sleep if this party goes all night."

"You know what?" Jake asked, leaning back and looking out the door. "It's been a long day and we're both beat. But the heat is clearly not your thing and it's only going to be hotter tomorrow. So let's be nocturnal. What do you say?"

Susan looked at her watch and sighed. "Okay. Why the hell not? If you can't beat 'em, might as well join 'em. It's not that late. I'll work up a second wind."

"That's more like it, partner. Let's do the sociable thing and join in the madness," Jake said.

Susan said, "Just give me twenty minutes. I need to finish setting things up here and then try to find a landline to call Amy."

"You got it. I'll use the time to get our cooking gear out of the car."

Susan took her pistol out of her duffel and handed it to Jake wrapped in a t-shirt. "There's no way to hide our weapons on us, so I guess we go unarmed. Lock this in the car, okay?"

Jake crawled out of the tent, stood, and took in the scene around him. The Howl was a carnival of light and motion; firelight, lantern light and headlights glowed from a thousand small camps. Music filled the amphitheater and people were dancing everywhere. Mimes and jugglers performed throughout the compound. Beach balls arched above the crowd as they were randomly batted from campsite to campsite. Jake's heart rate rose and the edginess that signaled an impending adventure started to bubble in his gut. He was anxious to get started. Maybe they would run into someone who knew Skutches and learn something useful. Three women in yellow and black butterfly body paint revealing bare breasts glided by and waved at Jake. Maybe they could have some fun while learning something useful, Jake thought. What the hell, it's The Howl.

Susan and Jake wandered down a makeshift avenue. It seemed like every campsite was having a party. After about two "blocks" they stumbled onto a shared open area. A small fire burned in the middle and several picnic tables had been set out around it in the sand. The sweet odor of weed grew stronger. The wandering electric guitar player performed on the other side of the fire for three retro-hippies, two male and one female. The two men had the stoner giggles over something that had just been said. Jake noticed some margarita mix, several Mexican beer cans, and a half-empty bottle of tequila at the end of the table. Perfect, he thought, as they were waved over by the large, busty, redheaded woman who introduced herself as Sara.

The guitar man's name was Steve and his friends were true throwbacks; except for the gray in their hair, bellies, and the roadmap faces—they were vintage sixties. Sara was in a short, loose, tie-dye dress and bare feet. One man, short and muscular, wore knee-high fringed leather boots and jeans, but no shirt. The other wore several leather and shell necklaces and a pair of cut-off jeans pinched tight under his hairy gut. They were working a joint around the table. Jake and Susan politely declined with each pass. Jake downed a couple of margaritas and was pleased to see Susan matching him drink for drink. He noticed a flush in Susan's face and a little more fluidity in her movements.

Steve moved closer to Susan and sat on the picnic table to serenade her. Between songs, he said he was a street performer in San Diego and had just met the other three. Steve said the two men were co-workers in a body shop in San Jose. With each additional drink, it became apparent that they were rivals for Sara's attention. Although she appeared to be doing her best to flirt with them equally, soon their jokes became taunts. Their pokes and pushes became punches and shoves. The palpable tension was escalating verbally and threatened to get ugly. Without speaking, as if they were reading each other's minds, Jake and Susan got up to leave. They thanked Sara for her hospitality, said goodnight to Steve, and walked out of the firelight.

"You boys behave or I'll spank you both," they heard Sara say as they left.

"Ooh, heck. We might have left just a little too soon." Jake said, walking backwards towards the group.

"Now *you* behave. You're working, remember? Let's head over to that circle of tents and vehicles by the wolf structure. Despite being zonked, Steve mentioned seeing a group there that fits the description when he was playing wandering minstrel earlier."

"I gotta say if he played 'Imagine' one more time, I was going to jam that guitar down his throat," Jake said.

"And if he asked me one more time if I wanted to look under his kilt, I woulda said, 'Wow, Steve, sure,' and then jerked him into a knot. Funny how guitarists think they get better with each drink and new song. My husband Keith was like that. Drove me crazy."

Susan was excited to have a possible lead on Skutches' location and was off at a fast clip. Jake trailed behind. They passed several tents, vans, and trailers and got dead-ended at an old school bus parked across the alley. Smoke and the rich aroma of cooking meat filled the air. A skinny, goateed man wearing only a leopard thong tended a grill by the bus.

Jake caught up to Susan as she tried to find a way around the bus. She decided to cut through a darkened campsite complete with a pick-up, a cooking fly, and a tent. Most of the truck was in the moon shadow of the fly. As she came around the back of the pick-up with Jake on her heels, the truck lurched on its springs and she heard a woman's cry. Out of force of habit, she pulled her flashlight from her hip pocket and pointed it at the bed of the truck. She was staring right at the ample and furry white ass of a man mounted on a woman from behind.

"Hey, what the fuck!" the man said.

"Oh, sorry," Susan said, shutting off the light. "Camper bed check."

Susan and Jake stumbled out into the next alley trying to stifle their giggles.

When they got out of earshot of the couple, Jake said, laughing, "'Camper bed check.' That's too funny. Damn. I coulda done without that view. I wonder if there's a sharp increase in pups born nine months after The Howl. Hey, look over there." Jake nodded toward a trailer with an attached awning dripping with multicolored lanterns. There was a gray-hair sitting sketching in a book open in his lap.

"That could be our prof," Jake said. Suddenly, Susan felt surrounded and very small. She and Jake skirted around four people on stilts in clown outfits and entered the light of the camp. Jake said hello and after some small talk asked if the man knew Professor Noah Skutches.

He chuckled. "It was all I could do to complete an undergraduate degree in under eight years. Name's Larry. I teach, all right. But not college. I teach people how to use software." Larry's wife came out of the trailer wiping her hands on a dishtowel. Larry introduced her as Rose.

"Did you hear about the excitement tonight?" Rose asked.

"You mean there was more excitement than all this?" Susan said gesturing with her hand at their surroundings.

"Oh yeah. A young man was riding his mountain bike through the crowd over there by the stage and a 'pirate' knocked him off, jumped on the bike and rode off yelling 'Arrgh!' Cracked two ribs and scratched up the bike owner pretty good."

"Haven't heard if he got it back," Larry said. "This ain't no Woodstock. Watch your possessions and your pretty wife, too."

Jake put his arm around Susan. "Will do, Larry. Thanks for the heads up."

Rose offered coffee but they declined, left arm in arm, and angled closer to the metal frame of the wolf.

One other camp caught their attention, but turned out to be a dead end. Susan grew impatient and insisted they split up to cover more ground. They agreed to meet back at their tent by midnight.

Susan had struck out on her solo search and, after returning to their camp, stretched out on top of her sleeping bag and fell into a light sleep. Around 1:00 a.m., she stirred. A roar of laughter had awakened her. She turned on the lamp and checked her watch. Where the hell was Jake? He was supposed to be back by now. She heard footsteps in the sand near their tent. The door was unzipped and Jake crawled inside.

"It's pretty steamy in here. Looks like you fell asleep." He crawled over her and sat on his bag. "I've been picking up some pretty interesting tidbits of information—had some fun, too. You should've stuck with me. I managed to stumble right into Skutches. I met a guy who fixed a flat for him when the prof first arrived. Guy led me to their camp. You know how it is when people are all having a good time and everyone's guard is down." Jake grinned. He took off his t-shirt and revealed streaks of paint on his chest.

"Whoa, Kemosabe. You did get into it, didn't you? What did you see?"

"I am trying to be very analytical here, officer, and not jump to conclusions. Nothing frivolous about this," he said, smiling down at his chest. "Unfortunately, I saw no sign of Lyn and no dog. There were three tents. One appeared to house the professor. The second holds White Wolf and that tall woman that I'm pretty sure Moody took to be Lyn in Yellowstone. Her name is Jennie. She appears to be the youngest— mid-twenties maybe. Jennie and I really hit it off," he said with a grin, as he slipped off his Birkenstock sandals. "The third tent belonged to a conservative looking couple in their thirties. They introduced themselves as Elizabeth and Edward. White Wolf busted their chops for their formality and called them 'Betty and Eddie.' Based on their jabber, I got the impression they handle technology for Lifewater activities. No mention of Fernando's death and no sign of his partner, Don. I bet he has left the group. At one point, White Wolf went over to Lyn's car and got out a bottle of wine. He treated the car as if it was his own. I even sat on the hood. Everything was so cool, normal, except ... no Lyn."

Concern rose in Susan's voice. "What do you make of it?"

"I honestly don't know. The car thing may not mean much. Kids loan their possessions to each other all the time. We'll know soon." Jake pulled his shirt over his head, lay back on his sleeping bag and started to pull down his shorts.

"Umm ... I think I should ... step outside for a minute, Jake, this is a little more than I bargained for and ..."

"Susan. It's a million degrees in here and we're married. Get real. Just take off your clothes and lie down."

"No, I don't think so."

"Your call." Jake pulled off his shorts. Susan tried to look away. Beautiful bod top-to-bottom, she thought. He slid the shorts over his ankles and lay down in his blue boxers.

"Hmm ... real nice. But all kidding aside there's married and then there's married. I'm not undressing with you in here." Susan sat upright and cross-legged. Her hair fell down from its makeshift ponytail and she shook it away from her neck. "I'm so friggin' hot," she said, lifting her hair.

Jake sat up. "When my boys complain of the heat, I blow on their necks."

"All Amy wants when she is hot is a cool cloth on her face." She reached into her duffel and rooted around for a clean red bandana, opened her water bottle and splashed water on it. She touched it first to her forehead and then to Jake's. She slowly sponged his face. Cool drops splashed on his thighs. Susan tucked the damp bandana down the front of her shirt. Jake scooted over to blow on her neck. She pulled back.

"Okay, that's enough, I think. We have to focus on business—need to get some sleep, if possible. Now, get out of here while I change."

Jake smiled innocently, and crawled out of the tent.

June 13
Tuesday

The new day was brilliant, sparkling and silver, and Lou awoke to the sound of waves slapping rapidly against the hull. But something was amiss; the stern was banging around. She grabbed her walker, went on deck, and almost lost her balance at the sight before her. Her boat's stern had been untethered from the dock and the bumpers had been tossed on board. She jarred at the sight of a pale fleshy thing on the deck.

She worked her way over for a closer look. A plucked goose, the kind from Chinese markets, lay on the deck strung noose-like to the traveler. A note was taped to its beak. It read:

"To the Messenger –
Stay with the flock and fly low over the water.
Break away to soar up only at your peril."

She nodded. PEA was very vigilant and very fast. It had taken them just hours to exert discipline. This, she knew in her heart, spelled the end of their trust in her and the end of her usefulness to them. She knew she had violated the code, but this hurt. It felt like losing an entire family. Well, like sacrificing one family for the other, her flesh and blood, Lyn.

She called her deckhand, Hap, and to his delight, gave him the week off. She forced herself to pack and made her way over to the salmon trawler. She'd tell the boys what happened with the goose without filling them in on who did it. She'd say she was going up the coast to relax. She found them having coffee down below. They came up on deck to save her unnecessary exertion.

"Louise, you're a force. But you're crazy to drive by yourself in your con ... after what just happened, even over to Gibsons. Why don't you let one of us go over with you, or follow you?" Doug said, handing her a coffee. "Whoever the assholes are who did this might trail you."

"Guys, no way. You're sweet just to look out for my Minerva. I'm at my best when in motion. Love the road, plus, I never travel without my shotgun. I'll be fine."

"Still, I just hate to see women alone on the highway ... Shit, if you only knew what I've seen."

"Read my thin old lips. You are dears but no way. I love your neighborliness, boys. Arrivederci. Remember to mow the grass and shovel the snow."

They laughed and, after insisting she eat the last doughnut in the box, sent her off.

She loved her old Dodge van for its clunky spaciousness. It was from the pre-minivan era, replete with Lazy-Boy type captain's chairs, a wooden console with cup holders, a large compartment for maps, and a wide deep dash housing enough storage in the glove compartment for all her old tapes. She'd renovated the back so her equipment, a small stove, and her cot could fit in easily with the third captain's chair. She'd even built in a locked gun box. The van was another little self-contained world where her needs were met with ease. Louise sagged into the driver's seat; she was ready to roll.

As she crested the hill of Granville Street, the sun hit the peak of Mount Baker and pointed her toward the chess game.

Susan was up with the gray-blue of dawn after a sleepless night in the tent. She scanned the camp as she brushed her hair and put it up in a ponytail, then grabbed a plastic container off the picnic table and walked past several still quiet campsites to the porta-potty and water truck area.

There was no sign of anyone from Skutches' group, but she did notice a bulletin board advertising the first day's events. They included lectures as diverse as channeling ("The Broad Band that is You!") and self-employment ("Sick of Working for the Man?"). A large black-and-white poster advertised a special evening program of Blues by Wild Child Butler and The Howlin' Wolf Band, with Sleepy La Beef. She noticed a session featuring the Virgin River Dam Protest was listed for 10:00 a.m. and Dr. Noah Skutches and Forrest White Wolf were advertised as the speakers.

After Jake's report last night, Susan was pretty certain that Lyn was not with Skutches and was nowhere near The Howl. Soon, she would know for sure. She filled her container, stood on the bumper of the water truck and, under the pretence of stretching, tried to spot Lyn Burke's car where Jake said it was parked among the hundreds of campsites sprawled across the chaotic compound. No luck. She squinted up at the sky as the sun rose over the rim of the rock bowl that contained the camp. The desert heat was already turning mean. The sky was a kiln-fired, ceramic-glaze blue, unmarred by a single cloud. Campers were beginning to stir. Susan could smell wood smoke and bacon frying.

"Nice morning." Susan jumped at the sound of a male voice behind her. It was Moody.

"Oh ... yes, very nice. But it's going to be a scorcher," Susan said.

He reached out his hand. "Name's Rank Moody."

Susan took his hand and felt a stiff piece of paper scrape her palm. "Susan Br ... Goddard, nice to meet you."

"Same here. Enjoy the festival." His eyes darted around the camp. "There's certainly no shortage of characters here."

"Characters, for sure," she said. "Characters everywhere."

As Susan hurried back through the campsites to the car, she passed people in various stages of dress, applying face and body paint and donning colorful costumes. A small-breasted woman in a thong sat under a blue tarp by a brown beater van, blowing up skinny balloons. Her better-endowed companion, wearing nothing but green body paint and a cowgirl hat, sat in a canvas director's chair drawing yellow flower petals that radiated out from her pierced nipples.

At their tent, Susan kneeled, reached in through the door, shook Jake's foot and whispered, "Jake … Jake, for God's sake, how can you stand this oven? Get up. I have a message from Moody."

Jake was lying on his stomach. He mumbled into his pillow, "What … from Moody … already? Whazit say?"

She unfolded the note. "Oh God, this is lame. Ha. It says we should attend the Virgin River Speech at 10:00 a.m. and meet him outside the entrance gate at 10:00 p.m." She looked up in disgust.

"That's it? That's my two hundred plus bucks worth?" Jake rolled over and sat up. "You've got to be kidding." He got to his knees slowly, rubbed his head and face. "Guess we're pretty much on our own here. Why would I expect better from Rank?" He pulled on some shorts and crawled outside.

He stood at the mouth of the tent beside Susan and stretched up on his toes. As a young couple, still in pjs, walked by on their way to the water trucks, Jake waved with one hand and wrapped his other arm around Susan, forcing her head onto his shoulder.

Jake said, "That looks more like a wife. Let's get some breakfast and prepare for that speech." He patted her on the butt.

Susan pressed her lips to his ear, whispered, "Fuck you, darling," and hip checked him.

"Whoa, testy before coffee," Jake said grabbing her arms. "What if I tripped you and you fell into that sagebrush?"

"I'd push you down in that cactus patch over there."

"Ouch," Jake said. "I keep forgetting I'm dealing with a rogue cop."

Susan and Jake waited for the program to begin. They stood fifty feet from the stage, sweltering in the crosshairs of the sun. As the crowd grew around them, Susan spotted Rank Moody, presumably trying to be incognito in tattered orange ski goggles, lurking on the fringe in the shade of a Fruit Smoothie tent. She looked over the crowd and was relieved to see many people in normal clothes. Her now dingy white blouse and jeans were not so out of place: they were just hot.

She stood behind Jake, noticed his tan and muscular legs below his running shorts and regretted not wearing her new shorts. Jake's ball cap had become as familiar as the blue of his eyes. Susan longed for a hat like Jake's to protect her eyes from the glare. She made a mental note to buy a Howl hat for herself and a t-shirt for Amy. Jake gestured over his shoulder to Susan as the people he had met at the Skutches camp approached.

By 10:00 a.m., a large and very colorful crowd pressed in around the stage, empty but for a lectern center stage. Skutches and White Wolf sat shaded by a tarp at the rear of the podium. White Wolf wore denim and a white cowboy hat. The Professor's outfit said safari. Both men wore dark glasses. Skutches sat slumped motionless, studying his notes on his lap, while White Wolf sat with his legs spread, glancing around the crowd and up at the high rocks behind the amphitheater. He chomped on a big wad of gum. His right leg bounced up and down at the knee.

Soon the couple Jake identified as Betty and Eddie scurried back and forth across the stage, looking very official in their khaki cargo shorts and matching Lifewater polo shirts. They wore headsets and appeared to be in communication with the audio technicians. Eddie approached White Wolf and Skutches and outfitted them with lavaliere microphones. Jennie perched on the front edge of the stage in a red bikini top and cutoff jean shorts. She had her hair pulled through the back of a Lifewater ball cap, a camera around her neck and a clipboard cradled in her lap.

Susan leaned up to Jake and whispered, "That girl you called Jennie is the woman in the pictures Moody shot in Yellowstone."

"Yup, and she and White Wolf are the bozos who almost hit us in Winston, but if either of them recognized me, they didn't let on last night."

Jake scanned the crowd. "What a bizarre scene this is."

Betty, Eddie, and Jennie were busy enlisting new volunteers to help recruit protesters after the speech. Eddie huddled up with a tall white man who wore a standard summer Federal Express uniform, but he had duct taped over half of the Fed Ex logo and it read, "Fed Up!" Jennie spoke with a short Hispanic woman who wore a thin strap t-shirt, a tutu, and no bra. Betty worked her way through the crowd and settled on a pale young African-American in a jester outfit, dreadlocks sprouting out from under his hat. While she was speaking to him, she was approached by a muscular young white man, dressed appropriately for The Howl in a rather skimpy wolf-skin loincloth. His chest and upper arms were covered in tattoos. Eventually all four volunteers were equipped with clipboards and Lifewater hats.

Professor Skutches approached the lectern and introduced himself and Forrest White Wolf. His speech proved dry and professorial. The rock walls muffled his monotone as he droned on about the effects of excessive silt and salinity on riparian areas and the destructive impact on native fish populations and migratory birds when a dammed river cannot follow its normal course of seasonal flooding. His face was mottled and flushed; his voice quavered in the heat and he seemed distracted and exhausted. Tutu yawned audibly near the stage and Fed Up drew circles in the sand with his right big toe. Jennie doodled on her clipboard. Finally, Skutches nodded to White Wolf, and as the young man strode confidently up and stood beside the lectern, the energy in the crowd pulsed upward.

"Does the word virgin mean anything anymore? Can no part of this miraculous gift from our Creator, our natural heritage, remain pristine and unspoiled? Does every single ecosystem have to be gouged and scraped, penetrated and raped, her plants torn out by the roots and animals driven out like my people?" One by one he was capturing the attention of the members of his audience.

"The Virgin River! This beautiful lady flows gracefully through Zion National Park, virtually untouched by human hands and unsullied by pollutants." He paused and removed his aviator glasses. "Now the defilers at Southern Desert Water Authority want to dam her so that the cancerous growth they call Las Vegas can waste her precious water on their unnatural lakes, lawns, golf courses, and casino fountains." White Wolf took two steps to the front of the stage. His voice boomed out over the camp. He had the crowd in the palm of his hand. "The last twenty-five miles of her languorous beauty, before her confluence with the Colorado

River, have already been lost to Lake Mead in what is called the Overton Arm; why must they take more? SDWA, an official department of the Nevada State Government, is acting in conjunction with counties in Arizona and Utah and is proposing not one, but two more dams on the Virgin and East Fork of the Virgin River. The first will spoil the Paiute Wilderness Area in northwest Arizona, the second, Zion Wilderness in Utah. I say damn them! Next week we are going to spoil their gangbang of our Virgin! We are going to disrupt their party. Our protest has been splashed all over the internet, Facebook, and Twitter and has been touted as one that will make Seattle 2000 seem like nothing."

A cheer went up. White Wolf was electric. More people wandered over at the sound of his voice thundering off the red rocks.

"This is where we draw the line in the sand! This is where the damming of rivers stops. These dams are going to have an irreparable impact on the wilderness and we want them stopped." Another cheer.

"The Southern Desert Water Authority, the group responsible for this outrageous crime, is an abomination. Many of the more passionate among us have said, *I am willing to die for this cause.* Thousands are heading to Utah to save the Virgin. Lifewater staffers and volunteers are among you with sign-up sheets that will also be used as petitions. Sign up and 'Save the Virgin'!"

The audience erupted with "Save the Virgin" chants. Enthusiasts thronged around the volunteers with the clipboards. White Wolf slid his dark glasses back on. He extended his hands slowly out over the audience, and then spread his legs in the manner of an evangelical preacher. Jennie beamed at him as a line formed in front of her. Skutches returned to the lectern to signal solidarity, but the moment belonged to White Wolf.

Jake and Susan worked their way forward to Jennie. As they reached the head of the line, she looked up and shouted over the crowd, "I remember you from last night, Chief. Where's your war paint? I don't think you ever mentioned your name."

"We had a good time, didn't we? I'm Jake and this is my wife, Susan. How do we join?"

"Well, sign right here to save the Virgin. There'll be an organizational meeting here in a couple of days. Watch the bulletin board for time and place."

"We will, for sure," Jake said, and signed with a phony last name. As another devotee with thick purple hair muscled her way in front of them, Jake called out, "Did you say your name was Jennie last night?"

"That's right, Jennie." She lifted her camera and pointed it at Skutches. "His assistant. See you soon. Nice to meet you, Susan. Save the Virgin!"

Betty and Eddie beamed at each other, flushed with excitement as the crowd crushed in to sign. Tutu, Fed Up, Jester, and Wolf Man faced lines of recruits fifteen and twenty deep. Jake and Susan turned and began to make their way back out of the crowd. White light flashed at the rear rim of the canyon. Jake and Susan froze. At the same instant, White Wolf wrestled Skutches to the floor of the stage and shielded his body. Rock splintered behind the stage as "pop, pop, pop" rang out from the rim and echoed several times.

"Someone is shooting!" Jennie shrieked and jumped off the stage to roll under the platform.

Jake instinctively pushed Susan down and yelled for everyone else to get down. Susan sprang back up immediately. They ran through the crowd, shoving people to the sand, demanding they drop. Moody, shielded by an RV, pointed to the high rocks. There was chaos in the crowd as some people dove to the ground and curled up and others crawled over them trying to reach shelter.

For a few seconds all was quiet, then Howl security vehicles, lights and sirens on full, rushed out the front gate. White Wolf stood up and dusted off his jeans. He helped Skutches to his feet. The professor immediately hurried off the stage. White Wolf waited until the area in front of the stage was clear and then called for quiet. He cleared his throat several times. There was something about his demeanor that caught Susan's attention. With a slight wheeze, but in a very calm and commanding voice, he told the audience that he thought they were all out of danger. Without hesitation, he attributed the "attempted murder" to the Southern Desert Water Authority and the powers that be in Las Vegas—those who wanted to "rape the Virgin."

"I will not be intimidated or deterred in my passion to save the Virgin River," White Wolf shouted and walked off the side of the stage. Susan followed, shielded by the crowd.

The lines in front of the clipboards swelled with angry converts and howlers huddled in small groups locked in animated discussions. Susan saw Forrest White Wolf pause, slip an inhaler out of his jeans pocket, and take a deep puff.

That night, rumors about the shooting occupied the full attention of the camp. Howl security had found no sign of the shooters, only tracks. The report made the rounds that a vehicle had approached and departed from the outside of the back wall of the rock bowl. Two sets of footprints led up the sand to a vantage point with a clear view of the entire amphitheater. There was nothing else, not even shell casings.

The local sheriff and his deputies were called to the scene and covered the same ground as Howl security. After interrogating over thirty people present at the time the shots were fired, the sheriff had no significant leads and little additional light was shed on the situation. The word was there were no reports of anything unusual on the highways near the festival, just the typical tourist and government vehicles. Most of the people in the crowd had been facing the stage when the shooting occurred and had seen nothing. For the most part, except for a few wild and unsubstantiated claims, requests for witnesses who had observed suspicious activities went unheeded. The sheriff's department vehicles could be been seen departing the area around the time the evening's cocktail parties were cranking up. Shortly after the officials left, the smell of marijuana once again wafted over the camp.

Just before 10:00 p.m., Jake and Susan drove out the gate and saw Moody's car idling beside the dirt road. They followed the green Suburban up behind a small butte a short distance away. The air had cooled a little and the pale night sky was already star-studded and sparkling with anticipation of the arrival of the moon. They parked out of view of the access road.

Rank Moody got out of his car looking the part of the desert rat in olive cargo shorts and a wide-brimmed canvas hat secured under the chin with a cord.

"So, how'd you like our little shooting party today?" Rank said.

"Very interesting sequence of events, if you ask me," Susan said.

"Yeah, it's the sequence that bothers me. I could swear the 'breed' was pushing the prof down before there were any shots fired," Rank said.

"What? Nah, that's not how it went down," Jake said. "I heard the shots and then saw Forrest go for Skutches. Not even White Wolf is macho enough to invite someone to shoot at him to make a point."

"No way, Goddard. It didn't happen that way," Moody said.

Susan said, "Well either way, what bothers me is, after the shots were fired, White Wolf never missed a beat. He came up with a prepared speech and nary a feather ruffled. After being shot at by a high-powered rifle? No way. For once, I agree with Moody."

Moody put his hands on his hips and nodded like a bobble-head doll. "White Wolf reacted before the shot, no doubt about it."

"I disagree. I think you're both jumping to conclusions," Jake said.

"Regardless of whether it was for real or not, this situation is beyond fishy," Susan said. "Some sort of game with lots at stake is being played here. Let's continue to observe the Lifewater folks over the next twenty-four hours and meet back here tomorrow night, same time, okay? And let's use extreme caution where White Wolf is concerned."

"Yeah right, we'll use extreme caution," Moody said sarcastically. "Gee, sounds like something I said about White Wolf in Winston." Before Susan could respond, Moody turned to Jake and poked him on the arm. "Hey, PI, you really earned your money today. You were a hero out there—runnin' around exposed, pushin' people to the ground. You could have gotten killed. I underestimated you. I hope the 'wife's' gonna reward you in that hot little tent." Susan stiffened.

Jake placed a hand on Susan's shoulder and replied, "You only have to be a hero when the situation calls for heroics, Moody." He had not missed Moody's hint regarding payment, however, and reached for his wallet for a second advance while making a mental note to contact Lou Cuvier about involving Moody. "Tell you what." He slapped the bills into Moody's hand. "I'm not even asking you to be a hero tomorrow. Just earn your damn money by telling me something I don't already know." Susan and Jake turned and walked to their car while Moody counted his money.

"I really don't know how much more of this situation or that asshole I can stand," Susan said. Moonlight flowed over the far eastern rim, bathed the rock and washed away the stars. "But I can tell you something you don't know, Jake. I won't even charge you."

"Make my day, partner?"

"Forrest White Wolf is an asthmatic. Saw him suck on an inhaler just after the shooting. No clue if that means anything but maybe he wasn't as coolheaded about the whole incident as he seemed."

"Good work. I didn't know that. And it's got to mean something." Jake stood with his hand on the driver's door and peered across the desert lost in thought. "But what?"

June 14
Wednesday

After another hot sleepless night, Susan spent most of the morning of the second day pacing around the camp trying to restrain herself. Moody had warned her in Winston about accosting White Wolf and Skutches. The thought that it could go very badly for Lyn Burke scared the hell out of her. She fretted over what she would want if it were her daughter. She knew Moody was right and hated that he was. His admonition was the only thing keeping her from marching into Skutches' camp and demanding to know Lyn's whereabouts.

God, she detested having to rely upon Rank Moody. The combination of stifling heat and his relentless garbage was really pissing her off. By mid-morning, when the sheriff returned to continue the investigation of the shooting, it was all she could do to keep from identifying herself as a police officer in need of support. But there was no telling how a small band of redneck cops would respond to her claims. If after twenty-four more hours of this madness there was no conclusive proof that Lyn was safe, she would try to persuade Jake to go to the cops before heading to Ashland Mine with Bev Witt—something that, at this point, she was dying to do.

Jake put together sandwiches for lunch and urged her to drink a quart of orange juice to combat dehydration. "One more day" was her mantra. Jesus, she thought, can I stand one more day in this furnace? She sat down in the sand in the scant shade of the car to drink. The heat, the sand in the food, the constant thirst—all evoked unpleasant memories of her childhood.

It was as if Jake had read her mind. He kneeled behind her and whispered, "Susan, I know this inactivity is driving you crazy. But, I have to tell you … I agree with Moody. It could be a costly mistake to confront White Wolf. He's definitely not what he appears to be. There is something very strange about all this. And I'm not just referring to The Howl. I've thought about it, and you're probably right about the shooting; it was staged, and you don't arrange to have someone shoot at you with a high-powered rifle to make a point unless you're into some serious shit. You said it yourself: where White Wolf is concerned, we need to proceed with extreme caution, for Lyn's sake."

Susan squinted up at him. "I can't decide if we should confront Skutches and White Wolf, go to the sheriff, or just wait this out a little longer—but this heat, and that asshole Moody, are driving me insane. I couldn't reach my daughter last night. I can't think straight. I'm dried up."

"It's frustrating not having cell service and the lines at the payphones are outrageous. Believe me, I'm pretty fed up with Rank's useless bullshit, too. This stalemate is makin' us all a little stir-crazy. So, I've got an idea. I'm beginning to believe Skutches is our best bet. I was lying awake last night and it hit me that Skutches was shaken up by the shooting. Like you said, Skutches didn't appear to know when it was coming—White Wolf did."

The orange juice and shade were helping Susan to feel a little better. "What are you thinking?"

"We have to find a way to speak with Skutches privately and, based on his stellar reputation, I think you're the key."

"Me? Why me?"

"Skutches is a fifth wheel in that cozy little group. The other night when I was in their camp, he seemed sullen and distant. I got the impression Forrest White Wolf had taken Jennie away from him. Based on what Hunter said about him, I'd guess Dr. Skutches needs an attractive female companion fawning all over him and telling him how impressive his data is."

"You can't be serious. Skutches likes young women and I haven't had a shower since we arrived, and…"

Jake put his hand on her shoulder. "You look great. I'm going to rig my solar shower and a tarp for a little privacy and …" Susan started to interrupt. "No, no arguments—go for a short run while I get you hooked up. Take a shower and put on some fresh clothes. You'll feel better. Later you make yourself up a bit and go flirt with the good professor. We have to lure him away from the group so we can question him about Lyn Burke."

"But you told Jennie we were married. Why come on to Skutches, if I'm here with my husband?"

"Hell, it's The Howl! A married woman flirting, especially with her clothes on, is nothing."

Jake was right. The run, the shower, clean hair, and clean clothing lifted Susan's spirits. The aqua tank top and brown hiking shorts she had hastily purchased in Salt Lake were a little tight, but considering her assignment, she decided that was a good thing. She began to view Jake's idea more favorably and felt that doing something, really anything, might help her frame of mind. Maybe Jake knew that. His perceptiveness about people was quite remarkable, she thought, a great asset in his line of work, and, no doubt, at the poker table.

The plan was for Susan to loiter where everyone had to go eventually: the porta-potties and water trucks. She'd approach Skutches, tell him how much she loved his presentation, and get to know him as well as possible in that brief encounter. Then she would invite him to come to their camp after dinner for a glass of wine. After one drink, Jake would make an excuse, leave, and join Moody outside the compound. If all went according to plan, she was going to invite Skutches to go for a drive away from camp to look at the moon. She'd take him behind the large rock where she and Jake had met Moody. Rank and Jake would then meet, greet, and interrogate.

Noah Skutches turned out to be a fairly easy catch for Susan and all went according to plan. Susan could tell his hopes for full body contact were dashed when she drove him around the rock and Jake and Moody were leaning against the green Suburban. Jake opened the professor's door. He got out wide-eyed and wary.

"What's this all about?" Skutches demanded. "We were just planning to look at the moon." Glaring at Rank, "I know you, you're Rank Moody—Sage Use. What do you want?"

Jake spoke first. "Professor Skutches, my real name is Jake Goddard. The other night when I was at your camp, I failed to mention we spoke on the phone once in Jackson Hole. This is Susan Brand. Susan is not my wife; she's a police officer in Jackson, and an associate. We are searching for Lyn Burke. I was hired by Louise Cuvier, who you know."

"Louise Cu … Lyn Burke? Has something happened to Lyn Burke?" Skutches asked.

"That's exactly what we wanted to ask you. Where is Lyn?" Susan asked.

Skutches removed his sweat-rimmed safari hat and smoothed his white hair. He looked first at Jake and then at Susan but avoided Moody's stare. "She's … she's acting as a front person for the Virgin River protest. We sent her ahead to research and photograph the remote wilderness and archeological values of the Virgin River drainages."

"When's the last time you heard from her?" Jake asked.

"I … Forrest White Wolf coordinated the trip—her field work is in a virtually inaccessible area and they will be out of contact most of the time—except there was one planned re-supply at the road-head. White Wolf reported Lyn was fine then, so …"

"Have you ever spoken to her since she left Jackson?" Moody demanded.

"No, I … now look, I will not be harassed by you, of all people. I have done nothing wrong here and I don't have to answer your questions. All I want is a successful and peaceful," he shot a look at Rank, "protest of the Virgin River Dam project and I'm certain that is not in your group's best interest, Mr. Moody."

Susan intervened. "Dr. Skutches, this is not about any environmental issue. Put yourself in Florence Burke's shoes. That poor mother hasn't heard from her daughter in almost three weeks, which just doesn't happen with Lyn. Plus, we are watching a suspicious man drive around in her car with another woman." Susan pushed a strand of hair behind her ear and continued to press. "Not to mention that Lyn was called to replace a young man who died violently. We need to know she isn't in danger and apparently you can't say for certain she isn't. If something bad has happened to that young woman, it will end your career." The professor looked startled, but he did not respond to Susan.

Jake explained what they had observed about the odd sequence of events around the shooting and finally got a reaction.

"So you think the shooting was staged and Forrest White Wolf was involved?" The professor looked off toward the horizon and gave his beard a few anxious tugs. "I don't know anything about any member of my group being in any danger. I have no idea if what you say about the shooting is true. I ... it just seems so outrageous and to what end would Forrest arrange to have us shot at?" He paused and stared at Jake and then at Susan. They waited.

The professor continued, "Forrest has been a good Lifewater member, far from perfect but certainly solid—an excellent recruiter." He stopped again, was lost in thought for a few moments, and inhaled audibly. "Look, Forrest has gone down to Las Vegas to try to raise money and do local news spots about the Virgin River protest. He's due back in a few days. I'll agree to one thing and one thing only. I'll try to pin him down about the location and condition of Ms. Burke and come by your camp when I have some information." He glared at Rank Moody. "But if this turns out to be just another Sage Use ploy—"

"I feel the same way as you about environmental issues, Dr. Skutches. Mr. Moody is involved only because I'm paying for his services." Moody flinched. Jake continued. "We have no hidden agendas. We're trying to find Lyn Burke for your old friend Louise Cuvier and her sister, Lyn's mother."

"And you must not discuss this conversation with White Wolf," Susan said. "If there is something shady going on, you are in danger yourself. You have no choice but to trust us. Like I said, we just want to be certain Lyn Burke is fine and that no one, you included, is harmed."

Jake took Moody aside and whispered, "How the fuck did White Wolf get by you without you seeing him go?" Moody shook his head. "I need you to stay out here, Moody, and make sure Skutches—in case he isn't being straight with us—doesn't try to run to Vegas to alert White Wolf. Can you handle that simple assignment?"

"How late do you want me to stay out here? It's already been a damn long day."

"Just until midnight. You owe me that after screwing up. I'll try to keep an eye on Skutches' camp from inside, but we can't let him sneak out."

"Okay, but I probably ought to charge you overtime."

"Give me a break. I'm getting low on cash and I haven't been able to reach Cuvier. Now keep an eye on the damn road until we're sure Skutches has settled down for the night."

Jake rejoined Susan and the professor and informed them he planned to walk back to camp.

Susan drove Skutches in silence back to the chaos of the compound and stopped at the concession area to let him out. She said, "Once again, Professor, I have to warn you to be very careful around Forrest White Wolf." He nodded and got out.

After parking by their tent, Susan opened the car door to let in some air, took a deep breath, and blinked her eyes to try and moisten them. She heard the sand crunch behind her and a hand touched her bare arm, turning her.

"Hey, Jake, I..." It was a stranger. "Who are you?" Susan asked.

A stocky woman with cropped gray hair and large silver hoop earrings sat in a wheelchair smiling at her. "Hey gorgeous, I'm Lou Cuvier—Lyn Burke's aunt. You must be Susan Brand."

Susan stared at the woman in disbelief. How can this case get any weirder? she thought.

June 15
Thursday

Susan dabbed at her forehead with a dampened bandana and squinted up at another cloudless sky. Jake was at the tankers getting water. She banged around the campsite preparing to cook breakfast, fuming at how unresponsive he had been in the tent last night when she expressed her concerns about Lou Cuvier. Client or not, in Susan's opinion Cuvier was a huge liability and impediment to their search. First, against Susan's better judgment, Jake had insisted on involving Moody; what good had that done? Now this aging hippy appeared to be joining their motley investigative team. And the damn heat … At least the thought of leaving in a few hours with Bev to case Ashland Mine provided some relief. She wanted two things with all her being—to find one child and return to her own.

Susan heard Lou cough and turn in her bunk, causing the van to shift slightly. Soon smoke billowed out the driver-side window. Jake returned and, just as he heaved two large water jugs onto the picnic table, Lou opened the driver's door and swung her heavy legs to a low stool. She was dressed in an extra large pink t-shirt that read, "Vancouver Harbor Tours" and knee-length khaki shorts. She crammed a tattered broad-brimmed straw hat on her head.

"To paraphrase my favorite, deceased, monkey-wrenching, desert-rat author," she said, taking in the azure sky. "Looks like another crappy day in paradise. May he desiccate in peace."

Lou's appearance surprised Jake. Her condition was much worse than he imagined from her emails. Her hair was thinning and she needed a walker as soon as she got out of the car. The weight brought on by middle age and immobility made her shapeless, and her voice was coarse and deep from smoking. Her one youthful touch was flamboyant jewelry; several silver hoops and feathered dream-catchers dangled to her shoulders. Her eyes, glacial pool blue, flashed with intelligence and humor.

Jake sank into a folding chair hidden from public view by his car, and began cleaning and reassembling his revolver. Lou shuffled over.

"You're quite the G-man, eh big guy, or maybe a real regular cowboy?"

He smiled and said, "Have gun, will travel, ma'am. I'm at your service. Sand is a bitch on artillery. Sorry we didn't get a chance to talk more last night. You turned in early." He returned to his task.

When she couldn't get more of a rise out of Jake, she worked her way back to the rear of her van, grunted down into her wheelchair and turned to Susan. "How do ya get a freakin' cuppa coffee around this paradise?"

Susan stood up at the mouth of the tent and put her hands on her hips as if to respond, thought better of it and went to the camp stove. "How do you take it, Ms. Cuvier?"

"Call me Lou and make it black, two sugars to keep me sweet, honey." Susan brought her a cup and went back to the tent without speaking. "Somebody want to explain to me what you two are doing sharing a tent?" Lou asked, then smiled into Susan's face as she went past carrying her duffle to the car.

"We're undercover—married," Jake whispered.

"Looks like you are more 'under covers,' than undercover." Lou grabbed Susan's arm as she walked back to the tent. "So, you're the cop Florence told me about. What the hell are you doing in the middle of this mess out here in Dante's Inferno?"

Susan kept her voice even, "Like I told you last night, I'm trying to find your niece, Ms. Cuvier. But fortunately, these are my last few hours here for a while. Sorry to have to go so soon after you arrived. If we had known you were coming—"

Jake interrupted, "Look, we are all here for the same reason, and we need to work together. Lou, you said last night you had information that could help us."

"I did? Oh yeah, right, I did. That's my boy. Cut to the chase. That's what I'm payin' you for. I do have information, but, goddamnit, let me get another cup of coffee and some more nicotine in me first." She tapped an unfiltered cigarette out of a pack.

Sitting in the shade of the van and sipping her second cup of coffee, Lou told of her close link to the radical environmental group, Planet Earth Alliance. Susan paused while packing her remaining belongings in Jake's car, listened, smiled, and said, "I'm certain you and our other amigo, Mr. Rank Moody, who's camped near the entrance, will have lots to talk about."

Jake shot Susan a look. "Uh, actually, I've been trying to reach you, Lou, to discuss my deal with Moody. I took the liberty to hire him to assist us on the case. He's an expert on eco groups and a veteran 'howler.' Been coming for years," Jake said.

"No problem, we can handle it later. Look forward to meeting him. It's only money and I don't much need it anymore." Lou coughed twice and rattled on. "I followed Planet Earth's activities in the news and on-line for years and just sort of got caught up in the movement. They are very savvy electronically, and very secretive. FBI has never penetrated them except for the occasional low-level scapegoat. PEA noticed my interest in them and gently reeled me in over time. I have never laid eyes on any of them. Don't know their names or anything about them. That used to bug me, now I respect it. It's one of the reasons they never get caught. My only connection was the internet. I was called upon, through encrypted emails from unidentified members, to use my communication skills in support of their actions. I accepted several assignments relaying messages to the media. It's been a helluva ride but I'm afraid it's over because I overstepped my bounds, electronically speaking, and received a severe warning from them in the form of a dead goose, but that's another story," Lou said.

"Did it ever bother you that you were condoning illegal activity?" Susan asked.

"Nope, the cause is just. I never gave it a thought. Otherwise, I'm just your everyday law-abiding citizen."

"Yeah, right," Susan muttered under her breath. She was ready to go. She slid into Jake's car, left the passenger door open and laid her head against the headrest. Lou pushed herself upright in her chair to respond, but before she could, Susan interjected, "Sorry, Lou, but I'm going to have to hear the rest of your story later. It's time for me to get out of this frying pan." Susan sat up, nodded at Jake and pointed to her watch.

Jake went to the tent to dig out his car keys.

Jake and Susan met Beverly Witt at nearby Cave Lake State Park, where he had spent the night in his truck. Jake thumped the big man on the back and told him to travel safe. Bev and Susan said goodbye to Jake and lumbered out of the parking lot.

Beverly Witt was in fine form driving his big rig through the desert with an attractive woman in the passenger's seat. He'd memorized every country song on the radio, claiming while crooning they were all about his life. He knew a thousand off-color jokes, many of which, to Susan's feigned dismay, involved boobs or blondes. Bev glowed. He confided that he had always felt the most at home behind the "19th wheel of an 18-wheeler."

The hours passed quickly. Susan filled him in on all that had transpired in the case since they had seen him. She completed her briefing and said, "This trip is only for reconnaissance, Bev. It should be an easy in and out."

"My experience, even the old easy in and out can get complicated, but I'm ready for whatever, as long as I've got my pretty side-kick … uh, excuse me, ma'am … boss." He beamed at her.

Except for one of Bev's country CDs playing softly, they drove in silence for a while and Susan dozed. Around 11:30 a.m., when she awoke and stretched, Bev popped the top off a cooler on the console and offered to share his lunch. "I always pack enough for company," he said chuckling. "Lots of company."

"Thanks. It all looks cold and delicious." She spread her fingers in the air currents emanating from the dash. "Your air-conditioning feels great," Susan said, holding her hair away from the sides of her head and then pushing the strands behind her ears.

The terrain rolled on in creosote-covered hardpan, cracked by the occasional dry streambed. Lavender mountains lined the horizon in serrated tiers. They polished off several turkey sandwiches and a bag of chips and a bottle of water each. Soon after eating, they saw signs indicating they were getting closer to Las Vegas.

"The weird thing about this country," Susan said, "no matter how long you drive, the mountains never seem any closer."

"It's true. They're always far away," he said. "This mind blowing country is the only thing that could ever make me believe in magic, or in God."

"Why in magic?"

"How else to explain nature's sleight-of-hand? Mountains that float on the horizon and never get closer, mirages, miraculous water holes, out-of-body experiences."

"In God?"

"Oh, I don't know, not because of the beauty. It's marginal, at best. I guess because of the size, the sameness. It's very spiritual. Strikes me that God might've had the foresight and the sense of humor to set aside a chunk of arid ground with no other purpose than to serve as a reminder that man can't find a use for, or a reason to fight over, every speck of creation." His voice quieted as he glanced out his side window. "Maybe this is what heaven is like—a place of desolate beauty that everyone ignores while on earth. Now that would be a good joke." He cleared his throat, and began to whistle quietly along with the music.

"It sounds like gospel to me. It's probably no accident Jerusalem looks a lot like this."

"Praise the Lord, the gospel according to Bev. Now that's a good one." He laughed from the belly and then fell silent.

Susan tried to gauge how far she could see across the desert. "The Indians have it right, you know. They believe this country is sacred. I was raised in the desert in a very Christian family. My father founded the

Salvation Army Mission on the rez in southern Arizona. My godparents were full-blooded Tohono O'odham. Like my father, I used to try to convince my Indian friends that the Bible had it right. Now, I believe, we were both right. Wild land is every bit as sacred as a church."

"Why'd you leave?"

"A dear friend we called Old Ruth was murdered when I was sixteen and my mother died from cancer just a year later. After they were gone there didn't seem to be much point. My younger brother Jack's way of dealing with our Mom's death and our father's religious rigidity was to drink too much, steal stupid shit, and light fires around the reservation. Classic minister's kid. Lord, he got some brutal whippings. He was killed by friendly fire during Desert Storm—ironic. I got real tired of the heat and the incessant preaching and joined the military just after high school." Bev nodded his head without comment.

Susan studied her hands and then looked out the front window. "When I was a kid, my favorite fort was Old Ruth's shed. It was full of dust-covered tools and old horse tack." She shared her memories of slipping through the partially sprung door and climbing around in the shed when she was trying to avoid her father. She said Ruth somehow knew when Susan was hiding in the shed and often invited her onto the porch for lemonade and cookies.

Susan described Ruth's weathered brown face and the fresh air smell of her worn cotton dresses. "She was a Christian. Otherwise, my father would've forbidden me to visit her. She always sent me off with a hug and the words, 'Bless your dear heart, and God love you.'"

"Sounds like a sweet lady." He pointed to a sign for Iron Springs. "We're getting closer to the mine."

"That's great, Bev. I've been curious about it since this whole thing started."

"And I'm curious about your childhood, you desert rat. Tell me more."

"One day in June when I was twelve, I was escaping the stifling heat in the shade of Ruth's shed. I crawled up on a shelf and pulled a broken pane of glass down on my head that sliced open my brow. The blood gushing down my face was more frightening than the pain. Ruth heard me cry out and in no time had me in the house, cleaned up, patched up, and cooled off with glass after glass of lemonade. I remember she burned a tuft of dry wild grass, wafted the smoke over my closed eyes with an eagle feather and told me how brave I was."

"Every kid should have a friend like that," Bev said.

"Yeah ... I was lucky to have her." Susan looked out the side window.

They began to see evidence of civilization—the odd abandoned shack and rusted out truck and then a sign: "Ashland Mine, Gypsum for the New Millennium – 4 miles." As the truck climbed a rise on the two-lane, they got a brief view of Lake Mead then turned down a wide, graded gravel road toward the plant.

"Wow. What a huge jewel of a lake, but I can't believe how low the water is. I haven't been here since I was a kid." Susan turned back to Bev. "What exactly do you expect in terms of the damage from the PEA attack?"

"Not a whole heck of a lot. When I called the plant manager yesterday to confirm this pickup he said the damage was mostly trivial, and the clean-up was almost complete." Bev adjusted the visor on his window. "Of course, it'll be some time before the buildings with graffiti can be repainted. What I hear from my drivers about the décor at Ashland, a little colorful guerilla artwork might just dress things up a bit. The main building was scarred, but not permanently damaged."

"Well, if the cloud of white dust over there is any indication, the mine is working just fine."

"I'm sure that cloud's a big part of the reason PEA came calling and left their little love note." They came up on another sign. "Ashland Mine, two miles. You ready, Boss?"

"I'm ready, Bev." She reached across and squeezed his massive forearm.

They drove in tense silence. When they neared the mine, Bev downshifted and said, "Let's do it." Susan felt her heart rate increase. She licked her lips and took a sip from her water bottle as the truck was waved through the security gate. Directly ahead sat a low landscaped office building, white clapboard with a circular drive in front, leading around the side to a parking lot. Otherwise, Ashland was a mosaic of metal, rock, sand, and dust—fine dust blowing everywhere and covering everything. The main plant buildings and piles of tailings were clustered behind the office complex. Susan noticed large sprinklers all around the site that were used to control dust and remembered Jake's comment about the excessive use of water. Ore cars sat on a spur of track. A crew operating massive yellow dozers gouged at a pit at the base of a mountain and filled dump trucks with crystalline material. Water trucks soaked the disturbed earth right behind the dozers.

Bev pulled his truck up to the office door and went inside to handle the paperwork. Susan eased down out of the truck and checked out the immediate area. An American flag snapped in the center of the driveway circle, its ropes clanging on the aluminum pole. There was no one around. She entered the building, ostensibly to find a ladies' room and a Coke machine, but really to snoop. When she pushed through the glass front door, she could see Bev towering over a smaller man wearing thick black-rimmed glasses sitting behind a desk in a windowed office. A hard looking receptionist—all hair, nails, and chewing gum—sent her on down the hall.

Susan emerged from the lavatory and turned into an alcove with a few Formica tables, folding chairs, a microwave, and coffeepot. The Coke machine stood in the corner. A muscular man in jeans, boots, and a white cowboy shirt was bent over, back to Susan, with his hand jammed up the chute.

He stood and, not noticing Susan, kicked at the machine. "Freakin' thing is worse than the slots for stealing your money." He straight-armed the dispenser hard and turned directly into Susan's face. She froze as he brushed by muttering, "Don't waste your money, lady." It was Forrest White Wolf. He showed no sign of recognition.

He swaggered up the hallway, turned into a room, and closed the door. Susan hastily poured coffee into a Styrofoam cup and followed. From outside the door, the voices were muted, but by easing closer to the door-jam, Susan could make out part of what was being said. There was at least one woman in the room. Susan ducked down in front of the door and pretended to be looking for a contact lens.

Planet Earth Alliance was mentioned several times. She caught, "Goddamn radical tree ... should be hung ... terrorists they are," in a man's voice she didn't recognize. He had an accent—Irish, perhaps.

The woman appeared to be running the meeting. Susan heard her say, "Mr. Liam O'Connor … finish the straw … cost be damned." One thing was for certain: White Wolf was not there representing the interests of Lifewater or any other environmental cause.

Susan leaned closer in an attempt to hear more. Suddenly the door swung open and she almost rolled into the room. Coffee spilled down the front of her jeans. In a blur, she saw White Wolf holding the door, a fat florid man in a white business shirt perched on a stool in front of a window, and a stylish middle-aged woman with brown hair, wearing a chartreuse pants suit at the head of the table. A third man, trim with salt and pepper hair and wearing a tropical shirt and linen pants stood at the front of the room. He turned toward a map on the wall and blocked Susan's view of it.

Susan stood awkwardly and put her hand to her eye. "Oh, ah … excuse me, I am very sorry and ah, very embarrassed. I just found a contact I dropped and am looking for the ladies' room." Susan searched from face to face.

The woman was the first to move and the first to speak. Her long designer nails tapping the metal tabletop sounded like rats on a tin roof. "That's all right, honey. The ladies' room is behind you, two doors down on the right, just before the snack room. It has a silhouette of a woman on it. You really can't miss it. Oh, I guess you already did, didn't you, sweetheart?"

"Please forgive me for interrupting." Susan backed out of the room and turned; eyes burned into her back. White Wolf closed the door. She rushed into the ladies' room to catch her breath and mop at the coffee on her jeans.

When she got back to the truck, Bev was waiting for her in the cab.

"Hey, you. Keep spending that much time in the john and I'm gonna start thinking some of those blonde jokes apply," he affected a stage whisper, "cop or no cop."

"Bev, listen to me. I just did something really stupid. There is something very strange going on here. I … I may have blown our cover. Let's get this done and get the hell out of here."

"I'm on it," Bev said, putting the truck in gear.

The loading of the truck went smoothly. Bev sat stolidly behind the wheel while Susan fidgeted in the passenger seat. She wore a suffocating surgical mask Bev had given her to prevent inhalation of dust. They had rolled up the windows and locked the doors. Susan rested one hand on the butt of her pistol, zipped in her duffle bag beside her on the console. As the cloud around the truck cleared, she could see the PEA logo sprayed crudely on the side of the main building. There were a few tall stacks of rubble. Otherwise, the plant was operating as usual.

A green light flashed, indicating the truck was full. Bev pushed out of his door with a grunt and went to strap down the fabric tarp over the load. Susan rocked in her seat and strained to see if anyone was coming toward the truck. Bev seemed to be taking forever.

A sharp rap on the door beside Susan startled her. Through the window she made out the grimy masked face of the operator of the front-end loader that had filled the truck. He pulled down his mask, smiled, and beckoned her to chat. She gestured to the mask and waved her hand in front of her face to signal that she didn't dare open the window. He tried to coerce her one more time with his broadest grin, but she shook her head. He shrugged and stepped down. Sweat ran down the side of her face into her mask. She unzipped her duffle a few inches. Bev Witt squeezed into the cab, announced their mission accomplished, and threw the big truck into gear. It began to jerk forward under the weight of the new load.

The truck rounded the office complex. There was no sign of the four people Susan had interrupted. As they neared the security gate, Susan's heart pounded and her throat closed. Removing her mask brought some relief and the security guard waved them through without any hesitation. Still Susan watched anxiously in the rearview mirror.

"How can security be this lax right after a terrorist attack. If this is heightened alert, they must have all been asleep on shift before," said Bev while chunking into the next gear. "So, what happened in there? Tell me the whole story."

"I saw Forrest White Wolf in the coffee lounge."

"White Wolf is here?"

"Hard to believe. I followed him to a small conference room. They saw me. White Wolf and the three people in the room saw me. He opened the door and I damn near fell at his feet." Susan wiped her face with her hand and pushed her hair behind her ears. "I made up a bullshit story about looking for the john. What if he figured out who I am?"

"Look, when you recognize someone, it is the hardest thing to believe they don't know you. But you told me White Wolf was up on the stage at The Howl. You were a face in the crowd. Now, darling, if you had had less clothing on like the majority of the Howlers, he might have remembered you. Don't worry about it." The big man winked and smiled.

They were a mile or so from the mine, passing through some barren hillocks, when a pop at the rear of the truck forced Bev to jolt to a stop.

"Damn tire must have blown," he said and started to open his door. Susan felt a blast of heat; the sun hammered into the cab.

"Don't go out there. Just drive on the damn thing."

"And ruin an expensive tire that I might be able to repair? No way. Don't be so jumpy, darling. We'll be fine." He reached over and patted her arm, then searched under his seat for a tire iron. Taking something to tap the tread was Bev's habit when he checked tires. He stepped down to the ground, came around the front of the truck, gave Susan the thumbs up, and headed down the passenger side of the trailer. She watched in the rear view mirror as he bent to inspect a tire near the back. Suddenly a heavy object struck Bev hard on the head. "Oh, God, Bev," Susan cried, struggling to get her pistol out of her duffle. The assailant struck again.

Bev reared up like a wounded bear and lashed back with his tire iron, shrieking "You son of a bitch!" The two exchanged several blows. Susan slammed the door open and leaped to the ground. As she raised her pistol, a vise-like hand clamped her throat from behind. Another grabbed her gun hand. She struggled and kicked backwards. She saw a dark figure in a cowboy hat and long black duster at the top of a nearby sandstone hill. The silhouette raised a rifle and aimed through a scope at the two men fighting at the rear of the truck. Susan tried to scream at Bev, but her shout came out as a squeak. Her legs began to weaken and bile burned her throat and mouth. She lashed back with her heel. A grunt told her she had landed a strategic kick, but the grip on her only tightened. A gash from another blow tore across the side of Bev's face. He fought ferociously. His attacker shoved him hard against the truck and pulled away. Bev lunged, but before he could make contact, a bullet pierced his chest and ripped a starburst across his back. The force of the shot pinned the big man back against the truck for a last heartbeat before he slumped to the ground, dead. Another squeak lodged in Susan's garroted throat as she watched the blood pool in the gravel beside the body.

Susan saw Forrest White Wolf drop the bloody pipe, place his hands on his knees, and suck air into his lungs. Susan flailed with her elbows and feet, but her limbs were like flesh stripped of muscle and bone. Her vision blurred. The hills swirled around her. The pistol slipped from her hand.

White Wolf straightened, coughed, and limped over to Susan and her assailant. "Looks like you've got a wild one there, Liam." He picked up her pistol.

Susan's rage tore the hand away from her throat. "You phony fuck, White Wolf! Everyone is on to you!" White Wolf smashed his fist into her temple and strong arms caught her body as it sagged backwards. Just before blacking out, her lips silently formed her daughter's name and her eyes locked on the shooter on the hill now turning to leave. The wind lifted the long coat at the leg, revealing a flash of green.

June 16
Friday

"By the way, I smelled something fishy about all this Virgin River Dam protest hoopla from the beginning and it wasn't from the usual floaters that surround my boat. It has not been trademark 'movement' from the get-go." Lou was on her third cup of coffee. A lit cigarette was balanced within reach on the edge of the picnic table.

"What was it that made you suspicious?" Jake asked. He was washing the last of their breakfast dishes. Between drags on her smoke and sips of coffee, Lou grabbed wet dishes from her wheelchair, toweled them dry, and stacked them on the table.

"Over the years, I've read about hundreds of protests in the planning stages and wished I could march in every one. This one is different—too well packaged, too smooth. It sounded more like the work of an ad agency than some of my good old anarchist buddies." She sipped her coffee, took a final puff, and stubbed out her cigarette in the sand by her chair. "Personally, I think the Virgin River Dam deal is bullshit. The Southern Desert Water Authority has always used it as a threat to get what they want from other water projects. I just haven't figured out why they are going to such extremes to bluff right now. It's almost as if they want to stir up a protest. Could be a diversionary tactic. Ha, that's a pun—water diversion. I don't know."

Two extremely tan and fit women walked by arm-in-arm. They wore saris below, nothing above. Their breasts hardly moved with their motion. They smiled at Jake. Lou grabbed his arm. When he reluctantly glanced down, Lou stared into his face and pointed to her eyes with two fingers.

"Speaking of diversions. Now pay attention!" Lou said, "I'm convinced the real issue is the new water treatment plant and tunnel being built in the Lake Mead National Recreation Area. The greedy bastards feel they need another tunnel—or straw, as they call it—to siphon off the requisite eight hundred gallons per person per day as Vegas grows at a rate of six thousand people per month. I admit those are pre-2008 recession figures but who's counting? Nobody seems to be talking about that new straw. It goes to the bottom of the lake. All the better to lap up the very last drops. Hey, are you listening to me?"

"Lou, you're paying me to observe. Of course I'm listening."

"From what I observe you observing, you ought to be paying me. Where was I? Oh yeah—the new straw. And as if that is not enough ... who am I kidding? With Vegas, there is never enough ... there's SDWA's proposed gazillion billion-dollar pipeline to fragile aquifers up here, the ground water from which flows where? Into the Colorado River! The Colorado River was recently named America's most endangered river by the American Rivers Organization. Did you know it costs one hundred and seventy-four million dollars and exclusive use of four of Boulder Dam's turbines every year to light up that darling of American cities? Lights are Las Vegas' signature and forty million human moths are attracted to them annually. But the water level almost dropped below the freakin' turbines recently. Lights and landscaping—for Christsakes, the reduction of lawns and landscaping alone could reduce the city's draw on Mead by ten percent."

Lou paused to catch her breath while Jake took her cup and refilled it from the pot. She fiddled with the silver bangles on her wrists while waiting and accepted the coffee without comment.

She resumed her lecture. "Excessive use of water and power from an oversubscribed river that is 97% smaller than the Mississippi, in a drought-stricken desert that gets an average of four inches of rain a year and is drier than North Africa." Lou sucked at her coffee cup.

"Interesting aberration brought to you by, who else, but our fellow men, as in, mostly fellow white men—always eager to make an easy buck and damn the collateral damage in making it." She scowled at Jake. He was banging things around, closing down the stove and the camp kitchen. "I've always said, the American Indians are going to have the last laugh around here after everything and everyone else has dried up and blown away. And by the way, I see Forrest White Wolf is here representing Lifewater. Now that's a joke if I ever heard one. I have some history with Forrest, y'know. Oh, yeah, I wouldn't trust White Wolf with month-old bait. He is as slick as they come and two-faced as the Jack of Spades. He will work both sides of the fence if it remotely involves personal gain or notoriety. To paraphrase Marlon Brando, I've seen the other side of his face and it ain't pretty."

"My feelings exactly," Jake said. "We think he staged a very public attempt on his own life on the first day of The Howl, to whip up support for his protest. And White Wolf is the person Skutches has entrusted your niece's welfare to, believe it or not—and is driving her car when he's not getting shot at."

Jake filled Lou in on the events surrounding the Virgin River speech and the shooting. "Too bad they missed. How is the professor? I must say if I wasn't so concerned about Lynnie's safety, I'd really be looking forward to catching up with Doc."

Jake asked, "If, in fact, this Virgin River Dam protest is bogus, do you think there is any chance Skutches is knowingly involved in the deception and your niece's disappearance? He's promoting this protest, and was very vague when pressed about Lyn. He thinks she is in Utah doing Lifewater research in the backcountry."

"Noah is a bit of a charlatan and he isn't the most ethical person you'll ever meet, but I know him very well. If he's promoting a protest of a project that's a sham, then he must be doing it innocently. When can I see him?"

"He promised to try to pin down White Wolf about the shooting and Lyn's location and meet us here with the answers soon," Jake said. "I recommend avoiding him until then."

"And what do we do while we wait, besides howl at the moon, that is?" Lou asked.

"Susan and I were discussing that yesterday morning. With White Wolf out of the picture for a few days and Susan gone to Ashland Mine, you and I could go over to Utah and poke around the Parunuweap Canyon, Misery Creek roadhead. You know, see if the car Lyn was supposedly driven down in gives us any clues. Check out local gas stations and the like for anyone who has seen her. With any luck, I'll find some cell service and check in with Bev and Susan about their visit to Ashland."

"As long as you're not asking me to go backpacking, I'm in. I'd just about do anything to know what's going on with that girl," Lou said.

"I'll tell Moody what we're doing. He ought to be able to handle surveillance here. Can we take your van in case we have to spend the night?"

"Spend the night—together? In the van? That sounds like a proposition. Hmm. First one in a long time. I'll have to give that some serious thought. Okay. Load up. Let's go."

June 17
Saturday

A searing white light awoke Susan, penetrated her eyelids, and forced them shut. Pain registered at the base of her skull, then in her right arm and back, and finally in her face. Gingerly, she palpated a bruise on her cheekbone. It was morning and she was lying on hard ground, a rock wedged under her shoulder blade. Her jeans and blouse were damp and dirty. Her skin was dry and starting to burn. She rolled over and removed the rock, then carefully opened her eyes. A lizard scurried away from her face and hid under a boulder. The dark edge of a departing storm lined the eastern horizon, and the only sound was the soft rumble of distant thunder. She blinked at the sun reflecting off the wet rocks. Two backpacks and a clump of brush partially blocked her view. She hoisted herself up on one arm to squint over them and saw a young woman, sprawled on her stomach. She was dressed in blue nylon wind pants and a brown fleece top. Who is this woman? Susan's mind was not fully connected. Where are we? She crawled to the woman and placed a hand on her back. The woman stirred and moved her head with a groan.

"Are you hurt, miss?" Susan asked.

"No ... no ... just stiff I think," she said, slowly rolling over, sand on her face and in her red hair. "But what about you? Your cheek looks awful."

"Lyn, it's you. I'm so glad to see you ... to see you alive. I'm Susan Brand. I've been looking for you." Her eyes searched the terrain, "But ... I just don't get this, and ..." Recent memory slammed her. "Oh my God, Bev."

Lyn gently touched the purple swelling on Susan's cheek. "I think you're in worse shape than me. Let's try to get you more comfortable. We'll talk later."

The women had spent their first few hours together tending to Susan's injuries as best they could, and getting acquainted with each other. It was mid-afternoon and they sat side-by-side with their backs against a boulder.

"What is the last thing you recall before waking up here?" Susan asked.

"Forcing down some cold macaroni and cheese in the hellhole where I'd been locked up. After that I felt dizzy and that's the last I remember."

They began to register the profound harshness of their surroundings. It was a vast stony wasteland to Lyn. But once Susan could collect herself and look around, she spotted a Joshua tree and was certain it was a sign they were in the Mojave Desert. Given what they could see from its edge, they were on top of a high, sandstone butte. Vegetation was sparse; stunted creosote bushes and cacti dotted the orange soil like so many old scabs. A yucca brandished its dagger-like foliage above them.

The morning storm had soaked their clothing and richly scented the air, but rainwater had filled only the smaller potholes; many larger ones still gaped, begging for more. Heat and exhaustion would prevent any significant movement for the rest of the day. They had to find shelter, drink, and begin to plan. They sat in the sand and dug through their packs. They discovered they had been filled methodically—but by whom and why?

Lyn pulled out a bag of dried fruit and nuts and said, "When we first spoke this morning, you mentioned someone by the name of Bev."

"Oh, Bev ... Beverly Witt was a sweet man who drove me to the mine in his truck to pick up a load of gypsum sludge." She looked hard at Lyn. "Your father's mine. Bev was just a good guy, and I'm responsible for putting him in danger. After we left with the load, Forrest White Wolf jumped Bev. While they fought, a man shot Bev from a nearby hill. Judging by his wound, I think he ... I'm sure he's dead. Someone choked me from behind and White Wolf gave me this." Susan touched her cheek. "That's the last thing I remember."

Lyn looked confused. She grasped handfuls of sand with her fists. Red hair framed her dirt-streaked face. "This happened near my father's mine? I'm so sorry he wasn't there to help you. And you say Forrest White Wolf was involved? That son-of-a-bitch." Her face quivered as she tried to hold back tears. "He's behind all of this and posing as an environmentalist? Son-of-a-bitch." She pounded the sand with her right fist and stared at Susan. "I had my own run-in with White Wolf."

"Tell me about it," Susan said, touching Lyn's arm.

"I ... I can't just yet. All I know is, I've been a prisoner in the bedroom of a cabin ever since my ... encounter ... with White Wolf, and I have no idea where my dog is, or how my family is, or ..." She started to shake. Susan moved closer and put her arm around her. "... Or why we are out here in this ... I just don't know ..." She looked into Susan's eyes and heaved out a sob.

"Shh, shh," Susan said. "It's okay. I've got some answers, I think. I'll tell you about them later on." She held the girl in both arms until Lyn's body quieted. "Do you remember anything that could help us identify any of your captors?"

Lyn shook her head. "I never saw or heard anyone. They used notes to communicate with me, and a dog door, a goddamn dog door, to slide me the worst food I've ever eaten. One of the hands I saw regularly had an ugly insect tattoo on it. That was my only human contact."

Susan suggested they focus for a while on the details of the present and continue to determine what was in their packs. They found some simple dried food, water for a few days, matches, a space blanket each, a good knife, water treatment tablets, a first-aid kit, sleeping bags and pads, sun block, hats, extra fleece, and nylon clothing. Even a little stove and pots. But no compass or maps, and no technology, not even watches. Someone wanted them to survive out here, abandoned.

Susan assessed their situation. Why keep them alive after killing Bev? Why tempt them with the false hope, and why out here? Lyn had been locked in a room for weeks by her kidnappers. What possible motivation did they have now to drug them both and drop them together on this butte?

Hours passed in a swirl of heat and dust as they rested and tended to their needs. In the early evening they found a shelter of rocks to protect them from the ascending wind. Susan was recovering a little and wanted to walk along the rim of the butte before dark and look for an escape route. She dug in her pack and donned a green nylon anorak to cut the wind. She hoped there might be arroyos, cracks, tracks, descending bands of outcrop rock, anything to serve as a way down. Before they got far into their search, the wind abated, but dusk soon closed in and forced them back to camp.

They scraped together a fire of twigs for the comfort of the aroma and dancing light, then lay on their sleeping bags waiting for sleep. The fire crackled and hissed softly.

"Susan, you awake?"

"Yes." Susan rolled up on an elbow.

"I hope there's a moon tonight. The sky is so black ... maybe because I've been cooped up ... but the openness, the vastness ... jeez. Don't you feel ... small and alone out here?"

"We are alone, but as I get to know you, I'm pretty confident we're gonna be fine. We'll be out of this soon."

"You really think so?"

"I'm betting everything on it, Lyn."

"My folks must be frantic by now. I've always kept in touch, no matter where I was." Susan rolled over and threw some more twigs on the fire. The flames flared and the wood smoke drifted toward them. It felt cleansing and reassuring to Susan.

"Like I said, when I spoke to your mom, she was very worried but seemed to be holding up well. And your Aunt Lou is doing all she can somewhere near here, working with Jake Goddard, the private investigator she hired."

"What a relief it was to hear that. You can't put much over on my Aunt Lou. And my dad, have you spoken to my dad?"

"Only indirectly. I ... don't really know anything about your father."

"What do you suppose White Wolf told Professor Skutches?"

"He told Skutches you were working in the Virgin River wilderness."

"Oh, great. Yeah, right. You don't think Dr. Skutches is involved, do you?"

"I can't say, Lyn. Your aunt doesn't think so."

They were quiet for a while. The moon began to peek over the eastern horizon—cold comfort.

"What are you thinking about, Susan?"

Susan sighed and rolled onto her back and threw an arm over her eyes. "To be honest, I'm not thinking very clearly. I feel so sad—and guilty—over Bev, and leaving my little girl, Amy. And I am so angry. I've never felt this angry in my life, even when my husband deserted me. I just can't shake it."

Lyn twisted over on her stomach and turned toward Susan. "I don't know if it helps but, I ... I know that you endured all this ... you risked all this ... for me. I can't begin to thank you."

Lyn started to talk about her ordeal. Everything she had been mulling during her weeks of captivity came out in a rush. She told Susan about being interviewed and hired by White Wolf in Las Vegas to replace Fernando Diaz. White Wolf said he had flown to Vegas for other business there and they decided to drive back to Jackson in her car. He had seemed knowledgeable and cocky, his behavior strange at times, but there had been no hint of the monster he turned out to be.

Lyn mopped at a few tears with her sleeve, sucked in a deep breath, gathered herself, and began to reveal the most painful parts of her recent memories, talking until she could no longer finish her sentences. Eyes on the sky and her hand on Lyn's arm, Susan took it all in.

Lyn remembered it was May 24th because it was just two days away from the fifth anniversary of when she got Mojo. It was mid-afternoon when they had left the interstate at Evanston, Wyoming, for a two-lane that wound back and forth across the Utah-Wyoming-Idaho borders. They passed through several high-valley, ranching communities, their hay fields stretching for miles to distant mountains. Monster irrigation systems rolled across the fields, tossing around snowmelt water. Mojo slept peacefully amid the gear in the back seat.

North of the ranch country, the road traversed a mountain pass and soon they wound through the talus-covered gray cliffs above the boiling white water of Snake River Canyon. By the time they had reached Jackson, the sun was disappearing behind the Tetons. The town was a blur of brightly lit businesses, gas stations, log hotels, and tourist attractions. It was high-mountain chilly. A bank flashed 48 degrees Fahrenheit.

Forrest recommended a place for Lyn to camp called Shadow Mountain in the national forest just beyond the eastern border of Grand Teton National Park. He said it was a little off the beaten track, but pretty and safe. Lyn dropped him off at a small motel on the northern edge of town—no camping for White Wolf two nights before a big media event—and headed out to find her nest for the night. Some of the group had gone ahead and would find her and introduce themselves, Forrest promised.

As she entered the national park, the view of the surrounding mountains left her breathless. She pulled over and gawked like a tourist. For several miles north of Jackson she had watched the eastern range turn to pink, then mauve and soft gray, as darkness seeped into the valley. Now she could also see the Tetons to the west and they were abrupt, commanding, and haloed in indigo. The entire range punched up from the valley floor aggressively. She liked the feeling of being surrounded by the mountains and felt exhilarated, but a little overwhelmed and harried. She didn't linger—she hated trying to find new places in the dark.

The camp hummed with purposeful activity. Tents were pitched at respectful distances from each other in an aspen grove. The trees bordered an open space where a fire burned in the center. Lyn loved the clean meadow smell of the place and the view of the Tetons, now illuminated by moonlight. Mojo loved the camp too, and he roamed from tent to tent, making new friends and accepting any and all treats. People milled about the common area and huddled around the fire, sipped drinks and compared stories.

In addition to Americans, there were lots of Canadians, including many Canadian Indians, a Costa Rican group, and clumps of Australian and New Zealand kids who were up mostly to ski bum, but who traveled the eco-circuit in the summer when they could.

A pretty woman named Jennie appeared at Lyn's side. She wore a gray hooded sweatshirt and jogging pants. She introduced herself as one of Professor Skutches' graduate assistants. She said Noah Skutches and some of the other members of the group were in town meeting the international press that had flooded Jackson Hole.

"This is way cool and I'm very excited, but I feel a little weirded out even being here under the circumstances. How's everyone handling Fernando's death?" Lyn asked.

"This is such an important event, I think it's keeping our minds off of it." Jennie said. "We're all doing pretty well, I guess. Except for Don Stein who was there at the time of the fall."

"Where is Don?" Lyn asked.

"He quit and headed back to Colorado," Jennie said. "He was so sad and none of us knew how to help him. But also he was pissed because nothing was being done about Fernando's death."

"I thought it was an accident."

"That's the official version. Donny is convinced Fernando was pushed." Jennie looked over her shoulder when she heard laughter. "Sorry to cut you short but I've got to get this ragged crew of mountain hippies organized into a protesting machine. Catch up with you later, okay? Glad you're here." Jennie smiled, waved, and walked over to a knot of kids chatting by an old VW camper.

Talk around the camp was focused on the water, the proposed Mackenzie pipeline, damage to habitat, climate change, and NAFTA. It didn't have the generic anti-establishment anger of Seattle, Quebec or Genoa—the sort that makes true environmentalists feel resentful, Lyn thought. This seemed planned, focused, and she felt charged like a solider preparing for battle. But she knew she had to sleep or she would be useless in the morning after two days on the road. Before climbing in her tent she looked at her watch—midnight. Time had flown and once again it was too late to call home.

May 25
Thursday

Lyn overslept and arrived a little late at the motel, but Forrest was cool about it. He offered her strong coffee and a shower. Clearheaded and refreshed, she plopped herself down on an armchair dressed in hiking shorts and a plain white t-shirt and toweled her hair. Forrest perched on the bed shirtless with his legs covered by a sheet, busily reviewing notes for his speech and gesticulating as he practiced sections of it silently.

Lyn looked out the window at the tree-covered mountains. "It was great to sleep near the mountains under the aspens last night. You should have come." White Wolf ignored her. "This country's an ornithologist's dream. Saw a Cooper's hawk nail a robin in mid-flight this morning. I can't wait to get to work on the birds of prey." She bent forward and turned her head from side to side toweling the water out of her hair and then sat up again.

"Mm," Forrest mumbled.

"It was such a whirlwind taking this job. And such bizarre circumstances replacing Fernando. But in just one day I feel better and more relaxed about all this. I met some great, committed people last night."

Forrest looked up at her and smiled. His hair was loose and down around his shoulders. "It's amazing country. Powerful country."

"To tell you the truth, night before last, in Provo, I was not feeling this good. You scared the shit out of me when I came back from my run and found you in my motel room."

"Hey, I was just messing with you. Seeing if you could handle a little stress. Consider it basic training for the protest tomorrow. Don't sweat it. And stop obsessing over Fernando. It's unfortunate, but it's history, okay?"

"Yeah. Newbie nerves, I guess. The whole thing is just freaking me out a little."

"Water over the dam, girl. We got big things coming up tomorrow. The bank president protest is major. Lots of media. Lots of action. You're going to love it."

"Well, yeah, I'm way into water conservation and am pretty steamed about the Mackenzie pipeline issues, but the media stuff is really a sidebar for me. I just want to see this United Global Bank guy realize what forces he's up against." She threw one leg up over the arm of the chair and started to towel off the back of her hair. "Fernando must have really been anticipating this protest. Was he?"

"Goddamnit, there you go again. You talked constantly about Fernando on the way up here from Vegas. I don't mean disrespect, but Fernando is dead. What difference does it make what he thought?"

Lyn looked perplexed. "I'm just concerned about doing a good job in his memory. And, I guess, as a climber myself, a little puzzled about the way he died. I hear his partner Don thought Fernando was murdered. I was thinking I might go out to the place where he fell. Just to look around. Do you think it was an accident?"

Forrest began to shake his head. "Forget about fuckin' Fernando, will you?" He put down his papers and took off his glasses. "Think about this. NBC and ABC are already setting up in front of Peter Dill's house and he thinks he's on vacation. And shit, with this place as a backdrop, it's gonna be beautiful."

White Wolf sprang off the bed as though some kind of switch had been thrown inside him. He wore only black briefs. Even though Lyn was taken aback and a little uncomfortable, she was transfixed by his physicality. The guy had a strong body, thickly muscled back, and narrow hips. He paced back and forth in front of her, and with each pass moved a little closer. He continued, his voice growing louder.

"This is Seattle, but way more cinematic. Way more dramatic. And way more important. I'm sitting real pretty. I'm in a position to stop the work on a goddamn pipeline! I could easily be on the national news tomorrow! God, I can not wait!"

He was virtually shouting now. Arousal seemed to have exploded inside him, and his eyes were flashing. He stopped in front of Lyn, legs akimbo, hands on his hips just above his briefs. Lyn tried to keep her eyes on his, though she could not miss the erection growing under the cloth. She was alarmed to see White Wolf's gaze taking her all in. It moved slowly down her neck to her breasts, her belly, crotch, and thighs. She moved her leg off the arm of the chair and shrunk back. Her heart spiked and she felt pinned in place. Fascinated yet fearful, she knew she was watching him transform himself into a primal force.

He balled up both fists and pummeled his thighs, stomach and chest in quick and startling sequence. Lyn sucked in her breath. Without releasing his gaze, he started backing up around the bed. He continued to punch the air and pound his body. His eyes never leaving Lyn's, White Wolf reached out and patted the bed and said with shortened breath, "Come over here." She sank further back in the chair and frantically began to plan her exit. He crossed back over to her, grabbed her chin roughly, and yanked her face up to his.

"I'm feeling good, darlin'." He pulled her head back by the hair and tried to thrust his tongue into her mouth.

Lyn twisted away and ran for the door, but before she could grab the knob, White Wolf leaped in front of her and blocked the exit. He put his hand gently around her neck and smiled.

"No, no, no. We need to celebrate, get a little more adrenaline flowing."

She pulled her head to one side, but his fingers tightened. He leaned in to kiss her and she clamped her mouth shut.

"You're a monster!" She hissed through her teeth. "Get the fuck away from me. Now!"

Forrest smiled and tightened his grip a little more on her throat, thumb digging into her windpipe. Lyn felt his other hand move under her t-shirt and cup her breast. He mashed it back against her ribcage and pinched her nipple hard, then began to turn her and walk her slowly back toward the bed. In her mind's eye, things fell to slow motion, as she strained to consider her options.

He released Lyn's breast and shot a brutal slap to her face. She stumbled back into the bathroom door and toppled to the floor. She gasped for air, held her throat, and choked out, "You asshole! What the hell kind of animal are you? Let me out of here!"

White Wolf wrenched her up to her feet, spun her around, and clamped her in a bear hug, so that he could avoid being kicked. He steered her toward the bed and threw her down, grabbing both of her arms in one hand as he did so and pulling them behind her. He jammed his knee into her back and pressed his mouth to her ear.

"You may think you have some choices here, lovely Lyn, and you do, but they are limited. And, one choice you don't have is making any more noise. You shut that pretty mouth right now, or you're gonna find it contains a few less teeth." He reached for a backpack by the bed. "I know you've been looking at me. You like what you see. And I'm just as good as I look. Now ... you want me or not?"

Lyn shook her head violently, but said nothing, now silenced by his threats. Tears welled up in her eyes.

"Okay, so you like to watch. That's cool, too. I can dig that."

He hoisted her up and slammed her into a chair facing the bed. White Wolf gagged her with a sock and duct tape, roped her arms behind her, and tied her to the chair. She stopped struggling and tried to think of a way out.

Lyn saw the corner of her tablet-phone in the outside pocket of her pack leaning against the leg of her chair. She wriggled cautiously, edging her hands toward the pocket, but sitting back in the chair made it nearly impossible for her to reach far enough down to grab the device. White Wolf's cold glare sent a shiver through her body. He was an agitated sexual predator trapping and mutilating his prey. She needed to move very subtly and hold his gaze without distracting him. If she could just unlock the phone function, she might be able to call an SOS to her mother.

Minutes were hours in her mind, but she finally pinched the corner between her middle fingers and eased the device out of her pack. She managed to slide the lock on the screen, activate the phone, open a recent voice message from her mother and hit "call back" but the device pinged, startling Forrest out of his rapture. He lunged at Lyn and yanked her bound wrists up behind her, wrenching her shoulders. She yipped and grunted, and spat part of the sock out of her mouth, then shouted, "Damn you!" He pulled the metal stylus out of the tablet's cover and flipped the device out of reach into her pack.

He pointed at her with the pen. "Almost, Lyn sweetie, almost, but nobody's coming ... At least nobody but me and maybe you, if you're lucky."

He sat back on his haunches with one arm propped on the bed, thrusting his erection up and down and breathing heavily. "You're getting off on this, aren't you? Lynnie likes to be tied up and watch. This is going to be one hell of a summer. I'll tell you what I'm going to do. I'm going to stop teasing and pop this cork for you to enjoy." He walked to the chair and locked eyes with Lyn, causing her to turn her head away. Inching closer to the side of the chair and her face and neck, he slowly rocked his hips into his grip. His tempo rose as his strokes increased and finally every muscle in his body tensed, rippling his stomach and forcing his head back. His hair brushed the middle of his back as a spasm shook him and a guttural sound pushed through his pursed lips. His upper body jack-knifed forward and, with glazed eyes, he watched himself finish. After a burst of breath, he shook his head slowly from side to side. "Shit, that was fucking incredible."

Lyn kept her eyes shut, trying not to vomit into the gag at the feel and the smell of him on her skin, praying that she had just heard the end of her torment.

June 17
Saturday Night

L yn was exhausted from dredging up the painful memories but wept in relief at finally having someone she trusted to talk to.

Susan put her arm over her. "I'm so sorry that sleazebag put you through that."

They lay side by side in eerie and elongated moon shadows for some time. Then depleted, they sank just below the surface of consciousness into eddies of disturbed and dream-laden sleep.

June 18
Sunday

Rest brought some composure to Susan the next morning. She and Lyn agreed that exploring for a few hours before the sun got too high, then resting until mid-afternoon, would help them conserve strength. Susan walked out after breakfast and paced along the edge of the butte. Far below, the desert undulated away in waves and washed up against other mesas in the distance. She knelt and sifted the sand, looked at insects, animal signs, and the sparse grasses. Clouds were forming to the west. In part, she was seeking information, but also she was seeking solitude, collecting herself.

After more than half an hour, Susan returned to the camp and plopped down beside her companion. "I think we should try to get off this rock pile and head south. If you look straight south from here you can see the sky change color just a little, I'm guessing from pollution, and you can see the hills diminish. I swear I even see a strip of blue—maybe a lake." She pointed at the horizon to the south. "We might be able to get to Vegas or some town near Vegas if we head that way, or at least Lake Mead if that's what I see. Then maybe we can hook up with my partner, Jake. He's good, Lynnie. If anyone can find us, Jake can."

"I want to believe that but … I can't see how we can begin to get off of here and get help." Lyn slowly turned in a circle looking out at the maze of mesas and valleys stretching away forever. "It has no beginning or end."

"It seems impossible, but there are probably remnants of ancient villages around here. If we could just find some paths, we might be in luck and also find water, especially if we find a trail where Kokopelli has been."

"Coco who? What's that?"

"Lynnie, don't tell me you grew up in Las Vegas and are a scientist and a rock climber and don't know about the Anasazi and Fremont cultures?"

"I guess my studies have been a bit narrow. I mean, I've heard of them sure, but I've mostly been in the mountains studying birds."

"But have you spent much time in the basins?" Susan asked.

"I'd have to admit, I've used the desert more as a gym for climbing day-trips than anything else."

"The desert is about to become your classroom then—for the most important class you ever take. And there will be a test." Susan gave Lyn a penetrating look and began, "Anasazi is Navajo for ancient enemies or ancient ones. Anthropologists call them Ancestral Pueblo people. They think Kokopelli was a wandering musician in the lore of prehistoric Southwestern Indians. He was a little hunchbacked Johnny Appleseed type who was conjured by the villagers to bring rain and to make things grow from seeds. He was sort of a fertility symbol playing a big flute, and frankly, was often depicted with an equally impressive erection." Lyn giggled and her neck and face flushed. "And here's the thing: they painted pictures of him, now called pictographs, on canyon walls or along the sides of the buttes like this one, to guide him on his journey. I often saw him as a child on the reservation. Between Kokopelli and the horse corrals on the reservation, who needed formal sex ed? If we can find his image or other similar signs somewhere, it might prove that we are on a route of some kind."

"A horny musician, I get it. Some things never change," Lyn said. "That's amazing, but are you sure that you're feeling all right? Are you sure you're up for exploring?"

Susan turned to her, smiling slightly. "I'm fine really—still a little dazed. No permanent damage, far as I can tell. Just a few injuries and stiffness from the fight." She delicately touched her hand to her face. "I think walking will work some of it out. Might even help with my frame of mind."

Susan was determined to set a healthy pace. But the butte top was wider than they had thought. Looking across its expanse was deceiving, like estimating distance across water. Although the women knew they must make their way south eventually, they followed the western rim to the north seeking a way off the butte. As they walked, Susan tried to remember landmarks such as large boulders, tall Mojave Yucca, and Joshua trees, but they often had to detour past steep canyons that had not been visible at the outset. By 11:00 a.m., when they stopped, they guessed they had covered only about a mile as the crow flies. And they still had not discovered a reliable exit. They returned to camp to wait out the mid-day heat.

The sound of synthetic new-age music pulsed from the main stage and ricocheted off the walls of the rock amphitheatre of The Howl. Lou sagged in a folding chair, cooling her face with a little battery-powered fan, recovering from the trip to Utah, and working her way through a six-pack. She fixed her gaze on the late afternoon sky and lifted her can. "I'm having one cold beer for every damn cloud I've seen since I arrived in this oven," she grumbled to herself. "The only thing clear around here is the freakin' sky and I'd kill for a rainy day."

Jake sat in the van, headphones on. Lou pushed herself up with a grunt, hobbled over and reached through the front passenger window to yank Jake's earphones off. "How the hell can you just sit there and listen to music? What, isn't 'Yawny,' or whatever the heck that amplified dentist's drill coming from the stage is, good enough for you? I'm worried. Skutches should have come by as soon as we got back!"

"Louise, chill, okay? This is how I think." Jake massaged his right ear. "I've got to piece this all together so it doesn't continue to feel like a maze."

"Well, I'm at my wits' end, that's for sure, and you're not keeping me informed. I'm sick with worry about my niece and have no earthly idea what to do next. All I can do is anesthetize myself." She took a last suck at her beer and burped delicately. "I know my sister is a mess, but now I'm certain she was right, damnit. I could shoot myself for not taking her more seriously when she told me about the voice message—"

Jake sat up in the seat and cut her off. "I haven't thought about that message since I read your early emails. You didn't seem to think it was significant."

"You're right, I didn't, because it was nothing but typical Florence drama, or at least that's what I thought at the time. Now I'm not so sure. It was on the first full day Lyn was supposed to be in Jackson. It was a message for Flo from Lyn but there was nothing, no voice, only background noise. In fact, my sister didn't think anything of it at the time and immediately deleted it. But later, after she hadn't heard from Lyn for a few days, she was suddenly hell-bent that weird call meant Lyn was in trouble. Typical of Florence, she immediately had this gut feeling Stanley was involved, but lately, it's been Stanley's fault when one of Florie's toilet paper rolls runs out, and Stanley doesn't even live there anymore. That's why I warned you about Stanley when I first contacted you, but in my heart I didn't really believe her. She has always been the queen of hysterical hyperbole. Now I could kick myself for not listening to her." She leaned closer to the window. "You're the hotshot PI. Can't we do something better than just sitting here listening to this crap music for Christsakes? Don't you care about my niece?"

"Goddamnit, Lou, that's not fair and you know it." He turned to face her squarely. She backed up. "Susan and I are deep into this. If we didn't care about that girl we sure as hell wouldn't be out here. We're both parents too. Believe me, I feel every minute trickling away like I'm the victim of freakin' Chinese water torture." He puffed out air and shook his head. "It's like this, Lou. It's a poker game. Unless I'm patient, systematic, and totally tuned in, if I fail to review every event and detail, I'll make an error—in this case, possibly a fatal error. Is the phone message important? I can't say for certain. Was it important to remind me about it? Hell, yes."

The band on the stage stopped for a break. There was a sprinkling of applause. Lou looked down as a gust of wind swirled dust around her feet. She nodded slowly. "Okay, I agree. I should have mentioned it and

I'm ... sorry. I know you care. I know you're worried about Lyn and I can see you're worried about Susan and your truck driver friend." She smiled and touched Jake on the shoulder. "That Susan seems like a good woman and a good cop. We snarled at each other a little, but two alphas sniffing around the same territory always do. I admire strength; she can handle herself."

Jake said, "Believe me, I'm just as exasperated as you, sitting around here not having a clue what to do next. Bev and Susan should have been here before you and I got back, and no word—that's way out of character for both of them. If I don't hear from them soon and if we don't hear that Skutches talked with White Wolf, I'm going to the Ashland Mine." He shoved his ball cap back and squeezed his forehead. "I've been going nuts since finally finding a payphone open last night and calling the trucking company. I cannot believe they've heard nothing since confirming with the mine that Bev and a female passenger picked up a load and left on schedule. Bev's dispatcher said she called the state police yesterday, but cops never do much in the first few days of a case involving missing adults. Look at the Jackson PD's initial response to your sister's report about Lyn. They treated it like a joke—except for Susan. Nevada State Police are on the lookout for the truck. That's it. I called the company again today at noon. Nothing new."

Lou shifted a little to keep her face in the shade of the van. "All right, let's try to work this out one more time. Hand me my cigs off the dash, will ya?" He slid out a pack and some matches. She lit up and inhaled deep. "Considering this latest information, or lack of it, and what we learned on our trip to Utah, which wasn't much considering we couldn't even find the coworker's car that Lyn was supposedly driven down in and that was allegedly parked at the trailhead, what's your current best thinking?"

"I wish I were thinking better. For starters, leaving the charger for my phone and iPad here and being unable to check messages while we were out of this shit-hole is just about my biggest fuck-up to date on this case." Jake fanned smoke from Lou's cigarette that had drifted in the window. "Being out of range here at The Howl is driving me crazy. It's like we have all this non-information. What do they call it in the military? 'Disinformation'? That's been the trademark of this case from the beginning, a missing girl whose father says she isn't missing, a wild goose chase with Rank Moody, and no car in Utah where it was reported that the car was parked. Sheriff finding nothing on the shooting here. White Wolf gone and Skutches late. No goddamn cell service here! No way to contact Susan. Plenty of nothing."

Jake got out of the van and started to pace. "Maybe there are legitimate explanations for all of this—maybe for none of it. Everything makes sense and at the same time nothing does."

He stopped and pointed at her van. "It's like that little convex mirror on your rearview." He bent toward the mirror. "You can watch everything that is happening behind you but what you see is really just a distortion of reality, and misinterpreting that information could kill you." He grabbed his jaw. "I look like shit." He straightened and turned to Lou. "But, I see one, or should I say, I smell one thing clearly—White Wolf's little shooting party here and Stanley Burke's bizarre behavior stink rotten. But why? We have just got to figure out why. Jesus!" He climbed back in the van, pulled his cap back down over his eyes, and reached for his headphones.

Later that afternoon, Susan and Lyn continued their exploration. Just as a dry wind was starting to swirl again, Susan found what she thought was a way down. She descended a steep track that began below a series of scrub-brush studded ledges, but turned back after a few minutes. She thought the path continued, but was not sure. They might be able to do it, but not without good concentration and they were tired. Lyn insisted on trying. The wind whipped her nylon pant legs. She moved slowly down the faint trail over precipitous rock slabs, facing into the slope, fingers and toes steadying her as she tried to keep as much of the soles of her running shoes on the rock as possible and descend without falling. But it was too steep and required balance and focus beyond her powers at that moment. The decision to spend another night on the butte was not easy.

Water in the potholes had evaporated and their supplies were getting low. They knew they'd have a tough descent and hike in the morning. On the other hand, another night of healing would be to Susan's advantage; she was aware she had become more tentative later in the day and her pace had slowed.

They returned to their camp, ate, built a fire, and tried to talk the puzzle pieces together some more before sleeping. Coyotes yipped, down where the two women so desperately wanted to go, far below.

The fire had burned to ashes as Lyn told Susan of the last fuzzy details of her abduction—vague and disjointed memories of a car and a plane. Then in silence, they watched the moon rise, and though waning, it looked huge on the horizon.

"I don't think, I … can talk … more tonight. I'm so tired," Lyn said.

"Girl, all I have to say is, you've been through a lot since you arrived in Jackson and you haven't even had a chance to buy a t-shirt." Susan smiled at Lyn and pushed her red hair away from her face. "We have to make sure you really get to see Jackson Hole when we get out of here." Susan stretched and yawned. "Let's go to sleep, huh? Tomorrow will bring fresh energy and ideas." Lyn hugged Susan, smiled lazily, flopped down, and rolled away from her, falling asleep in seconds.

June 19
Monday

While the decision to remain did help strengthen Susan's and Lyn's resolve and concentration, the third day on the butte was miserable and threatening. As they hiked, the sky filled with dark thunderheads and produced skirts of rain that tailed away before they brushed the ground. The wind gusted up. Although she kept up a bold front for Lyn's sake, Susan was still weaker than she wished, and needed more water than they could afford. They found a faint path that started in a descending crack and took them about three hundred feet down a slope that ended abruptly in a sheer face. Perched on the edge of the cliff, like an omen, was the rib cage and skull of a Bighorn ram. They were rim-rocked again with nowhere to go but back up. Worse, they were on a west face and the wind leaned on them relentlessly as they climbed. Only determination got them safely back on top. By 2:00 p.m. they were back at camp, thirstier and more disconsolate than ever.

Susan's frustration and dehydration translated into a pattern of alternating anger and silence, Lyn's into hyperactivity and noise. "We are getting so nowhere! I feel like some kind of puppet!" Lyn scuffed twigs with her shoes, threw rocks over the edge of the butte, and lobbed screams at a remorseless gray sky. "Why are you doing this to us?" She ranged around and finally slammed herself down on a sandy patch in front of a boulder. Her hand shot up, fingers spread. She stared wide-eyed at a palm full of cactus spines, jerked her hair over her face, and started to cry.

Susan watched Lyn until she stopped. Then she rose, approached her, stooped in front of her, and took her hands. While picking the spines out of her palm, she counseled the young woman. "Lynnie, you have to reserve strength, no matter how wigged out you feel. This desert will beat you down in no time at the rate you're going. If you don't respect it, it will take and take and give nothing back. I'm scared too, but I … wait … listen … what's that?" She turned one ear to the west. A bird called, and then faintly, a rumble rose in the distance. "I think I hear a plane."

They stood and concentrated on the sounds underneath the incessant growl of the wind. Susan perceived a rising drone. Then they saw it. It was an official looking helicopter—maybe Bureau of Land Management out patrolling. Soon it was right over them and the roar was deafening. Lower and lower it circled, dipping in toward them from a variety of angles as though checking them out. Awash in relief, the women flailed their arms. Lyn jumped and yelled. Then both hunkered back to await the helicopter's landing. It descended and briefly hovered around fifteen feet. Lyn and Susan couldn't see in the dust the propellers churned up. Suddenly motor pitch and volume changed, air velocity surged, and the helicopter swung up and away. The women choked and screamed in indignation. Renewed isolation slammed into them and pushed them to the ground.

Silence had returned, the chopper was gone, taking with it their confidence and hope. They were exhausted and humiliated. But when the dust cleared they saw something on the ground and scrambled toward it. Lyn sat on the sand and pulled a pack onto her lap. After a few silent moments she said with dull recognition, "This is my pack. I haven't seen it for weeks." Lyn slowly removed sleeping pads, plastic bottles of water and some dried food. She drank and passed the bottle to Susan. Lyn hugged the empty pack to her chest and, feeling a hard object press against her ribs, held it up for inspection. "There's something else in it." She began opening zippers and Velcro tabs, reaching deep into the recesses of the pack. She felt around. Her eyes got wide. "My tablet," she said. She pulled a rectangular object from the pack. "They overlooked it." She turned the electronic device over and over in her hands as if it were a precious gem.

"What is it?" Susan asked.

Lyn looked at her, eyes wide. "It's an electronic tablet. But it's also a smart phone." She opened the vinyl cover. "It used to have a metal pen for my graduate school notes on digital textbooks and doodling and the like."

"Oh yeah. I know all about that. Your mother gave it to you. And I think I know where the stylus is too. Somehow Moody ended up with it. White Wolf must have dropped it along with your ... uh, I'll tell you all about that later. What I want to know is can you make a call from here?"

Lyn activated the device and grinned. "Shit, Susan, there's a little battery left and, look, I have a few bars of coverage. I can make calls anywhere there is cell service, but a text message is even more likely to go through."

"Let's give it a shot. Type in this number."

Susan recited Jake Goddard's cell phone number and dictated a brief text. Lyn's fingers flew back and forth across the screen.

By mid-afternoon, food and fresh water gave the women a new perspective. And although they now were sure they were being monitored, the outside chance that they had sent a text message before the tablet's battery died lifted their spirits as well.

Susan's thinking sharpened and narrowed to a singular essence: the will to survive. She was filled with cold determination to get them off the butte alive. She and Lyn repacked and reorganized rations, particularly water.

"We're a hell of a team, you know. You make me believe we can do this. I really think we can." Lyn said.

"I know we can do this, Lyn. Let's finish up here, rest for the remainder of the day, and start moving tonight. Until we're safe, we'll be nocturnal— less heat, less chance of detection. We'll be a pair of night critters."

"Right. A couple of wise old owls," Lyn said.

"Yup, and something's telling me I need to make a few adjustments, sister." Her face hardened as she jammed clothing into her pack. "I can feel endlessly guilty, stupid, angry—and none of it will help us. What I need is my full power—pedal to metal. It's been too long since I felt it. Now I need it." She looked at Lyn. "We are getting the fuck off this pile of rocks!"

At sundown, after their rest, the two women shared a reassuring hug and a determined high five, shouldered their packs, and started to move. The night sky was clear with sparkling stars and a bright quarter moon illuminating the terrain. Susan kept silent about her fears that there might not be a way out of this prison. But if they could get off the butte alive, she'd keep the North Star behind her and plot a general direction south. She'd find good daytime shelter and help Lyn keep hydrated and as cool as possible. If they were lucky, they'd eventually find more water. She felt like Old Ruth was guiding her every move now and was amazed at what she could recall of her teachings. And to her surprise, she found herself reciting the 23rd Psalm in her head. She smiled, thinking how pleased her father would be. But the most important thing was to focus. It was critical that she miss nothing, and that they keep their minds off the danger that lay ahead. She had to look for signs of the ancestors but also assume the role of spiritual pilot.

They picked their way through creosote bushes and around shoulder-high boulders.

"Anthropologists think many modern tribes descended from the Anasazi," Susan said.

"Were they all over the southwest?" Lyn asked.

"No, just the Four Corners area of Utah, Colorado, New Mexico, and Arizona. But, those ancient southwestern civilizations that were not specifically Anasazi, such as the Fremont in this area, were all influenced by Anasazi culture. People tend to romanticize the Anasazi because they were so advanced and because they disappeared under such bizarre circumstances."

"So what happened to them?" Lyn said, while gingerly holding a handful of yucca spikes for Susan to pass under safely.

"There's a lot of debate about the end of that era, a couple of hundred years before Columbus. Apparently within a forty or fifty year span, they simply evaporated. Some anthropologists think nomadic enemies drove off the Anasazi; others feel that mismanagement of natural resources was the major problem. Another interesting theory, that's getting a lot of play these days, holds that it was an intense and prolonged period of drought that got them."

"The parallels to today are a little scary, aren't they?" Lyn said.

Susan stopped and looked out over the darkening emptiness of the valley floor. "You know, the Fremont people grew crops around here. Seems unimaginable that this area could have been fertile." The moon cast a milky light on the smooth sandstone in front of them. Except for the sparse shrubs, the ground looked like pictures Susan had seen of the lunar surface.

"What could the farms have been like in this gnarly landscape?" Lyn asked.

"Apparently they captured and stored the water in natural pockets on the tops and in the canyons of the mesas. They also understood some principles of irrigation. Corn was their staple. But there is evidence of beans and other legumes too. Like the Anasazi, the Fremont are famous mostly for their dwellings and rock art, but you know they were amazing conservationists, and because they needed to store their food and water—decent potters," Susan said.

The night air was sweet. Susan relished its cool wash across her skin. She relaxed, let Lyn's voice and the breeze flow around her, and began to find a steady rhythmical pace across the uneven terrain. Susan was no stranger to scrambling around on butte tops and hoped they'd have better luck getting off from the northeastern side. It was slightly less exposed and might slope more gradually to the plain below.

She was right. By midnight they were looking down at a descending sweep of overlapping rock layers, like an armadillo's back, that began at the base of two cliffs. Susan knelt and began to crawl around searching along the top edge of the face.

"Whatcha doin', wild woman?" Lyn asked. "You look like you're getting ready to howl at the moon."

"Jeez, I don't think I have a single howl left in me. I'm looking for signs of the ancients or large animals. If we find either, we know we have found the way."

"And if we find neither?" Lyn asked.

Susan sat up. "Well, let's see, if there are no signs, it doesn't mean this route won't get us off the butte; it is just a bit more of a gamble that we might get rim-rocked again, is all." She continued searching behind bushes growing along a low rock ledge that branched horizontally above the face.

"I get that tracks, scat, and broken branches indicate an animal trail, but what sort of sign of man are you looking for?" Lyn asked.

"Sometimes you find a little pictograph, like I was telling you about Kokopelli, or some other kind of symbol. Usually under a protective ledge." She scrambled into a small alcove and pulled the branches of a shrub away from the base of the rock wall. "Yes!! Somebody else has been here."

"Recently?" Lyn asked.

"Well, yes, more or less," Susan said over her shoulder. "I'd say about eight hundred years ago, give or take." She sparked up a grin.

"That's not funny!"

"But don't you see, it doesn't matter, if this was a trail off the butte then, it probably is now unless—"

"Unless, well, go on, give me the bad news, unless..."

"The Fremont often used log ladders, many of which no longer exist, in steep places. And sometimes large fins of rock provided a route, but have since been frost-wedged off, leaving sheer faces where once there was a steep trail."

Lyn got on her knees beside Susan. "Show me what you've found."

"Right here behind the brush growing out of this crack, an animal, maybe a bighorn, is painted on the rock," Susan said.

"An animal?"

"Yup. Legend says if you find a sign of the ancestors, water can't be too far away. With the occasional side-trip for hunting, all travel in the desert is either to or from water, right? Makes sense." Susan smiled. "Also, the artist had to get up here somehow. This might be a way off the butte."

Lyn pushed back on her heels and howled. Then she hugged Susan hard and pounded her on the back. Holding her at arm's length, she said, grinning, "Let's go, girl!"

They had to drop about ten feet onto a sharply angled upper slope. Lyn let her pack slide down the cliff face and held her breath, hoping that it would land without going into a roll. It nudged into some brush. Susan's pack plopped nearby. Lyn was a pretty skilled climber and she was able to reduce the distance of her fall by nearly half by finding some small holds for her feet in the rock face. Susan could not duplicate the moves, however, and jumped the whole distance. Although she was able to roll as she hit the ground, she cried out and came to a stop holding her ankle.

They fashioned a triangle bandage out of a t-shirt and bound the injured ankle. Susan refused to rest. She limped on with the shoe on the bandaged foot loosely laced. A large spire to the east blocked the moonlight, and the rock sloping directly below them was in darkness.

The moon shadow hampered their vision. A combination of walking, groping, sliding, and down climbing took them another three hundred yards or so. Suddenly, Lyn stepped one foot into nothingness before she sensed a void. A quick sit down and clutch at a sturdy creosote bush saved her. She was on the edge of the second cliff. She rolled over onto her knees, crawled up the slope and tried to collect herself.

Lyn's laugh emerged in a tight squeak. "No grabbing onto roots, they always tell climbers. The girls in my college rock climbing class got a chuckle out of that one. Whoa, that was close."

Susan tossed a pebble over the edge and listened for the impact. This time the cliff was too high to descend in a controlled fall. Susan said, "Maybe this is the type of rock face that had fissures or chimneys where the Fremont used narrow ladders up the middle. I'll bet there's something like that around here. We know they got to the top somehow, right? Can you try to find a crack while I rest this ankle?"

Lyn had to crawl slowly and work at keeping her body weight uphill to avoid a fall. Shallow indentations were easy to confuse with true breaks in the rock. It took almost an hour, but she returned to Susan having found an opening.

"It's only a fair crack. I mean, it starts out good and narrow, but who knows what happens further down? So much of it is in shadow. I could see the bottom, though; it is out of the shadow and in the moonlight. At least, if we make it, we will get out of this darkness. You up for trying it?"

"I'm up for anything that goes down, Lynnie." Susan limped behind Lyn to the crack.

"Of course, you realize we don't have a ladder around, or any of those old-school ancestors to make one," Lyn said. The opening was about the width of a narrow doorway. "We can inch down Spiderman-style, bracing our butts and backs against one wall, and hands and feet against the other,"

"You make it sound so easy." Susan peered below and nervously pushed her hair behind her ears.

"It is, really. I used to practice it all the time in the doorway of my dorm in college. No sweat." Moisture glistened at her hairline.

Again the packs went down first, and provided more information about the length of the cliff. It was one hundred feet at most, they thought. Lyn led so she could help Susan from below if need be. She was immediately swallowed by the darkness at the top of the crack. She sang as she went to calm her nerves and reassure her friend. Susan waited for Lyn's signal. About twenty feet into the chute, she called for Susan to begin her descent.

"The surface is a little rougher than I expected," she called up. "Go slowly and try hard not to slip. The rock will tear you up if you slide far. Feel for little ledges and holds. I think your ankle will be fine—this is a piece of cake."

"Okay, here goes," Susan squeezed into the slot. "Ooo, a little tough on the hands and ankle but, I'm okay. It's just so tight ... up here." She was already breathing heavily. "Does it ... get any wider ... where you are?"

"It's about six inches wider than up there. I'm resting my butt on a nice little ledge. I'll reserve it for you." A dark shaft gaped below Lyn's perch. Lyn strained to hear her companion's movements. Susan was going slowly and resting often. Her breathing came in short gasps, masking pain. A coyote called in the distance.

"Do you hear that coyote, Susan? He wants to sing for you when you get down." No response from above except scraping and hard breathing. She was getting closer. "How ya doing? How's the foot?" No response. "Susan, you okay?"

"I feel like I might slip and hit you. Move down. I'm going to step on your head. God, I can't stop my arms and legs from shaking."

"You're doing great. Don't worry about me." Though Lyn had confidence in Susan's strength, she knew she should probably go ahead and call back instructions about the section below. "I think I will do the rest now. You're going to love this ledge. I just wanted to be certain you were managing. I'll let you know when…"

Pebbles and sand started to rain down on Lyn's head. Susan shouted, "I can't…" She slid down on Lyn. Both women cried out in pain.

Lyn dropped several feet, tearing skin off her palms and scraping her right shoulder before twisting and wedging her body across the crack. Susan's full weight was on Lyn's head and left shoulder, bending her neck at a painful angle. Lyn did not have good purchase with her feet and was holding up Susan with her arms and knees. They slipped another two feet. Lyn fought the chalky taste of panic in her throat as she looked down the chimney into a void. Her hands were jammed against the rock on the other side but her feet flailed for a hold.

"Pull up with your arms! Get your weight off me. I have to brace my feet or we're going to fall."

"Oh, shit, Lynnie, okay, okay here goes…" Susan forced out a long grunt and pulled her feet up, followed by her hands, causing great pain in the right one. Lyn got her feet securely placed on the rock.

"Good, I'm okay. I can support your weight if you want to catch your breath, but only for a minute. Put your hurt foot on me." She felt Susan's foot shaking on her shoulder. "That's it. Deep breaths—we're fine—we just need to rest and breathe a little."

Susan muttered something.

"What did you say?"

Susan responded through gritted teeth. "I said, 'Fuck fear, fuck evil!'"

"Thatta girl. And fuck that evil asshole White Wolf," added Lyn.

After they collected themselves and Susan was positioned on the ledge, Lyn worked her way down the last eighty feet to the bottom. She shouted for Susan to follow, only then noticing the pain in her hands, knees, and back. Lyn watched Susan and could see that she was totally focused. Susan ignored her pain and laboriously leveraged down. She dropped the last few feet and, favoring her hurt ankle, rolled on soft sand into the moonlight. Susan got to her knees and touched the sand gratefully with both palms, then staggered to her feet and gave Lyn a big hug.

"You totally killed on that rock, Susan."

"We did it, girlfriend. We kicked ass. We're down. Thank God!"

"And thank you, Anasazi," Lyn said, grinning.

The two women, skin abraded and covered with dirt, sat against the cliff and celebrated with water and dried fruit. They were off the top of the butte. The rest of the way was an easy scramble down the stair-like overlapping strata of rock. They looked out at a stark and beautiful landscape of moonlit slopes, ridges, and dark arroyos descending to the desert floor. Susan was still not certain of their location, but they were free to run, hide if necessary, and for the first time in days, free to dictate some of the terms of their own fate.

Liam O'Connor's pilot, Rick Sanders, entered the air-conditioned trailer squinting as his eyes adjusted to the bluish caste of the interior light. It was like being under water—cool and a little blurry compared with the artificially lit yellows and reds outside. O'Connor, his supervisor, was facing away, speaking on the phone. He'd had a large window installed in the back wall of his office so that, day or night, he could gaze at his beloved tunnel project without venturing into the heat.

As Sanders stepped forward, he noticed that the fat Irishman was doing his weird one-handed knuckle-cracking thing. O'Connor trusted Rick, so Rick was taken for granted and often overheard private conversations. Sanders took the nervous knuckle popping to mean O'Connor was talking to his boss, the so-called Water Witch, the Director of the Southern Desert Water Authority.

"No ma'am, you really don't need to concern yourself overly about this. The deal is as solid as can be. A veritable pot of gold in our hands. When we meet with them, you'll see they are being very solicitous and very discreet. They'll leave no trace, believe me. These people need us. They're desperate for any excess water we can send downstream their way. The yakuza's plans for a massive development at the Salton Sea are top drawer, every detail thought of, but they cannot do it without our water. No way. It'll fail like all previous attempts to develop that thirsty area for anything other than a few dry land crops. And—" He paused, sucked in his breath, and adjusted his sitting position in the leather chair. "No. I haven't had to budge on price. They're in a weak bargaining position. Yes, my figures are accurate. The boys have done impeccable research. Golf courses, casinos, subdivisions, fountains—the whole nine yards. All require our water. Beautiful design. Everything is under control. You can just come in and close the deal. So, if that's all, I'll be—" O'Connor leaned forward and rubbed his eyes with one hand, then popped two knuckles. "Why the butte, ma'am? Well, there was no more room at the inn, so to speak. It was one thing to keep a kid here, a seasoned cop, another altogether. So, we have them where we want them and can use them as we see fit to best suit our purposes. Two terrorists caught in the act, media will love it. They will not escape, I assure you. I plan to hang them out to dry for one more day, scoop them up, and then maybe they have an unfortunate accident attempting to monkey wrench our straw project. When it's to our advantage, I will put their lovely bodies before the media, as the ecoterrorists they are. I'd just ask you to keep Stanley placated and at a distance, if you would. Don't need additional distractions right now vis-á-vis him sniffing around worried about his daughter. Tell him she'll be fine. Ha! We're lucky as hell he never heard what happened to the truck driver so close to his mine. But then who gives Stan much credit for brains? Glad there are so many abandoned shafts around there that can swallow a semi … excuse me? Now see here, there is no way they can elude my men and our technology, no way in hell." He grimaced, held the receiver away and gave the phone the finger. "Yes, ma'am, will do. You have yourself a good night. Don't worry about a thing. You bet. Goodnight, now." He hung up. "Jesus, Mary, and Joseph, what a paranoid meddling bitch. What I wouldn't give to—"

The pilot cleared his throat. "You called for me, O'Connor? You want another run?"

O'Connor spun around in his swivel chair. Deep circles formed troughs in the swollen flesh around his eyes. "God, lad, don't sneak up on me like that!" He coughed wetly and cleared his throat, undid another button at the neck of his shirt. "I don't know, Rick, lad. If we go at night, we'll attract attention with our lights as well as our sound. But we need the chopper here on site during the day ... can't go flapping all over hell's half acre pursuing those two. Not that I'd mind a closer look at those lasses' asses ... enjoyed seeing their surprise when we did the drop yesterday." He cleared his throat again.

"The straw is already leaning too heavily on general SDWA resources and is way the hell over budget, and our goose is still at least two weeks away from laying her golden egg when the tunnel is due to be complete and the water flows. I could gleefully strangle that goddamn White Wolf for adding this fucking complication, but we'll just have to make the best of it now, won't we? And knowing our boy Forrest, he will land on his feet, after giving his knees and elbows a bloody good scraping, that is."

Sanders had long ago learned it was best to stick to business when dealing with his boss. "The wind isn't that strong tonight, and it's coming from the west. Most noise'll just sail out over the desert. I'd like to see if they're still on the butte, or, if not, if I can pick up their trail."

"All right then," O'Connor sat back in his chair. "Do a short run just before dawn. Just one, mind you." He widened his eyes in mock surprise. "Why, I'll be curious to see if the desert heat has sucked the juices out of our two plump little prickly pears. But who knows, by now they might be surviving like kangaroo rats, burrowing in the sand and recycling their own piss like the good little environmentalists they are." He waved the pilot away.

June 20
Tuesday

In the early hours of the morning, the two women stood in the middle of a dry wash in the bottom of a shallow canyon. Lyn had taken off her shoes and pack and paced slowly back and forth, letting the cool softer sand massage her feet. Susan sat on a rock and rubbed her ankle.

"This place reminds me of something out of Star Wars," mused Lyn. "All we need is a little Starfighter, or whatever they're called, that could lift us up and away into that indigo sky—or at least elevate us to a point where we could see where we are."

"I think I know where we are, more or less. Well … less," Susan replied, groggy with fatigue, "but maybe tomorrow, er, I mean later today, we can climb up to the top of these walls and have a real look. And a listen. Sometimes, if the breeze is low and coming from the right direction, you can hear trucks and cars on the … the … highways."

Barely an hour later, having just crawled in under an overhang at the mouth of a small alcove, they did hear motor sounds. But not of ground vehicles. The SDWA copter was flying low, coming from the area of the butte. They scrambled as far back into the shadow of the overhang as possible, hoping their footprints were invisible in the early gray light. For twenty minutes, the roar ebbed and flowed as the chopper nosed around them, dipped into the canyon and out. When it hovered in one place, it swished its tail back and forth impatiently, blowing sand, dust, and detritus everywhere. It seemed to Susan to be a mechanical hound, a huge metal search beast that could smell their presence. Finally, the helicopter's drone trailed away, leaving her with the eerie sense that it knew where they were and where they were going, but was simply returning to base to fuel up and plan the details of their recapture.

Stanley Burke was lost. Every time he drove to Henderson it looked different, was different, because subdivisions had popped up literally overnight. The houses were virtually identical and lined up like boxcars with orange tile tops. The director had asked him to meet at Pumping Station Seven at 9:00 a.m.; it was already 9:15 a.m. and he was driving aimlessly through labyrinthine streets. He had asked three separate people watering and working on their lawns how to find the station. They had no clue where their water came from.

Finally he rounded a bend of houses that he could have sworn he had driven around before. Ahead he saw a two-story concrete building with large pipes, like tentacles, sprouting in every direction. Number Seven stood at a cul-de-sac in front of two bare hillocks. Burke recognized the director's parked Buick with the SDWA insignia. As soon as he opened his door he heard water gushing out of a canal between the hills behind the building. It was sucked down into the station by a gaping concrete mouth.

The director waved from the structure's front door and walked out into the sun, putting on her Ray Bans. She was wearing a creamy Armani suit with a lacy brown camisole exposing lots of surgically enhanced and suntanned cleavage.

Stanley Burke was an attractive man, over six feet tall. He had thick salt-and-pepper hair and a ruddy face with a strong jaw. Expensive silk tropical shirts and linen pants were de rigueur. Once at a consortium party, and after several drinks, the director whispered to Stan that she found him to be a bit whiny and wishy-washy for a successful businessman, but that she liked him in a big sister kind of way. That is, she said, nearly flooring Stan, a big sister contemplating unzipping her little brother's fly and showing him a thing or two.

They walked on a concrete path by the canal behind the pumping station. Water splashed and rushed just below their feet. This was how the director made an impression. She loved to have these chats with the music and power of liquid gold playing in the background.

"It's good to see you, Stanley. You look fit as usual."

"I work pretty hard at it. Thanks for noticing." He patted his flat stomach. "How you been?"

"Well, Stanley, well. As I like to say, as long as there is water in the well," she gestured toward the flow, "I do very well. Are those circles under your bedroom brown eyes?"

"Actually, I haven't been sleeping. All this tunnel business has come way closer to home than I imagined when I joined the consortium. I'm concerned about Lyn."

"And that's exactly why I asked you to come and see me today. I wanted to reassure you. What with that beautiful daughter's unfortunate involvement, I felt I needed to give you an update and fill you in on a few details we don't normally share with our business partners. Unfortunately, I wasn't able to tell you the whole story when your daughter was detained."

"Florence is beside herself and, in addition to filing a missing person's report, has involved her pushy sister who has hired a private detective. I told you about my attempts to scare off the cop assigned to the case. Well, they appear to have failed. She called my wife. Sounds like she is still on the scent. Christ, a small-town cop. Are you sure Lyn is well hidden and well taken care of?"

"I gave you my word your daughter would be taken care of from the beginning and she has been. Her situation is like living at a spa for God's sake." She studied the nails on her right hand. "I should be so lucky. She will never know who captured her and why, and she will not be harmed, I assure you." The director touched his arm, smiled and looked into his eyes. Moving water thrummed hypnotically beside them.

"I ... I'm sorry. I just need reassurance. She's my little girl after all."

"Typically, Stan, the seventy-some businesses in the consortium that range, as you know, from mines to casinos, are responsible for marketing, public relations and financial support of our projects. You all are kept, as is in your best interest, on a need-to-know basis, but I feel compelled to tell you everything, given the circumstances. The Colorado River Compact members have not formally approved our new water appropriations as of yet. States both upstream and down are concerned about our growth and future consumption. That is just a matter of inconvenience and negotiation but it could mean nuisance lawsuits and additional expense. And expense is the problem. This project was approved with a 1.9 billion dollar budget but we are looking at serious overages due to delays, material costs skyrocketing, and a myriad of other problems completely out of our control but for which we are being held totally accountable. We are talking close to sixty million. So far, I've been able to keep that out of the public eye."

She stopped, turned, leaned down in front of him, and fished a pebble out of her red Ferragamo flat with long lacquered fingernails. He could see between two internally supported mounds of flesh, all the way to her wrinkled navel. She stood, tossed the pebble into the water, and continued walking.

"Sixty million is a lot of money," Burke said. "What do you plan to do about it?"

"We have secured business arrangements with some Japanese officials to offset at least half of the overage."

"What sort of 'arrangements'?"

"Well, they need—truly are desperate for—what we got—water. Good ol' H_2O for a major development in the Salton Sea area. Their sources are oversubscribed and for the most part badly polluted. When the new straw is complete, it will be a fairly simple matter to route some of our water south to them. Let's just say we are negotiating arrangements that we don't want the CIA, FBI, or even the EPA, to know about."

"Let alone any of the granola organizations that are constantly breathing down our necks."

"Exactly, Stan. But we are confident that we can complete the straw, deliver the additional water you and other local businessmen must have to continue growing, and, after the usual inspections and initial monitoring, hide the Japanese activity."

"The good news is, soon we will be able to return your daughter—happy, healthy and none the wiser. The bad news is…" she grabbed his arm hard and drilled a look into his face, "now that you know all this, I'm going to have to kill you." Stan recoiled. The director's pancake crinkled into a grin. "Just kidding. But what you now know could hurt you, so keep it close to that wonderful hairy chest, hmmmn." She caressed the front of his silk shirt.

Burke collected himself. "How much longer is all this going to take? When will my daughter be released?"

"We just need another week or so. The Virgin River decoy is working nicely to keep the enviros distracted."

"But, can you absolutely assure me she is being treated well?"

"Absolutely. We will have all this behind us shortly, and look." She put her arm around his waist and turned him toward the canal. "This gorgeous stretch of Lake Mead water flows through the old straw under the River Mountains. It's nothing compared to the private little river we are going to send up your way when the new straw is sucking. Won't that be great for Ashland Mine?" She drew air down deep through her nostrils. "Smell the water; doesn't it smell wonderful?" She pushed her right breast hard against his arm and gazed into his eyes. "There are those who think vice is the smell of money in Nevada. They're so wrong." She inhaled again. "This is the smell of money."

It was the last morning of The Howl and still no word from Susan and Bev. Jake had packed up his camping gear and stuffed a few last objects into his car. He left the tent for Susan in case she returned. He kneeled down in front of Lou's wheelchair and handed her a set of keys.

"These two are for my Airstream. There are extra hook-ups at my site."

Lou said, "After this dustbowl, a little onboard water and power for AC will be welcome relief. Swear to God I saw the Joad family—you know, from *Grapes of Wrath*—pulling out this morning. Had a mattress and rocking chair on top of a loaded pickup truck. Probably headed for Cal-i-for-ni-a." She took a swig of the beer gripped in her hand.

"You should be fine in Salt Lake until I get back from Ashland Mine. If all goes well, I won't be that far behind you getting home. If not ... this all stinks, Lou, I'm going to find out what the fuck is going on if it kills me. "

Lou grabbed the bill of his cap. "Not so fast, Superman. I've got something else to add that I haven't told you. It's kinda out there but it's been eating at me since I left Vancouver and I don't dare reveal everything I suspect about it. Nor do I, under any circumstances, want Rank Moody to know about it. He may be working for us but, like you said, he bats for the other team. I got it from some very cryptic messaging on the internet—" An approaching vehicle interrupted Lou's thought. "Well, speak and the devil appears," she said.

The green Suburban was doing well above the posted camp speed limit. Moody braked hard, shut off the engine, and jumped out. "White Wolf came back briefly, but he's left again in Lyn Burke's car."

"Alone?" Jake asked.

"Yeah, I think so." Moody said. "There was no one in the passenger seat. The back was full to the ceiling with his crap. Looks like he's not coming back. Guess he's howled himself out, and I can't find Skutches anywhere."

"Stink just got worse," Lou said to Jake.

Jake snapped into action. "Okay, now listen—we have to move fast. White Wolf won't know Lou's rig. Rank, you and Lou follow him. I'm going to the mine to look for Susan and Bev, as soon as I figure out what happened to Skutches.

"10-4, Sherlock. Now we're talking!" Lou wrestled her bulk in behind the wheel and, cigarette clenched between her teeth, turned over the engine.

Jake added, "Meet us at the—"

"No way! That's a crip van," Moody barked.

Lou yelled over the revving engine, "The politically correct term is 'mobility impaired' and this baby is 'mobile' cuz I just had her 'repaired.' Now get yer ass in or get out of the way." Moody cursed her under his breath, angrily grabbed his daypack, camera, and binoculars out of the Suburban and got in the van. He sat staring straight ahead like a petulant child.

Lou called out the window. "I don't have time to, uh ... elaborate on that hunch of mine from off the internet," she tossed her head slightly toward Moody, "but if you don't hear from me sooner, meet us tomorrow morning at the Lake Mead Boulder Beach Visitor's Center no later than 5:00 a.m. sharp. I will tell you everything I suspect then. Unless I miss my guess, there's a summer solstice sunrise party planned with a little early Fourth of July thrown in at the lake. But remember, no later than 5:00 a.m. And don't be anywhere near the straw after that. That is critical." She pulled down her visor and through the driver's window handed Jake a piece of letter-size paper folded in half. "Here's what I found. I'm counting on your geology training making sense of this. We'll see if our two interpretations agree." Lou reached down beside her seat, flipped over a plaid blanket, pulled up a shotgun, and brandished it out the window at Jake. "Glad I brought Matilda. Boat or van, I never go waltzing without her."

"Whoa," Jake said recoiling. "Do not, I repeat, do not engage White Wolf—tail him only. Lou, Rank, you read me?"

Lou flashed her biggest smile and hit the gas, jamming Moody back against the seat. "TTFN," she called as they spun away.

Moody struggled to get his seatbelt buckled. The beer had relaxed Lou's approach to pothole management and, as they bucked up the road, he hoped the belt might prevent his head from slamming into the roof.

They reached the pavement. After barreling along for several miles, red rock cliffs and canyons whizzing by on both sides, there was still no sign of Lyn's car. They flew through a mountain pass and then bucketed up on the isolated junction where U.S. 6 and U.S. 50 headed east and U.S. 93 branched right and continued south. Although there was no sign of White Wolf, Lou slowed just enough to bank around the turn, run the stop sign, and swerve onto 93.

"How do you know where to go? Are you out of your mind or just drunk, lady? Jerk could be going anywhere from here."

"I've been doing some hard thinking over the last few thousand miles. I got this bird's number and I have just figured out his flight plan. Besides, sure as shit flows downhill, most traffic in Nevada goes to Lake Mead or Vegas. They must have planned it that way. And mister, I'm as sober as a Mormon judge."

They pursued in silence for several minutes. The road ran straight through a wide sagebrush valley dotted with black cows, platted with green fields, and ringed by rugged snow-covered mountains.

"Bucolic, eh?" Lou said. "Too bad those cute critters are the problem. Agriculture uses ninety percent of the water in the West and much of that goes to growing feed for cattle."

"I could go for a burger," Moody snapped.

They climbed over a low pass and looked down on a car several miles to the south.

"Mitsubishi at twelve o'clock," Lou announced.

"Well, I'll be damned, you've got the green weenie in your cross hairs," Moody said.

"White Wolf is no environmentalist if that's what you mean. He's an opportunist, plain and simple." Lou told Rank what she knew about Forrest White Wolf. Then she turned and bore her blue eyes into him. "I've never understood your problem with environmentalists, anyway."

While keeping White Wolf in sight, Lou was reminded there was pretty much nothing she and Moody agreed upon except that Forrest White Wolf was an imposter. In fact, Lou was so immersed in verbally sparring with Moody she drove right past the lead car. White Wolf had pulled to the side to relieve himself. Moody shrunk down, but White Wolf's head was turned away as he was focused on other matters. Dusk was fading to dark.

"Now, what the hell are you going to do?" Moody asked. "You passed the son of a bitch."

"I'm going to pull over up here a ways and enjoy the pretty Joshua trees while you hide in the back. It wouldn't do for us to get ahead of our prey. Though, it'd be kind of funny if we beat him to his destination, huh? This is the gambling state, right? I'd bet money he's headed to the new tunnel being dug from Mead to Vegas."

In a few minutes, White Wolf was back on the road. He paid no attention to the van pulled off at an overview. After several uneventful hours of driving, the Mitsubishi left the main highway and headed down the access road to Lake Mead. Night enveloped the desert, making it easy for Lou to hang back and keep her quarry's lights in view. A flat plain in the otherwise convoluted terrain suggested they were nearing the lake. Soon the dark edge of the water was in view. The little car followed the shoreline west and then south for several miles and stopped at the gated construction site for the new straw on the arc of Boulder Bay. Several well-lit cranes reached to the sky above concrete trucks, heavy equipment, and trailers. The reflection of a rising waning moon shimmered on the lake behind a partially completed three-story structure. Next to the building, a helicopter sat on a concrete pad painted like a bull's eye. White Wolf was waved through the security gate; he drove a short distance to a doublewide trailer.

Lou and Moody backtracked up a hill to the parking lot of a fish hatchery above the tunnel construction site and waited for White Wolf to reappear. Dromedary Peak loomed high on the mountain range behind them. Beyond the construction site to the south, several horses swished their tails and huddled together in a corral bordering the lake.

Moody scanned through his binoculars. "Car's parked by a trailer. Might be an office. I really don't have a good view. White Wolf must have gone inside."

"That building under construction has got to be the water treatment plant," Lou said.

Moody nodded, put down the binos, and after a few minutes of staring out the window, picked up a tattered scrapbook off her dash. It was filled with news clippings. "What's this? Happy memories of fire bombings?"

"I've never vandalized anything. I don't even know who the PEA members are. I just pass on information in a timely fashion. I first got involved in November of 1996."

"Wasn't that the Forest Service truck torching in Washington?"

"You got it. You know your stuff—pity you're on the wrong side. And to think I'm paying you. Could cost me my green card."

"But let me ask you," Moody said. "What's arson of a cotton gin, as in California, January 2000, got to do with genetically altered cotton? That's ridiculous."

"Like they say, they are 'the burning rage of a dying planet.' And they do get creative sometimes, bless their hearts, but as you know, nobody has ever been hurt—"

He cut her off. "So far, no one has ever been hurt, but it's really only a matter of time until some poor innocent bastard gets his ass caught in one of their—your—direct actions."

"Well now, Mr. Moody," she said, staring him down, "that'd be really unfortunate, wouldn't it? Truth is, to date, and I admit there is a faction that wants to go further, their credo rules out injury to any living being, no matter how much they might need injuring. No, really, your crop crushers, your frankenfooders, fur protesters, mink releasers, and your fire bombers—although I don't know any of them personally—I love them all, because they care, and they are willing to act upon that caring. They work in the shadows, with total anonymity and zero recognition, fueled only by their passion."

"Gimme a break … they're criminals," Moody sneered.

"I prefer to think of them as civil dissidents. But that notebook won't help you with your vocation. I collect police blotter blurbs from papers around the country, off the Internet. It's not that I enjoy other people's misery. It's just that the reports are, for the most part, pretty damn funny," Lou said, adjusting her turquoise necklace.

Moody read, "'March 17th. A fight broke out between a woman in a wheelchair and another woman. The woman in the wheelchair was missing both legs and one eye.'"

"That is definitely one of my favorites. I'll put my money on the woman in the wheelchair. Reminds me of something I'd do, read the next one."

"'A woman reported that a dog bit her on the finger while she was trying to help it after she had run over it with her car.'"

"Now there I think I'd bet on the dog. It was obviously much smarter than the woman. Uh oh, looks like our boy is on the move again." Lou swung her seat around under the wheel and started the engine. Moody focused his binoculars. White Wolf got back in the car. He drove to the boat dock beyond the office, parked, unloaded a very heavy sleeping bag out of the rear of the car, and carried it to the larger of two speedboats. He untied the boat, jumped on board, started the engine, and backed away from the dock, the boat growling and spewing water.

Lou started her engine. "Do you know what the definition of 'lymph' is?"

"No, I don't guess I do."

"It's someone who walks with a lisp, ha, ha … got that one off the internet, too. I surf, therefore I am. Let's go partner." She accelerated to keep pace with the boat as it headed south along the shore. Its wake trailed out, luminescent in the moonlight.

Traffic was light on the highway. The van's view of the lake was unimpeded, except for a few moments when the road wound behind rounded buttes. Lou whipped her chunky vehicle around bends and over inclines. In less than twenty minutes, the boat approached the end of the lake. Lou had stayed with it, but knowing it could go no further than the booms protecting Boulder Dam, wrenched her vehicle off the highway at the last overview before the road dropped down to the new bridge downstream from the dam. Metal towers, linked by high-tension wires, marched up the cliffs from the dam like gigantic warriors. Moody jumped out with the binoculars just in time to see the boat go out of sight behind a large outcrop overlooking the dam—Promontory Point. In a few minutes the boat was racing back toward the straw construction site. Lou and Moody drove back to their lookout at the hatchery, parked, watched, and waited. Lou lit a cigarette.

Minutes after docking the boat, White Wolf got into the Mitsubishi, drove past the guard station, and turned out of the compound, towards Las Vegas.

Lou stubbed out her cigarette and started the van, preparing to pursue again. She checked her watch and said quietly, "Whatever he loaded in the boat didn't come back from the dam. It's time to stop that son-of-a-bitch, and sooner than later is our only choice now." She hit the gas.

Moody grabbed the ceiling handle and braced as the van swerved out of the hatchery. He steeled himself for another insane ride and muttered, "Christ. How the hell did I get myself into this?"

"I can't answer that, bud. But I will say this: get ready, because we are about to dive in the deep end, and it is lousy with sharks."

"Goddard said not to approach White Wolf."

"Did he?" Lou said. "You know, when you been on this gorgeous ol' planet long as I have, you're lucky if you can remember what you had for breakfast." Lou stared straight ahead and pointed the van down the hill after White Wolf.

The Water Authority Director chose the Bellagio in Las Vegas as the meeting place. Her guests had requested opulence and she presumed the Bellagio—originally built for a billion-and-a-half—would fit the bill. Also, she valued the effect quiet but efficient air conditioning and the view of majestic fountains had on negotiations in the blistering and searing Nevada climate. She always appreciated the extravagant use of water for aesthetic purposes, and the Bellagio was an ersatz Lake Como. It, like the other new hotels, was meant to re-create another world entirely. But unlike the Venetian or the Mirage, Bellagio admitted real sunlight wherever possible and projected a subtlety that made it classier. There were more open terraces and gardens, as well as the choreographed fountains. The Water Witch had secured a corner conference room decorated to resemble a fifteenth-century palazzo—cream and caramel-colored marble, oriental rugs, and a lush red cloth on the conference table.

When the yakuza bakuto from Kyushu Island walked in, stood by the door, and introduced themselves, the first thing everyone noticed was their appearance. The leader, Mr. Kuroda, was almost six feet tall, and all three walked with an uncharacteristically wide gait for Japanese men. They were dressed and groomed impeccably—colorful silk suits, beautiful Italian leather shoes, subtle diamond cufflinks on Mr. Kuroda, manicures, and two hundred dollar haircuts. They were cordial and their English was impeccable. The Water Witch was in a tailored gray business suit and a white silk blouse. O'Connor, in slacks and a blazer, looked at a disadvantage. She glanced at his apparel with mild distaste and noticed him attempting to remain cool. Although a little tense, he looked like a man who felt he was in the driver's seat and liked it. The Witch sat down at the table, hoping to signal the beginning of business, but the men remained standing. And then the tapping began. She drummed her fingers and admired the tiny Japanese flags that adorned her nails.

Mr. Kuroda ignored the director and offered his first conversational comment to O'Connor. "Mr. O'Connor, I believe I saw you in the rose garden last evening. Do you enjoy flowers? Do you like this hotel?"

"Yes, it is very beautiful. But I spent most of my evening in the art gallery. I'm afraid I do not appreciate the flowers as much as I might."

"Really ... the Vermeers? They are exquisite, are they not?"

"Yes, indeed, Mr. Kuroda, I'm pleased to hear that you know the Western masterpieces." O'Connor was relaxing, but the longer he pattered on, the more she tapped. "Holbein and Vermeer are two of my favorite Baroque artists. I love the delicacy of shadow and gesture. Pure genius. The hotel gallery did a nice job illuminating the little oils with ambient light, don't you think?"

"You sound very knowledgeable, Mr. O'Connor. Are you an artist?"

"Just a bloody dabbler, I fear. I hope someday to set up a studio at my cabin north of Vegas overlooking the Timpahutes Mountains—"

"Uhhh ... hmmmm." The Witch interrupted O'Connor. "Oh, excuse me. I didn't mean to interrupt. Do you gentlemen need anything before we begin? Tea, for instance? Are you comfortable?"

"No, thank you. We are most comfortable. We find it hot, of course, coming from the southern islands originally and more recently from Hawaii." Mr. Kuroda smiled. "Shall we move to the table and begin to speak of our business?"

"Please." O'Connor gestured them ahead of him. The Director nodded. O'Connor hesitated, then rose and brought a tray of ice water and glasses to the table. The three men all drank before settling to their work. One of the three, Mr. Ugaki, who appeared to be the accountant, was beginning to perspire despite a room temperature of seventy degrees.

"Gentlemen, please do not stand on ceremony here," the Water Witch said. "You are most welcome to remove your jackets if the heat bothers you. This is quite acceptable in the West. We are a little more relaxed than in New York, or Hong Kong, or Tokyo."

The accountant smiled his thanks at her, pushed back from his laptop, and began to remove his jacket. The Witch noticed that the tip of his left little finger appeared to be a prosthetic. Mr. Kuroda, still without making eye contact with his hostess, spoke sharply. "No, thank you. Not just yet."

The accountant pulled his jacket back on.

Their transactions went smoothly. The Witch forced herself to drum less and even smile occasionally. They covered virtually every point of negotiation on the sale of water treatment technology as well as the sale of water. The Japanese had money to burn, and were prepared to pay any price to move business along. Only when they got to timing, and firm dates for diversion of water to their development at the Salton Sea, did Mr. Kuroda slow things down. He needed water to his development in southeastern California no later than the end of August.

O'Connor and his boss explained repeatedly that covert sales of surplus could only begin after they'd passed all inspections and operations were no longer being monitored closely—after water had been flowing for three months at least, and that their taps weren't going to be turned on until mid-July at the earliest.

The Japanese reacted poorly to this. They were not pleased at the influence that regulatory bodies had in the States. Nor were they convinced there wasn't a way around the regulations. They interpreted their hosts' position as a negotiating stance only and they offered more money.

The accountant began to perspire heavily. He removed his jacket and started to roll up his shirtsleeve so that he could manipulate his keyboard more easily. The director stared at Ugaki's right arm. It was completely covered in ornate tattoos from an inch above the wrist up. Quickly Mr.

Kuroda admonished his colleague in Japanese and Ugaki rolled the sleeve back down.

They failed to come to an agreement about dates and decided to meet again later that day. The Japanese yakuza felt they were offering the Americans the time needed to consider any and all expedient measures and they were not willing to be patient. They wanted illegitimate water immediately and their offer was too good to turn down—an additional thirty-five million. It would go a long way toward wiping out the overage on the tunnel. The director wasn't flinching. O'Connor looked elated but a bit overwhelmed.

A meal arrived and after eating and more polite conversation that O'Connor forced himself to manage graciously, and from which the Water Witch noticed she was largely excluded, the three businessmen prepared to leave. Mr. Kuroda bowed and asked O'Connor to think over the offer, promising to return that night at eleven.

"Sexist pigs!" the director said after the yakuza left. Her nails drummed the tabletop. "Don't they realize we are taking huge risks involving ourselves in these negotiations, alone? I agree that laws are meant to be bent, but hell, it sounds like they don't have any laws governing this sort of thing in their country."

O'Connor shook his head. "Let it pass, ma'am. A minor hiccup, considering the size of their current offer, I'd say. What time do you want me here this evening?"

"I want you here at ten forty-five, Liam, and I will close this deal if it takes us all night. I want you to keep your mouth shut. Those bastards will deal with me or they won't deal at all." She ran all ten fingers through her stiff hair.

"That's your call, but I think you're making a big mistake."

"Well, then, so be it. Their goddamn Salton Sea Resort can turn to dust like all the others before it, for all I care. We won't sell them our technology or a drop of water. They can damn well launder their ill-gotten gains somewhere else." Again, the tapping. "I'm going to go change my clothes and go to the shooting range to relax a little and think. I'm working on one hundred straight bulls-eyes, Liam, thirteen to go. Aren't you proud of your boss? You should get back to work. I believe you still have two very wily little creatures out there who have outsmarted you once, and who, you have assured me, could never get away from you a second time. And they fucking well better not!" She stood and walked to the door. "I've got to go do some more massaging of the regulations, if you know what I mean. See you tonight. Wear a suit." She slammed the door as she left and the crystal chandeliers tinkled.

When O'Connor returned to his trailer it was already late afternoon and the tunnel construction workers were piling into their pickup trucks and heading out for the night. He sat at his desk and sighed, scratched his belly, and then picked up the phone to call Sanders. While waiting for the pilot, he looked at his mail.

Soon there was a rap on the trailer door. Sanders walked in and sat across the desk from him.

"Rick, my boy, I hope you brought your A game this evening. I want those two bitches caught and the Witch off my ass. Tonight. Da'ya hear, lad?"

"Yeah, I hear. It's not like I haven't been trying. Somehow they must have gotten off that goddamn butte. Beats me how, but they're still out there, I'm sure of that. That's unreal—two women, shit. Not sure I could get off that rock without cashing in."

"You might just be cashing in, son, if you don't bring them in tonight."

Sanders was accustomed to the fat Irishman's threats. "I've spent almost three hours in the air and figure that there are only two possible ways to civilization. Hiking northwest from the butte would bring them to an old county road within a day or two. But that route is rough as hell, strewn with huge boulders and thick brush. Going due south, following a series of washes, will bring them to the highway. The arroyos and dry washes are a maze of dead ends and box canyons and they might waste days going off-track, but I'd lay money on their picking south, especially if they were able to get good bearings from the top of the butte."

"Now you're talking, Rick. That's what I pay you for, boy. Now go get in that helicopter—"

Sanders interrupted and rambled on. "They must be heading to Lake Mead. I can fly over them until the cows come home. All they have to do is duck under an overhang when they hear me." None of this guesswork impressed the fat man. He was sick of listening to it. Histrionics being his motivator of choice, he stood and slammed both meaty palms on his desktop, bouncing the phone.

"You make damn sure they don't get away again on my watch!" he shouted, red faced.

"Shit, boss, it's a waste of—"

"The only thing being wasted is my time. I'm supposed to be negotiating a lucrative deal with a bunch of Japanese, uh, officials tonight." He dropped back in his chair. "Christ, at least it might keep my mind off the two female thorns in my side." He pointed at Sanders. "Now get your ass up in that bird. I have orders from Her Majesty to report back to Bellagio—in a suit, mind you—and endure what promises to be a night of smiling, nodding, and cringing at the maddening tap, tap, tap of those damnable fingernails. Now, you bring me those bitches."

For the first time in days, Jake had a few minutes to think without distractions. A few clean-up crews worked their way around the grounds. With the festival ending at noon, most of the howlers had left and the camp was less chaotic. Jake paced back and forth by his car, lost in thought. Lou and Rank had been gone several hours, following White Wolf. While scouring the camp for Skutches, Jake learned from Jennie that White Wolf had come flying back into camp, ignored her, and taken the professor off in the car. He returned alone, in an ugly mood, and, refusing to answer her questions, packed and departed in a rush. She had not seen him or Noah Skutches since.

Jake knelt down by the tent, picked up a stick, and drew patterns in the sand. One thing was obvious; it was time to act, even without anything close to a clear picture of what cards his opponents were holding. Jake's only option was to go to Ashland Mine. Everything led back to Stan Burke. His plan was to briefly observe the mine. If he saw nothing suspicious, he'd corner Burke and demand an explanation for all the events surrounding his daughter's disappearance. Susan had been way ahead of Jake on this one. It was long past time to confront Stanley Burke. He threw his few remaining items into the Subaru, left a note for Susan in the tent telling of his plans, then drove out of the amphitheater and headed south.

Even in the relative cool of the cave's shadow, the desert air wrapped itself tightly around the women as they rested. Its hot clutch nearly smothered them. Dreams of searching and escaping rampaged through Susan's brain and deep sleep was impossible.

Lyn's dreams were of her parents and Aunt Lou. The images washed in and out of her mind and she groaned on her dusty sleeping pad as the air temperature climbed. She couldn't get her father to comfort her or help her interpret a map, though she pleaded with him to do so. Dogs barked incessantly somewhere. Aunt Lou, young and strong, was running, sometimes away from Lyn, sometimes beside or toward her. Her mother floated, faceless, and gestured across the canyon. She would not be still long enough for Lyn to speak to her.

Susan's dreams had little line or form. She stood on an arid plain watching the sky change from blue to a searing yellow and then to vermilion. The sky was descending and exerted weight, pinning her down. She heard Amy singing somewhere. Clouds formed, roiled, then rained fat dark-red drops onto her face, chest, and arms. The viscous liquid streamed down her forearms, pooled in her upturned palms, and drained through her fingers.

Sometime mid-afternoon, Susan awakened to an unfamiliar stillness. No motor sounds, no wind, no rumble of thunder. She gazed out from the shade of their shelter at shimmering red rock. A row of cacti stood guard between her and the streambed, and the slope opposite rose high enough to prevent her from seeing over its top. Everything she looked at ignited some vague fear in her; she felt frayed like a worn-out rope.

She sat and stared. Her years of living as a girl with native myths resurrected old memories. An elder neighbor, a cousin of Old Ruth and a skilled tracker and hunter, told her once, "The land tells a story if you look past the big picture to the small detail." Focusing her mind even more on details might do some good. She needed to engage the hunter's state of full alertness that she had been taught as a child. She decided to try to scale the bank as soon as the sun started to go down, and maybe learn more about the way out. Her ankle was swollen, but she could rotate it a bit and wiggle all her toes. She'd force herself to manage. In the meantime, while she waited for Lyn to awaken, she examined the cave wall behind her and the floor of the alcove for miniscule messages. She sifted sand through her fingers and was pleased to find a black and white striped potsherd the size of a silver dollar. After studying the fragment of pottery, she searched further and discovered a small round stone and then a broken arrow point.

"I'm so thirsty. I could drink a lake dry. I hardly have to pee, and I've been sleeping for what, six hours?" Lyn said, sitting up on her pad and shaking an empty plastic water bottle. "We're probably rationing the food okay, but our water ... I'm concerned about our water."

"Before 'Good Morning' or 'Hello' you start talking about your stomach. You're such a kid!" Susan grinned at her companion as she sat looking groggy and dazed. Her skin and lips were burned, dirty, and cracked; her red hair was knotted and snagged. Cuts criss-crossed her arms and legs.

"It's afternoon now anyhow, and you're right, all I can think about is water, plunging into water, drinking all my belly can hold. I swear I will never underestimate the importance of water again. God, I hope we can find a spring or a seep today ... or tonight. How's the foot?"

Susan leaned forward and massaged it. "Not bad. A little stiff. We'll see what happens when I start to put weight on it again. I'd really like to climb the bank of the wash over there and see what's around us."

Lyn regarded Susan closely. Her facial bruises were still livid. Her blouse was torn at the breast pockets and her jeans were filthy. "And how about the rest of your body and soul?"

"Oh ... I'm still in shock, I think. I had nightmarish dreams and I can't stop thinking about ..." She smiled ruefully. "But it's a new night and we have a project we gotta work on here."

Lyn shook out her hair and tied it back with a piece of cloth; she put on her cap and sunglasses and crawled over to Susan's side. "You gave me good advice about conserving energy yesterday. But you better practice what you preach. Now ... let's get some fuel into us."

They choked down some dried fruit and nuts and rationed themselves each a cup of water. They were trying to manage on two small meals a day. And they'd have to find water and help soon. While they waited for evening, the hours plodded by at dirge tempo. As the late afternoon sun cast the high rocks of the bank of the arroyo into relief, the women started slowly up it. Almost immediately Susan was favoring her ankle and had to sit. The steep angle caused too much pain. Lyn felt like she needed to move and started scrambling up quickly. The temperature was dropping a little and cooler air crossed her sweat-soaked back, but the rock was almost too hot to grasp. Nonetheless, within five minutes, she was more than halfway to the top.

"Hey, this isn't bad at all. Lots of good footing. Way better than the climb down the butte. And my shoulder ..." Lyn froze in mid-sentence. She heard a soft shimmer just above and to her right on the rock where she was placing her hand. "Susan," she shouted in a stage whisper, "I just heard a rattle!"

"Oh, yeah, Lynnie. I'd guess there're lots of snakes around here, it's probably a diamondback. You've surprised him and he's warning you. Just remove your hand slowly and back away. Climb down. And watch where you put your hands and feet." Lyn virtually flew down the hill to Susan's side. Susan got up and reached out for her hand.

"There now, it's a perfect relationship, he warns you, and you avoid him. You're both doing the polite thing." Susan was still eager to get a view from the top, but nothing could convince her companion to go back up. There was no alternative but to follow the main wash and their instincts, blind to the larger landscape that held them captive. But it was imperative that they move. They had roughly three days to find water, or else die in the desert.

Shortly before dusk, after several hours on the road, Jake checked his map while driving and figured he was approximately ninety or so miles from Iron Springs and the mine; Vegas was another twenty miles beyond that. The car was climbing up a steep mesa with a view to the south of chaparral the color of lemon when he was startled by an electronic beep. Cell service at last and there were messages. With one hand he scrolled down past several voice messages from Rachel. He switched to the text messages app on his screen and saw that he had several new texts. The light on the phone blinked off and he looked up just in time to yank the car back over the centerline before an on-coming mud-covered pickup shot by. He slowed and found a firm patch of shoulder sand.

He switched off the ignition, unlocked his screen, and pushed the button to select his text messages. There was a new message that started, "Lyn/Sue okay." Jake's chest constricted. The message continued: "Descending butte ... N.E. Vegas ... N. Mead, approx ..." It was truncated, but it was like a treasure in Goddard's trembling hands. Sweat beaded on his forehead. He plugged in the number of origin on the text and tried calling it but an automated message told him the user was out of cell range. He grabbed his map. I-15 and U.S. 93 formed two sides to a box around the area described in the message. Susan and Lyn were somewhere in approximately sixty square miles of rugged backcountry with limited access. He felt the tightness in his chest relax and a sense of, not elation exactly, but direction, clarity. It was still a huge gamble, but at least he had a shot at success. But where was Bev? His heart hammered and the trembling returned anew.

He focused his mind on the message and on the terrain. Another look at the map and he noted there was only one unpaved road that led up into the high country in the center of the targeted area. North of I-15 and

Lake Mead, halfway across the "box," was a four-wheel drive road that dead-ended near something called Mormon Peak.

It took Goddard another half-hour to find the spur road. It began at an isolated ranch exit and initially ran perpendicular to the interstate before turning due north into the mountains. He followed it for a few miles with I-15 still in view. Dark was fast approaching as he pulled off the dirt road to get his bearings. In the waning light he could see the discrete island of treeless high country ahead, the highest point of which had to be Mormon Peak.

He was stowing his map when a dirty white pick-up truck left I-15 and headed his way. As the truck approached, trailing dust, Jake could see the driver was alone. The truck passed and Jake jolted when he saw a SDWA seal on the side. The pick-up headed out the road toward the peaks and grew smaller with distance.

When he felt it was safe to pursue, he reached behind the passenger seat, grabbed his Browning 9mm, and laid it on the console next to him. For miles there was nothing but rolling desert terrain until he passed a sign for The Carp Buffalo Ranch. The weathered sign told of the dangers of buffalo and warned that trespassers, if they survived, would be prosecuted.

Following the truck up into the high desert, Jake turned off his headlights and relied only on the moon. The terrain grew more rugged as the road climbed steadily and twisted through washes and around outcrops. Joshua trees stood out on the ridges like disjointed bottle-washers. As the road approached a jumble of house-sized slabs, the surface went from sand to rock and then from rock to boulder. Jake wrenched the little station wagon around boulders as large as the car, wincing when chassis metal screeched across rock. His palms were slippery on the wheel. The truck had higher clearance and was pulling away from him. He fell even further behind as his car alternately wallowed in sandy dips and bucked over large rocks. Panic started as a tingle in his groin and crawled up his spine like ants. He accelerated recklessly, bouncing the little car from rock to rock in an effort to catch up. His brain screamed conflicting alerts. You'll lose him! You'll get stuck!

The Subaru lunged up a low slope of rock and tipped over the front edge. Goddard hit the gas as the back wheels spun and the car slammed sideways with a metallic "chunk" and high-centered on a point of rock. He twisted off the ignition, banged out, and kicked the front tire. "You stupid fuck!" he shouted as much at himself as the car. He ripped off his ball cap, slapped it on the car's fender and stared ahead. He was stuck right in the center of what, according to his map, was the only road in or out. The stars, though relatively dim in the moonlight, still mocked him with their brilliance.

He had few choices. He tucked his pistol in his belt, got out his flashlight and started up the road on foot toward the mountains, now dark silhouettes in the distance. Suddenly he heard a huffing sound just off the road to his right and swung around with his pistol at the ready, snapping on the light. Beyond a sturdy fence, a large brown shape moved slowly away from him, a bull bison. It paused, snorted, and lumbered out of view. Jake sat on a boulder to calm his breathing and get his bearings before resuming his pace.

The two women began their evening's hike in silence. Susan rolled a smooth round pebble between her fingers. Out of respect, she'd tucked the potsherd and arrowhead back in the sand where she'd found it. She struggled to ratchet up her senses to detect water. By now the sounds of dusk were becoming familiar; changes in bird calls, the rustle of small nocturnal animals. Lyn asked about one lonely echoing call that descended the musical scale in short bursts.

"Canyon wren," Susan said. "One of my favorites when I was a kid … and really good news, now that I think about it, because they hang out near water. I think we're close to water."

"Of course, I know the canyon wren. Ha. That's funny. For a second, I thought it was a flute. Duh. I'm like, oh, a flute … great. As if there'd be a flute player out here. Maybe that randy Koko guy, right? I'm getting really spacey—like I'm floating in a tunnel. I hope you're right about the water, but I'm trying not to get my hopes up."

The wash divided again and again and deepened into a true canyon with sheer sandstone walls. The women struggled to identify the best route. Several times they headed down what seemed to be the main branch, only to discover they were in a box canyon. Each time they backtracked, their spirits sagged. Trapped in a maze, their frustration mounted. Susan had to rest her ankle every thirty minutes.

During one such break, Susan said, "Lynnie, one of the things police work teaches you is to review what you know over and over, in different sequences. Now, I realize you don't want to focus on White Wolf, but let's discuss him one more time."

"It's really hard for me."

"I realize that, hon. This won't take long, I promise. Knowing what White Wolf did to you and to me, do you think he could commit murder? Is he that crazy?" Susan asked.

"Oh, yeah. I'm convinced he was involved in Fernando's death."

"He's clearly not operating alone. You know I saw him speaking with two men and a woman at your father's mine just before Bev was killed and White Wolf punched me out."

Lyn stood and glared at Susan. "If he was meeting with people at Ashland, it must have been without my father's knowledge. I don't agree with my father's politics or choice of business, but he would never associate with a scumbag like Forrest White Wolf. Never." She started to walk and Susan followed.

"Okay, let's try another tactic. Can you remember any hints about Fernando's death that White Wolf might have given you?"

"He refused to talk about Fernando but was clearly unmoved by his death. I could kick myself for not reading that danger sign. I believe White Wolf pushed Fernando and there can be only one reason. Fernando must have somehow learned that White Wolf was a fraud and, who knows, maybe that the Virgin River dam project is bullshit, too."

The two were so busy talking and so used to twists and bends in their path that they failed to notice when the walls of the wash narrowed and deepened even more. They were walking in a winding slot, about as wide as a one-lane road. Moonlight reflected in tiny crystalline specks on its walls and sandy surface. They began to slow their pace as they dealt with their confusion. What stopped them, though, was the faint gurgling sound they could hear from around the next bend.

They dropped their gear and hurried toward the sound. A glistening pool appeared before them in a shallow depression at the base of a small alcove in the canyon wall. Monkey flowers and small deciduous bushes surrounded the spring. Ferns grew on the damp rock.

"This water is the best thing I have ever felt or tasted," Lyn said. She bathed her swollen hands, Susan her feet. They filled their bottles at the source, drank and refilled. Susan fished the little stone from her pocket. It was rounded by water. A stream had originally formed it. It was a little detail, a tiny oracle. The potsherd too, had been a clue about the proximity of reliable water. They both served as a reminder that now that they had found water, she had to be all the more alert and prepared for danger. The women lingered at the edge of the spring, drinking or splashing whenever they felt like it, their thoughts spilling out at random.

"Amy would love this. Swimming in a magic pool by moonlight. She used to be happy in the bathtub for hours." Susan cupped water in her hands and dripped it on her hair. And then a few moments later she took a long sip and held up her bottle and sighed. "Here's to you, Bev."

Lyn knelt by the water, dipped her head in the little pool and came up sputtering. "If Mojo were here he'd be up to his ears trying to bite stones off of the bottom." Susan started to tell her about the round stone and potsherd when a related memory bubbled up and burst into her consciousness.

"Lyn ... Lyn. Please come away from the water for a minute. Bring your bottle." Lyn, looking confused, stood up. "Please ... come away from the spring—just give me a minute to explain. There is something we need to do ... for the spring." Lyn looked quizzical, twisted water out of her hair and walked across the wash to Susan. "I just remembered something important. The Tohono O'odham fear too much water as well as too little. They have great reverence for the balance. They were always cautioning me and the other children to not drink too much water ..."

"Oh that's a myth about drinking too much when you're dehydrated—as long as you start slowly," Lyn interrupted.

"No, no, you don't understand. It is not about that. It's about respect and humility. They believe using water with arrogance and self-indulgence is asking for serious trouble."

Lyn looked closely at her friend. "Susan, come on."

"No, Lyn. Hear me out. They told this story of a vain teenage boy who ignored his elders' warnings and wasted water constantly, washing himself and his possessions. One crystal-clear day he was going again to a spring in a dry wash, like this, for more water when he was swept away and drowned in a flash flood. Please indulge me. Just out of respect and gratitude, let's just put some of this water in our bottles back in the spring."

Susan approached the pool as if she were entering a church. Lyn followed tentatively. Susan slowly poured the contents of her bottle into the small spring. The water splashed and rippled. Susan turned to Lyn. She reached her bottle toward the spring and tilted it, but before any water escaped a sound sent a jolt of adrenaline through her. Not the helicopter, not now! But it wasn't the helicopter. It was a large pickup truck. It turned around a sandstone fin and bounced over the rocks, sending sand and pebbles flying out of depressions. They were paralyzed in the headlights, totally exposed. The walls around them were too steep to climb and running back up the canyon was out of the question. They stood by the spring—Susan threw her arm around Lyn. The immense vehicle clawed its way toward them and jolted to a stop at twenty yards. The driver was a young man, alone. He leaned out the driver's side window without smiling and said, "Thought you two could use a cold drink and a ride."

Susan and Lyn looked at each other. Lyn waited for a sign from Susan. Even though all Susan's systems were calling for extreme caution, she realized they had no choice but to go with the stranger in the truck. In fact, on one level, she had been expecting him. Susan nodded. They retrieved their packs, lifted them into the bed, and climbed in the cab. Lyn sat in the middle. The driver pulled two quarts of Gatorade out of a cooler behind the seat and handed them each a turkey sandwich as well.

The man seemed very uncomfortable shifting into reverse next to Lyn's thigh. He apologized awkwardly when he accidentally bumped her knee. It was dark in the cab but Susan made out that he was wearing old tan canvas shorts and a plain white t-shirt, and he had a tattoo on the back of his right hand. He backed the truck down the canyon.

"We were hiking and we got lost a few days ago. How did you happen to find us?" Susan asked.

"Oh … I been scouting bighorn and I saw you … from up on a nearby butte. Thought you looked kinda lost and tired," he said, briefly glancing sideways at the women. The truck bucked back over a large rock.

"Scouting game in the middle of the night?" Susan asked.

"All the good kills are nocturnal this time of year. Everything in the area eventually ends up at that spring. Predator and prey alike." Susan pressed her elbow into Lyn's side.

The driver backed into a side spur, turned around, and headed down the narrow main canyon. They rode in silence, the women wolfing down their sandwiches, until Lyn blurted, "Where are you taking us?"

"Where do you want to go?" the man asked. Lyn shot Susan a glance.

"Oh, the … the rest of our group is at Lake Mead, near where the Virgin River empties into the lake. Can you take us there?" Lyn asked.

He smiled, for the first time. "I can, but you'll need a Hummer, 'cause that spot you described has no road access and you ladies don't look in any shape to hike in."

"What she means is … they're on houseboats and we need to go to the nearest marina," Susan said.

Again the driver was quiet, but the light from the dashboard revealed a slight smile lingering on his face and it put Susan on alert. The canyon widened. In the headlights, red rock gave way to eroded shale and limestone hillocks. Susan could feel Lyn's tension and sensed that Lyn was studying the man surreptitiously. Susan rested her head against the passenger window and tried to remember the details of the land at the north end of Lake Mead.

A loud click by her ear caused Susan to jerk upright. The driver's arm had brushed a button on his armrest and the doors had locked automatically. Lyn glowered at him for a second and then drove her left foot onto the brake, hard. "What the fuck?" the driver shouted. The truck slid sideways on the sand and shuttered to a stop.

"I recognize that tattoo on your hand, you bastard! You're one of the animals who slid food through the door." Lyn dove across him trying to get to the automatic door lock. "Let us out, now. Unlock the door." Susan began pulling frantically on her door handle.

Sanders pinned Lyn's arms across his chest, "Hold on, hold on ... listen to me. I'm here on my own. I want to help."

"Right, you scumbag. How do we know we can believe you?" Susan demanded.

Lyn tried again to pull away. "What's in it for you?"

"Hear me out. If you can't trust me, then I'll let you go. I'm not exactly sure why I'm doing this. Okay, I was ordered by my boss to bring you in. Normally, I'm just a guy does his job and goes home to a couple of beers." He looked at the women for a reaction and eased up on Lyn's arms. "Bottom line, you two impressed the shit out of me. I thought you'd end up at that spring. When I headed out, to be honest, I wasn't sure what I was going to do if I found you. But then when I drove up and saw you so scared and worn out after all you'd been through...shit, I don't know. Fuck the boss! Where do you want to go?"

Sanders released the young woman's arms, and Susan reached for Lyn's hand and held it tightly in her own between their hips. "We need to see what's happening at Lake Mead, right, Lyn?" Tears welled up in Lyn's eyes and she struggled to swallow. She nodded her assent.

"We don't have a choice but to trust you. But we're two and you're one, so just drive us straight to the marina," said Susan, glaring across Lyn at the man. "If you are jerking us around I will do everything in my power to kill you."

Sanders nodded at Susan. She saw a change in his eyes. They had gone cold. He turned out of the rubble onto a steep ramp of rock and picked his way downhill around boulders. After dropping into a sandy wash, Sanders stopped the truck and shoved the stick into park. He reached down between his legs and grabbed a small cloth bag. Its contents were heavy. Leaning back against the driver's door and smiling slowly, he pulled a handgun from the bag.

"Thought my little game would make it easier to bag you two. You threatening to kill me, officer—now that took all the fun out of it." He wiped his mouth with the back of his hand. "You know, I got to thinking while I was driving, shit, maybe you could kill me. You're pretty tough, a cop and all. Go for my throat or something. You're not as easy to deal with as when I flew you out here in the helicopter and you were all drugged up. And hey, by the way, you have really nice tits under that shirt." He gestured with the gun. "I had me a little peek, before. You were in la la land. Sweet. Anyhow, let's save them till later. It's time to stop playing around and get serious." He turned the pistol in his hand. "This Glock of yours is a honey, ma'am. Real nice. .40-caliber, right?" He reached behind Lyn and placed the barrel against the back of Susan's head. "Now, please don't make me mess up this truck. Just got it detailed. My boss is looking forward to seeing you. Okay, Red, you're going to work the gearshift. Put this baby in drive." Lyn looked with desperation at Susan who nodded tersely. She wrestled the truck into gear.

Fearing he might recognize her van since she'd been following him for hours, Lou tailed White Wolf at a more discreet distance. The blue car left the Lake Mead area and cut through the mountains toward Las Vegas. Towering rock walls and barren hillocks were backlit by the glow of the city to the west. More cars began to enter the freeway. Lou relaxed a bit with this additional cover and moved a little closer.

White Wolf was driving erratically. Just as they entered the Las Vegas Valley and could see the ubiquitous lights, he drifted off onto the right-hand rumble strip and remained off course for several hundred yards before jerking the car back into his lane.

"What do you think our activist friend is up to now?" Lou asked. "If I were him, I'd be thinking about a place to bunk. He's had a long day."

"Hell, we've all had a long day," Moody said.

"I hear that." Lou yawned. "And I sense our boy is either getting very tired or drunk or both. And that means he's vulnerable. It shouldn't be long before he finds a hole to crawl into for the rest of the night." She checked her watch. "Think he's expecting visitors at this hour?"

At the first exit with lodging, there was a massive digital sign pitching cheap rooms, $5 slots, and $10 prime rib dinners. White Wolf turned off the highway and shot up a short access road to a garish three-story wood building with faux columns and a portico surrounding the entrance.

White Wolf squinted against the bright lights and lime green of the motel corridor and stumbled a bit as he searched for his room. He dropped his duffle in front of a door and tried his card repeatedly with no luck. In his peripheral vision he noticed a white haired women in a wheelchair, being pushed by a man in a hooded sweatshirt and ball cap. He dragged his duffle down one more door, checked the number, tried the card, and got a green light on the second try. Yawning, he pushed the door open and reached for his duffle on the floor. The wheelchair was passing behind him. He could hear the old lady yawn. When he straightened to go in his room, a hard object jammed into the small of his back.

"What the—"

"Don't turn around. Keep your mouth shut and walk slowly into the room," Lou whispered.

White Wolf did as he was told. Moody rolled Lou into the room and closed the door behind them. White Wolf lowered his duffle onto the bed.

"Now you can turn around," Lou said. He pivoted, launching the duffle in an arc toward Lou's head. She ducked and Moody pulled back as it whizzed in front of his face; it thumped harmlessly against the wall and plopped to the floor. White Wolf stared dumbfounded down the barrel of the shotgun in Lou's hands.

"I will shoot you." Lou shifted in her chair and pushed the shotgun closer to his face. "You get to be my age and debilitated and realize you no longer have much to lose, Forrest. Now, you listen to me. If you don't do as I ask, or if you try anything that stupid again, I will shoot you with both barrels."

"Who are you?" White Wolf asked, incredulous.

"I'm Lou Cuvier. Remember me?" He didn't respond. "No? You should make a point of remembering the people you spit on. What is it about you and faces? I understand you shoved a pie in this gentleman's face recently." Moody removed his hood and ball cap.

A look of surprised recognition came into White Wolf's eyes. "I do remember you, lady, from way back … and we all know your friend here. What do you want with me?"

"I'm still an environmentalist, Forrest, but I'm not here on such a noble mission as you. What is it now? 'Save the Virgin,' right? That'd be a first for you, for sure. Tell me, Mr. White Wolf, what is an environmentalist doing entering a tunnel construction site and using their equipment like he works for them? We didn't do things that way in my day." She glanced at her watch. "But, I'm here as a very worried old Auntie. Lyn Burke is my niece. You've been enjoying her car. Where is she, Forrest? Her mother is very worried and I want to take her home."

"You're Lyn's aunt?" White Wolf licked his lower lip. "Damn, that's great. She's a hell of a young woman. You must be very proud of her."

"Cut the bullshit, asshole. Where is she?" Moody asked.

"She's … she's back from Utah and is out in the desert near here with a good friend of mine. SDWA is required to hire folks like your niece and me for … for impact studies. She should be back at the straw soon. The super told me on the phone that he sent his pilot out three hours ago to pick them up. We can ask the super at the straw when to expect her."

Lou pressed. "Hmm, must be the 'friend' who supposedly accompanied Lyn to the Virgin River area? The guy gets around. Where is Dr. Skutches?"

White Wolf shrugged and looked out the window and back at Lou. "Not sure. Still at The Howl at the Full Moon Festival, I guess."

"What were you doing in that boat at the dam?" Moody demanded.

"Oh … checking water levels. It has an impact on construction schedules at the tunnel."

"Checking water levels in the middle of the night? Interesting. You have an answer for everything, don't you? And, I'm certain you know the true answer to my question about my niece." Lou said. She looked at her watch again and felt panic rising up in her for the first time. "We're going to the straw, Forrest, and you better not be lying about Lyn being there soon. Now move! We don't have all night. Walk in front of the chair and do not get more than five feet away from me." White Wolf paused a minute and, deciding the old lady wasn't bluffing, shook his head and did what he was told.

Sanders' truck clawed out of a wash and then began to ascend a long rise that climbed up toward a jumble of two-story rocks before leveling off beyond. Once again, the ride got very rough.

Susan felt the barrel of the pistol bump her head when the truck lurched over a slab. "Damnit! You're going to crack my skull with that barrel."

"Pray that's all I do, lady."

Susan turned her head toward Sanders, as if to relieve the pain from the bump, and eyed the hand on the pistol. His finger was not centered on the trigger. Her Glock wouldn't fire unless his finger was centered. She calculated the risk involved in trying to grab the gun. Her pulse drummed in her ears. The truck lurched again. Susan struggled to think straight as Lyn looked at her with terror in her eyes. Susan's head felt swollen and her cheek throbbed. She was nauseous from the headlights bouncing on the surrounding rocks and bushes and the constant swaying of the vehicle. The truck bumped hard again and whined under the stress of climbing the final pitch of steep terrain. Sanders fought the wheel with one hand. The road flattened at the top and the lights settled back to level, illuminating the entrance to a narrow passageway in the wall of boulders. Sanders steered slowly through the slot. On the other side of the massive rocks, the headlights spilled on the body of a man lying prone across the road. Susan yelled. Sanders reacted and slammed on the brakes. Jake jumped up and lunged toward the driver's door, shielding his eyes from the glare and aiming his pistol at the driver. Susan grabbed

Sanders' wrist with both hands and sank her teeth into the flesh below his thumb. The pilot shrieked and drove his foot onto the gas. The truck bounced toward Jake, but he leaped to the side, holding his fire as the vehicle charged by. As Susan wrestled the wrist and bit harder, Sanders squeezed off two deafening shots past her left ear. The first bullet penetrated the front window. The second went through the roof. Jake sprinted after the truck and, reacting to the shots, fired once at each rear tire, but missed. The pain caused Sanders to lose control of the wheel. The truck lurched into a ditch and sideswiped a boulder. He cranked the wheel and fishtailed back onto the road.

"Lyn, help me!" Susan hissed through bloody teeth. Lyn looked like she was fainting into Susan's lap but then twisted and kicked at Sanders' face with her left foot, catching him under the chin and jamming his head hard against the side window. She wrenched the gearshift up into neutral. The engine roared, just as Jake appeared at the window and placed his pistol outside the glass two inches from Sanders' temple.

"Drop it! Goddamnit! Drop it now!" Jake yelled through the glass. "Take your foot off the gas." The engine quieted. The pilot let Susan pull the gun out of his injured hand. She reached across Lyn and pointed it at his chest, holding her ear with her other hand. Lyn reached up, switched off the engine, and lay shaking with her head in Susan's lap.

Sanders sat in the corner, scowling and gripping his bleeding hand. Jake ordered him to unlock the doors, get out, and lie on the ground, face down.

Lyn sucked in breath after breath. "Oh my God! Is it over? Is it really over?"

Susan shook her head to stop the ringing and put her hand on Lyn's shoulder. "It's over, sweetheart. That's my partner, Jake. Good to see him, huh?" With trembling fingers, she brushed Lyn's hair from her forehead. Lyn sat up and began to rock, hugging herself. "You did great. You were amazing," Susan said. Tears ran down Lyn's face.

Susan eased out of the truck, went around the hood, and stood beside her friend with her Glock trained on Sanders. She put her arm around Jake, "You never looked better, partner." She looked down at Sanders. "We just bagged the pilot who stranded us on a butte and has been hunting us since we escaped." She looked at Jake. "Turned the tables on the hunter. I was pretty sure if we found water, he'd find us. I just wasn't sure what we were going to do then. Glad you showed up."

"Excellent work, officer. Good to see you. Damn good to see you." He smiled at her and she detected a quiver at the corners of his mouth. "They shot Bev, Jake," Susan said. "He's dead."

Susan stared into Jake's eyes as they dampened; he exhaled a ragged breath and worked his lower jaw. "I'm very sorry," Susan said. He brought his free arm up around her waist and squeezed. Lyn had collected herself and slid out the passenger side of the truck.

"So, you're Lyn Burke. How glad I am to see you, too," Jake said.

"Thank you soooo much," she said, running around the front of the truck. "You two are my heroes." She hugged their necks throwing them off balance.

Suddenly, Sanders was up and running toward the edge of the road. "I'm sorry, I'm sorry," Lyn cried. Sanders rushed straight into a green and gold patch of teddy bear cholla, beavertail cactus, and Spanish bayonet, rolled like a linebacker and came up on the fly, bleeding and howling, spikes of plant material stuck in his arms and legs. He was exposed in the moonlight and searched desperately for cover. Susan ran to the edge of the road and took aim. Lyn kneeled, held her ears, and closed her eyes. The cop lowered her gun as Sanders scrambled under a fence and zigzagged like a spooked hare, disappearing behind a large lone boulder on the sandy flats.

"'Don't throw me in that briar patch,'" Jake said, coming up beside Susan.

"Well, that solves one big problem, doesn't it?" Susan said.

"He's hurt, unarmed, and ill-equipped," Jake said, watching the boulder for any sign of Sanders. "Let's just see if the pilot can find his way back to civilization without the aid of high tech equipment. Turn and burn, you son-of-a-bitch." He turned to Susan. "Bev would've laughed his ass off seeing him go through that cactus. "He used to say 'turn and burn' when I was about to lose a poker hand."

"No doubt about it," Susan said, putting her arm on Jake's shoulder. "Bev would have loved being here for this." They stared at the rock in silence for a few moments. "Burn in hell!" she said.

"Come on, partner. Let's use his truck to get me unstuck and then disable it. We've got bigger game to hunt down at Mead than ol' Br'er Rabbit out there."

They turned back to Lyn but a sound stopped them short.

A bellow and a roar came from beyond the fence.

The tattoo of hoofs on rock was met with a scream.

"Lynnie, stay here," Susan shouted.

She and Goddard picked their way around the cactus patch and climbed up a short bank to the fence.

Approximately fifty yards away, Sanders lay at the feet of three agitated bull buffalo.

A cloud of dust rose around the animals as they gored and trampled him.

They lifted and tossed the broken body back and forth on their horns like a rag doll.

The largest bull threw the body to the ground in a lifeless heap.

The animals stood panting over the body briefly and then shuffled away.

"There was nothing we could do," Jake said.

"It's God's call now," Susan added.

Jake and Susan rejoined an anxious Lyn. A shake of Susan's head told the young woman it was over for Sanders. The three climbed in the truck and drove to the Subaru in exhausted silence.

June 21
Summer Solstice
Wednesday

Lou shielded her eyes from the lights as she eased the van up to the booth at the tunnel security gate. White Wolf was in the passenger seat. Rank Moody sat behind him with a blanket over his lap.

"This is off limits to the public, ma'am," the guard said before she could get her window down.

The nub of the shotgun poked through the seat into White Wolf's kidney. He squirmed away. "It's okay," he said, leaning down so the guard could see his face. "My car died and this nice lady is giving me a ride back to the office." Lou flashed the guard her best smile, made sure he saw her white hair, and fiddled with her favorite silver necklace. The guard raised the gate.

Three tanks on long metal stilts, gaping concrete mixers, several dump trucks, and piles of building materials lined the entrance road. High above the earth, a steel beam dangled from a crane. Still as slate, the lake's surface mirrored the shoreline, reflecting the gallery of concrete, iron, and steel. White Wolf pointed to a doublewide trailer up the road adjacent to the large unfinished water treatment plant. The trailer's interior light flowed out from a single window under an attached ramada. Lou pulled under the ramada, opened the van's automatic door behind her seat, and worked the wheelchair lift to the ground. She slid out of the driver's seat and into her chair and rolled herself around the front of the van to the passenger side, not once taking her eyes off White Wolf. She gestured to Moody to arrange the blanket and shotgun on her lap. He slid out, tucked her in, and got behind her, ready to push. For a moment, Lou shifted her gaze toward the mouth of the tunnel, then, focused, cleared her throat, and signaled White Wolf to get out of the van. They went up a short gravel path to the ramp into the trailer.

The trailer door was unlocked but O'Connor was not inside. White Wolf approached the desk with a swagger and leafed through a file on the blotter.

"Your boss isn't here, Forrest, nor is my niece." Lou raised the gun. "What's your plan now?" He looked at the ceiling for a second and then reached for the desk phone. "Look, I ... I was told she'd be here. Lemme make a call or two."

"To whom? Nobody can help you faster than my shot can blow you away. And the two of us can be out of here in no time."

Forrest's eyes darted from Lou to Moody. "Just let me call the superintendent. He's the one who knows for sure. I'm just a consultant on this operation."

"All right," Lou nodded, "one call. Put the damn thing on speaker. I want to hear his voice."

He dialed. The phone was answered on the second ring. "Mr. O'Connor. This is Forrest White Wolf."

"White Wolf, what the Jesus are you up to at this hour?"

White Wolf glanced toward Lou's lap then turned and looked out the window. "Mr. O'Connor, I'm here in your office with Lyn Burke's aunt. She's very concerned about her niece. I told her Lyn's back from Utah and working here now and that you sent someone out to pick her up tonight."

"You did, did you, Forrest?"

"Yes, I said you'd be glad to show Ms. Cuvier here that Lyn is fine and is doing field research for us."

"Really. Research, huh? You told her she was doing research? Put her on, you imbecile."

"Uh, it's on speaker now, sir."

His tone sweetened abruptly. "This is Liam O'Connor. How can I help you?"

"I need to see my niece immediately, Mr. O'Connor."

"Yes, well, I'm sorry to disappoint you, madam, but your niece did not come in from the field today. She sent word to me earlier that she found some fossils and she wanted to stay out a little longer and study them. They should be back soon. She's in great shape—a strapping healthy young woman, that's sure. She did a fine job over there in Utah, I'm told. You must be proud of such a goal-oriented and bright—"

"Please forgive me, Mr. O'Connor," Lou cut him off. "But this is urgent and what you are telling me just doesn't seem right. For starters, what the hell does SDWA have to do with activists from Lifewater?" She glared at White Wolf. "Also, my niece usually calls my sister and me regularly, you see. Why hasn't she called since returning from Utah?"

"Ma'am, there are just a few hours until I get into the office. I will be happy to do what I can when I get there. Now, if—"

Again, Lou interjected, "I suppose you have a point. We'll be here just before dawn, waiting and if my niece is not here, the police will be our next stop."

O'Connor's voice was icy. "As you wish, Ms. Cuvier. Goodbye." He hung up.

Lou dropped the blanket. "Forrest, come right over here by me." White Wolf did as he was told. "Now, no more of your crap. You know more about my niece than you're admitting. For instance, you know she doesn't study fossils. She studies hawks. You also know there is no way she'd work for the SDWA. That's like oil and water. No way in hell. You know exactly where she is 'in the field.' You know exactly what mental and physical condition she is in. You are going to tell me where she is and prove she is safe. And I'll tell you something." She checked her watch. "It is 4:32 a.m., you are going to die in sixty minutes unless I have the information I want before then."

White Wolf tried to stare her down, but couldn't. She heard his bowels gurgle; he knew she wasn't bluffing. "Uh ... maybe she's already at the tunnel," he blurted out in a desperate attempt to buy time.

Trying not to disturb the two women asleep in the back, Jake eased his car into the parking lot next to the yellow brick Visitor's Center overlooking Boulder Bay. He reclined his seat and tried to doze but sleep evaded him. He looked in the rearview mirror at Susan and Lyn, partially illuminated by the parking lot lights. Lyn's cheeks were scraped and bruised, her hair a mass of tangles. She slept a deep drug-like sleep—stretched out, relaxed as a baby, her head in Susan's lap. Susan was sitting up, knees tight together, one arm across Lyn's torso, the other close at her side. Her hands were dirty and cut, and her fingernails, usually so well manicured, torn and caked with blood. Her face twitched as she slept, her mouth and brow tightly drawn. To Jake's eyes, although still beautiful, she had aged ten years in less than five days. He kept picturing her smiling down at him from her horse's back—strong, proud, and pretty.

Worry and admiration swelled up in him, but fear and concern pressed him harder. They lit up his brain like a pinball machine. Lou and Moody were still out there with White Wolf, and Lou's cryptic reference to fireworks at sunrise echoed in his ears. According to a sign by the entrance to the Visitor's Center, the sun was due to rise at 5:35 a.m., now just a little over an hour away. Where the hell were Moody and Cuvier? Jake reached up on the dash and snatched the piece of paper Lou had given him when she left The Howl. He couldn't make it out in the semi-darkness. He grabbed his binoculars and pistol and slipped out of the car.

Jake went through the breezeway of the Visitor's Center and out past a garden of saguaro cactus, palm trees, and desert plants, which led to a viewing terrace. Propping his elbows on the log railing, he scanned the surrounding landscape and lakeshore below. High above him to the left, backlit by the garish lights of Las Vegas, were the barren River Mountains, capped by rounded Dromedary Peak. Jake raked his binos from the top of Dromedary, down the still-dark slopes, and along the arid foothills and dry washes that eventually terminated at the shore of the lake. He could make out several islands and peninsulas breaking the smooth surface. Power towers originating at the dam assaulted the mountain range through a high pass and headed on to Vegas. Lakeshore Drive, parallel to the shore and half a mile back from the water, curved over several foothills, past the mouth of the tunnel and the fish hatchery, and toward Las Vegas Bay—the arm of the lake that reached out closest to the city. Vegas sprawl, including a small artificial lake and housing development in what was formerly a wash, pushed right up against the boundary of the Lake Mead Recreation Area.

He swung the binoculars back to the bright lights of the tunnel construction site. A litter of garishly lit machinery and partially completed structures stood in stark contrast to the emptiness of the surrounding terrain. Following the lakeshore south, past the barn and corrals of a trail-riding concession, he looked in the direction of Boulder Dam. He could see the gargantuan transmission towers ascending both the Nevada and Arizona sides of the lake and, peeking out from behind a ridge, the top of a multi-storied casino. Promontory Point, a towering peninsula, hid the dam from his view.

Jake bristled at the sound of a motor. Headlights swung past him, locked briefly on his car, and were extinguished. A young man in a green uniform, with a ponytail and thick glasses, got out of a Park Service truck. He grabbed a mop and bucket out of the bed and entered the women's restroom. Jake exhaled, bent his head from side to side, and panned across the straw site and nearby shoreline one more time. At the sound of footsteps, he spun around.

"Whoa, Susan, you scared me," he said quietly, putting his index finger to his mouth and nodding toward the Park Service truck.

"Sorry, I should have spoken," Susan whispered.

"You doing all right?"

"I'll be all right when I'm home with my daughter. It was great to hear her sleepy voice on the phone. Even Chuck sounded good to me." She shivered and yawned.

"Couldn't sleep?" Jake said.

"Not really. The truck lights woke me from weird half dreams ... and just being this close to that prick White Wolf makes me uneasy." She looked down toward Lakeshore Drive. "I just hope Lou hasn't had a run-in with him."

"Lou said to meet here no later than 5:00 a.m., roughly thirty minutes from now. We should know more soon. She said something about 'an early Fourth of July celebration' with the sunrise today." Jake tapped his iPad. "I just checked the Boulder Dam webcam. Dam's lit like a stage set—nothing going on over there." Jake unfolded the piece of paper Lou gave him, but it was difficult to see. "Lou gave me this note. Let's move under that light and see if we can make any sense of it."

They walked back toward the building. Jake noticed Susan was still limping. The partners perched on a bench under the arch of the breezeway. The bucket scraped across the floor in the women's room. A coyote yipped in the distance.

"Thank you, song dog," Susan murmured.

"What?"

"When I was about at my lowest point during our climb down off the butte and pretty certain I was going to fall, Lynnie heard a coyote and said it was singing to me. My childhood friend, Old Ruth, used to say that. It helped."

Jake opened the folded piece of paper. Its only marking was a design. The only word, "sunrise."

"What do you make of this? It looks to me like a spiral with a dagger through it from the bottom."

Susan yawned, "Oh, excuse me. Here, let me see it." She studied the paper. "Looks like rock art—a carved petroglyph or drawn pictograph. The dagger from the edge to the center usually represents a spear of sunlight and the spiral—I'm not certain what it means, but you see it a lot in the Four Corners area. It could be the Anasazi symbol for the summer solstice."

"Which is today, right?"

"Is it today? June, what, 21st? I guess it is. There are several ruins around the Southwest where the spirals have been carved into rock and sunlight on the solstice moves across it to the center. There's a famous one … uh … somewhere in New Mexico, I think."

Jake stared at the paper for a moment. "I've seen that petroglyph at Chaco, but there has to be more to it or Lou wouldn't place so much importance on it. What else?"

"Why didn't Lou just tell you what she thought it meant? Why waste time playing these stupid games?" Susan asked.

"She was about to when Moody drove up. Can't blame her for not trusting Rank. Probably the old PEA cloak of secrecy at work. Before she took off after White Wolf, she promised to explain it all here this morning."

Susan pushed her hair behind her ears. "Pure speculation, but some believe rock art is like ancient road signs and the spiral also stood for a journey, or the way ... maybe the way to water. Pretty damn important in a desert. Lyn and I saw a pictograph on the butte and I had a hunch it meant a way down. Luckily, the ancients didn't fail us. That's about all I can suggest. You were the geology major. Does it ring any other bells?"

"With this kind of pressure, I'm hearing nothing but the clock. I'm afraid most of the symbolism you're suggesting has been debunked by scholarly research, but, shit, I don't have a better idea, suppose you're right. A journey, water, the summer solstice—but what does it mean to Lou, I wonder?" He looked at his watch. "Christ, we don't have much time to figure this out. I wish to hell Lou had given me more to go on." He scanned the road with his eyes and noticed the first hint of dawning light across Mead to the east. "Better yet, I wish she'd show the hell up and tell me what she thinks this means." He adjusted his cap and stared at the paper. "I've studied rock art a bit too; it can be fascinating. But right now, just friggin' frustrating."

Susan stifled a yawn. "Spiral, spiral, spiral down. What does the goddamn spiral mean? I'm just not thinking straight right now."

"Wait a minute," Jake said, "let me Google it." He fired up his iPad, typed in "rock art," and studied the different website choices, quickly settling on Wikipedia. He opened it, scrolled down as fast as his eyes could scan, and then tapped the screen with his index finger. "Says here native lore suggests the spiral also stood for a journey to the center. Does that help?"

"Yes, in the sense that the soul is at the center of us all and the life journey spiral leads inward—that's what I learned as a child. But there are thousands of modern versions of these tales, Jake. Every teller made changes in the old days—that's what they were supposed to do. That's how they made the story their own. So, it's a maybe, at best. I mean, to indigenous people, for that matter, it could mean a journey through rock from the center of the earth through the hole where mankind entered this earth—the place of emergence, where they left evil behind. The creation myth."

"Oh, yeah ... the *sipapu*. I remember reading about the spirals that represent the origin of man somewhere in an article on rock art. So ... we have the way to water, a journey to a center, maybe down through some rock. When I think of a pathway or journey through rock I think of a cave, or ... a tunnel."

"You know, that just has to be it—some subterranean river or waterway," Susan said.

"And we have a dagger of light in the spiral to represent the summer solstice and the word, 'sunrise,' which, according to my watch is now less than an hour away." Jake turned the paper around in his hand until the dagger was at the top of the spiral. "Jesus. The dagger looks like a split or wide crack when you turn it this way. A crack in the spiral. A crack in the rock—in the tunnel. Holy shit!"

"Lou thinks the straw is going to be blown up at sunrise," Susan said.

Jake jumped up and checked the lake for movement. Nothing. Then from behind the construction office trailer he saw Lou's van heading along the shore toward the mouth of the straw.

"Look there." He handed her the binos. "Lou's van just entered the tunnel mouth area. See it? How the fuck did she get in there? There's no sign of Lynnie's car or White Wolf, though. Lou doesn't know you two are safe." He glanced at his watch, took Susan's hand, and started to walk her to the car. "I'm going down there. You stay here with Lyn."

"Not on your life! White Wolf might be there. The thought of messing him up is all that's kept me going this week. Let's go."

"No way. Not gonna happen. You're injured and weak. Dehydrated and exhausted. You're not yourself. Your judgment's way off. What you're proposing is a violation of police procedure and you know it. And you have an agenda—apart from getting revenge on White Wolf, you want to rescue everybody, mess up all the bad guys. Be seen as a good parent and a good cop again. Well, forget it." Jake gripped her shoulder and she shook him off.

"Don't tell me what I want! And like you don't have an agenda, Goddard? I thought we were partners. Who do you think you are? The Lone friggin' Ranger? It just so happens I know of some demons you'd like to kill off, too."

Jake blanched. "What the hell is that supposed to mean?"

"What do you think Rachel and I talked about back in Salt Lake, the doilies we were making? Church covered-dish recipes? She is scared shitless that you think you can cure yourself of your problems by gunning them all down."

Jake turned away from her and spoke slowly. "Please show some restraint, and some faith in me one more time. I need that more than any other kind of help you can give me right now." He turned back to face her, then stepped forward, and pulled her rigid body into a hug. "Susan, I'm amazed by your strength. I was … so relieved when I saw you unhurt in that truck. But I'm the stronger of the two of us now. You've got to know that."

She pushed back. "If I don't go, it's because I decide not to go. Because I deem myself unfit for the duty. Are we clear on that?"

"Clear."

"Good. Then I will remain here with Lyn and rest, eat, and drink a little more. But I'll be watching from the overlook and when I'm ready, I'm back in this full bore. Agreed?"

"Agreed."

"Sun'll be up soon. Get going," she said, looking up into his face. "And try to think of something more original and less dangerous than lying down in the road to stop a truck, okay?"

He grinned and turned his palms up. "It was an all-chips-in moment. I bet the ranch."

"Yea, well, you almost bought the farm. It was a little too much like something I'd do," Susan said. "Jake … be careful." She turned and walked to the car carrying the binos.

Jake slipped his gun into his belt in the back and eased through the shadows. The windows were down in the Park Service truck. He took one step into the light toward the truck when a screen door slammed open. He jerked back and hugged the brick wall. The janitor heaved a bag of trash into the back of the truck, loaded the sign indicating the restroom was closed for service, then headed back inside.

Jake crab-walked to the truck and crawled into the driver's seat. He pushed a hat, a radio, and a clipboard with some papers attached across the seat, sat up, turned the key, and dropped the truck into gear in one motion. As he pulled away, he saw the janitor run out the door, a mop in one hand and a bucket in the other. Jake figured, with the guy's radio gone and the center locked, he had at least fifteen minutes, more or less, before rangers could be notified of the stolen truck—maybe another fifteen before they could find him. But the real deadline was sunrise, now just thirty-five minutes away.

As he approached the construction site, he donned the Park Service hat and switched off the two-way radio. "How's it going?" he asked the guard at the gate.

"Not bad for a long hot night. Almost too quiet. Could use a little excitement." He scrutinized Jake closely. "What brings you down at this godforsaken hour?" The guard was mid-forties, heavyset, and had thick hairy arms covered with tattoos exposed below the sleeves of his blue polo with the SDWA logo.

"I was cleaning the restroom at the Visitor's Center and got a call about a dumb ass drunk boater who tied up here by accident. Puked his guts out on the dock. Typical shit for this time of year." Jake smiled and turned and stared at the gate, trying to will it up. The guard studied Jake.

"Better you than me, buddy. How come you're out of uniform?"

Jake looked down at his t-shirt and hiking shorts. "Oh, I … I got a bunch of crap on me earlier tonight and didn't have a clean set. Hell of a way to start a new job," Jake said, drumming the steering wheel with his thumbs.

"Guess there ain't nobody to impress but the critters this hour," the guard said. He reached to the lever to raise the gate but stopped and turned again to the window. "Hey." Jake had revved the truck's engine and almost plowed through the gate.

"You heard any ball game scores tonight?" he asked, shaking an old radio on his counter. "This bugger ain't worth a shit."

"No, I haven't had mine on." Jake swallowed to force the pitch of his voice down. "I gotta get this job done quick, buddy." The gate eased up and Jake started through.

"I was wondering how the Dodgers did, is all," the guard shouted after him.

Jake scanned the property and checked his rearview mirror to see if there was trouble behind him at the guard station. None. The guard had bought it. In a few seconds he was at the trailer. He stopped briefly, but there was nobody at the office. Lou's van tracks were visible in the sand.

Easing the truck back into gear, he headed along the lakeshore toward the mouth of the tunnel. He passed a sign extolling the virtues of a safe job site.

Dirt embankments rose up on either side of the road as it curved inland for a few hundred yards. When he emerged from between the banks he saw Lou's van at the top of a spillway. The concrete ramp disappeared, like a snake's tongue, into the yawning mouth of the tunnel. The mouth was half covered by a chain link gate. In front of the tunnel Jake could see Moody, Lou in her wheelchair, and White Wolf, spread eagle, facing the gate. Jake parked beyond the van, leaped out, pulled out his pistol, and sprinted down the steep ramp. As he neared the mouth, he saw that Rank Moody had chained Forrest to the fence.

"Well, look who's here. Stole a government truck, eh, cowboy?" Lou said.

"What ... the hell ... is up ... Lou?" Jake gasped.

"Mr. White Wolf here keeps tripping up in his story." She gestured at him with the shotgun. "We think he killed Noah and dumped his body down by the dam."

Moody said, "He went out in a boat with a heavy object and returned without it."

"I never touched Skutches. You're crazy. Both of you." White Wolf wheezed and coughed violently.

Lou straightened up in her chair. "Also, I've had my fill of his lies about Lyn. I'm pretty certain this sick prick knows where she is and I plan to get it—"

"I hope you're wrong about the professor, but we have Lyn. She's with Susan and she is fine—roughed up but in good spirits."

"Well, hallelujah!" Lou said, grinning. "Guess we don't need ol' Mr. Big Bad any more." White Wolf's body went rigid.

"But you could be right, as far as I know, Skutches hasn't been seen since our friend here left The Howl in such a hurry." Goddard walked over to White Wolf, grabbed his braid, and yanked. Forrest winced and yelped. "Also, Susan told me the pervert got himself off while Lynnie was tied up and forced to watch." He pulled again and then released the hair. "Later, one of his buddies shot and killed Bev Witt near Stan Burke's mine and brave Forrest here punched out Susan. Then they damn near killed the two women by stranding them on the top of a butte." He looked at his watch. "Let's get the hell out of here. It'll be light in less than twenty minutes. Release him, Rank. But keep your eyes on him."

"Copy that," Moody said. "Let's get outta here." He approached White Wolf.

"At least that's some good news—Lynnie is alive and well," Lou said. "That girl is tough as shoe leather ... runs in the family. I'm so relieved, Jake. And I'm real sorry about your friend, Bev." White Wolf grunted and pulled against the chains but Lou shifted the gun toward Moody. "Not so fast, my friend. I've got other plans. You two boys better run along. When that sun peeks up over the lake, unless I misread the signs, things are going to get real interesting around here. I want to make sure our perverted and murderous friend doesn't miss a thing. Sick animals need to be put down—or, in this case, blown up. It's the humane thing to do."

Moody spun around to face her. "What the hell are you talking about? Have you gone completely nuts?"

"Lou thinks Planet Earth Alliance plans to bomb the tunnel at sunrise," Jake said.

"Brilliant, Holmes! That's my best guess based on what I was able to dig up off their websites. And for which I'm paying a high price.

Sad to say, they won't have any use for me after that violation of protocol."

"But there's no sign of them around here," Moody said, looking around wildly.

"Never any sign of them," Lou said. "That's why they never get caught. Don't forget, the tunnel runs for miles under the mountains but the security is only here at the mouth. And you've seen how stellar that is."

"PEA, shit! I'm out of here," Moody said, "I want no part of this." He turned and lunged up the spillway.

White Wolf strained against his bonds, rattling the fence. "Let me go, goddamnit!"

"The only place you're going is sky high, then straight to hell," Lou hissed.

"Lou, listen to reason. You can't do this to yourself and, tempting as it may be, you can't do it to White Wolf either. Give me the key."

"Sorry, Jake—Enviroactivism 101. Carry lots of chains and open padlocks cuz you never know when you might need to attach yourself to something to make a statement. But never, ever carry the keys. Makes it too easy to change your mind or have the authorities reach in your pocket and change it for you."

"Jesus Christ, Goddard, can you hurry the hell up?" Moody yelled, pacing in front of the van.

The outline of the foothills was emerging against a paling sky. "You better go. Here, take these." Lou handed him her car keys. "The guard thinks we were dropping off White Wolf and is expecting us to leave. I'd guess the park is already looking for that missing truck. You'd better get under the covers on the bunk. Guard will assume it's the old lady, all tuckered out, after a night of playing Good Samaritan."

"I cannot tell your niece I left you here, Louise. She'll never come to grips with this, and I'll never forgive myself. You're her family—her mentor. Why are you doing this? I don't understand you." He gripped her arms, but she shook him off and sat up straight in her chair.

"Some of us have to be the first to go and others will follow. For every one of us who dies, thousands of people will finally wake up. The greens are losing the battle. The horse is out, Jake, and measures like recycling and no idling are closing the barn door—an inch. We're running out of time." She pointed at White Wolf. "This gorgeous planet is sick and people like our friend here and his greedy partners are the virus. I'm old and ill and I've been cast out by my PEA family. The planet will be better served by my death. Lynnie is strong. She'll do just fine."

"No, Lou … please."

"You can stand around here and argue with me, but you only have fifteen minutes, more or less, and, if you remember, I can be pretty stubborn."

"I'm not leaving here without you." Jake grabbed the handles on the wheelchair and began fiercely pushing up the hill.

White Wolf shook the fence and yelled, "You're wasting your energy. She's whacked. When the crew arrives and I'm freed, the old bitch is gonna get what she deserves!"

"Listen to him. Turn around. Let this old bitch get what she deserves." Lou banged the barrel of the shotgun against the arm of the chair. Jake kept pushing up the hill. "There isn't time. Take me back. I should have padlocked my chair to the fence. I don't want to change my mind." Jake leaned against the chair with everything he had, while Lou balanced the shotgun on her knees and tried in vain to apply the brake. "Goddamn brake never did work right!"

Jake had bulled his way halfway up the hill when he slipped on some gravel, stumbled and partially recovered, giving Lou just enough time to lock on her faulty brake. When the chair dug in, his feet slipped again, causing him to lose his grip and fall on his knees. Lou whipped the chair around to face downhill and aimed her shotgun at Jake's chest.

"Goddard, shit, do what she asks and come on," Moody roared from the van.

"You crazy old fuck!" White Wolf raged from below.

"I appreciate the sentiment, I really do. You're a good man, Jake Goddard, and a good investigator. And that Susan Brand—one heck of a fine cop. I made the right call when I found you on the web and hired you, didn't I? Pays to advertise. Now, as for my last wish." She smiled. "I get one, right? You mustn't tell anyone, and especially Lynnie, that you suspect her father was involved. It'll kill her. Please, grant me that. Stan is corrupt, greedy as hell, but he's not a murderer or a kidnapper. He must have been desperate to fall in with such a bad crowd. Now go, Goddard." Jake raised his hand in protest. "No, my mind is made up. Get out of here, while you still can." She released the brake and started to roll toward the gate. Jake dove at the handles and missed. When the chair picked up momentum, Lou dropped the shotgun and made a slight correction with her hips, aiming herself straight at the opening of the tunnel. In a few soundless seconds, she had careened past an incredulous White Wolf and was swallowed by the gaping mouth of the straw.

"Lou!!" Jake yelled, as her chair disappeared into the darkness.

"Get your ass in this van, Goddard! She's gone," Moody bleated from the driver's seat. Jake checked the time, turned and ran up the spillway, jumped in the passenger seat, and handed Moody the keys. Moody tried to get the key in the ignition but dropped the set on the floor. He and Goddard both reached for them at the same time but Jake got to them first. He sat up and passed them to Moody. Moody's hand shook as he tried again to get the key to slide in. He felt the shotgun barrel press against his temple.

"Just call me Houdini," White Wolf said, dropping a chain and lock on the concrete. "That padlock is a rusted piece of crap. Two barrels, gentlemen. One for each of you. The sun's coming up, it's going to be a beautiful day—say good morning—and say good-bye."

Moody was sweating profusely, shaking violently, and muttering what sounded like a prayer. "Please, no..." White Wolf pulled the trigger. There was a click. A shot exploded, and then another. White Wolf's body rolled across the hood of the car and slid to the pavement. Susan ran up and kicked away the shotgun. She held her Glock on White Wolf. Jake leaped out, rushed around the front, and knelt by White Wolf, feeling for a pulse at his neck. Blood slicked the concrete under the van like leaking oil and a small red rivulet dribbled down the spillway toward the tunnel.

Susan pushed her hair behind her ear, bit her lip, and tried to swallow. "I got him ... I ... think I ..."

Jake pushed up from the body and stood, staring. "You killed him, partner."

Susan and Jake seemed rooted in place, neither moving nor speaking.

After a few moments, Rank Moody cleared his throat and interjected in a tight, squeaky voice, "Uh, folks, uh … we really need to get out of here."

Jake squeezed Susan's arm. "Yeah, Moody's right for a change, we really do need to go, now." He turned toward the van but stopped. "How'd you get in here, anyhow?"

"I just badged the lazy stiff at the gate and told him I was looking for a stolen van and had seen one that fit the description turn in here. He didn't even question me—except to ask if I had heard any baseball scores."

"Damn, you're good," Jake said.

"Where's Lou?" Susan asked.

Jake jerked his gaze to the tunnel. "This is the way she wants it. I'll explain later, let's go."

Jake jumped in the van and crawled back to hide in the bunk. Susan ran up the road to where she had left the car.

The sun's rays were just beginning to knife across the surface of the lake. The van and car raced into the parking lot of the Visitor's Center. Goddard and Moody leaped out of the van and Susan sprinted from the car to the overlook. A few solstice lovers had gathered and were chatting excitedly. Lyn rushed up to Susan, wide-eyed. One solitary white male in workmen's attire stood quietly to the side of the overlook. Susan noticed his left hand resting on the log rail was missing two fingers. Her focus racked to three park vehicles approaching on the road below with their emergency lights flashing.

"If Lou's information was incorrect, we're going to have a lot of explaining to do," Susan said.

"What information did Aunt Lou give you?" Lyn looked from Jake to Susan. "Where is she?" They turned toward the lake without responding.

As the rays of the sun lit the west shore of Lake Mead, a flash of light erupted from the tunnel mouth. A plume of white smoke and a stentorian boom followed. The sequence was repeated a dozen times as a necklace of explosions worked its way up the tunnel into the mountains toward the foot of Dromedary Peak. At each blast, the ground rose up and then sank into a lengthening trough of debris. Lyn, Susan, and the men watched, speechless, from the overlook. In a few moments, all was silent.

The park rangers whipped around, switched on their sirens, and headed off toward the collapsed tunnel. Susan, Moody, and Lyn turned and walked toward the cars. In the breezeway, Lyn called back to Jake to ask again about her Aunt Lou, but a strange rattle cut off Jake's answer. The spikes on a yucca plant in the demonstration garden were vibrating. Jake felt a shudder beneath his feet and heard a distant engine. "I don't think it's over," he shouted, pointing toward the mountains to the north. A plane the size of a small airliner rode over the uplifted terrain and dipped toward the water near Crescent Cove. It carried a large cylinder below its belly and soared like a pelican close to the lake's surface on a direct course to the dam. When the plane got within a few hundred yards of the dam, the cylinder dropped away as the plane lurched up, engines screaming.

"Jesus," Jake said. Because the dam was out of sight, Goddard quickly selected the Boulder Dam webcam site on his iPad. The site blinked to life on the screen in time for Jake and Susan to see the device hit the water, bounce over the security boom, skip twice more, slam into the face of the dam and then disappear under the surface. Nothing. Then water boiled against the dam's face followed by an explosion and concussion. Cracks ran up the face of the dam and the thinnest concrete at the top began to fail. Water streamed through the cracks and down the face of the massive structure. Slab by slab, huge pieces of concrete crashed down the steep face of the dam to the river below. Soon a waterfall was formed over a small concave break in the center of the structure. Dust billowed upwards in a thunderhead as massive chunks of concrete and house-sized boulders settled into a newly formed cataract below the dam. Another heartbeat of silence held the witnesses immobile before the surface of Lake Mead surged with a triumphant roar. A tidal wave rebounding from the initial blast and intensified by the narrow gorge leading up to the dam slammed back into the newly formed notch in the damaged dam—water and debris blasted hundreds of yards downstream. Nearby, power transmission towers buckled at the knees and toppled in sequence, then cables fell and crossed, sending sparks and flames dancing along the downed lines. The webcam image blinked and went black.

O'Connor walked out of the Bellagio just before the rising sun struck the city. The famous fountains on the man-made lake were greeting the day lustily, choreographed to a Strauss waltz. A soft breeze carried a spray of mist into his face. Those Japanese are tough hombres, he thought. They had negotiated all night without ever showing the slightest fatigue, but he was beat. He had begged off early to go back and check on White Wolf and that bizarre incident involving the aunt. The Water Witch seemed to have things well in hand. He whistled along with the music and fountains while strolling beside the lake toward the parking garage. Thunder rumbled in the east, stopping O'Connor. It seemed an odd sound so early in the morning.

In an instant, the wind sharpened and small waves on the lake broke over the edge to splash on his shoes. The rumble rose to a bellow, the sound of a thousand rampaging beasts. O'Connor stopped in his wet tracks and loosened the grip on his briefcase. He looked to the east. A large chasm was forming in the mountains. The high ground above his new tunnel collapsed like old casinos detonated for new development. Massive boulders settled into the newly formed trough. One by one, the lights of the Bellagio went out, and the fountains sputtered and died. The multistory monolith, THEhotel at Mandalay Bay, went black as if one switch had been thrown. The strip was dark and it was dry. Slackjawed, O'Connor had only one dull thought, which he spoke aloud. "Fuck. We're fucking ruined."

June 23
Friday

When Lyn called her mother and complained that media people were hounding them, Florence suggested they spend some time at the family mountain retreat in Utah. Jake and Susan agreed that it would be a good way to escape and unwind.

Like many places in the southwestern corner of Utah, Brian Head is a refreshing aberration. Jake said it was always a pleasant surprise to first-timers visiting that quirky area—especially for those coming from the Nevada desert. Susan had no idea that southern Utah had a legitimate ski area. She had heard that St. George, lying just to the south of the ski resort, was a winter haven for retirees but knew nothing of Brian Head. To her delight, the country became more mountainous as they climbed out of St. George toward Cedar City. The high land north of Cedar City was a lush paradise compared to the desert. When they drove into the alpine village, Susan opened the car window and inhaled deeply.

Later, after settling in, Jake and Susan sat on the deck, Jake in newly acquired running shorts and a teal t-shirt, Susan in tan hiking shorts and a yellow polo. To the east, they could see the vertical bands of the cliffs of Cedar Breaks, a dramatic escarpment of sheer red rock. He relaxed in a rocking chair; she swayed gently on a freestanding porch swing.

The air carried the scent of rich soil. Mountain bluebirds flitted across the deck. Bright scarlet wildflowers bloomed around the log house. The breeze whisked the tall pines and a mountain stream gurgled along the Burkes' property, separating them from the nearest neighbor's cabin, barn, and corral.

Jake looked out over the valley stretching below to the desert and at a few cumulus clouds in the distance. He spoke softly because Lyn was napping in her room upstairs. "I love being up high in the mountains. From here, you can see where weather begins and ends."

"You're preaching to the choir, brother. You can breathe the air, wear a sweater, snuggle up by the fire," Susan said, smiling at him. "I'm a mountain person, for sure. Damn, it was hot and dry down there." She stopped swaying and looked out over the desert. "But you know, after this experience, I don't feel the same way about the desert. I guess I learned you're just as controlled by something you're running away from every day as you are when you're living it every day." She swallowed and nodded. "And out there I felt like maybe …" She inhaled. "Maybe I can forgive my father … some day."

"You must be excited about seeing Amy tomorrow."

"I can't tell you. I could've reached through the phone and hugged Earl when he offered to fly her down to Salt Lake to meet me. Amy and I will have the night in the city and then the whole glorious five-hour drive back to Jackson to catch up. My daughter is the therapy I need right now."

They enjoyed a comfortable silence broken by Jake. "When I was getting gas in town, all the talk was about Vegas and the Colorado River. The guy at the checkout counter had the television on. You should have seen the pictures. The edge of Las Vegas has a new valley all the way through the mountains to Lake Mead. What a mess. Power out. No air conditioning. Lucky nobody was killed."

"That just can't be good for business," Susan joked.

"I turned on the news when I got back here to the house. Wall–to-wall coverage. They reported Vegas has no reliable potable water source. The level of Mead is rapidly heading back to original river levels as the overtopping water erodes the damaged concrete. It's going to take years to rebuild infrastructure and get the city up and running again. Could be five years for the dam. They must be cyber-celebrating at Planet Earth Alliance."

"As usual, they planned it and timed it for maximum destruction to property—minimum loss of life. What are they saying that bizarre thing was that hit the dam?" Susan asked.

"An old DC 3 flying out of the Mexican desert and retrofitted to carry a dambuster bomb. Jets out of the Tucson AFB scrambled to intercept after the drop but failed to catch it."

"Dambuster?"

"Yeah. Who would have thought? PEA defeats all these modern high-tech security devices using World War II technology." Jake formed an invisible cylinder with his hands. "Plane comes in low and fast with a cylindrical bomb spinning backwards underneath. The bomb is dropped and bounces like a skipping rock on the water over all surface booms and underwater deterrents, and when it hits the wall of the dam, because of the backspin, dives to the foot before detonating. The explosive device used a shaped charge to intensify the damage."

"Okay, help me out here—shaped charge?"

"It's a technique used in the military, as well as in oil wells and quarries. An explosive charge with a shaped cavity to focus the impact of the explosion. PEA said the bomb had a name—Edward. CNN thinks it's for Edward Abbey. You saw the outcome." He had something else on his mind; Susan watched his face and waited. A big smile broke out. "The media are reporting that a Liam O'Connor and everyone else at the highest echelon of the Southern Desert Water Authority have been suspended and are under investigation. Someone apparently tipped the FBI that those good citizens had been in negotiations with the Japanese mob. My guess: the tipster was a PEA hacker. The higher-ups at SDWA are looking at serious jail time and futures as felonious supermarket greeters."

Susan shook her head in disbelief. "O'Connor? He was with White Wolf in that meeting at the mine. I overheard that ... that godawful woman mention his name. I hope they string up all those scumbags."

Jake continued. "Turns out that SDWA, even though they did not have permission from the Colorado River Compact to siphon more water out of Mead through the new straw for their own use, was in negotiations with the yakuza to provide water to their proposed development at the

Salton Sea. The plan involved using partially abandoned canals to deliver the goods. News claimed that the Japanese wanted to turn Bombay Beach into another Vegas—named Funabashi Beach—but they needed SDWA water to do it."

"I just hope the Feds get to the bottom of the whole stinking mess," Susan said bitterly.

"It may be water over the dam, Susan—pun definitely intended. The tsunami blasting downstream from Mead took out every manmade structure in its path and just arrived at the Sea of Cortez. The destruction included the head gates controlling the diversion into the Imperial Valley. The Salton Sea is filling and predicted to quadruple its current size, equal to 1905 when the original engineering screw-up caused the entire Colorado River to pour into the Salton Basin, forming the lake. The Japanese development is already under yards of water. It will be years before the water recedes. Hey, tell you what, I'll sell you some Salton Seaside property in Indio."

"They wanted water …. Sad to think of all those towns and farms being flooded in the Imperial Valley, but you're saying the Colorado River is running free to the sea from below the Grand Canyon. First time in what—eighty years?" Susan said.

"Since the thirties—yeah." Jake added. "With the usual identify-as-many-villains-as-possible mentality, the media's pegged Lou Cuvier and Forrest White Wolf as the evil ecoterrorists." Susan shook her head again. "They took what remains there were and the manner in which they were discovered as a statement. Compared them to suicide bombers, admitting that they could not have planted the explosives alone, but assuming both died by choice in the attack. That creep O'Connor was condemning Lou and White Wolf in an interview on television today in an attempt to turn the attention away from the corruption around the straw and him, I guess."

"Maybe hypocrisy, corruption, and murder are what it takes to move up the career ladder around here."

"Just as we feared, they found remnants of Noah Skutches's clothing and skull by the dam when the water level was lowered. Fox News said it was believed White Wolf killed Skutches because, they speculated, Skutches refused to go along with blowing up the straw."

"Well, at least they got that right. Sort of," Susan said. She got up, walked over to the rail of the deck, gazed out over the valley, and sighed deeply. "I was no big fan of Lou's and I don't condone her choices. But, I will say this—I have a much deeper understanding of her passion and commitment. I hope I never take water for granted again. Now you say she's being blamed by those assholes ... God. She'd be pissed about the authorities taking such a simplistic view."

"PEA claimed credit for the bombings, and it didn't take a brilliant federal agent to connect her with them."

"You're right. It's the conclusion they'd draw based on her history. Easy, tidy."

"Yeah, well here's the kicker. Moody's face was all over the screen. He claims that he was very close to exposing Lou, White Wolf, and the whole plot."

"I thought from what you told me that he performed pretty well as Lou's sidekick."

"He did. Or so he told me. But the cameras really seduced him; he was just the same old, self-serving Rank working the best angle. I have to admit you had Moody pegged from the beginning."

"Basically useless."

"Yep. Couldn't even chain the bad guy to a fence."

"One of the few consolations Lynnie might draw from her aunt's death is that you were there and saw what she really wanted. If Lyn didn't have the truth from you to cling to ... I don't know, I think she'd be facing a long run of confusion and grief."

"I've got to tell you, Lou's death was one of the most impressive acts of courage I've ever seen. She chose her own destiny and went out ... well, with a hell of a bang. Moody's a cowardly bastard by comparison. He hasn't even spoken to me since the explosion—too busy pumping himself up in front of the Feds and the media. To think he could publicly sully Lou's memory like that. She deserves better. Of course, she was no longer useful to him as a cash cow." Jake went over, stood beside Susan, and put his hand on her arm. "I'm glad you agree we should honor her last wish," he whispered.

"I agree ... don't like it much, but agree ..." she dropped her voice "... that we should not tell Lyn or the authorities that we think Stan Burke smells in this. But it stops with Burke. After I get rested and collected and confer with Earl, I'm going after Bev's killer, and if Burke gets swept up in that net, then so be it. I'm going to take down the guy in the black coat that killed Beverly, whoever he is." She bored her eyes into his. "And ... I might need your help."

"I'm there for you, anytime," Jake said. "Well anytime, after several days at home with my boys. Rachel says Clint's coming down for a few days to 'celebrate my survival.'" He glanced away from Susan.

"Are you going to stay at the house?"

"Yeah. I guess so."

Susan studied his face for a few seconds and then thought it best to change the subject. "I'm convinced Burke and SDWA staged the ecoterrorism attack on Ashland, probably to smear PEA and for the insurance." She crossed back to the swing, sat, and pushed hard on the deck with her feet.

"I noticed PEA never took credit for that one. That speaks volumes," Jake said.

Susan said, "I'll bet it was those same upstanding citizens who faked the shooting at The Howl."

A gust of air blew the manes and tails of four brown horses in the corral next door. They whinnied and paced by the fence, staring at the deck as though waiting for the next part of the story. "Sounds like they agree with you," Jake said, sitting back against the deck's railing and crossing his arms.

Jake thought of Lyn Burke. "What do you think, as a mother of a daughter, I mean? Lyn is resilient ... but is she going to be okay?"

Susan shrugged a little. "Hard to say. It's going to take time to get past it. Her parents are obviously not going to be much support. I can help the best I can from a distance. You know, call and check on her. I could use a woman friend myself. Hey, maybe the two of us could go camping in the desert," she said with a grin. "She saved my life ... and I guess I saved hers."

Lyn walked out on the deck, stretching. She had on a blue tank top and green pajama bottoms. "Speak of the devil, how long have you been awake?" Susan said smiling at her. She yawned, flopped down beside Susan, and gave her a big hug.

"So how are you doing, girl?" Jake asked.

She exhaled. "Hanging in there, I guess. I keep thinking about Aunt Lou." She fingered the fringe of the swing's cushion. "And I'd feel better if I knew what happened to Mojo. I suppose Forrest ... got rid of him back in Jackson." She moved in tight against Susan and rested her head on her shoulder.

Susan put her hand on Lyn's hair. "You'll think of Lou every day, but the pain eases in time. She was one gutsy woman. And maybe you're better off not knowing the details of Mojo's death, honey. Moody finding his tag means whoever dropped it, and it was probably White Wolf, did not want Mojo's body identified."

"Did you have any suspicions about White Wolf when you first met him?" Jake asked.

"He was just really arrogant, you know, being such a good looking guy, and so full of himself. And I did feel uneasy about the whole death of Fernando thing. You know, like Forrest was hiding something. When he broke into my room in the motel and joked about it—that really put me off. But he always smoothed the waters and charmed me. It wasn't 'til he got so abusive that I realized he was one perverted asshole." Lyn was steady but her voice was low. "Jake, I'm a little scared about the whole FBI and Homeland Security thing. I was part of the Skutches group, and Lou was my aunt, and that interrogation was heavy. They seemed more interested in me than in you or Susan or Rank Moody."

"Lynnie, you've got to look at this from a political perspective. Even though your story doesn't jive with the official version coming out of the Southern Desert Water Authority, it's really just a question of manpower and resources. The local and state authorities are dealing with, what ... a billion plus in damages and power outages from California to Texas? The FBI is trying desperately to put a face on PEA and arrest someone.

They have nothing substantial to connect you to that organization. The federal agents probably don't want to go through the red tape of having to deal with an extraneous case after PEA claimed credit. When they tally all that up against so little real evidence, they will realize that you are not worth the effort or expense. The truth is, in the face of such monumental destruction and property loss, your situation is inconsequential to them."

"And what about someone being arrested for the deaths of Fernando and Bev Witt—and for the way Susan and I were treated by Forrest's cronies? Maybe my father can help me go after the sleaze bags White Wolf answered to."

"Oh ... your father might be too ... close to the situation to help much. Your best bet there is your friend, Susan."

Susan nodded and rose to her feet slowly. She thought it better to head off any discussion of Stan Burke involving Lyn. Jake noticed her vibrancy and vitality had returned. With her hair tied back in a ponytail and a spray of freckles across her peeling nose, she looked like she could be Lyn's blond sister.

"Okay. I'm going in to make one of my famous apple pies. Wanna help, you two?" Susan headed toward the door to the kitchen.

"Sure, I'll help. I don't want to miss a chance to demonstrate how sensitive and domesticated I am," Jake said.

Susan turned to Lyn. "Feel like some pie-making therapy?"

"Okay if I beg off? I think I need a walk—maybe I'll head up the creek over there by the fence and check out the birds."

"Good plan," said Susan. "We could all give our minds a rest. In fact, after all this talking, I'd like to propose a moratorium on debriefing until the dessert is eaten. Sound fair?"

"Sure, but just one last question. Earlier, Jake did I hear you say the Colorado is running free all the way to the sea?"

"You heard that from upstairs?" He glanced at Susan before responding. "That's right, Lyn. All the way to the Sea of Cortez," Jake said.

Lyn smiled. "Aunt Lou would've called that a happy ending."

They sat at the picnic table on the deck. Jake opened a bottle of white wine. After a toast and Susan's short eulogy for Bev, they ate dinner in silence.

Jake still had evidence of flour on his cheek and collar from Susan's playful dusting during the pie production. Lyn had changed out of her hiking clothes and back into her green pajamas.

The sun descended over the desert and painted the bottoms of the few puffy clouds on the horizon. The air was high-mountain clear—the evening shadows deep and long.

Jake broke the silence, "Uh hum. Since we have agreed to a no shop talk rule until after dessert, I've got some silly games my boys just love. Wanna try one?"

"Sure, this silence is too loaded," Lyn said.

"Okay, here goes. I make a disgusting sound and you have to top it."

Susan rolled her eyes and shook her head. "I always wondered what sort of uplifting activities went on in boy households. I feel sorry for Rachel." After a few minutes of raspberries and sundry other gesticulations by Jake, quickly topped by Lyn's raucous armpit farting noises, Lyn was declared the winner and they were on to the next challenge.

"How about the old spoon on the nose trick?" Lyn asked.

"I'm an Olympic level nose-and-spoon guy," Jake said, exhaling on his spoon. "I'll bet even Susan can excel at this one." Susan tried it and they all giggled when the spoon immediately fell clattering to her plate.

"Okay Lynnie, it's you and me. Ready? You're the official timer, Susan. Annnnd...*go!*"

Lyn tried to suppress her laughter, but the spoon fell at the twelve-second mark.

"*Ha!* The master prevails. You know if you're ever going to win at this, you have to control your laughter. This is serious stuff. Nothing funny about it."

"Okay, okay, best three out of five wins," said Lyn. "There's no way you can do this one."

"What?"

"Well it's sort of a variation of the gross noises trick. Call it weird body feats. I'll do something weird and you have to match it if you can. You know, like turning your tongue upside down, stuff like that. But you can't use your hands. I'll go first." Lyn drew her hair back from her face and wiggled her ears.

That cracked them up.

Jake turned red in the face and wiggled virtually everything but his ears. They laughed some more.

"Nope, no ear movement noted. You lose that round. Okay, your turn."

Jake reached his right hand over to his left shirtsleeve and pulled it up to his shoulder. He sat perfectly still and struck a pose like The Thinker. Then his bicep began to jiggle and bump. "If I had a hula dancer tattoo, I could make her do all kinds of sexy moves."

Susan interjected in her best "bimbo" voice, "Ooooo, Jake. You are soooo buff. Love your arms, honey. And you two are soooo talented."

Lyn pointed at her right bicep just below the blue tank top, stared at her slender arm, and began to grunt.

"First, you have to have an actual bicep. You gave it your best shot, but the twitchometer records no movement." She slid her left hand under her right bicep. "Hey! No using the other hand or any other jiggling agents," cried Jake in mock protest. "We're tied."

"No way." Lyn bounced up, held her arms out straight and started to jump up and down on flat feet. Everything on her body that could jiggle did jiggle. Biceps included. "I declare victory for Aunt Lou and all womankind." She whirled around, danced in a victory celebration, and fell back in her chair. Jake laughed. Susan looked perplexed.

Lyn suddenly got very quiet. The day's last light and lamps from the interior of the cabin illuminated the deck. Susan served their pie and they ate in silence.

Lyn stretched her long body. "That was the perfect pie and the perfect distraction. Thank you both so much. And, okay, I admit I cheated on the last one." She yawned. "I'm pretty beat. Let's call it a tie and a day, okay?" She hugged Jake, gave Susan a kiss on the forehead, and went off to bed.

Jake got up and poured another glass of wine while Susan paced in thought. She stopped behind the rocking chair and grabbed the back.

"Jake, when Lynnie was jumping around in her green pajama bottoms, something hit me. It's almost hard to believe—but I can't shake it. The woman I saw in the meeting room at Ashland. She might be the one who shot Beverly."

"Why do you say that?"

"She was wearing a green pants suit. Tonight, when Lyn was spinning around, I remembered something—I saw a flash of green under the duster the shooter was wearing. I assumed it was a man because of the cowboy hat and long coat, but now can't say for certain."

"That's a little hard to imagine, that the woman in that meeting murdered Bev with a high powered rifle. Of course, the way things have gone in this case, it's certainly worth a follow-up—starting with determining who she is, but ..." Jake got silent. "But ... I'm sorry, it's ... it's still hard for me to talk about Bev." He crossed the deck to the picnic table and stared out toward the desert. "More wine?"

"No, I'm good, thanks," Susan said.

"Can we, uh ... take a break from all this again, and just let it percolate a bit? We both just need to think," Jake said.

Susan went off to take a shower. Jake felt the relief of the alcohol. It allowed his mind to leave Bev for the moment and relax into the anticipation of days ahead. He could easily justify a long catch-up period at home before accepting any other clients. More than anything, he wanted to play outside with the boys, and smell the sun on the back of their necks. Maybe he and Rachel could somehow reconnect. If she'd just tone down the proselytizing a little, maybe he could even attend church once or twice. Do some house projects for her—that'd shock the shit out of her—take the boys camping, fishing, whatever, just be around his family. Then he thought about Susan again. He had been thinking about her a lot.

Jake saw a shooting star. He went over to the edge of the deck to get a better view of the sky and leaned out on the deck railing. Susan came out of the house in a bathrobe and bare feet. He didn't hear her approach.

On impulse, Susan put her arms around him. "Jake, I just ... I just need some contact. You don't even have to turn around. Just let me hold you ... for a few minutes, okay?" She moved closer and put her head in the middle of his back, then slowly squeezed tighter and pressed her hips against his buttocks. With an attenuated breath she slid her hands down to his hips.

Jake turned and grabbed handfuls of her wet hair with both hands and kissed her gently, then hard, then hungry and deep. Susan responded by putting her hands on his butt and pulling him into her. Jake stared into her eyes, his breath coming faster. His hand slipped inside her bathrobe. He felt the weight, the firmness of her breast. His fingers and thumb closed around an erect nipple. Susan leaned up into him and bit his neck. The phone rang—they froze—it rang again. Jake stepped away, paused and looked hard at Susan, his lips trembling, and then hurried inside to answer before the phone woke up Lyn.

June 24
Saturday

It was a gloriously bright and cool mountain morning. Susan, Jake, and Lyn drove together down to the St. George Airport. The phone call had been Lyn's mother. The Las Vegas Airport had reopened and she suggested that Lyn fly home. Susan told Jake it might be best if she were to fly to Salt Lake to be there when Amy arrived. She gently refused Jake's offer to have them stay at the Goddard's house. Lyn's flight was first. After they parked and entered the small ultra-modern terminal, Jake went to find a monitor to double check her gate.

Lyn and Susan sat down across from each other in a seating area just outside of security. Susan took Lyn's hands in hers. "You know what, Lyn? I could use a woman friend. Are you available?"

Lyn's eyes filled. "Are you kidding? You're stuck with me for life." Her words came out in a rush. "I can't even think of a way to describe how connected I feel to you. It's on the molecular level. And I don't know how to thank you ... I—"

"You're my desert angel, Lynnie."

"And you are so my desert warrior."

They held each other's gaze; both fought tears and then embraced, long and tight.

Jake returned with the gate number and he and Susan gave Lyn a send-off of hugs and well wishes. They all pledged to get together again soon for more apple pie and gross body tricks. Lyn looked happy and relatively rested as she waved and went through security to board and fly home.

Then things got difficult. Jake and Susan couldn't agree on a time to see each other again. Susan turned away and headed for security in frustration and anger. She came running back.

"I feel like shit," he said. She tried to apologize. He shook his head and began to refuse the apology, but his throat closed. She reached for his hand, but he could only squeeze hers perfunctorily.

"We can't do this, can we? At least not now," Susan said. He was not able to answer. Not able to move. "I won't stay long at your place, I promise. Just long enough to pick up my truck, then I'm gone." She kissed him on the lips and headed to security without looking back.

That afternoon, Jake seemed to float in a trance as he headed down the state road away from Brian Head. He had never in his life been more off balance or confused. His only clear thought was of Susan—he longed for her strength, her common sense. He craved her touch. He reviewed the mental snapshots of their brief sensual contact over and over. But he also needed his boys right now like he had never needed them before. Heading due west into the sun, the visor was useless and he was blinded by the brilliance. It was difficult to see the road signs. He came to a stop just before the on-ramp for I-15. A billboard advertising The Oasis, a casino in Mesquite, popped up in front of him. Just beyond it was a green highway sign that read, "North—Salt Lake City—235 miles, South—Mesquite, Nevada—109 miles." Alone at the intersection, he put on his right turn signal, and sat for a full minute without moving, the turn indicator blinking. He leaned forward, pulled his wallet out of his hip pocket, and checked his cash. "Rachel won't mind if I take just one more day," he muttered to himself—and turned left toward Nevada.

Susan's plane landed in Salt Lake and she hurried out of the E terminal toward the ramp to the D terminal, the appointed meeting place. She waited by the entrance to a café and scanned the crowd. She caught a glimpse of Earl's cowboy hat coming around the corner. He was wearing a daypack and carrying a wooden canoe paddle. When Amy saw Susan she broke away from Earl's hand and sprinted to her. Susan noticed there was no trace of a limp. They clinched. Susan lifted her daughter off the ground, spun her around once, and let her slide down her front to the floor. Susan held her at arms' length. "I swear you've grown three inches in a week." She hugged her again. "I missed you so much."

"I missed you too, Mom. Are you all right?" Amy asked, as Earl came up grinning.

"Best ever Amy, right now, I am the best ever." She reached an arm out to Earl's neck. "Good to see you, Chief. Thanks for this." Susan nodded toward Amy.

"No problem, Brandy." He grinned. "She's a real pain in the you-know-what, but Chuck's family was happy to put her up and I loved my flight down here with this little trooper. Caught up on all the gossip." He patted Amy on the shoulder.

They walked toward the moving sidewalk leading to baggage claim and the exits. Susan had one arm around Earl and the other around Amy. The Chief stopped. "Oh whoa, wait a minute." Travelers rushed around them like water. "I almost forgot. I have an official presentation from the department. Carried this stupid thing on the plane. Darn near took an old lady's head off with it." He handed her the canoe paddle. "Officer Brand, you have earned the stern."

Susan studied the paddle; everyone in the department had signed it. "I don't get it. I haven't canoed in ... oh ... Earl. Ha, that's great. It's about your parable, isn't it?" His face lit up with a grin. "Earl, that was the best damn parable I've ever been lectured with—you really ought to be a preacher." She put her arm in his arm. "But let's go before you're tempted to start the sermon." Amy ran ahead and jumped with both feet onto the moving sidewalk.

.

OUR CHARACTERS RETURN IN

Some Say Fire
by Gregory Zeigler

READ A SNEAK PREVIEW NOW

Hell yeah, revenge is sweet. Especially when it rights a horrific wrong after a protracted wait. Susan felt exhilarated and vindicated when short squat Billy Longbraid shuffled into the Pinal County Superior Court looking like an orange duck. He was about to hear his sentence on a plea bargain. His court-appointed lawyer, a tall ruddy man named Patrick Templeton, claimed Billy's youth in 1986, combined with drug addiction, had driven him to "commit his offense." That offense being to pick up a stick of firewood and crush the back of Susan's dearest friend's skull.

Since the age of sixteen, Susan had literally dreamed of—and back then even prayed for—the day she would arrest Ruth Patricio's killer and avenge her senseless death. Today was sweet. And it helped to have Jake there to share it. The gavel banged and Longbraid was escorted out, eyes on the floor, to begin a sentence of twenty years without parole—right there in Florence, Arizona. The judge retired to her chambers. The lawmen, lawyers, and a few spectators headed out of the courtroom. The air conditioning hummed.

"He'll be what, sixty-something when he gets out?" Jake said, putting his arm around Susan's shoulders.

"Only if he's a very good boy in lockup," Susan said. "Why couldn't he rob her without killing her? Knowing Old Ruth, she'd have given him her dearest possessions."

"Maybe because clubbing her from behind was easier than looking her in the eye." Jake squeezed Susan's shoulder.

"I can't say I feel the anger toward him I always thought I would. He's a pitiful loser."

"That's good. That's healthy. You spoke with action. Anger will only poison you. It can't hurt or teach him. Now Billy has twenty years to think and maybe even learn something."

"Or not. That's between him and his ... whatever."

"This calls for a celebration. I asked Wanda to hang out with Amy at the Airstream until nine. They're going to start stowing her stuff for the haul back to Hanksville tomorrow. Let's just hope 89 north of Flag is open again."

"That's some pretty bad fire up that way. Kinda scary to think of driving through it. With a kid, I mean," Susan said.

"Not as scary as driving through Phoenix."

"It's nothing to joke about. I read in this morning's paper six people died in that man-caused conflagration. Hell of a way to go."

"I just hope they catch and string up whoever started it—like that hunter who ignited the Rim Fire. Careless asshole almost cost us Yosemite. We can check ADOT for road openings online tomorrow morning. What do you say to some Mexican?" Jake said.

Susan pushed her blonde hair behind her ears and blew out a breath of air. "Only if it comes with air conditioning and a pitcher of frozen margaritas."

"You gave the sheriff the proof for the collar, you call the shots." They stood to go out into the June desert heat.

The next morning was classic Arizona—clear, dry, and hot. There was no discussion about the route home to Hanksville, Utah. U.S. 89 north of Flagstaff was still closed because of forest fires and heavy smoke. The news reported visibility near zero in the vicinity of Sunset Crater volcano. That left only one choice if Jake, Susan, and Amy were going to make it home that day.

Jake drove, heading north across the desert on a circuitous route that at least avoided Phoenix. The Airstream gleamed in the sun. Soon they were climbing through forested foothills north of Globe. Susan rode shotgun. Amy snacked and exchanged texts with friends from the back of the Suburban.

"The air in this boat sure isn't working great," Susan said, lifting her hair off the collar of her teal polo shirt.

"What would you expect from a '97 with over 200k on her?" Jake lifted the brim of his black and yellow Pittsburgh Pirates ball cap and glanced in the rearview. "Look how nice the Airstream's tracking. Truly looks like a silver cloud. I love her brand name. Always love telling people—'57 Flying Cloud. I've had Majestic since starting college in 1989 and this purple bucket's the best tow vehicle I've ever owned."

"It's maroon—one of my top five favorite colors. So can we fix the air situation?"

"Sure." Jake lowered the front two windows with the buttons on his armrest. Hot air blasted in. "There you go."

"Very funny."

Jake grinned at her. "I may have a little problem with gambling but your jones is air conditioning. You're an AC addict. Been a little tougher to get your fix since the massive power outages from the dam bombing, eh?"

Susan shot a look that could chill a room in Yuma in July. "You try growing up in the *Arid-zona* desert with a preacher father who loves to give blistering sermons in the sweltering heat." She smiled. "Hey, it's one of the reasons we went north. If I hadn't moved to Wyoming and joined the Jackson PD, I would've never met you. I don't know what I was thinking—letting you charm me into quitting and moving half way back to hot ol' Hanksville. But I rest my case. You should be damn glad I hate heat."

Jake shook his head and chuckled. "Thank you, counselor."

"I'm getting a headache from all these trees flashing by."

"Spoken like a true Wyoming girl," Jake said, turning to Amy. "Growing up tree deprived." He pointed out the windshield. "This is Tonto National Forest. Every bit as mountainous and forested as the Flagstaff area but, thankfully, not as visited because of the reservation and no interstate," Jake said.

"Hmm, Tonto—maybe they should call it Johnny Depp National Forest," Susan said.

Jake smiled. "You'd like that, wouldn't you? You'd pay to watch that guy food shop."

"Yesss, sir, I would." Susan pushed strands of blonde hair behind her ears and looked in the rearview at Amy. "We're having us an adventure, eh kiddo?"

Amy grunted and turned back to her cell phone. She slapped it down on the seat beside her. "An adventure with no cell service. I'm bored."

"Listen Miss Eleven-Year-Old, you're darned lucky to even own a cell phone," Susan said.

"Who needs cell? Look." Jake nodded out the window at the steeply sloped conifer covered mountains. "Check out that pretty creek gushing through those huge boulders. Adventure begins where cell service ends."

"Why don't you try and draw the stream, honey?" Susan said.

The road began a corkscrew climb, slowing the rig and working the motor. The temperature dropped a bit with rising elevation. Susan hung her arm out the window and let the current flow over her hand. Although the forest was stressed from prolonged drought, the faint scent of pine filled the car. At a mountain pass, they saw a sign that read: 'White Mountain Apache Tribe Welcomes You.' And then a second that read: 'Break a Treaty; Break the Law.'

As they descended the pass, Susan heard a whining engine on her side of the road. A cloud of dust rose through the forest from a gravel track that intersected just ahead. A small blue pickup flashed through the trunks of trees separating the two roads—a cluster of bandanna-adorned heads visible in the truck's bed.

"Better get these windows up before that dust drifts over," Jake said, raising the windows.

"Watch out for that truck. It doesn't look like it's going to stop. Probably a bunch of lit-up braves playing weekend warrior," Susan said.

"It damn well better stop. I have the right of way." The pickup was drawing even with Jake's rig. A grim, dark, soot-covered face perched behind the wheel. Three other men crouched in the bed from which a harsh red glare emanated, thick smoke trailing behind the truck like a flag.

"Jake!" Susan yelled. He stood on the brakes and the rig shuddered to a stop as the truck shot out of the side road. A short burly man stood up, braced against the cab, and hurled a lit flare at the Suburban. The flare spun on the hood, spouting flame and smoke, and then rolled off. The truck shifted gears and raced around the next bend.

"Christ," Jake said. "Is that flare in a safe spot?"

"Yeah, I can see it on the shoulder. Shouldn't ignite anything."

Jake gunned his engine, bucking the Flying Cloud to life. "I'm going to try to at least get a plate."

"Let it go. We're in the middle of nowhere," Susan said.

Jake banked around a curve. The Flying Cloud leaned but tracked and settled back to level. The trees fell away on the downhill side, revealing a panorama of the valley. The blue truck was visible, two tight switchbacks below.

"I'm not letting it go." The Suburban picked up speed.

"Now this is an adventure," Amy said. Susan turned to check her daughter's seatbelt. The road-cut rock whizzed by in a blur. Susan braced. She could see thousands of feet to the rocky bottom of the mountain. Jake steered around another turn.

"This is insane. We are on a reservation mountain road in pursuit of Indians, with no authority and no back-up," Susan said.

Jake wrestled the wheel and rounded another curve. Susan's magazines flew off the dash to the floor. "I'm not going to confront the jerks. I just want to find out who they are. Get the binos out of the glove box. See if you can get the plate." Jake sped up through a straightaway that dipped like a roller coaster track.

"Woo hoo!" came from the back seat as the rig crested the hill and leaned into another bend. The vintage Airstream mirrored every move flawlessly.

Susan tried to focus the binoculars while fighting the bouncing of the car. Jake hit another descending curve hard, downshifting to brake. The trailer jackknifed a little on some gravel but corrected immediately. Just in time. A semi-truck lumbered into view in the uphill lane.

"Yeah, baby!" Amy said after righting herself.

"Okay, I've got it. Amy put this on your phone."

Amy fumbled for her cell. "Go Mom."

"Arizona JBB … JBB3202." She put the binoculars on the seat between them and squeezed Jake's arm. "Now will you slow down, please?"

"Got it," Amy said.

Jake steered the rig over to a passenger-side pull-off perched above the valley. The blue truck had disappeared. The trailer groaned as the rig eased to a halt.

They climbed out of the car. Amy brushed crumbs off her short white shorts. The wind exhaled in the pines and a rivulet of water in a draw beside the road giggled its way down-mountain. A red-tailed hawk shrieked above.

"I can't wait to write this 'What I did last summer' essay," Amy said. "Chased Apaches with my Mom's boyfriend's Airstream."

"Jake, what on earth were you thinking? I'm afraid to even look inside the trailer."

"Pissed me off. They could've hit Majestic with that flare."

Amy burst out laughing, Jake chortled, and finally Susan smiled and shook her head. "What a cowboy." She caught Jake with her glance. "You know who would've loved this?"

"Yeah, I do," Jake said, casting his eyes skyward. "He'd be laughing his ass off."

"Beverly would have loved this," Susan looked up at the top of the mountain and noticed a billowing cloud ascending. "Is that smoke up there?"

Jake grabbed the binos off the front seat and studied the pass. "It sure as hell looks like it." He rushed around the front to the driver's side. "Let's go. We need to get to cell service or to Show Low to report a fire and four punks in a pickup."

"Yee haw," Amy said, jumping back in the car.

Acknowledgements

I worked on *Straw* for a decade, and was constantly amazed at how helpful people were with my research. So, from the owner of the gun store in Clayton, Georgia who let me handle his Glock (9mm), to the golf course contractor in California who told me how to steal dynamite, and all those in between, I'm deeply grateful. I also received expert advice from retired police officers Ed Burts, Dave Griffin, and Suzan Fuhrmann.

As the book neared completion, I enjoyed invaluable guidance from Todd Wilkinson, Gerry Spence, Patrick Foley, Gillian Rose, John Willott, Joverne Burnside, Arun Batavia, David Swift, Noah Waterhouse, Mary Correia-Moreno and Jim Griffin. Thanks also to Ken Wright of Raven's Eye Press and editors Heather Bennett and Lindsay Nyquist. I'm indebted to Mary Moreno for sharing her Tohono O'odham heritage with me, to Annabel for her expertise on all things middle school, and to Karla Swiggum for introducing us. I'm grateful to several longtime friends for reading various drafts over the years: Dimmis Weller, Lindsey Gilbert, Tom Jackson, John Hebberger, Valerie Schram, and Clint and Virginia Grosse. And I always draw inspiration as a writer from my writer daughter, Jameson.

And finally, *Straw* simply would not have happened without the excellent editorial work and advice of Ruth Ann Penny and Tim Sandlin— or the love and undying support of she to whom this book is dedicated.

About the Author

The *Straw That Broke* is Gregory Zeigler's first environmental thriller. He is also the author of the travel memoir, *Travels With Max: In Search of Steinbeck's America Fifty Years Later*, and has enjoyed speaking all over the country about his American adventure.

Gregory Zeigler is a life-long educator, writer, speaker and environmentalist. He is a former NOLS instructor and Executive Director of the Teton Science School in Jackson, Wyoming. Zeigler holds a B.A. from Washington and Jefferson College in Washington, PA, and a Masters of Education from the University of Utah.

Throughout his career as a teacher and school head, Gregory presented papers at national educational conferences and published numerous articles on historical and educational subjects. He has acted professionally on stage and in film, including appearing alongside NFL great Lynn Swann in an Instructional Television production, Arts Alive.

Gregory and his wife Dimmie have three adult children: Jamie, Alex, and Wil. When the Zeiglers are not gallivanting about in their Airstream Bambi named Winnie, they reside in Jackson Hole, Wyoming.

Raven's Eye Press

Rediscovering the West

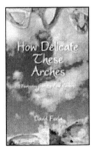

Sometimes Creek:
A Wyoming Memoir
by Florence Shepard

The Monkey Wrench Dad:
Dispatches from the
Backyard Frontline
by Ken Wright

Smoke Signals
by M. John Fayhee

Livin' the Dream:
Testing the Ragged
Edge of Machismo
by B. Frank

How Delicate These Arches:
Footnotes from the Four Corners
by David Feela

Visit www.ravenseyepress.com
for a complete listing of our titles.

CPSIA information can be obtained at www.ICGtesting.com
Printed in the USA
LVOW12s0301200116

470767LV00003B/5/P